IN BETWEEN
MEN

Books by San Culberson

IN BETWEEN MEN

THE NICK OF TIME

Published by Dafina Books

IN BETWEEN MEN

San Culberson

KENSINGTON PUBLISHING CORP.
http://www.kensingtonbooks.com

DAFINA BOOKS are published by

Kensington Publishing Corp.
119 West 40th Street
New York, NY 10018

ISBN-13: 978-0-7582-1523-9
ISBN-10: 0-7582-1523-1

First trade paperback printing: December 2007
First mass market printing; December 2010

10 9 8 7 6 5 4 3 2 1

Printed in the United States of America

*For my mother, Emmer Lee Culberson,
resting in peace.*

Speak up, girl. He can't hear you crying.

Chapter One

"Shoot her, Mama! Just kill her!" Hope Williams looked down with amazement at the little girl who couldn't have been any more than five years old. She could tell by the bloodthirsty expression on her otherwise angelic-looking face that the little girl was dead serious. Hope focused again on the "mama" standing near the front bumper of a gleaming white Mercedes. The woman had a tight grip on the hobo bag that was wrapped over her shoulder, and it wasn't hard for Hope to imagine her pulling out some sort of automatic weapon.

The nasty remark she had been about to make died a quick death. She was not about to get herself killed in a parking lot shoot-out . . . especially considering she didn't have anything to shoot with other than her mouth! Yeah, the other woman was wrong . . . she had parked too damn close to the yellow line. Hope always—always—parked squarely between the lines. And it wasn't always easy in the big-assed Navigator her husband insisted she drive. She took a deep breath before attempting to reason with the woman again.

"Look, I'm just saying that I can't get into my truck. Will you *please* move your car over? I don't want anything to happen to your paint job or mine." Hope said it with as much pleasantness as she could muster, but she couldn't control the slight roll of her neck.

"I ain't movin' a goddamn thang! And I *don't* give a fuck about yo paint job, but lemme come outta this bitch and find a scratch on my car." The "bitch" she referred to was the exclusive boutique Hope had just left. "You betta get in the best way you know how. Bring yo ass on here, Shairaqetria!" She grabbed the little girl's hand and walked away, not even looking back to see what Hope *might* do.

Hope felt the rough-and-ready young girl that she used to be before she left the mean streets of South Dallas pleading with her . . . *Come on, Hope, you don't have to take that shit! Kick her ass! Fuck up her car.* When the former Hope realized that the *mature* thirty-four-year-old Hope wasn't going to take her advice, she gave up with a disgusted sigh. *Damn, girl, how you goin' let her do you like that?* The memory of the little girl pleading with her mother to commit murder kept her quiet. Her mother had always said the apple doesn't fall far from the tree.

She walked to the passenger side of her truck and pressed the small button on her keychain to open the door. She draped the garment bag across the seat and climbed in and over the center console to get to the driver's seat, cursing under her breath the entire time. The tears that stung the back of her eyes were from anger and frustration.

The engine sprang to life when she turned the key in

the ignition. She backed out without looking and whipped the big Navigator around in the parking lot like it was a two-seater Porsche. Hope glanced at the small clock in the dashboard as she turned onto the street, and realized that she should have been back in her office thirty-five minutes ago. The drive back to the bank would take at least fifteen minutes. "Damn!" she muttered again under her breath.

If she hadn't spent the last hour in the small, over-priced boutique trying to convince herself not to blow her clothing budget, she would have avoided the nasty confrontation because she would have been where she was supposed to be . . . sitting behind her desk. She wasn't happy about the fact that she had spent a small fortune on a dress she would wear three times max. She couldn't wear it to work and she *certainly* couldn't wear it to church. Hope glanced at the satiny black bag next to her and decided that the bag had probably added about twenty-five percent to the price tag.

Her lips curled defiantly as she came to the first stoplight and reflected on the last ninety minutes. The dress looked *good* on her, and she had been at the bank long enough to take a long lunch every once in a while. "And you *should* have beat that heifer's ghetto-fabu-lous ass! Since when did you start letting people talk to you like that? And that badass little girl needs an ass-whoopin' too!" Since no one was in the truck to hear her profanity, she continued her tirade for a few seconds longer.

From the time she had thrown the covers back that morning, Hope had been pissed. The kids had been fighting, and by the time she realized there wasn't any milk for cereal it was too late for her to cook anything. She had been forced to wait in the drive-thru line at

McDonald's. And her husband, Ray, had waited until that *morning* to tell her that they were invited to an anniversary party that *night* and that *he* wanted to go. She hated going out on Friday!

The driver behind her pressed long and hard on his horn. She refocused her attention on the traffic light and saw that it was green. "So what! You can't control my fucking driving!" Although she was yelling at the top of her lungs, her voice didn't penetrate the two tons of steel that surrounded her. Hope pressed *longer* and *harder* on her horn before pulling off at a snail's pace.

Her hand was positioned to respond to any sign language that he cared to offer. She was not going to run from a fight two times in less than fifteen minutes. But the other driver moved into the next lane and passed her without so much as a glance in her direction. She was instantly ashamed of her irresponsible and juvenile behavior.

What if he had been one of those road-rage maniacs they're always featuring on the news? I could have been shot and killed, and no one would have ever seen how good I look in my new dress. My three children would have been left without a mother and Ray would have been forced to start cleaning up after himself. Ray cleaning up was such an impossibility that she laughed out loud, and suddenly the angst that she had been experiencing all day melted.

Her moods had been changing so rapidly recently that she had talked to her best friend Stephanie about the symptoms of premenopause. Stephanie had convinced her that at thirty-four she was much too young, and suggested instead that Hope was on the verge of losing her mind. "You just *crazy*," were her exact words. Hope's thoughts shifted again.

Going out on Friday wouldn't be so bad if I didn't have to rush and do everything. She pondered. *I could have a glass of wine, listen to some music, give myself a facial . . .* Hope leaned over and grabbed the cell phone from the side of her purse before she had time to dismiss the plan forming in her head. She called her office and counted four rings before her secretary answered.

"Security National Bank." The secretary's voice was clear and professional.

"Helen, this is Hope."

"Oh, hi, Hope."

"I'm not going to be able to make it back in to the office today." She started to make up an excuse, but decided not to. She didn't owe the woman an explanation, and she hated to lie unnecessarily. But her voice did hold just a hint of *"it's something personal, I don't care to discuss it"* softness. "If anyone calls with an urgent question, and I do mean *urgent,* you can page me; otherwise, I'll see you on Monday morning."

"Okay . . . I hope everything is fine?" There was a slight question in her voice, but Hope ignored it and looked again at the garment bag to her right.

"I'm sure they will be, thanks, Helen." She ended the call and chuckled to herself. *I didn't lie; things will be all right if Stephanie comes through for me.* She mentally crossed her fingers as she made a second call. The phone rang five times before her friend picked up.

"Hey girl, what's up?"

Hope chuckled some more before answering. "You and that damn caller ID." Hope was not a fan.

"I know you didn't call here to talk about my caller ID. What do you want?"

"I want you to stop being so rude, but I called because I'm looking for someone who can use a thousand dollars." Hope knew Stephanie would take the bait.

"I know a lot of people who could use a thousand dollars. Myself first and foremost."

Hope sighed deeply. "Well, girl, you're in luck because I'm *so* tired, I'll pay you that just to keep my kids overnight."

Stephanie laughed into the phone. "Your cheap ass wouldn't pay a thousand dollars for a first-class trip to the moon."

Hope laughed back at her. "This is true, but I will buy pizza for you and your hungry monsters if my kids can spend the night at your house. Please, please, best friend . . . only *real* friend." Hope pretended to beg as she continued to maneuver through the light midday traffic. Stephanie didn't say yes immediately.

"What are you doing that you have to get rid of your kids for the *entire* night?"

"Ray and I are going to Ralph and Lisa's tenth anniversary party. That is, if you can baby-sit," she pleaded some more.

Stephanie tried to sound disgusted, but Hope knew that she didn't really mind. "Bring 'em on. The more the scarier. I'll just throw them in the back with my three monsters."

"Thank you, thank you, thank you!" The appreciation in her voice was heartfelt. "I'll drop them off at six." Hope was starting to feel like butter. Anticipation flooded her body, and suddenly she was really looking forward to getting dressed up and going out. "Girrrlll, you ought to see the dress I just bought."

Stephanie, who was seven months pregnant and showing it, sighed into the phone. "If I can't wear it, I don't want to see it."

Hope had a clear picture of her friend's big, round belly. "I feel you, girl. I'll let you wear it *after* the baby is born." Hope laughed.

"After this baby is born, I'll be wearing nursing bras and stretch pants." Stephanie sounded cheerful about it, but Hope remembered what it felt like to be seven months pregnant and mother to a newborn. The flashback of midnight feedings and engorged breasts sent a slight shiver up her right arm.

"Been there, done that, glad to say I won't be doing it again." Hope's baby-making days had ended with a snip of scissors and a flick of her doctor's wrist twelve minutes after David had been born three years before. Hope was about to inquire about Stephanie's pregnancy, but her friend cut in before she could.

"Girl, I have to go, the buzzer is going off on the dryer. Just bring them on by, and don't forget to bring a super-large pizza with everything for the adults who don't have any sort of social life that doesn't involve minors, and some buffalo wings, and some cheese sticks too."

Hope laughed. "See you later on." Hope pressed the End button on the cell phone and tossed it back into her purse. She made the first possible turn, got on the expressway, and headed toward her home in DeSoto, Texas, a suburban community thirty-five minutes from downtown Dallas. She smiled as she always did when she thought about her home. Their five-bedroom house took up two lots in the center of a cul-de-sac. She and Ray had looked at dozens of houses before finding the one they fell in love with. The backyard had been the selling factor. The original owners had built a tropical pool with spa and waterfall in one corner, and had installed a large sandbox complete with swings and jungle gym close to the back fence. It was an idyllic spot for young children and lovers.

She was thinking about her boys as she turned onto the cul-de-sac, and made a quick decision to take them out for ice cream right after school . . . *mother guilt.* Whenever she knew she was going to spend any amount of time away from her kids (and with the exception of work, she rarely did) she felt compelled to do something special for them.

She pulled into her driveway and pressed the garage door opener. She frowned when she saw that Ray's car was parked in the garage. *Damn! What is he doing here in the middle of the day?* Her thoughts were uncharitable, but she didn't care. She had been looking forward to spending some time alone in her home . . . something *else* she rarely had a chance to do.

Hope noticed that her next-door neighbor, Margaret, was pulling weeds out of a flower bed. The woman was wearing a flower-patterned bonnet that tied under her chin. *She probably ordered it from some Ladylike Living magazine.* The thought of it caused Hope's eyes to roll. Hope Williams was an anomaly in a neighborhood full of "soccer moms" and PTO volunteers. Most of the women were like Margaret; they stayed at home and tended their flowers and their children and their husbands. Hope had heard that some of the women had recently started a pinochle club. Rumor had it that a select group of women met every Wednesday for a game of cards and a cold lunch. It didn't bother Hope that her invitations to join the other women in their pursuit of happiness had trickled to none a long time back.

She decided to leave her truck in the driveway and turned the engine off. Before she could open the door properly, Margaret was running across their yards like

Chicken Little. *Why the hell is she coming over here?* Hope tried to smooth the irritation from her face. The bonnet looked even more ridiculous on closer inspection. The hand she waved in Margaret's direction said "hi, but I'm really too busy to talk to you right now."

"Hi, Hope." The short run had made Margaret breathless. She was still carrying a small trowel in her hand. She looked at Ray's car in the garage and then quickly back at Hope. "Hi, Hope," she said again.

"Hi, Margaret." Hope wondered how much neighborly conversation she would have to endure before she was allowed to go inside.

"You're home early today." The petite redhead smiled warmly at Hope, apparently unaware that she was a nuisance.

"Yeah." Hope smiled back with exaggerated politeness. "We have plans tonight and I'm a little tired, so I decided to come home and get some rest." Margaret pointed to the garment bag in her hand.

"Not too tired to shop I see."

Hope's fake smile widened genuinely. "*Never* too tired to shop."

Margaret's look was almost envious. "Well, before you go in why don't you come over for coffee. I'm finished with the yard."

Hope looked at the small containers of Mexican heather that Margaret had deserted. "Looks like you have quite a bit more to do." *What part of "I'm going to get some rest" didn't she understand?* Hope wondered, but kept the smile fixed on her face.

"Well, I'm *almost* finished, and I could use some adult company." Margaret looked again at Ray's car. "Why don't you just come in for a minute . . . show me what you bought?" She sounded almost desperate.

Is she that lonely? Hope wondered. "Another time, Margaret." The other woman started to protest, but Hope waved and walked through the garage without looking back. The sound of the alarm greeted her as she pushed the door open. She hurried over to silence it before looking around her living room as she always did. Hope *loved* her home. She tried not to make it a habit to love *things,* and the house and its contents were definitely *things.* But two years ago, after she had *finally* finished furnishing it, she sat down on her jewel green sofa, looked around at all the things that had been chosen so carefully—from the mahogany coffee table to the three identical silver frames that held each boy's "first photo"—and gave herself permission to love this one thing . . . her home.

Five bedrooms, four and a half baths, hardwood floors where she wanted them, a Jacuzzi tub! It was a mansion and a haven to a girl who had grown up in the housing projects of South and West Dallas. It took six months of living in the house before she stopped feeling like Weezie from *The Jeffersons.* She was definitely a woman who had "moved on up." A hissing noise somewhere toward the bedrooms broke her train of thought. She had almost forgotten Ray was at home. She put her purse and the garment bag on the sofa.

"Ray?" she called out as she walked to the back of the house. As she got closer to the master bedroom the hissing noise became louder. "Ray," she called loud enough for him to hear and respond. When he didn't, the hairs on the back of her neck stood up and she stopped in front of her bedroom door. Her thoughts moved immediately to the negative. *Maybe Margaret was trying to keep me out of the house for a reason . . . maybe she knows something I don't know.* Hope's heart

started pounding faster as she turned the crystal doorknob that led to her bedroom. It was like she was playing the lead role in a second-rate soap opera. *Lord,
don't let this be something I can't handle*, she prayed
silently before pushing the door open.

Her eyes immediately went toward the bed. It was
empty, the covers rumpled just as she had left them that
morning. She felt a strange mixture of relief and disappointment as she let out the breath she had been holding. Then she laughed; Ray was not the cheating type.
He was more likely to be holed up with a sports magazine than with another woman. *What was I thinking?*
She half snorted.

A quick scan of the room revealed the source of the
hissing noise. In the corner closest to the door was the
battery-operated car that her youngest son had gotten on
his birthday. The spinning wheels made the hissing
sound because the wall prevented the car from moving
forward. She picked up the toy and turned it off. "This
is why they're always asking for batteries." She held it
in her hand as she walked to the nightstand and picked
up the telephone and called her husband on his cell.

"Ray," she almost whined into the phone. "Where are
you?"

"What do you mean where am I? I'm working."

"Your car is still in the garage," she accused.

"That's because I'm riding with Jacob today . . . in-
troducing him to clients."

"Oh. Is that the new guy?" Her husband was regional
supervisor for a large pharmaceutical company.

"Yes, it is. Is there anything you need?" His tone
probably sounded patient to anyone around him, but
Hope knew it to be patronizing.

"No, I was just calling to make sure everything was

all right. I thought you were at home, and I was calling your name, but you didn't say anything." The silliness of her statement embarrassed her.

"Well, I'm not at home, and everything is fine. I'll see you later." He hung up before Hope could say good-bye. She stuck her tongue out at the phone before putting it down. She took the batteries out of the car and tossed them into her nightstand before putting it back in the boy's room; then she went to get the garment bag that she had left on the sofa.

Back in the bedroom, she looked longingly at her unmade bed before starting her normal home-from-work routine. Her jacket and her new dress were hung in the closet, and after removing her skirt and her lavender silk blouse, she tossed them in the dry-cleaning bin. As she was turning away from the bin, she caught a glimpse of herself in the long rectangular mirror positioned above the double sink. She stood in her bra, pantyhose, and three-inch black work pumps.

Hope was thirty-four years old, mother to three boys, and her dress size was holding steady at a size eight. She moved her long fingers over the stomach that was as flat as it had been when she was a freshman in college . . . *well, almost as flat.* A smile crossed her face; she was pleased that her hard work at the gym had paid off. Seven months after David, her youngest son, had been born, she was disappointed to discover a lone stretch mark had remained on her smooth brown belly.

She had managed to escape the marks of childbirth with the twins, but David had been leaving his mark on her since birth. Her only consolation was the fact that the mark was so faint that Ray probably didn't even know it was there—that and her beautiful baby boy, of course. After her final postpartum checkup, her ob-gyn had proclaimed that she was made for having babies. She told *him* that she was made to have *three* babies.

Her eyes and fingers traveled upward and settled on her face. Her skin was literally the color of ground nutmeg. There were no lines on her face, and no blemishes . . . this time of the month. Her dark brown eyes were evenly spaced and her lashes were thick and very dark. She had been very attractive her entire life, but when she hit thirty, she had crossed the line from very attractive to stunning.

She put her hands in her hair and smiled at herself again. When she met Ray she had been a twenty-one-year-old senior at the University of Texas, and her hair was always caught up in a ponytail that extended past her shoulders. *Then*, he was always complimenting her on its lush thickness, telling her that she looked *so* sexy when she wore it down. Eventually his sweet talk had worn *her* down, and she had foregone the practicality of her ponytail and started leaving it loose for love's sake.

Throughout their ten-year marriage, she had had four inches taken off the top and two inches off the sides, and an inch here and an inch there until she had arrived at her current ultracontemporary style. Her hair was very short . . . so short that when she had gotten it cut to its current length, Ray didn't say a word about it for twelve days. But *she* loved it, and had maintained the same style for over a year. It was relaxed, and special styling products kept it as glossy as pressed satin. Her bangs extended about an inch and a half past her hairline. Her hair stylist had expertly shaped and tapered the sides and the back. At its longest point, her hair was shorter than her pinkie.

If there was one thing she would change about her body, it would be her breasts. After providing sustenance for three hungry boys, and after twelve years of being a *major* source of amusement for a grown man, they would not be mistaken by anyone for those of a twenty-one-year-old. But they were small enough to have weathered the storm without *too* much damage. She still went braless . . . occasionally . . . *to bed, mostly*, she thought to herself wryly, before kicking off her shoes and carefully removing her pantyhose. As always, she checked her backside before turning away from the mirror. Her *ass* was a work of art.

After slipping on a pair of shorts and a T-shirt, she thought about the housework waiting for her. She could use this free time to start a load of laundry, clean the kids' bathroom, clean the refrigerator, or vacuum . . . or she could *actually* take the nap that she had promised herself. A tired sigh escaped her before she walked to the nightstand, set the alarm clock, slipped out of the clothes she had just put on, and slid her naked body between the rumpled sheets. Decision made.

Hope turned on her back and stretched like a cat. She moved her hands along the sides of her waist, appreciating the soft, smooth feel of her skin. She crossed her hands over her thighs, and massaged some of the knots that were left from her latest trip to the gym. Seemingly of their own volition, her fingers found the juncture between her legs. She caressed herself before rolling over on her stomach, keeping her hands and fingers in place. Hope moved her hand and fingers firmly and insistently for several minutes before she found quick release and peaceful sleep.

Chapter Two

The alarm woke her two hours later. She flung the covers back and sat on the side of the bed and stretched before picking up the clothes she had discarded earlier. After taking five minutes to wash her face and brush her teeth, Hope dressed in jeans, T-shirt, baseball cap, and sneakers before walking out the door.

She made the trip to the boys' school in less than ten minutes. As she walked into the double doors she caught the lingering smell of something that she couldn't put her finger on, but it was the same smell that had lingered in the halls of every elementary school she had ever been in.

Her twins, Karl and Jordan, were in the second grade, but were placed in different classrooms. David, her three-year-old, attended the cooperative day care housed in the north end of the school. She knew they would not have a problem foregoing after-school care at the Y in order to go out for ice cream. She walked down the familiar halls to collect her children, and fif-

teen minutes later her boys were safely buckled in the
backseat, talking excitedly about ice cream and sleeping over with their good friends.

Hope pulled into an empty parking space in front of
the ice creamery in the shopping strip across the street
from Southland Mall. The twins were unbuckling their
seat belts before she had the truck in Park. "Don't you
open that door!" she warned. "And haven't I told you
not to unbuckle your seat belt until *I* say so?" At seven
and a half years old, the boys knew a rhetorical question when they heard one.

They waited on the edge of their seats for either
more fussing from their mother or permission to open
the door. She gave her best frustrated-mother sigh before saying, "*Now* you can get out of the truck." The
twins were out of the truck and into the store before
she made it around to the passenger side to help David
out of his car seat.

She looked at the back of their heads through the
glass front of the ice cream shop as she walked toward
the door. They were not identical twins, but they were
close enough. Same height, same slender build. Their
facial features were arranged differently, but they were
both good-looking boys. *Good genes,* Hope thought
proudly as she opened the door.

David pulled his hand from hers and wasted no time
joining his brothers at the counter. The man behind the
counter looked up at her and gave her the sort of smile
that she had been getting since she was fourteen years
old . . . twelve, really. "Are these your boys?" His voice
was friendly, but Hope pretended to be seriously considering what to have and answered without looking up.

"They are."

"They sure are lucky to have such a pretty mommy."

This time she did look up. "They are." Hope smiled coolly. His smile widened. Apparently he didn't know that he was flirting with himself.

"I'm Terrance Oliver, the owner."

Hope looked back down into the freezer and kept her voice cool. "Really? We're in here all the time . . . I've never seen you."

His smile was self-satisfied. "This store practically runs itself. I spend the majority of my time at my other *two* stores." If he was waiting for her to be impressed he had a long wait.

"Do you know what you want?" Her question was directed at all three boys.

"Can we have a banana split?" Jordan was the unofficial spokesperson for the brothers, and he sounded as if he expected her to say no. Hope knew a good mother kept her children guessing.

"Sure." She smiled at him and rubbed her hand across his head. They excitedly told "the owner" what flavors they wanted. She even let David have a banana split even though she knew there was no way he could finish it; he was on an eternal quest to keep up with his big brothers. Besides, she couldn't just tell him no without an explanation; he demanded answers. He was *definitely* his father's son.

"The owner" gave the boys their banana splits and put the caramel sundae that she ordered for herself on the counter. When she took out her wallet to pay him he held up his hand in protest.

"No charge." He smiled a smile that Hope objectively thought might be considered seductive . . . by someone interested in being seduced. She smiled back as she continued to count her money.

"My *husband* warned me never to take ice cream from strangers."

He leaned over the counter slightly. "We don't *have* to be strangers."

Hope gave him her best "don't be ridiculous" laugh.

"Yes . . . we do." She tossed sixteen dollars on the counter and went to join her boys.

They made it home before Ray so she sent the twins to their room to pack an overnight bag for themselves and for their younger brother. After David's third birthday, she had converted his bedroom into a playroom and moved the three boys into the same large bedroom. The smallest bedroom was used as a guest room, and the other had been converted into a well-equipped home office.

She was in the master bedroom making the bed when Ray got home. "The boys say they're spending the night with Stephanie?" He waited for her to explain as he loosened his tie and tossed it on her freshly made bed. He didn't like the boys to spend the night away from home unless it was absolutely necessary.

"Hello to you too, Mr. Williams." She picked up the tie from the bed and threw it back at him. He caught it, threw it back on the bed, and started to unbutton his shirt. She walked closer to him and tangled her hands in the springy hairs on his chest. Ray was definitely in the upper echelon in terms of physical good looks. He kept his 6'2", deep chocolate frame in top condition. The thick, neat mustache drew attention to his even white teeth. He kept his hair low with weekly trips to the barber. They had been instantly attracted to one another. "I just wanted to spend some time alone tonight with my lover." He tossed his shirt next to his tie and ignored her remark.

"Why are they spending the night with Stephanie? Can't Renee baby-sit?" Renee was their regular baby-sitter, a nineteen-year-old college student. Hope leaned in closer to kiss him, but he stepped away from her. "Stop it, Hope." Ray sat on the side of the bed to remove his pants. Her hand fell to her sides. One of the unspoken rules in their marriage was that they only played when *Ray* felt like it. She screwed up her face at him playfully, determined to keep the evening light.

"I thought it would be nice for us to have the house to ourselves after the party tonight."

He looked a little more interested. "Do I have to drop them off?"

Hope nodded and spoke slowly. "Yeah, at six o'-clock." Looking at Ray's well-built body brought back some of the edginess she thought she had taken care of earlier. She moved until she was standing between his parted legs and slipped her hands into the fly front of his boxer shorts. He responded instantly. *Playing* was one thing . . . *fucking* was another. Ray looked pointedly at the open door. They could hear the children laughing and arguing in the other room.

"All right," he warned, his voice a little deeper, "don't start something that you can't finish." She bit her lip, pretending to consider her options, and removed her hand from his underwear, but not before stroking him teasingly. "I thought so." He smacked her bottom lightly as she walked out of the room to referee the argument between the boys that had gotten progressively louder.

* * *

At eight o'clock, her children were safe at her best friend's house, her husband was on his way back from the gym, and Hope was relaxing in a soapy tub. She reached over and drank the last sip from her second glass of wine. Feeling good! She decided to get out of the tub before she turned into a prune. Ray walked into the room as she was going through her underwear drawer. "We're leaving in forty-five minutes, Hope," he warned. He had on sweatpants and one of his workout T-shirts. She turned back to choosing underwear.

"I'm almost ready, Ray." He was always complaining about her holding them up when they went somewhere, even though she usually spent no time getting herself ready because she was solely responsible for making sure the boys were presentable.

"What about your hair?" he asked casually as he walked away from her. Hope turned around, one hand on her bare hip, giving him her full attention.

"What *about* my hair?" *I'm tired of his damn snide comments about my hair. Everybody and their mama likes my hair, but he can't say one nice fucking thing about it.* Her eyes challenged him to say something that she didn't like, but he smiled, he didn't want to argue.

"I like it when you put that mousse stuff in it and wear it kinda spiked." He kicked off his sneakers and left them on the floor. Hope heard him laughing quietly behind the bathroom door as he closed it. Ray was always saying something she didn't expect. It amazed and sometimes angered her that he *still* had so much control over her emotions. Hope went back to choosing her underwear again, but there was a soft smile on her lips.

She needed "barely there" underwear for her new

dress. She didn't really like to wear thongs, and her lowest-cut bra was not cut low enough to accommodate the plunging V neckline of her dress. She closed the drawer without removing any underwear. Decision made.

For the next fifteen minutes Hope expertly applied her make-up, and after spiking her hair in a few strategic places she was pleased with the woman reflected back at her when she looked in the mirror. Her make-up made a bold statement, a perfect complement to the boldness of her dress. Deep red lips were the focal point on her face. A little foundation gave her skin a satiny sheen, and her lids were brushed lightly with bronze shadow. Velvet black mascara made her lashes so thick and long they almost looked false.

Hope took the black patent leather stiletto heels she had decided to wear out of the closet before stepping into the dress that she had draped across the bed. She slipped the shoes on and took one final look in the mirror. A wide smile spread across her face.

The dress was simple elegance. A sleeveless, black, tightly woven Italian knit number; the neckline plunged to the bottom of the valley between her breasts. And of course it clung to *every* curve of her body. She knew she would not be making any new friends among the other women attending the party tonight. Ralph and Lisa's friends tended to be on the stiff side.

She sprayed her pulse points with a citrus-scented perfume to complement the lotion she had applied earlier, slipped silver cuff bracelets on both of her wrists, diamond studs in her ears, and *voila* . . .

Ray walked out of the bathroom fully dressed. Black designer pants, T-shirt, and sports jacket. His shoes were polished to a high gloss. He looked good and smelled good and she told him so. She pretended that she was a model on the catwalk so he could appreciate her dress and her body fully. "What do you think?"

"It looks like something a teenager would wear," was his dry response. She was suddenly glad she had spent the money on the dress. She pretended to flick a piece of lint from the front of her dress and asked just as dryly, "Really? Do you think a teenager would be able to afford a dress like this?"

"I'm not *even* going to ask you how much you spent on that dress." He fastened his watch as he said it.

"Good." She stuck her tongue out at him like she had seen David do when he wasn't looking. She wasn't worried about Ray. She had seen the look in his eyes when he had walked out of the bathroom.

Chapter Three

Ray had a hard time finding a parking space when they got to the party. Cars lined both sides of the street in the upper-middle-class neighborhood. He ended up parking four houses down and they walked the short distance to the front door. Obviously the party was already in full swing.

He rested one hand lightly around Hope's waist and used his free hand to ring the doorbell. Their hostess, Lisa, opened the door for them and greeted Ray with a hug. Someone who didn't know better could have mistaken the smile that she gave Hope for warm. Hope knew better.

"Hope, I'm so glad you guys could make it." As she spoke her eyes took in Hope's appearance from head to toe. "Oh my God! I'm surprised Ray let you out of the house in that." *She must think Ray is my daddy.* "Ralph would never let me out of the house in a dress like that." The only thing Lisa and Hope had in common was the fact that their husbands were employed by the same pharmaceutical company. In fact, the two women didn't like each other at all. Hope and Ray had been discussing that very thing on the drive over, and she had promised to be "nice." *Whatever that means.*

Hope looked Lisa up and down. "I'm *sure* he wouldn't." Hope's smile was just as tight as her hostess's. *She can take that any way she likes, but if she's smart she'll take it how I mean it.* Ray pressed his fingers in her side to remind her of her promise. *I like her less every time I see her. Who would wear polyester slacks and an outdated sequined top to her own anniversary party?* Hope's thought continued unchecked until Ray lied and told Lisa that she looked good, then steered Hope toward their host.

In Hope's opinion Ralph and Lisa were total opposites. He was easygoing and modest, and unlike his wife, very likeable. Hope smiled brightly at the short man with the bald spot. As she did she could *feel* Lisa's disapproval. She leaned closer to Ralph and hugged him as Lisa had hugged Ray seconds before. "Happy anniversary, Ralph." They straightened themselves after the short hug.

"You're looking like a model tonight, Hope." Hope smiled her thanks, and Lisa moved even closer to her husband. Just for the hell of it Hope leaned back in and kissed Ralph on the cheek. She smiled to herself when Lisa grabbed Ralph's hand and pulled him back.

"Ten years, right, man?" Ray reached over and the two men shook hands in greeting.

"Ten long years." The two men laughed at the old joke. Lisa's face softened and she punched her husband playfully in the shoulder. He caught her hand and brought it to his lips. "And if Lisa will have me, I pray it'll be another ten years and another and . . ."

"Okay." Hope held up her hands, laughing. "We get it." *He actually loves this bitch,* she thought to herself. It didn't really surprise her. She had stopped wondering a long time ago what attracted people to one another. The amount of animosity she felt toward Lisa at that moment surprised her. *Just because I don't like her doesn't mean she's a bitch. Well, she is a bitch, but that shouldn't concern me.*

And right then, the "bitch" in question was looking at her husband as though he was the captain of the basketball team and he had just asked her to the prom, and he returned her look twofold. *So? Ray and I still look at each other like that . . . sometimes.* "Make yourselves at home," Ralph said as he pointed to a far corner in the room. "Everything is laid out over there, and you know where the bathrooms are." Of course they did, they had visited the home on several other occasions. The couple loved to have parties. The doorbell rang again and their host and hostess were off to greet their other guests.

"You want a drink, babe?" Ray's hand still rested on the small of her back. She looked up at him and smiled. She loved it when he called her "babe."

"Yeah." He surprised her further by brushing his lips across her cheeks before leaving. While Ray was getting their drinks, she moved closer to the nearest wall so that she could get a good look at the party going on around her. Lisa had done an excellent job setting up for the party. It was being held in the "grand room," a popular feature in the custom homes that could carry a price tag anywhere from 400,000 to 700,000 dollars. There was a buffet set up in the center of the room, complete with linen tablecloths, candlelight, and fresh flowers. And from where she stood it looked as if

Ralph and Lisa had bought out a small liquor store. Those who didn't know would assume the party had been catered, but Hope knew that Lisa had done it herself. B. Smith didn't have *nothing* on Lisa, Hope admitted to herself grudgingly. *I could do the same thing if I had no kids and nothing but time on my hands.*

The furniture that normally filled the room had been arranged into several intimate seating areas. Soft music filtered through the surround sound system, and the well-dressed partygoers were involved in various activities. Eating, drinking, dancing, talking softly to one another . . . a few were playing some sort of game in the small library just off the main party room. Hope saw some familiar faces in the crowd and waved whenever she caught the eye of someone she knew. Ray was back soon with their drinks.

"What's this?" she asked as she took a sip of the creamy-looking drink.

"Baileys and cognac." He had poured himself a whiskey.

"Mmm." Hope smacked her lips. The drink was delicious. "Thank you, it's good. I think I have a new favorite drink."

"I knew you'd like it. By the way, what was that comment about Lisa for?"

"Considering the way she looked at me and the comment that *she* made, I thought that I showed quite a bit of restraint. And by the way, Ray, she looks ridiculous."

"She does not. She's dressed *conservatively*. I know you're not aware of this, Hope, but some women feel that it's appropriate to dress more conservatively as they get older." He took a drink of his whiskey and smiled in the glass. The drink that he had given her was already having an effect. She knew because she couldn't do anything but laugh back at the comment that was obviously for her benefit.

"To each her own."

An hour later, Hope was halfway through a third Baileys and cognac that she poured herself and Ray was off somewhere talking pharmaceuticals. She had spent part of the last hour playing Taboo in the library. Her husband had watched for a while before going off to talk shop with some of the men who worked for the same company.

She was accustomed to being left alone at parties, and after so many years she had learned to sit back, enjoy the music and the company of other people. When she wanted something she knew how to get it, and if she needed Ray for anything she knew where to find him. She was not a wallflower by any means.

Al Green's voice filled the room; Hope was mouthing the words and people-watching when she felt a light touch on her shoulder and a deep voice. "What do you know about Al Green? You must be, what, twenty-five?" After so many years of looking like she was a lone woman at a party filled mostly with couples, she had also mastered the polite brush-off. She turned around, a small smile already on her face, but for some reason, the words that she had been about to utter died in her mouth.

"It's not polite to ask a woman her age, but if you must know, I'm twenty-three," she said instead. Maybe it was the look in his eyes that made her take an instant liking to him. It was not the "come on" look that she was accustomed to getting. His eyes were filled with laughter and the laughter spilled out at her comeback. He had approached her teasingly, as though they were old friends. Hope couldn't help but notice how attractive he was as he held out his hand in introduction.

"Anthony Bolden."

"Hope Williams." Hope held out her hand also, and was surprised when he captured it in both of his.

"This is one of my favorite songs. I could tell it must be one of yours too. I saw you light up from across the room. Would you like to dance? We can still catch the last part." She didn't allow herself to consider the fact that he had been watching her from across the room.

"No, thank you." Hope hadn't danced at a party in years. Ray didn't dance, and she would feel awkward dancing with another man without Ray's permission with him somewhere in the room.

"Okay," he said, accepting her answer without trying to change her mind. "How do you know Ralph and Lisa?"

"My *husband* and Ralph work for the same company," she said without hesitation. So far, he didn't appear to be flirting with her, but she wanted to make sure he was fully aware of her status as a married woman before they continued their conversation. He nodded, showing no reaction to her words. Hope thought about the platinum and diamond anniversary band Ray had given her on *their* tenth anniversary. *He probably already knew that I was married.*

"What's his name? Maybe I know him."

Hope frowned at him, confused. "Whose name?"

He laughed at her. "Your *husband*." He put the same emphasis on *husband* as she had.

"Ray Williams. Do you?"

"Do I what?" He was teasing her.

"Do you know my husband?"

"I've never met him, but I have heard Ralph mention a Ray on several occasions."

"Maybe you'll get a chance to meet him tonight. He's a great guy." *Now, why did I say that?*

"I'm sure he is." He laughed some more. Hope was sure he was wondering why she had made that last comment about Ray being great. That twinkle was back in his eye . . . he was teasing her again. Tension she hadn't realized that she was feeling left her body.

"What about you?" he asked and sipped from the bottle he held.

"Am *I* a great guy?" Hope asked and they both laughed. *We're not flirting . . . we're having a good time.*

"It's obvious that you're not a guy." Hope wasn't sure, but she thought he gave her the quick once-over as he spoke. *Maybe he's flirting just a little bit*, she admitted to herself. "I meant what do you do?"

"I'm a loan officer at Security National downtown."

His smile widened . . . if that were possible. "So we have two things in common, then; Al Green and the banking business."

"Oh really?" Hope waited for him to explain.

"I'm an investment banker. Ralph and I went to graduate school together." Hope noticed that the hand holding the light beer was well manicured.

"Do you work downtown?"

"Downtown *Houston*. I'm just in town for the party."

"Really." She was interested in all aspects of banking and was about to ask him about the industry in Houston and the ins and outs of being an investment banker when she felt heavy hands on her shoulders. It took her a second to realize that the hands belonged to Ray. "Hey, honey." She smiled back at her husband and leaned into his chest. He massaged her shoulders for a second before speaking.

"You need another drink, babe?" He didn't look at her when he asked the question; he was looking at the stranger standing in front of her.

"Thanks." She handed him her empty glass and decided to introduce him when he didn't move. "Oh, honey, this is Anthony Bolden, he and Ralph went to graduate school together." The two men shook hands. "Anthony, this is my husband, Ray Williams."

"Good to meet you," Anthony said as they were shaking hands. Ray didn't have too much to say to Anthony; in fact, he didn't say a word.

"Babe, come over here with me. I want to introduce you to some people." Ray placed his hands around Hope's waist, preparing to lead her away. She smiled at Anthony a final time.

"It was nice meeting you. If we get a chance later on, I'd like to talk to you about what's going on in the banking industry in Houston and a couple of other things."

"No problem." He had the same warm smile on his face as they walked away.

They left the party at close to two in the morning. Hope was sincere when she thanked Lisa for throwing such a nice party. On the way to the car Ray held her close to him to protect her from the cool night air.

"You looked good tonight, baby." Hope was sitting on the side of the bed removing her earrings. Ray was walking toward her naked. Her expensive dress was in a heap on the floor.

"That's not what you said earlier," she reminded him.

"I didn't *say* you didn't look good. I *said* that the dress looked liked something a teenager would wear." He stood over her and placed his hands on her shoulders. She liked the way his hands felt on her bare flesh. "What I neglected to say"—he slid his hands down and cupped her breasts—"was that if a teenager came at me wearing a dress like that, looking like you looked tonight . . . *I'd fuck the shit out of her!*" He clenched his teeth as he said the last part for added effect. His fake growl made them both laugh. A tingling had started between her legs when he started walking toward her. His groin was positioned right in front of her face. She could easily take him into her mouth, but she wanted to finish the game he had started. She laughed softly.

"How would you fuck her?" She tried to pretend to be disinterested, but Ray slid one of his hands from her breast and found the moistness between her legs.

"Well, I wouldn't take my dick out too soon." He stroked her as he talked. Hope parted her legs slightly to allow him better access.

"Why not?" She took the bait.

"Because she might get a look at how big it is and get scared."

Hope pretended to inspect the object in question. "Maybe so," she conceded, "so how would you fuck her?"

"Well . . ." Ray pushed her back on the bed. "I have a little trick that I would use to relax her."

"Show me." Hope's eyes were closed in anticipation. Ray knelt in front of her and blew air gently across her thighs.

"Say please." She didn't oblige until he captured some of the moistness he had discovered earlier with the tip of his tongue. He lifted her legs and placed them on his shoulders. Hope locked her legs around his neck, moving closer to the source of her pleasure. When he felt her moving more insistently, he lifted his head slightly to ask . . .

"Are you going to come for me, baby?" Hope nodded in response. Her hands found the top of his head and pushed down, encouraging him to use his mouth for something other than talking. Deliciousness coursed through her and her body jerked in response. Ray stood up and kissed her deeply. She accepted his tongue gladly. "Can you taste that?"

Hope smiled lazily as he continued to kiss her. "You . . . are . . . so . . . *nasty*."

He kissed her along the side of her neck. "But you like it, don't you, baby?" He moved her up farther in the bed as he prepared for his own satisfaction.

"I love everything you do to me, Ray."

He slid smoothly inside her. "I want you to come again for me." His voice was husky and seductive. She could barely speak. His strokes were strong and confident. After more than twelve years of lovemaking he knew how to please her.

"I want to." He pressed a little deeper inside and she knew she would.

"Whose pussy is this?" His mouth was against her ear and he took the opportunity to sweep his tongue across the sensitive skin.

"Ours, baby." She bit and stroked the parts of his

body that she had access to. He slowed his movements deliberately.

"*Whose* pussy is this?" he asked again.

She enjoyed the slow swivel of his hips, but she knew and he knew also that she needed a different stroke to achieve the result she was after. She put her hands on his hips and attempted to drive him deeper inside her, but he only pulled out farther.

"Whose *pussy* is this?" he asked a final time.

"Yours, baby, yours."

Chapter Four

At ten the following morning, Hope stepped off the treadmill and wiped the sweat from her forehead with the towel that she retrieved from the handle. Forty-five minutes ago the gym had been filled with people getting in an early morning workout. Now the circuit training area was almost deserted and Hope could use the weights without worrying about somebody wanting to "work in." She worked her upper body for twenty minutes before moving to her favorite ab machine.

Truth be known, she wasn't fond of *any* of the machines, but over the years she had made her peace with the ones that had proven to give her results she *was* fond of. She exhaled one last time, stood up, and wiped down the machine. At the *end* of a workout she always felt great.

Women in various stages of undress were positioned around the locker room. Hope took off her workout clothes and stood under the shower to rinse the sweat off before putting on her tank-style swimsuit. Today there was enough time in her schedule for her to spend a few minutes relaxing in the sauna.

Waves of heat and steam greeted her when she opened the door to the coed sauna. She found an empty spot on one of the benches and sighed as she sat down. Karl had called at around eight that morning to make sure that they wouldn't be picked up too early because "Aunt Stephanie" had promised to make pancakes. She had assured him that he would be there for the promised pancake breakfast before hanging up. Going back to sleep after that was impossible, so she put on her gym clothes, got some post-workout clothes, and left the house.

It had been an excellent decision to send the kids away for the night. Ray and she had done some memorable things the night before. Rarely did she get the opportunity to spend time alone with her husband. Their time together was mostly family time . . . G-rated movies, school functions, church . . . *When the kids are with his mom this summer, maybe I can convince Ray that we should spend a week alone on some tropical island. Yeah, right!* She shook her head at the thought and leaned back into the heat.

Her kids greeted her with hugs and kisses as soon as she walked into the home of her best friend. The two women had met at freshman orientation at UT. They hit it off immediately and had been pleased to discover that they were assigned to the same dorm room. They continued to get along well, even though their backgrounds were so different.

Stephanie's family was solidly middle class and had

been for at least three generations. Her father was a dentist and her grandfather had been a mortician. Her parents had started saving for college before she started kindergarten. Hope had moved into the dorms almost straight from the projects and had qualified for all the financial aid that the state of Texas had to offer. After that first year, they had moved off campus to a nearby one-bedroom apartment and had continued to share an apartment until Hope and Ray had gotten married. Bad romances, academic probation, pregnancies, and life's many pitfalls had only strengthened their friendship. Hope had been the one to tell Stephanie that her mother had been killed in a car accident, and Stephanie had been in the hospital two and a half years ago when Hope's mother had taken her last breath. There wasn't much that they didn't share with one another.

After prying David's sticky hands from her bare legs, she sat down at the kitchen table and demanded coffee.

"I'm the one who's pregnant," Stephanie complained halfheartedly as she went to pour Hope a cupful. "You should be waiting on me. Help a big round sister out!"

"I am helping you out, girlfriend. You need the exercise." Hope blew out her cheeks and rubbed Stephanie's stomach as she placed the coffee in front of her. Her friend just smiled at her and sat down.

Stephanie was pregnant with her fourth child, and as with the other three pregnancies she had been exercising regularly and eating good, healthy foods. She was 5'3" and in very good shape. Stephanie and her husband, Lamar, had three boys also. Hope knew that most people thought the fourth pregnancy was a relentless effort on their part to add a girl to the mix, but the truth was they planned to have *at least* six children.

They believed that it was their responsibility as educated black folks to raise as many "bound to be successful" black children as they possibly could. In order to do that, they had foregone many luxuries they could have otherwise afforded. When it was time for them to purchase their home, they had searched for and found a modest house in a stable neighborhood. Stephanie had decided not to go back to work after their first child had been born. Five days a week and one Saturday a month Lamar drove the fifteen minutes to the dental practice that he shared with Stephanie's father. In the summer they took their children on special family vacations to broaden their outlooks and to supplement what they learned throughout the year. They lived modestly and saved almost every extra dollar for their children's education.

We could send a child to Harvard with all the money we spend on unnecessary things, Hope admitted to herself as she considered her friends' lifestyle. In reality she wasn't worried about the kids' school because she and Ray had a sound financial plan. Plus, she rarely made purchases that weren't budgeted . . . other than the occasional overpriced dress.

Toys were strewn all around Stephanie's kitchen, something Hope would not be able to tolerate in her own kitchen. *I'm not trying to be Ma Walton . . . and I did get my money's worth out of that dress last night.*

"What are you smiling at?" Stephanie had a smile on her own face, ready to share her friend's amusement.

"Just thinking about last night." What part of last night would remain her secret.

"Did y'all have a good time?" Hope nodded and took a few minutes to give her the highlights of the party. "How was Lisa?" Stephanie knew of Hope's strong dislike of the other woman. Hope looked around the kitchen to make sure there were no children lurking in the background before responding.

"*Still* a bitch." She curled up her lips in distaste to illustrate her point. "If she didn't give such good parties, I wouldn't have anything to do with her." Stephanie laughed as she was supposed to, then got up to respond to a third call of *"Mommy!"* Hope drank the last of her coffee before getting up to join the fray in the back of the house.

They made it back home around lunchtime. Jordan, Karl, and David jumped out of the truck and ran over to their father, who was just finishing his weekly yardwork. Hope waved at her husband and went inside to start her own weekend chores.

Later, Ray suggested they spend the rest of the day in the backyard. He grilled hamburgers while the boys divided their time between the swimming pool and the jungle gym. Hope spent most of her time refereeing the frequent arguments that broke out between the boys, but she did manage to finish a few chapters in the book that she was reading in relative peace.

By early evening the boys were exhausted and their arguing was nonstop.

"*Mommy!* Jordan keeps splashing me and I told him to stop!" Karl shouting.

"But he splashed me first!" Jordan whining.

"First of all, stop that whining. Second, it's time to

go in anyway. Get out of the pool and go start your baths." Mommy sighing.

"David." She raised her voice in order to get the attention of her younger son sitting in the sandbox. "It's time to go in." She knew David was tired when he got up without argument and started toward her.

"It's Saturday . . . Can we stay up late?" Karl again. Both boys were looking up at her like wet puppies. They were exhausted, but they would never admit it.

"I know it's Saturday, and you know tomorrow is Sunday. We're going to early service tomorrow."

"*Aww, man*! We never get to stay up late." Jordan this time. Tuning out the boy's complaints was a skill she had mastered years ago. Hope was determined not to be irritated by the fact that Ray wasn't at home to help with the boys. After the burgers were done and they had all eaten, he had decided to go to Oak Cliff to play basketball with some of his friends.

"Ray," she had said when he told her of his plans, "I thought we were going to spend the day together." He had given her his "don't start" look.

"We *did* spend the day together . . . and *now* I'm going to play basketball." Hope had started to say something, but she knew from experience that they would just end up arguing and Ray would *still* go to play basketball. So she had given him her "whatever" shrug and went back to reading her book.

And now I'm stuck here with three grumpy-ass boys.

Let it go, Hope; remember, you weren't going to let irritation get the best of you. The voice in her head was starting to be such a constant presence that Hope was thinking of giving her a name. She had considered "Screw that," since it was the phrase that usually came to her mind after the inner voice offered unsolicited advice.

"Please, Mommy! Please!" Hope was brought back to the present by the unrelenting whining of three little boys. They were following her through the house and pulling on her like little leeches. The patience had been officially sucked from her. She turned around suddenly and in her quietest, fiercest mommy voice . . .

"Jor-dan. Karllll. Da*vid*." Each name was pronounced with exaggerated distinction. "If you don't stop that whining *right now*, not only will you *not* get to stay up late, you will go to bed immediately after you take your baths. I said *no* and I mean *no!*" Then the boys made their way to their room without any additional comment. "Jordan and Karl, use the shower in the guest room and help your brother," she shouted after them.

As soon as they were out of sight she felt guilty. She hadn't shouted at them, but she had used a voice usually reserved for behavior more serious than simple whining and begging. She was not above apologizing to her children, especially when she knew they were not the root cause of her irritation.

The boys were busy getting their sleeping clothes together. Their fierce whispering stopped when they noticed their mother standing in the door. "Hey, guys." She smiled warmly at them to let them know that she had overreacted and that they were not in trouble. "If you hurry with your baths, we have time for some ice cream and a cartoon." She was rewarded with *"Yeahs!"* and big grins. Feeling a little better, she walked away. She loved her boys to death, and there was nothing that she wouldn't do to make them happy . . . *except* let them stay up late on a night when she was dead tired.

* * *

Three hours later the boys were fast asleep and Hope was freshly showered and fuming. Ray had been gone for five hours. She knew that the drive to Oak Cliff was fifty minutes round-trip from their house.

"They don't play four hours and ten minutes in the fucking NBA!" Hope muttered under her breath. She checked the clock again to make sure she was right about the time. She considered making herself a drink, but dismissed the idea immediately. Drinking to ease tension was the first step to becoming an alcoholic, in Hope's mind. Her thoughts then turned to the two gallons of ice cream in the freezer.

"And if I ate Häagen-Dazs every time Ray pulled some shit like this, I wouldn't be able to fit through the front door. And I won't give him the pleasure of having one more thing to complain about."

After the twins had been born, she had done her share of raging at Ray. Complaining, or "bitching," as he called it, that he needed to do more . . . that he should be more considerate of her needs . . . her feelings. Her mother had told her that she just had the "baby blues" and that they would pass. Hope hadn't argued with her mother, but she knew what she had was the "I just had these two babies and my husband ain't doin' a damn thing to help blues." Her mother had been right about them passing, though. Once Hope had gotten it in her mind that her "bitching" wasn't going to do anything to change the situation, and in fact, it seemed to make Ray more resistant . . . she just stopped.

She had tried to focus instead on the positive aspects of her life . . . she'd had *three* healthy boys, a nice place to live, a good job, a man who could tie her body in knots and with the swivel of his hips have her feeling as loose as a goose. She had decided to leave well enough alone. Ray had been happy, grateful even, and Hope had been *happier . . .* for a while . . . until she realized that she hadn't *stopped* bitching, she just did all of her bitching where Ray couldn't hear—*in her head.* Her silence was more dangerous than her complaining.

Hope shut down her brain as best she could. She sat on the edge of the bed and massaged her temples, trying to alleviate some of the pressure that was continuing to build. By the time she heard Ray pull into the garage she was lying prone on the bed, covering her eyes with the palms of her hands and fighting back tears of frustration. She did some deep-breathing exercises she had seen on TV.

Ray walked into the bedroom. Hope heard when he kicked his gym shoes off. She didn't get up from the bed . . . she couldn't get up.

"The kids asleep?" To her he sounded refreshed and full of energy. That pissed her off further. She fought to keep her voice under control.

"You know they're asleep, Ray." Her voice was tight. Still, she didn't change her position.

"What's wrong with you?" He had the nerve to sound really confused. *That's right, Ray*, she encouraged him silently, *walk in here all happy and pretend you don't know what's wrong.* She sat up on the bed and looked him straight in the eye.

"What's wrong with *me,* Ray, is that you leave a family barbecue that *you* suggested and don't come back for *five hours.* What the fuck is wrong with *you*?" Hope stood in front of Ray with her arms crossed over her breasts, waiting for an explanation. She hadn't meant for the profanity to slip out, but it had been right there on the tip of her tongue. Ray's face lost its pleasant, relaxed look and was suddenly scrunched up in anger. He hated it when she used profanity, especially on the rare occasions when it was directed at him.

"You *know* where I've been, Hope. I was gone a little longer because after the game we went back to Rodney's house to play cards. If you needed me for something, you should have called. You know I always have my cell phone with me." She took no pleasure in the fact that he hated explaining himself more than he hated her use of profanity.

And she *had* known all along how to reach him. She wasn't mad because she thought he had been out screwing or drugging or gambling or drinking . . . and she hadn't been on the verge of tears because she thought his car had crashed through a barricade on the freeway.

"I shouldn't *have* to call for you to come home, Ray. The fact that you were at Rodney's house is not important. What is important is that you think that after all these years you still have the freedom that you did when you were a teenager. Do you think it's right, Ray, that I spend my weekends caring for our children—and when I say 'our' I don't mean 'our' as in me and the fucking man next door, I mean 'ours' as in me and you—and you are free to come and go as you please. If you want to play basketball, you play basketball. If you want to go to the gym, you go to the gym. If you need to work late, you work late." At some point during their short conversation, Hope had decided to forego her no-bitching policy for good.

He didn't respond to her tirade. Instead he said, as

though she was a lunatic that he was forced to live with, "You need to lower your voice before you wake the kids."

"If I wake the kids, I'll put them to sleep . . . like I do every night." But she did lower her voice. She didn't want the kids to be witness to their argument. It was really her argument, because as she spoke Ray was walking toward the bathroom.

"Hope, if you need some time for yourself, take it. If you were worried, I'm sorry. But I'm a grown man, and until that changes I will do whatever the hell I want." With that sarcastic bit he closed the bathroom door. And then there was nothing left for Hope to do but get in the bed. Her bitching had been as effective as it had been when she had given it up—not at all. But at least she had the satisfaction of knowing that he had been disturbed, if just briefly.

And she felt better. She smiled to herself when she recalled the look on his face when she had asked, "What the fuck is wrong with you?" *If I knock him in his fucking head I bet I'll get some respect and consideration around here.* Hope giggled aloud as she imagined the look on Ray's face if she got after him with the *famed* cast-iron skillet.

She got control of her glee and held perfectly still when Ray pulled back the covers on his side of the bed. He moved close to put a firm hand on her shoulder. His voice was warm and conciliatory as he spoke. "Hope, you know I don't mean to upset you. If you want to know where I am, call. If you need me to do something with the kids, you need to say so. I love you, baby. I don't like it when we argue." When she didn't respond, he started to stroke her back softly; he even went so far as to nibble her bare shoulder.

After a few more tries he sighed in frustration and turned his back to her. She knew that he wouldn't compromise his pride and *actually* beg. And if he knew her better he would know that she would not be swayed just because he approached her with soft words and a hard dick. Especially when she knew the only reason he was even attempting to apologize was his hard dick. Hope continued to take deep, quiet breaths until she fell asleep.

Chapter Five

The next morning she and Ray sat side by side on one of the front pews at Greater Lakeside Baptist Church, argument unresolved. They had made it to church in time to get the boys settled in children's church and to find decent seats for themselves at the always packed nine A.M. service. The couple hadn't spoken two words to each other all morning. All of their communication for the last couple of hours had been through or around their kids.

"Ask your dad to pour you another glass of juice." Hope.

"It's almost time to go. Are you boys ready?" Ray.

Hope looked at Ray out of the corner of her eye. He looked good in his lightweight tan suit . . . face smooth . . . smelling like the spicy cologne she had given him on his last birthday. She had told him on several occasions how good he looked in that particular suit . . . she would bet her offering money that he had worn it deliberately.

As they made their way to their seats, Hope had noticed the surreptitious glances of more than one woman. She knew that there were women in and outside the church who would like to be sitting where she was sitting. She remembered how pleased she had been the first time Ray approached her.

He had asked her out at their first meeting. She had been having coffee with Stephanie at one of their hangouts on campus when she noticed a tall, good-looking man walking toward them. Both she and Stephanie had been quiet and polite when he told them he was a graduate student working on his MBA. Stephanie and Lamar had been dating for six months and the writing was already on the wall, so a slow smile warmed her insides when he directed his attention toward her. She had been impressed with his directness and his confidence . . . *The sexy smile he added to the mix didn't hurt*. She had said yes almost too quickly when he asked her to go for a movie. And after two years of intense dating, Ray had gotten his MBA and asked her to marry him.

When her mother was alive, she had lost no opportunity to tell Hope how lucky she was to have found such a "rare" thing as a good-looking, hardworking man. Hope had felt lucky herself. She had been a silent witness to her mother's relationships throughout her childhood. After all those years she still cringed inside when she thought about some of the things her mother had experienced at the hands of mean-spirited men. Men who had never been hardworking *and* good-looking . . . who, in Hope's opinion, were often neither.

In the end, her mother had decided that hardworking was better than good-looking. And Hope had been thrilled when she had met and married Arthur six years before her death. Hope tried to force thoughts of her mother out of her head so that she could get back to being mad at Ray.

She turned her attention to the sermon. She *needed* a good word that morning. Instead of the "good word" she was looking for, the minister was talking about the members' fiscal responsibilities toward the church. *What the hell kind of sermon is this?* Hope wondered. *That's why I hate this damn church.* Hope's thoughts continued irreverently. When the minister called for all of the women to bring their charge cards to the altar, Hope groaned to herself and tuned him out as she did most Sundays. It was *Ray's* church anyway. She had told him that she felt like her spiritual needs weren't being met at Lakeside, but Ray didn't like change, and they continued to attend. *And I go along like the good little wifey that I am*, Hope thought cynically.

The minister's voice droned on in the background and her train of thought returned to her mother.

Pearl Barker had found herself all alone when she had given birth to her only child at nineteen. Her family had never been supportive, and Hope's father had left before the rabbit could have a proper burial. She had raised her child with no help from friends or relatives and only occasional help from the government. She had lived to see Hope finish college, and had been present at the birth of all three of her grandchildren. In Hope's opinion her mother's life had been a success. The tragedy was her death. Just as she was beginning to see the fruits of her hard work and faith, cancer struck.

And her so-called relatives had the nerve to come to the funeral pretending to be grief stricken. Asking to come back to the house . . . Hope suppressed the old bitterness that she had always felt toward her mother's relatives. She switched gears and contemplated more pleasant memories. By the time the minister was doing his final altar call . . . *people this time* . . . Hope was planning her wardrobe for the coming week.

"Hope . . . Hope." Ray finally succeeded in getting her attention. "Service is over." He held out a hand to help her up. *Now, why am I mad at him? Oh yeah, his lack of consideration.*

She shook her head in resignation. At this point her marriage had everything in common with a roller coaster—up, down, sudden unexpected turns. When the ride was over, the mostly uncomfortable riders got back in the long line, over and over again, determined to make it through without screaming and without that awful lurching feeling in the pits of their stomachs. They looked up with envy at the riders who had conquered the roller coaster . . . the ones who threw their hands in the air and whose screams were joyous.

She had read books and articles about women and men being from different planets and she agreed wholeheartedly, but she hadn't figured out why she had to do all of the commuting in her marriage. Hope sighed and took the proffered hand. She couldn't stay mad forever . . . she had a life to live and a family to raise.

Chapter Six

Hope walked into the bank earlier than usual on Monday. The weekend had ended on a positive note. After they had gotten home from church, the boys had changed their clothes and Ray had taken them to the movie they had been begging to see. She had used those precious alone hours to start dinner for the family and straighten the house a bit.

When they got back home the boys told their mother the best parts of the movie. To her it seemed as if Ray was waiting in the background trying to determine the climate in the house. While they were gone, Hope had replayed the events of the night before and had decided to leave well enough alone. Her bitching hadn't helped, and Ray had been *slightly* apologetic. She had cooked up a pecan pie, his favorite, as a peace offering. And when the boys had gone to bed, Hope had given him a little something to help him get to sleep.

She acknowledged the people already at the bank as she made her way to her office. She had been promoted to senior loan officer three years previously and was now responsible for overseeing the work of the eight loan officers at the bank. She had to be well versed on current state and federal lending regulations.

Hope attended frequent meetings with other senior officers at the bank and held her own meetings to update her staff on new bank procedures and to review productivity and default rates. Occasionally she worked loans that exceeded the lending authority of her staff.

Working at the bank had suited her well over the last years . . . especially the hours. She was always available for her family during the evenings and on the weekends, and because of her seniority she was able to take an occasional afternoon off without drama. Recently, however, she had been contemplating a career change . . . something more challenging.

After so many years at the same bank, she could do her job with her eyes closed. On a couple of occasions she had mentioned to Ray that she would like to go back to school. He agreed that she should make a change, but his idea was that she should quit work altogether. She had dismissed the idea immediately—she had no intention of staying at home—and continued to mull over her options.

Hope was working double-time to clear her desk of paperwork left behind on Friday. She barely acknowledged Helen when she stuck her head in to say good morning. She took calls, signed papers, and double-checked the work of one of her staff members who had been making some costly decisions for the bank until close to lunch. As she was just about to take a break, the phone rang again. "This is Hope."

"Hope, it's Rob." Rob was one of the men on Hope's small staff.

"Yes, Rob?" As she spoke, Hope used her feet to search for the pumps that she had kicked off earlier.

"I have a client here who has some questions about a mortgage loan that we weren't able to approve."

"Can't you answer her questions?" Hope didn't try to hide her irritation, and Rob answered somewhat defensively.

"Well . . . I have attempted to answer her questions, but she's asking to speak with someone else."

She could hear the tension in his voice. She rolled her eyes toward the ceiling, further irritated.

"Walk her down with her application." Hope shook her head as she placed the phone back on its cradle. Occasionally her job forced her to deal with individuals who couldn't take no for an answer.

She had on her game face when Rob introduced her to the bank's would-be client a few minutes later. Hope looked down at the folder that Rob handed her, searching for a name. "Thank you, Rob." The smile that she directed toward the woman didn't reach her eyes. "If you'll follow me, Ms. Rendale." When they entered her office Hope motioned for the woman to sit down. "How can I help you?" Hope took her seat and conducted a fifteen-second assessment of the woman sitting across from her. Late thirties/early forties, African American, neat figure, decent dress . . . stressed.

"I was turned down for a home loan and I would like a more detailed explanation as to why."

Hope added intelligent to her assessment. The woman sat very still in the leather chair, but her breathing pattern told Hope that she was either nervous or trying extremely hard to hold her anger in check. Hope hoped that it was nervousness she detected. *I'm in no mood to deal with an angry sister*. After reviewing the application for a few seconds, Hope looked up.

"Ms. Rendale, your loan application was processed and according to our guidelines you don't qualify. You have four charge-offs and several slow pays. I'm sure you know that your credit rating is very important consideration when you are asking for a loan—"

The woman interrupted her before she could finish. "I *paid* two of those accounts in *full* and I showed that man the canceled checks to prove it. The other two I'm making payments on. And if you will check the dates, you'll see that those slow pays were over *two* years ago." The woman raised her voice slightly and was moving her head back and forth with emotion.

Don't get mad at me . . . shit, Hope thought to herself, but her face remained professional.

"I understand *that*, but unless you make arrangements with your creditors, that negative information will remain on your credit record." Hope shook her head in a way that she hoped said, "I'm sorry, now please get out of my office." The woman did not get up. "And as it stands," Hope continued, "we *cannot* approve your loan."

"I'm an RN. I make enough money to pay that mortgage. I pay more than that for rent now and have been for over two years. Call the manager at my apartment complex. She'll tell you that I have *never* been late with my rent." The woman was trying to keep it together, but Hope heard the hint of pleading in her voice.

"That's not something that we do. And your income is not in question. What I would suggest is that you contact these creditors about removing that information from your record. If you ask, the ones that you're still paying may allow you to settle with them for a reduced amount. If you do that, we may be able to reconsider your application at another time with that new information." Hope kept the "I'm sorry, but there is nothing I can do" expression on her face.

The woman reached for her purse on the floor and Hope thought she was getting ready to leave until she put her hand in it. *Lord, don't let me die over a $95,000 loan,* Hope prayed quickly as she pushed her chair back. *If she wanted to shoot somebody she should have shot Rob . . . Damn.* The woman tossed what appeared to be bank statements across her desk and stood up. Her expression screamed angry.

"I've been banking here for eight fucking years! The *one time*"—she held her index finger and moved it back and forth—"the *one time* I come here for any damn thing, y'all can't help me. I don't need you to *reconsider my application at another time*." She changed her voice to mimic Hope. "I'm supposed to close at the end of the week. You think they'll put off selling that house if I tell them you *may* reconsider me? I've been promising my kids that we would have our own house since their father died."

The woman was on her feet now in front of Hope's desk, tears of frustration streaming down her face. "I told them that I found us a house. Now I'm supposed to go back and tell them we have to wait some more?" When the woman had started cursing, Hope had decided to forget professionalism and have security remove her from the bank. But the tears had started immediately after. Frustration and disappointment, Hope understood.

"Ma'am, I'm sorry, but the bank did not ruin your

credit. We would be happy to give you a loan if we could. We *can't*." The finality in Hope's voice must have gotten through to the woman. She took several calming breaths and reached for one of the tissues on Hope's desk to wipe her face. Hope stayed still behind her desk, waiting for her next move.

"I apologize. I know that the bank is not responsible for my credit or my children." She smiled tightly, obviously embarrassed. Once she had composed herself, she turned as if to walk out of the office, but turned around just as Hope was about to let out the breath she had been holding. "Not that you care, and not that it matters, but my husband and I had been saving money in this bank for years to buy a house for our family.

"And then one day about four years ago somebody gave him some drugs . . . and he liked it. He spent the next two years feeding his habit, smoking up our money and our dreams, and I spent the next two years trying to hold my family together, lying to my children and to my relatives about what was going on. And then he died. I've been trying to fix this mess. I'm sorry again about walking into your office and making a scene, but I just didn't want to go home and admit to my children that I told them another lie." She wiped at the tears that had formed again in the corners of her eyes and walked out.

Hope sat back in her chair after the woman left, staring at the door that she had closed behind her. She stood up and walked around her office, gathering the papers that the woman had strewn over her desk and the ones that had fallen on the floor. They were bank statements. Savings and checking account statements. When Hope had all of them in hand, she sat back down and leafed through them.

At one point there had been a substantial amount in the savings account. Certainly enough for a down payment on a house. The records showed increasingly large savings withdrawals; at one point the account had been depleted. The checking account had been overdrawn on several occasions around the period that the woman had talked about. She appeared to be getting her financial life in order. The most recent savings account statement showed a balance of $6,200, and the checking account was in good standing with the bank.

Hope dropped the papers on her desk and leaned back in her chair. She had been blessed financially, she knew. With their combined salaries they were able to live a very good lifestyle. In fact, they could live the same lifestyle if she quit work as Ray had been after her to do. But she had had enough financial worries growing up to really empathize with the lady. Her mother had struggled to pay the light bill, the phone bill, the rent . . . and Hope could not recall one time when anyone had given her mother a break. She had always managed, but it had not been easy.

Her situation is entirely different from my mother's, though, Hope thought to herself. *It's not like she doesn't have a profession, and even if she can't buy the house now, she can buy it in a couple of years.* She recalled the look on the woman's face as she had left her office. Beaten, was how she had looked. Hope didn't want the loan refusal to be the straw that broke the sister's back.

For some reason, Hope felt guilty. She didn't cause the woman's problems and had just been doing her job when she reiterated what Rob had to have explained to her, but still . . .

Her thoughts kept going back to her mother. She remembered being a little girl sitting in her mother's lap as she tried to explain her situation to the "welfare lady," as she was commonly called in the projects. As young as she had been then, she had still felt how much it galled her mother to answer the questions of the women who were often rude and uncaring.

Ninety-five thousand dollars was not a lot of money for a house in today's market, and the amount was *well* within her lending authority. Hope continued to finger the documents as she considered . . . *If I wanted to, I could call her up and tell her we would approve the loan pending the home inspection*. Hope knew intuitively that the woman had not been lying and that she would make every effort to meet the mortgage payments.

She put the papers down and doodled absently on a sticky pad as she considered doing what she had never done before. A few minutes later she was dialing the woman's home number. Decision made.

Chapter Seven

Thirty minutes later she was waiting for her friend Tabitha at a restaurant near the bank. They arranged to have lunch on Mondays, whenever Tabitha was in town and not off making purchases. She was a buyer for a large department store. As usual, Tabitha was ten minutes late and counting. Hope sat in the small Italian restaurant reviewing the menu that she knew by heart when Tabitha finally arrived, fifteen minutes late.

"Hey, girl." Tabitha sat down in a rush and tossed a shopping bag on the floor. She was a beautiful woman, the product of an on-again, off-again romance between a black Trinidadian man and an Indian woman. She smiled so wide that her crimson-stained lips almost got lost in the deep dimples that marked both of her cheeks. Hope was not in a smiling mood.

"If you can't get here on time, Tabitha, you could at least call. What took you so long *this* time?" Hope didn't really want an answer.

"Girl, I brought you something from New York, and

I had to run back to my office to get it." Tabitha reached for the shopping bag on the floor.

Hope sighed in frustration. She refused to be appeased so easily. "I'm starving! And I've spent half of my lunch hour sitting here waiting for your ass." Hope was unaware that she was rolling her eyes slightly as she spoke. She reached for the shopping bag, but Tabitha pulled it back.

"Look," Tabitha warned, "don't bitch at me like I'm Ray. Last time I checked, I wasn't gettin' my pussy from you." Tabitha didn't believe in gender discrimination, as she called it, when it came to choosing her lovers, and Hope was one of the few she shared this personal tidbit with. Hope snatched the bag and laughed softly as she was supposed to.

"For your information, I don't *bitch* at my husband." She stuck her tongue out at the other woman for added effect.

"See, that's your problem."

Hope caught her breath as she pulled a pale cashmere scarf from the bag. "This is *absolutely* beautiful. A gift?" she asked hopefully, thinking of her extravagant purchase on Friday.

"It is if you change your attitude. I got it from one of the designers that I saw last week." The "freebies" were one of the many fringe benefits of Tabitha's job.

"For this," Hope put the scarf back in the bag and placed it next to her chair, "I'll excuse your tardiness." Hope smiled genuinely at her friend. "Thanks, it was just what I needed."

"I won't *even* touch that," Tabitha teased.

"Please don't." Hope laughed some more and sat back in her chair. The two women had become friends six years ago when Tabitha had worked at the bank for a short while. When she left the bank for a starting position at the department store that had turned into her current "dream job," they had started seeing each other regularly for lunch.

Tabitha had been very frank with Hope about her sexual orientation or *nonorientation* a few weeks into their friendship. And when, by some of the remarks she made, it appeared that Tabitha was testing to see if Hope's river flowed in both directions, Hope was equally frank when she had shut her down.

Tabitha motioned for the waiter and he took their order. "What's wrong with you today?" She sipped from her water glass as she waited for Hope to answer.

"A lady came into my office a little while ago wanting a loan." Hope shook her head as she replayed the scene for Tabitha. By the time she had finished the story, the waiter had their pasta salads on the table.

"So," Tabitha looked confused as she stabbed some of the spiral shaped pasta with her fork, "are you saying you gave her the money?"

"I left a message on her home answering machine telling her that I'd take care of it." When she considered the possible ramifications of what she had done, Hope lost her appetite.

"Unless the banking industry has changed since I've been gone, that's illegal. You just can't give somebody money 'cause you feel sorry for them . . . not the *bank's* money."

"Well, I *did*," Hope said defiantly. *For somebody who is so "free" sexually, you sure are conservative in other areas,* she thought to herself. "You sound like I lent her *your* money."

"You *did* lend her my money! I still have an account at that bank."

Hope covered her mouth to quiet her sudden loud laughter. She laughed until tears formed in her eyes. Here she was telling one of the bank's depositors that the senior loan officer was making illegal lending decisions based on emotions. Tabitha had to laugh herself.

"You better hope she makes those mortgage payments." Tabitha spoke as if Hope was a mischievous child.

"No, *you* better hope she makes those mortgage payments. I don't have an *account* there." She stuck her tongue out again and dug into the salad. Laughter improved her appetite.

When the clock struck five, Hope let out the breath she had been holding all afternoon. She had told herself that if the bank's president hadn't marched into her office by that time, waving documents and demanding an explanation, he wasn't going to. Ms. Rendale had returned her call shortly after she had returned from lunch. Hope had been embarrassed by the extent of the woman's gratitude. When their call ended, Hope had been more certain than ever that she had done the right thing. Good or bad, access to money always brought changes to the lives of people who didn't have much of it.

She looked around her office to make sure everything was in place before she shut down her computer. Since she didn't have to pick the kids up from the Y until six, she decided to stop by the grocery store to get something for dinner that they could fix together. Helping out a fellow sister seemed to give her a burst of energy.

*   *   *

When she made it to the Y, David refused to give her a kiss. "You're late, Mommy." His lips were stuck out like a petulant child. Hope reminded herself that he was a petulant child. She smiled to herself; of her three sons, David was most like his father, and therefore the most challenging to her. She shook her head as he walked past her, making his own way to the truck. The twins allowed her to rub their heads affectionately. Karl and Jordan were unusually quiet.

"What's wrong?" The question was directed at both of them. They looked at each other in a way that told Hope that they were keeping something from her. "What's wrong?" she repeated with a little steel in her voice. They looked at each other again; Jordan as usual was the first to speak.

"We got our progress reports today." Hope used the keyless entry to open the truck door for a whining David. She held out her hand for thin slips of paper before she allowed the boys to climb into the backseat. Jordan's progress report (the last one of the school year) was great as usual . . . well above average in all areas, good conduct. Her eyes immediately sought the math grade when she looked at Karl's report card.

"Damn," she muttered under her breath.

Math—D
Karl needs additional help in this area. Please call to schedule a parent/teacher conference. His test scores are low.

A little bit of Hope's energy left her. *His conduct is good, and he's making the grade in his other subjects, but that math . . .* She cut her thought off midstream. Better to focus on the positive. "You guys are doing a great job and I'm proud of both of you." She saw the doubtful look that Karl gave her from her rearview mirror.

"I don't like that math grade, Karl, and I'm going to meet with your teacher to see what we can do to help you bring it up. When things don't come easy to you, it doesn't mean that you can't do it; it means you have to work that much harder. Okay?" He nodded back at her. "I had a hard time with fractions when I was learning too." Karl relaxed visibly and sat back in his seat.

"I'm hungry, Mommy, can I *pllleeease* have a snack when we get home?" David changed his tactics when he saw that he wasn't getting his mother's attention.

"Maybe."

The boys were more hindrance than help in the kitchen, but Hope allowed them to "cook" the tacos anyway. She was doing the dishes and the boys were finishing up their baths when Ray got home. "Hey, baby." She wiped her hands on a dishtowel and went to give her husband a proper greeting. He barely looked at her. It was obvious that there was something on his mind.

"What's for dinner?" He loosened his tie as he asked the question.

"We made tacos. I left some for you. I wish that you had called to let me know that you would be late."

"I was very busy, Hope." She didn't like his tone, she didn't know if he was irritated at her reference to his lateness or at the fact that she had prepared tacos for dinner.

"Is that all we have to eat?" *You live here too; you know that's not all we have to eat,* she thought.

"No, if you don't want tacos I could make you

something else," she offered, proud of herself. *I'm such a good wife.*

"You knew I wasn't going to eat those tacos when you made 'em." Ray looked at her as if he were the leader of some free nation and her choice for dinner was some sort of communist plot against him. *Now if I can do it, why can't he keep his smart-ass comments to himself?*

"You're right, Ray. What do you want?" *I am not going to argue with Ray Williams today.*

"You can make me a hamburger." He put his jacket on one of the chairs at the breakfast table and sat down to look through the mail.

What's the difference between a taco and a hamburger? Not much. Hope laughed to herself.

"What's this?" Ray was holding up the boys' progress reports.

"Oh . . . the boys got their progress reports today." She had intended to talk to him before he saw the reports.

"Did you see that Karl got a D in math?" *That's right, Ray, focus on the negative.*

"Yeah, but I'm sure he can bring it up." Her tone and her facial expression said "let's not panic." But Ray, *as usual*, paid no attention to her body language. He stared at her angrily. Hope sighed inwardly and rolled her eyes toward the ceiling.

Everything was always *her* fault. When David had stepped on a piece of glass in the kitchen it was her fault first, because *apparently* she hadn't swept the floor well enough, and then again because according to Ray, she "shouldn't let those boys walk around barefoot." If Ray couldn't find a tool he needed, it was *her* fault. She had struggled with that one for years, until she had come to the conclusion that Ray thought she was taking his wrenches and hammers to the pawn-shops in South Dallas. And his clothes . . . *oh* . . . that was another matter altogether.

"What?" Hope held her body defensively.

"*This* is what I've been talking about, Hope." He placed the progress reports back on the table and tapped on them with two fingers. "You spend all your time at that bank when your son is failing school." He looked at her as if he expected her to say, "*Yeah, baby, you're right, you've been right all along. I'm quitting tomorrow.*"

"Ray, I spend my time at *that bank* because that's where I work." *I guess I am going to argue with Ray Williams today.* "And Karl is not *failing* school. He is just having some difficulties with fractions."

"The *point,* Hope . . ." Ray spoke slowly, as if he were dealing with someone with limited mental capacity. *Oh, now I can't even pick out the relevant points of a conversation,* Hope thought sarcastically.

". . . is that your children need you at *home.* How far do you think Karl will get if he goes through school making Ds and Fs?"

Hope threw her hands in the air in frustration. "Oh my God, Ray, a D on a progress report in elementary school will not go on his permanent record!" Hope made quotation marks in the air as she said *permanent record.* And because she already knew the answer she asked, "If you're so concerned about our children end-ing up on skid row, why don't *you* stay at home?"

"And if I did, who would support this family? *You?*"

She really, really didn't like the disdain that he made no attempt to hide. "What the *hell* is that supposed to mean?"

His look told her that she knew what it meant, but he didn't say it. "Nothing, Hope." The fight suddenly went out of him, and he held up his hands to let her know that their argument was over. "I just had a very bad day, maybe I *am* blowing this out of proportion," he conceded. Hope was more than willing to let the argument drop. She didn't want to spend another evening fuming when she could be resting her head on her husband's shoulders. He looked tired and it had been obvious when he walked through the door that something was wrong.

"What happened?" As soon as the words were out of her mouth, she could have kicked herself for asking the question that she had promised herself that she would not ask again a thousand times. The answer was always the same.

"I don't want to talk about it." He got up from the table and walked toward their bedroom.

He doesn't want to talk about it, Hope repeated to herself. *As if our lives aren't linked . . . as if I don't have a right to ask him about the things that affect the quality of our lives together.*

After so many years of marriage, she still hadn't figured out how to be a supportive wife to a man who refused to talk about what bothered him. Who could get downright nasty if she pressed the issue. The last of her "energy burst" dissipated and she did what she had started doing about two years ago to shield herself from the hurt and disappointment she always felt when he shut her out—and it *was* a shutout, no mistaking it.

She took a deep breath, turned around, and went about her business. And on that day, her business was finishing the kitchen and helping her sons with their homework. *Good wife be damned. Ray will just have to make his own hamburger.*

Honey lips touch me
everywhere.
Finally, I have the
soft love that I
need.

Chapter Eight

Hope tried to control her excitement as she kissed David a final time before closing the back door of her truck. Ray was taking the boys to Atlanta to visit his mother. For the last three years, the boys had spent the first two weeks of their summer vacation with their grandmother. The drive up was a perfect opportunity for Ray to spend some time alone with his boys, and Hope had *never* looked so forward to time by herself. Ray looked a little impatient as he waited for Hope to finish her warnings and kisses.

"Now do what your grandmother tells you"—kiss kiss—"Call me every night"—kiss kiss—"You guys look after your little brother"—kiss kiss . . . kiss kiss kiss.

"Hope, that's enough. We need to get on the road."

"Okay, okay." She moved a few steps so she was standing directly in front of her husband. He was standing beside the truck waiting for *his* send-off. She didn't know what kind of send-off he expected, be-

cause things had been cool between them for the last
two weeks—not cold, just cool. So as not to disappoint
him in case he was hoping for a warm send-off, and
partially because she felt guilty for being so ready to
get rid of his ass for a few days, Hope wrapped her
arms around his neck and kissed him in a way that she
almost never did in front of the kids.

She put all of the sensuality that she suddenly felt
into the kiss. Teasing the roof of his mouth with her
tongue . . . sliding her arms from his neck to his back .
. . pressing her body as close to his as she could get
with clothes on. And when she felt his response—
hands on her ass, a slight movement of his hips, the
bulge in his denim shorts—she moved away slowly and
looked at him teasingly with her bottom lip caught between her teeth. "I know you have to get on the road."
She used his words. "Y'all be careful, and call me
tonight." She stuck out her tongue at him, and he
couldn't help but smile.

He got into the truck and buckled his seat belt before he said anything. "Be ready when I get back on
Monday night."

"Ready for what?" she asked, feigning innocence.
Ray pulled off as she waved to the kids for the last
time.

She walked back into the house and then practically
skipped into the master bedroom. Hope looked at the
unmade bed and an uncontrollable urge took over. She
jumped lithely on the king-sized bed and then proceeded to jump up and down as she allowed the boys to
do every once in a while. After a couple of minutes,
she allowed her body to fall freely back into the down
comforter. For the next three days she would be as free

as a bird. She closed her eyes and allowed herself to relish the possibilities.

During the last couple of months she had been busier than usual. Busy at work. Busy helping Karl bring up his math grade. She had presented the final report card to Ray triumphantly two days before, proud that Karl had brought his grade up to a B. She shook her head as she remembered the expression on Ray's face. He had looked almost . . . disappointed. She had smiled at him and made a comment about how skid row had been staved off for another year.

Her ongoing sarcasm hadn't done much for her marital relations over the last weeks. In her mind she had been giving Ray a taste of his own medicine. Not letting any perceived slight pass, making plans without consulting him, looking at him like he was crazy when he asked her to do something. And instead of teaching him a lesson as she had initially planned, she had fallen into a pattern.

As one day turned into two and two weeks turned into four, she had to remind herself that the no-nonsense, sardonic-smiling, distant woman walking around her house was not who she was. And the light had not gone off in Ray's head as she had hoped it would. Apparently Ray hadn't noticed any change in her behavior, or worse . . . he didn't care. On the other hand, the boys had noticed that something was different about their mother. David had been whinier than usual—if that were possible—Karl had worked almost *too* hard to bring up his math grade, and she had caught Jordan warning his brothers to "just do what she says" on more than one occasion.

Somebody on the outside looking in could have

come to the conclusion that she was a "bitch in train-ing." And since being a bitch had not been on her "things to do" list, she had decided that she would take her three days of solitude to reevaluate. She just hadn't figured out what exactly she needed to reevaluate. What she did know was that her current tactic had not improved her marriage—even temporarily—and that it was definitely messing with her kids' peace of mind.

But before she got down to her serious soul search-ing, she wanted to do some serious dancing. She rolled over and picked up the phone on the nightstand. She dialed Tabitha's number and wiggled her toes expec-tantly as she waited for her to pick up.

"Hello." Tabitha's voice was groggy. It was clear that she had been sleeping. Hope checked the time 8:17 A.M.

"Get up, girl, I need to talk to you."

"Hope?" Tabitha identified her voice. "What are you calling here so early for?" Tabitha made no attempt to hide the irritation in her voice. On weekends she had a ten/ten/ten rule in terms of telephone calls. Don't call her before ten A.M., don't call her after ten P.M., and don't call her more than ten times a day. Hope didn't care. She needed a partner in crime, and if anyone was up for a party it was Tabitha.

"What are you doing tonight?"

"I don't know. Why?"

"Because I want to go to Clyde's and I want *you* to go with me." The mention of the latest hot spot for Dal-las's "urban professionals," *i.e.* people of color, got Tabitha's attention. Hope had been listening to the radio spots for the club for the last three weeks. Tonight she wanted to be an "urban professional" and put all thoughts of "Mommy" and "wifey" out of her mind.

"Since when did Ray start allowing you to go club-bing?" Tabitha sounded leery.

"How many times do I have to tell you . . . Ray does not run my life." Hope wasn't too sure how true that was anymore, but she said it anyway.

"Oh, that's right." Tabitha did not respond to her statement and formed her own conclusion. "He's gone to Atlanta with the boys. When the cat's away the mouse will play."

"Look, I don't have time for your played-out clichés. Do you want to go or not?" She was hoping that Tabitha would say yes. There weren't too many other people she could ask. Stephanie wasn't much of a partyer . . . plus her baby was due any day.

"Why do we have to go to Clyde's? Everybody and their mother will be there tonight."

Hope took that for a yes. "Because I've never been there. And *I'm* inviting you, so I get to choose." Hope realized she sounded like Jordan when he was trying to get his way. "Now, what time are you picking me up?"

"You *know* that I'm not driving all the way out to the boonies to pick you up so that we can drive all the way back downtown. The club is about ten minutes from my house. Be here at ten o'clock."

"Ten o'clock?" Hope complained. "That's too late! I thought we could go shopping and get something to eat before we went to the club."

"Don't expect me to baby-sit you all day because your man is gone. I already have plans for an early dinner, thank you. You better grab a sandwich on the way over here."

"Well, if you're going to go out with me after the dinner it can't be *that* serious. Why can't I join y'all?" They had been friends long enough for Hope to feel comfortable enough to invite herself along. Tabitha laughed mischievously on the other end of the line.

"Believe me, you don't *want* to come along on this dinner date."

Hope laughed back at her friend. "You're *so* nasty." Hope shook her head and continued to laugh affectionately as she ended the conversation. "I'll be there at ten."

Immediately after ending the first call, Hope rolled over onto her stomach and dialed Stephanie's number. Stephanie's eleven-year-old answered the phone after only one ring. "Rodney, how are you doing, honey?"

"Fine, Aunt Hope. You want to talk to my mom?" he asked hurriedly, eager to get off the phone.

"Well, if *you* don't have a minute to talk to me you can put your mother on the phone." Rodney hesitated. Hope knew he was considering whether or not he could spare some of his precious eleven-year-old time. Apparently he could not.

"She's in the back. Hold on," he instructed. He dropped the receiver and shouted, "Mom, telephone!" There was a two-minute wait before Hope heard Stephanie's voice.

"I got it. Hang up the phone, Rodney!"

"Is that girl done yet?" Hope asked before Stephanie could speak. Lamar and Stephanie had decided to find out the sex of their fourth child at the last minute. Tamara Nicole Turner was two days overdue.

"Girl . . ." Stephanie sounded exhausted. "She's a diva *already*. Having us wait until she's ready to make her grand entrance. If she's not here by tomorrow . . . Monday morning, I'm checking myself into the hospital and I'm not leaving until she comes. It's too hard walking around one hundred weeks pregnant with these boys pulling on me." Hope laughed, enjoying her friend's feigned misery. She knew despite all of her complaints that Stephanie was beyond thrilled to be having the daughter she had waited so long for.

"What has Lamar been doing?"

Stephanie made a "do you even have to ask?" sound.

"Girl, pleeeaasse." Stephanie stretched out the last word. "He's worse than these boys. You would think that this is his first child. He's been walking around here getting in my way and talking to L.J. about how he needs to treat the baby." The love Stephanie felt for her family was evident in her laughter.

"Do you need anything?" Hope asked as she started to rise from the bed.

"No thanks, I'm okay. Have you changed your mind about coming to the hospital?" Hope would be god-mother to Stephanie's first daughter, and Stephanie had been trying to coax her to witness the actual birth.

Ever since she was nine years old and had accidentally seen a woman giving birth on a documentary for PBS, Hope had been squeamish about childbirth. She had closed her eyes when each of her own children had made their appearance in the world, and had requested in advance that they not be placed on her stomach all bloody and slimy as they had been on the show. *Seeing some things too early can scar you for life,* Hope thought and shivered in distaste as she remembered the show.

"Look, I love you to death, but I just don't think that my seeing you all spread-eagle and bloody is going to strengthen my relationship with my goddaughter-to-be." She said the words gently, so as not to offend. She knew from firsthand experience how sensitive pregnant women could be. "Some things should just be between baby's Mama and baby's Daddy."

"When you put it that way, I see your point." Stephanie still sounded a little disappointed and Hope felt bad—but not bad enough to change her mind.

"I'll call you later on," Hope promised.

"Okay, talk to you later." Stephanie was yelling instructions to someone before she could hang up the phone.

Hope looked at the textured ceiling as she considered what she would do for the next thirteen hours and eighteen minutes. She thought of and quickly dismissed going to a spa. A person had to be in the right mood to have her body picked at and squeezed by strangers . . . and she was not in the mood. Shopping, maybe? The movies?

Even though she thought of herself as an independent woman, Hope really didn't like going to the movies alone. And since she and Ray had different taste in movies she had missed seeing many of the ones that had caught her attention. She saw what Ray would consider "girly" movies when she could arrange a common time with her girlfriends . . . about three a year. On the rare occasions that Ray suggested they go to a movie together, it went without saying that he would choose what they saw.

"Why can't I go alone?" she wondered aloud. "I'm a big girl, and if I'm going to make some changes in my life, why not start there?" And when she could think of no good reason not to, she decided to go to see the romantic comedy she had been dying to see for about a month. She glanced at the clock again. The box office wouldn't open for at least another three hours, so she went into the kitchen to do something she had wanted to do for a lot longer than a month.

Hope hummed as she opened the door to reveal the contents of the massive refrigerator. She pushed some items around until she found the bottle of champagne that Ray had brought home from work. The pharmaceutical company had been having some sort of champagne giveaway for its top salespeople, and Ray had grabbed a couple of bottles for himself. She took out a jar of maraschino cherries as an afterthought. After opening the champagne, she took the champagne, the cherries, a family-sized bag of potato chips, and a beautiful crystal flute back into the bedroom.

With the cherries and champagne, she made herself a pink champagne cocktail, popped open the bag of chips with a big bang like she had seen the boys do, and settled back into the bed to watch music videos. She looked at the clock on the nightstand yet again to confirm that she was drinking champagne at nine o'-clock in the morning. *Life isn't so bad,* she thought smugly. *For lunch I'm having Frito pie with extra cheese and onions and a strawberry shake . . . no . . . strawberry and chocolate mixed,* she decided.

Chapter Nine

Hope drank the entire bottle of champagne for breakfast and fell into a somewhat drunken slumber. Later she saw a movie—not the romantic comedy; it was no longer showing at any of the theaters close to her—and found a restaurant that sold Frito pie. Though she had promised herself that she would leave her soul-searching/decision-making process for the next day, she couldn't help but think about her situation as she drove home later that afternoon.

She knew that if her mother was still alive she would tell her to be thankful that her life was going as well as it was. Her kids were fine, her job was stable, she was healthy . . . she had a nice house and good friends. Her marriage was . . . the word *decent* popped into her head. Lost in her thoughts, she took no notice of her surroundings as she pulled the truck into the garage and let herself inside the house.

She felt momentarily sad at the thought that *decent* was the best that she could look forward to. She wondered at what point her marriage had gone from great to good to decent. She put her keys and purse on the table and went to the refrigerator.

Decent is good, she comforted herself as she took vanilla ice cream from the freezer, then put it back when she remembered the shake she had just a couple of hours before, then took it *back* out because it hadn't been vanilla and one scoop wouldn't hurt. *No, decent is not good*, she corrected herself—soul searching was not effective if it wasn't honest—*decent is good enough*.

She decided that if she had to choose one thing in her life that was the root cause of her discontent—she wasn't ready to label herself as unhappy—it would be her marriage. And if she had to choose two, her job would be second on the list.

Hope knew of women whose relationships and marriages could be featured on one of the trash talk shows that she watched surreptitiously whenever she got the opportunity. *Having an opinionated, controlling husband is not the worst thing that I could have. He could be a womanizing homosexual drug addict who likes dressing up in women's clothing.* Hope smiled widely as she imagined Ray sneaking out of the house with his big feet hanging off the back of a pair of her high-heeled sandals.

By the time she sprinkled pecans on her scoop of vanilla ice cream turned chocolate sundae, she had decided that she didn't have a *real* problem with Ray being opinionated. *Hell, he can even be controlling if he wants.* She made a short mental list of some of the things and people that Ray could control. *He can control the kids. He can control the people he supervises. He can control the chlorine level in the pool. If only he wouldn't try to control every damn aspect of my life.*

Hope laughed out loud as she took her sundae into the bedroom and sat on the edge of the bed.

She started a second mental list as she licked the chocolate from the back of her spoon. *He wants to control my career, my hairstyle, my thoughts, and my friends* . . . Hope knew that Ray would have a fit if he knew she was going out with Tabitha that night. He had let her know in no uncertain terms that he did not approve of her lifestyle.

Hope finished her ice cream and allowed her list to become more creative and outrageous. *He wants to control my skin-care regimen . . . the brand of douche I use . . . how often I douche . . . the toenail polish I wear . . . the way I wipe my ass* . . . Hope fell back on the bed laughing.

The sad truth was, though, Ray really did want her to use a brand-name douche. She had discovered that fact two years into their marriage. She had fished an unopened four-pack of Walgreen's Spring Mountain douche from the trash. She had assumed that Ray had tossed it mistakenly, but he had told her "Massengill is better." And she "should spend the few extra cents for a quality product."

Apparently, he was more of an expert on feminine-care products than she was. She had refused to argue over something so *stupid*. So to save the peace, she had started buying *his* brand. She rationalized that he should have *some* say in the matter . . . after all, in those days he was spending almost as much time tending to her vagina as she was.

In the beginning of their marriage, it had been easier for Hope to work with what she had then considered Ray's little idiosyncrasies . . . his many little idiosyncrasies. Now it wasn't so easy; in fact, it wasn't *easy* at all. She had adjusted her habits and tastes in a thousand different ways to accommodate her husband. And for what? So that he could find a thousand new things that need changing.

Hope knew she was being a little unfair to Ray; it wasn't *his* fault she had started off their marriage being so accommodating. Her mother had *always* said, "Give a man an inch, and he'll take a mile." Or was that a yard? Hope couldn't remember. *Well, anyway*—she shook her head mentally to get herself back on track—*he's taken more than I wanted him to take.*

As the afternoon turned into early evening and evening turned into night, Hope continued her soul searching/reminiscing. When she was making the final turn to get to Tabitha's town home a light went off in her head. Her career and her marriage were inextricably linked. When she had felt most happy at work, she had felt most happy at home.

At one point her job had been challenging. She had been learning something new almost every day, working her way up the corporate ladder. Ten years ago the possibilities had seemed endless. Her days had flown by, and at night she hadn't had as much time to pick apart and analyze everything her husband did or said to her.

Take the movies, for instance. Ten years ago if Ray hadn't wanted to see a movie that she wanted to see, no big deal. She could call up Stephanie or one of her other girlfriends and they would go together. If Ray spent a night out with his boys, she went out with her girls, and if her memory served her correctly she had come in later than he ninety-five percent of the time.

Of course, she hadn't had children then, and neither had any of her friends. Children made it a little harder to leave the house at the drop of a hat—*at least for me,*

Hope thought somewhat resentfully. She couldn't change the fact that she was now a mother of three . . . wouldn't even if she could. But she *could* change her career.

She hadn't *intended* to stay at the bank for so long. She had planned to model her career after some of the women she had read about in business journals. By forty she had thought that she would be a vice president of *something. At the rate I'm going now*, Hope thought, *the only thing that I'll ever be vice president of is our community association. That is, if I work hard and learn how to play pinochle.*

But once she had started having her babies, the pace at the bank seemed to suit her needs. Ray had been working long hours and the kids needed someone there. And naturally the responsibility fell to her, the person with the nurturing heart and the milk-filled titties . . . the wife . . . the mother.

What to do? What to do? Hope tapped her fingers on the steering wheel as she waited for Tabitha to buzz her in through the security gates. Her littlest baby would be starting kindergarten in the fall, and Hope knew there was enough money coming into their household to hire someone to take up some of the slack if she decided to go back to school.

Go back to school? Is that what I need to do? she questioned herself. *Maybe not, but it's what you want to do.* She played a game of devil's advocate as she waited for Tabitha to come out.

Ray would have a fit.

Not if you presented it in a way that would be beneficial to him.

How could I do that?

Talk to him about how you've been feeling. Tell him

you'll be happier, he'll be happier, and the kids will be happier if you could fulfill one of your dreams.

Whatever!

Remember, Hope, there was a time when your power of persuasion over Ray was strong. Take that shit out of the closet, dust it off, and make him see the light. You can catch more flies with honey than you can with that tart-ass vinegar you've been using.

Maybe so. She nodded her head decisively just as Tabitha opened the passenger side door. *Maybe so.*

The two women walked into the club at about a quarter after ten. Since she had invited Tabitha, Hope paid the thirty dollars it took for both of them to get in. They stood for a moment at the entrance, absorbing the atmosphere. The place was packed! Wall-to-wall "urban professionals." Brothers were leaning over well-heeled sisters, whispering sweet nothings or nasty tidbits into their ears. The waitresses maneuvered their way through the crowd, holding the drinks like the experts they were. Hope wondered if they were cold in their short skirts and halter tops or if constant movement kept them warm.

People struck familiar poses along the walls. There was the pretty boy, standing nonchalantly near the front door so that he could get a look at every woman walking through the door, and more importantly, so that every woman walking through the door could get a look at him. There was the club regular, a man who probably left his wife and children at home alone every weekend so he could foster the relationships he had formed at that club and every other club in the city. And of course there were the women scorned, women recently divorced or dumped, determined to show their exes that they were still desirable and they were moving on with their lives. Too bad for them that the looks on their faces gave them away and that their exes were usually off with their new women and not in the club.

If she had to, Hope would categorize herself with the bored wives, out to see if the scene had changed since the last time they had ventured out. She was both disappointed and pleased to see it had not. She looked behind her and saw that Tabitha was searching the room for an empty table. Hope smiled in the dark, smoky room. Tabitha would be in a class by herself: the sophisticated bisexual indulging her less fortunate married friend by going to a place that she would not frequent under normal circumstances.

Hope tapped Tabitha on the shoulder and pointed to an empty table near the back of the room. The two women forged their way through the crowd, trying un-successfully to avoid booty-to-booty contact with their fellow clubgoers. Almost as soon as they sat down one of the scantily clad waitresses approached their table. "If you ladies would like something to drink," she paused as she placed napkins in front of them, "the gentleman to your right says it's on him." She waited with a small smile for their drink orders.

Both women glanced to the right, searching for their proposed benefactor. Their eyes settled on a man who looked to be in his early forties, graying hair, with a great smile.

"Two apple martinis," Tabitha ordered for both of them. The waitress sashayed away to get their drinks.

"Now why did you do that?" Hope questioned her immediately after the waitress left. "Now he's going to come over here and spend the rest of the night hounding us. That's not worth fourteen dollars to me." Hope shook her head and looked at Tabitha accusingly.

"He was going to come over here regardless." Tabitha smoothed her long hair. "If we had said no he would have come over to ask why we turned the drink down. If you're going to dance, you may as well dance with a brother who's willing to spend a few dollars." Tabitha was unrepentant. And her theory *did* make a little sense. "Besides," she added, "he won't hound us. He's not the type."

"How did you know that?"

"I just know. I know people." Tabitha waved thanks across the room as the waitress placed their drinks on the table.

"What is this?" Hope asked as she sipped the drink.

"An apple martini. It's what all the cosmopolitan people are having these days." Tabitha laughed at herself and took a drink.

"This is so good." Hope took another sip. "I'm *sooo* lucky to be in the presence of *such* a sophisticate." Hope raised her hands and bowed her head slightly, pretending deference. She was ready to have a good time.

"Yes, you are." Tabitha raised her eyebrow haughtily. They laughed and then quietly enjoyed their drinks and the R&B music that surrounded them. Tabitha was right about the man not hounding them. He had continued to sit alone at his small table, looking around the room and moving his head slightly to the music.

"I'm starving," Tabitha said suddenly as she drank the last of her martini.

"I thought you had dinner earlier?" Hope waited for an explanation.

"I didn't have time to satisfy *all* of my appetites tonight, so I had to make a choice."

"Okay, my interest is piqued. What *did* you end up doing tonight?"

"Oh no, sister!" Tabitha laughed and shook her finger playfully at Hope. "First of all, you *know* what I did tonight, and I'll be more than happy to share the details, but first you tell *me* what happened the last time Ray fucked you." Tabitha knew Hope would never reveal the details of her sex life with her husband.

What she doesn't know, Hope laughed to herself, *is that it's been a while since we've done anything worth keeping secret. But that's about to change.* Hope remembered her earlier resolve.

"You have a filthy mouth. I'm gonna start hanging out with the women from the church." The threat was insincere and Tabitha knew it. She picked up her martini, thinking that she would order another.

"My mouth is *not* filthy." She deliberately misunderstood her friend's words. "I brushed my teeth and gargled afterward."

Hope's laughter at Tabitha's unexpected words caused her to choke slightly on her drink. The last sip of her martini spewed from her mouth into the air. Hope was too amused to be embarrassed and both women laughed until tears formed in their eyes. They were still laughing as their benefactor approached.

"Excuse me. You ladies seem to be having such a good time, I had to come over to say hello." His voice was deep chocolate and got the attention of both women immediately. Hope patted her eyes with the napkin that her drink had rested on. *Oh my God! The man is gorgeous!* Apparently Tabitha thought the same thing because her shoe was making repeated contact with Hope's bare ankle.

"Hello," they said in unison. Hope looked at her friend and saw the wicked gleam in her eye. *See . . . I need to go home right now.* Tabitha stood up and extended her manicured hand.

"Tabitha . . . and this is my friend Hope." She nodded her head back toward Hope, exposing the smooth brown column of her neck. She smiled in a way that could only be considered seductive before she sat back down. Standing had served two purposes. One, it had allowed their "friend" to see that Tabitha had no "lumps" and that all of her "bumps" were in the right places. And two, it allowed her to reposition her crossed legs so as to maximize the view of her shapely thighs. Hope did not stand when the man turned to her.

"Thomas Matthews," he introduced himself and Hope shook his hand briefly before placing her hands demurely on the table. His smile encompassed both women. "You ladies mind if I join you for a moment?" He waited respectfully for their answer. Hope was about to invite him to sit down when Tabitha intervened.

"That depends . . ." She let her voice trail off. His look said okay, *I'll take the bait.*

"On what?"

"On whether or not you can . . . entertain both of us." Tabitha said the word "entertain" to let him know that it could be replaced with the verb of his choice.

"I'll do my best," he promised as he sat down. The waitress came back and they ordered another round of drinks.

*   *   *

For the next thirty minutes the three of them listened to the music and made small talk. Tabitha was flirting outrageously with the man. Initially her double entendres made Hope a little nervous. She didn't want the man to think that he was sitting between a couple of "freaks." But by the time she finished her second martini, she was relaxed and enjoying the interplay between Tabitha and Thomas. So much so that when Tabitha suggested they all dance together, Hope headed to the dance floor in front of them.

Hope moved with the beat of the music as she walked toward the circular maple dance floor. Thomas stepped ahead of her and cleared a space for them near the DJ booth. Hope was aware of the covert glances of both men and women. When it became obvious that two women would be sharing a dance partner, the looks of the women nearest them became openly disapproving. Black folks just didn't do that sort of thing in Dallas nightclubs.

Blame it on the martinis or blame it on the unexpected surge of adrenaline that Hope got from breaking an unspoken rule, but she decided to give the people something to curl their lips up over. She made eye contact with her friend in the dark nightclub and they smiled mischievously at one another. They were on the same page. They moved closer to the man between them, leaving him just enough room to move comfortably.

Hope gave herself over totally to the music, dipping and swaying as the beat called for. She and Tabitha synchronized their movements so that when one woman moved back the other moved forward. Thomas managed to pay equal attention to both women. He danced confidently, placing his hands lightly on hips

and shoulders at various points. It was impossible not
to notice the trio. It was all innocent fun, but those who
wanted could easily get the wrong impression. People
continued to look as they danced to a second song and
through a third.

When the DJ mixed a very popular slow song over
the final beats of Toni Braxton's latest single, Hope
knew it was time for her to sit down. She swiveled her
ass a final time and gestured to let Tabitha and Thomas
know that they should continue without her.

As Hope sipped on a fresh martini she watched her
old friend move sensuously against their new friend on
the dance floor. She smiled when Thomas leaned in to
whisper who knows what into Tabitha's ear. Tabitha
was the biggest tease Hope had ever encountered.
Hope had discovered, on the few occasions that they
had gone out together to a nightclub, that Tabitha took
great pleasure in saying *just* the right thing to make a
man to conjure up all sort of wicked scenarios in his
head.

She also knew that when Tabitha felt Thomas had
been properly titillated, she would become bored and
gracefully extricate herself from the sensuous web she
had woven. They would dance some more, maybe have
another drink, and when it was time for them to
leave—(on past occasions around one thirty)—Tabitha
would pretend to be *so* regretful that she could not
spend the night with the man. She was not *all* talk, but
she was discriminating with her action.

And as Hope predicted, it happened. Thomas had a
knowing look in his eye as he kissed both women
lightly on the cheek and thanked them for their company like a true gentleman.

Tabitha wanted to stop by the ladies' room on the

way out of the club, and Hope followed her in. Two other women stared at them rudely as they were checking for empty stalls. The two women stopped their preening to look at Hope as she went to wash her hands.

"Excuse me," one of the women said.

Hope looked around to be sure the woman was speaking to her before answering. "Yes?" Hope shook the water from her hands as Tabitha was coming out of the stall.

"That was my ex-boyfriend that you and your friend was just dancing all over."

Hope dried her hands . . . obviously this urban professional was looking for some drama. "Your ex? I'm sorry it didn't work out." Hope tried to keep her voice level; she wasn't looking for any drama.

The woman looked at her and then Tabitha and directed her next question to both of them. "Are y'all planning on hooking up with him after the club?"

Hope started to answer with a simple no, but at that point Tabitha took over.

"Didn't you say he was your *ex*?" Tabitha didn't wait for her to respond before going on. "Then don't fucking worry about whether or not we're hooking up with him." The look she gave the woman was full of disgust. "Let's go, Hope."

Hope followed her out of the club a little embarrassed at how harshly she had addressed the woman. "Damn, Tabitha," Hope said when they reached the car. "Did you have to be so mean?"

"Hope, that woman wanted to kick your ass and mine too, and she would have tried if we had given her a chance. That's your problem; you gotta learn how to cut shit off before it gets out of hand."

* * *

Hope sat straight up in the middle of the bed some-time before dawn that same morning. Her heart was beating fast and the hair at the nape of her neck was damp with perspiration. She was disoriented. When she realized that she was in her bed she looked around for Ray and remembered he was gone. She had been dreaming. Not a nightmare . . . but the dream had disturbed her nonetheless. She took a few seconds to process the dream in the dark room, and fell back into a troubled sleep.

Chapter Ten

Late Sunday evening, Lamar called to let Hope know that Stephanie was *finally* in labor. Hope waited at home for a few hours before going to the hospital. She wanted to give the baby ample time to slide out. Her timing was perfect. When she got to the hospital, Tamara was well on her way to becoming acquainted with her new world.

Hope was directed to Stephanie's room by one of the nurses at the nurses' station. She knocked lightly on the door. When she heard Stephanie call "come in" she opened the door quietly and peeked into the birthing room. Her eyes immediately took in the fact that the baby was cleaned and swaddled. *Thank God!* Hope thought as she moved in to get a good look at the closest thing to a daughter that she would ever have.

She smiled at Stephanie before she looked down into the scrunched-up face of her goddaughter. Her skin was red and splotchy, and Hope saw that there was not much hair atop her head. *But she has potential,*

Hope decided. She touched the area of the receiving blanket nearest Tamara's foot affectionately and turned her attention to her best friend.

She leaned in and touched Stephanie's cheek to hers. "You did it, girl." She kept her voice low so that she wouldn't disturb the wonder sleeping soundly on Stephanie's breast.

"Yeah. I'm glad it's over. They had to go ahead and do a C-section." Stephanie fumbled with the control on the side of the bed until she was in a more upright position. All three of Stephanie's sons were delivered via C-section, but when the doctor explained to her that there was no reason she could not opt for a vaginal delivery, she decided to go for it.

"What happened?"

"The doctor said that she was experiencing some distress, and that to be safe they wanted to just take her. It was fine with me, because after two hours her mommy was distressed too." Stephanie looked down at her daughter and used a *goo-goo* voice as she said the last few words.

"So basically, you've been miserable for the last few days when you could have just made an *appointment* to have the C-section that you ended up having anyway."

"Girl, I don't *even* want to talk about that. I'm just glad it's *over*. I've been so tired these last few days— no, not tired, *miserable*, that I haven't been able to think straight. But now it's okay because Mommy has her baby girl." Goo-goo talk again.

Hope looked at the woman who had been her friend for so many years as she looked down on her new daughter. She looked tired. She had a new mother glow, all right, but it wasn't the one that was portrayed on TV or in magazine ads. Though Stephanie was very attractive, she wouldn't be entering any beauty contests that day or any day soon.

Her face was swollen and she had bags under her eyes. Her lips looked dry and slightly cracked. She had had the presence of mind to have her hair braided a couple of weeks before her due date so at least it was caught back in a neat ponytail. But there was no question that as she looked down at her first born daughter that she was glowing. Hope thought what made women beautiful immediately after giving birth and the days after was relief, pride in themselves and in their newborn, and all the hope and possibility that flooded through their bodies with a first cry.

And though it wasn't true in the conventional use of the phrase, she said to her friend, "You look good." She couldn't hold back her laugh when Stephanie gave her a *girl, please* look from the corner of her eye. "Well, at least your coochie is still intact," Hope offered.

Stephanie laughed at Hope's unexpected statement. The laughter caused her to grimace at the pain, and she placed her hand on her sore abdomen.

"Girl, don't make me laugh. My *coochie* is still intact, but I'm as sore as hell." Periodically, whenever the subject of family size and her friend's desire to have "a mess of kids," as her mother used to say, came up, Hope teased Stephanie about how much her vaginal muscles would have been compromised if she hadn't been forced to have C-sections from the start. Hope had delivered all three of her boys vaginally, so she had and still did depend on Kegel exercises to keep her coochie at an acceptable circumference.

Out of respect for Stephanie's stitches, Hope changed the subject. "Where's Lamar?"

"He went to get something for us to eat. I'm starving and I refuse to eat *anything* in this hospital after what I've been through."

"I feel you, girl. The boys okay?"

Stephanie laughed again at the mention of her sons, this time a soft chuckle.

"Girlll, Lamar called the boys at his dad's house right after Tamara was born to let them know everything was all right. And Benjamin asked him to come and pick him up. Not so that he could come to the hospital and see his new sister, mind you, but so that he could take him home because he forgot one of his game cartridges." Benjamin was their middle son and had been the least excited about the pending birth. Hope laughed as she walked over to the sink and used the disinfectant soap to scrub her hands. She walked back to the bed and picked up the still-sleeping baby girl without asking. The rest of her visit she would spend bonding with Tamara.

She sat down with the baby in the rocking chair that the hospital provided. After positioning herself deep in the chair, she rocked the baby confidently. Though she wasn't *technically* a new mother, she too was filled with hope, possibility, and excitement because of this new life and the new life that she was planning to make for herself.

Chapter Eleven

The following Monday Hope sat at her desk surfing the Internet. The bank frowned on Web surfing that wasn't job related, but Hope had found that browsing through various sites was a stress reliever of sorts. Ray was due back home later that night, and since she hadn't figured out the best way to tell him of her newly made plans, she needed a stress reliever.

She was treating herself to a fantasy lux-shopping spree. Checking the designer Web sites for the latest fashions, she found a dress on clearance for 8,500 dollars that she just had to have, so she added it to her already full shopping cart. When her grand total was inching close to the 90,000-dollar mark, she emptied her shopping cart and found another Web site. She typed www.AfrAmerbankers. com and the familiar green and purple home page popped up almost instantly on her computer screen.

The organization had been established several years before, and Hope had joined the year before, but so far the extent of her involvement had been just what she was doing, checking the site for information on African Americans who were making waves in the business, and looking over their upcoming events. She moved her mouse and double-clicked on the coming events icon. Since it was a nationwide organization, the different chapters were always hosting one event or another. Her interest was piqued when she saw that the Houston chapter was holding a panel discussion on Friday at the Omni hotel from nine A.M. to three P.M.

Taking Our Place
Banking Opportunities in the 21st Century
The banking industry is growing and there are
many opportunities for African Americans in the
field. If you are currently in the industry or you
are considering a career change, please join us
for an eye-opening afternoon.

Hope sat back in her chair and thought for a minute. Then she picked up the phone and called the number posted on the page for those who needed additional information. As she waited for the phone to be answered, she came to the conclusion that finding out about the seminar was a sign—a sign that she was making the right decision.

I rarely check that Web site . . . The discussion is in four days . . . The kids are at their grandma's . . . It's in Houston! I could take a cheap flight and be home before dinner, and if the title holds true it's exactly what I'm looking for. Hope's thoughts raced as she mentally checked off the points that led her to make the phone call. She took a deep breath when the phone was finally answered. *Please! Please! Let there still be a slot open.*

Hope smiled widely a few minutes into the conversation after getting more information and finding out that, "Yes, there are a few spaces still available. I can get you registered over the phone with a major credit card." Hope nodded silently as she reached into her purse for her dark brown leather wallet.

Yep! God is definitely trying to tell me something.

Ray called Hope just before she left her office to let her know that he would be home a couple of hours earlier than he had originally planned. She stopped by the liquor store and bought a couple of her favorite bottles of red wine and decided to replace the bottle of champagne that she had had for breakfast on Saturday. When the salesperson told her the price of the champagne, she shook her head politely. If things went as she planned, Ray would forgive her. *Hell, he might even forget that he had it cooling in the refrigerator.* Hope paid for the bottles of wine and left the store.

At eight o'clock Hope was bathed, shaved, and ready to be laid. It had been a long time since she had used her feminine wiles for anything, so she had decided to take the casual approach with Ray that night. When she heard the garage door open she took a deep breath. She needed Ray to be in a good mood. The night would go so much better if he was.

Hope went into the kitchen and positioned herself in front of the open refrigerator. When Ray walked in he was presented with a nice view of her backside. She was wearing a thigh-length silk robe. The robe was black and patterned with green and purple hibiscus flowers. She had left the belt untied so that it would trail down, directing the attention from her ass to her calves.

"Hey," was the first thing Ray said when he walked in the door. Hope smiled to herself. He was tired; she could tell from the sound of his voice . . . but not *too* tired. She heard the rattle of his keys when he threw them on the kitchen counter. Hope grabbed a gallon of milk from the refrigerator and turned to greet her husband. She smiled sweetly when his eyes widened . . . slightly. Apparently, he was playing it casual too.

Another reason she had left the robe untied was to get her money's worth from the overpriced underwear she had on. Both panties and bra were a cool lime green color that complemented the flowers in her robe. The thong panties were cut very high and accentuated the curve of her hips beautifully. The bra snapped in the front, and though her breasts were fully covered, the material was so sheer that her nipples were clearly visible.

She closed the refrigerator door with her foot and Ray's eyes were drawn to the flexing muscles of her inner thigh. *Maybe this underwear is not overpriced*, Hope reconsidered. *You have to pay to play*. She was smiling wickedly to herself as she continued to smile sweetly at her husband.

"Hi, baby. How was your drive back?" Hope placed the milk on the counter nearest him. She knew he could smell her perfume . . . she had dabbed his favorite on *all* of her pulse points. She leaned in a little and placed a kiss on his cheek. "You look tired." She waited a minute for his response before walking to the cabinet where they kept their glasses.

"The trip was fine. I made good time because the

traffic was so light." Ray leaned against the counter. Hope could feel his eyes on her as she stood on her tip-toes to get a glass. He hadn't taken his eyes off her since she had turned around. She didn't really *need* to stand on her tiptoes to get a glass, but doing so made her robe rise just enough for Ray to see that her ass was bare . . . except for the tiny little string that was tucked safely between her cheeks.

"Good." Hope turned slightly to make eye contact. "I'm glad you're home. I missed you." She looked at him seriously for a moment . . . she *was* serious. Throughout the weekend she had thought constantly about how good things used to be between them. She felt that with enough effort it could be that way again.

"Do you want something to drink, honey? A sand-wich maybe?"

Ray ignored her question. "Is that new?"

Hope looked down at herself as though she had for-gotten what she was wearing. "Yeah, I picked it up a couple of days ago. Do you like it?" She looked him directly in the eye and waited for his answer. The tip of her tongue appeared to moisten her lips. They laughed at the same time. *Okay . . . maybe the tongue and the sultry voice was a bit much,* Hope admitted to herself. Their love games had been played too many times be-fore for her coyness to be anything but amusing. She had let Ray know early on in their marriage that he had a wife who would basically give it to him anytime he wanted it. She had also let him know early on that *how* she gave it to him was another matter altogether.

He walked to her, took the glass from her hand, and placed it on the counter. He put his hand inside the open robe and ran it along the smooth lines of her waist and hips.

"I like it," he answered softly. He brushed his rough cheek against her smooth one and she held her breath. *Ooh baby, that's what I like.* "You smell good."

Hope put both arms around his neck. "How were the boys when you left them?" *Oh . . . real sexy, Hope.*

Ray put his mouth against her neck. His kisses were butterfly soft. "I don't want to talk about the boys. I want to talk about how good you feel. With my eyes closed I can't tell the difference between the silk and your skin."

Okay, Hope rolled her eyes to herself and looked at Ray in disbelief. *Is he trying to sound like Barry White or Billy Dee Williams?* She didn't spend too much time thinking about it because the truth was, it really didn't matter to her . . . she liked it. She liked the way her husband's mouth felt against her skin, she liked the corny compliment, she liked the fact that Ray was trying to catch *his fly* with honey, and she really, really liked the familiar warmth that was coursing through her body.

Ray slid his lips across her cheek and traced the lines of her mouth with his tongue. Hope sighed and settled into the feeling. One of the hands that had been moving along the side of her body found its way to her backside. Ray spread his large hand and alternately squeezed and caressed the warm skin. He found the little piece of silk that joined the back of her panties to the front, and hooked it with a finger. He followed the string until it ended. Hope opened her legs just enough to allow his knuckle to make contact with the flesh that *really* was like silk . . . wet silk. And then he kissed her.

She realized they had never fucked on the kitchen floor . . . but she was willing.

"I missed you *so* much," she moaned. *Wait a minute, didn't I already say that?* The thought occurred to her as his tongue made contact with the roof of her mouth. She was unaware that she opened her legs just a tad bit more because her thoughts were focused on sensations, and the fact that no one . . . *no one* had ever had power over her mind and body like Ray had.

Just when her legs were about to buckle, Ray ended the kiss. Hope looked up at him through half-closed eyes. Ray had a half smile on his face. "I'm going to take a shower, babe. I think I will take you up on your offer to make me a sandwich. Bring me some orange juice too on a tray." He laughed slightly and turned away toward the bedroom. Leaving her hanging.

Hope stood for a moment with her mouth slightly open and then she smiled at Ray's retreating back. *I did offer to make him a sandwich. That's fine.* She shrugged her shoulders. *Sandwich now . . . dessert later.*

A few minutes later when Ray got out of the shower, Hope and his sandwich were waiting for him on the side of the bed. Ray had tucked a towel securely around his waist, and the stark whiteness of the cotton looked good against his dark skin. He picked up the tray and sat next to her.

"We don't have any pickles?" Ray looked at her with raised eyebrows. Hope knew it was a rhetorical question. They had three boys—they always had Popsicles, potato chips, and pickles. She let him know with a look that she wasn't going back into the kitchen for a pickle.

"That's okay," he said as he bit into his sandwich.

"It's good, baby. Thank you." Ray kissed Hope lightly on the cheek before he took a second bite.

I know it's okay, Hope thought even as she moved her body behind his in the bed.

She kneeled behind him and placed her hands on his shoulders. Then she kneaded the tension from his shoulders as he made short work of his sandwich and drink. He broke contact with her hands for a moment to place the tray on the floor when he finished.

"Did you miss me?" Hope's mouth was close to Ray's ear, so she caught it between her teeth.

"I wasn't gone long enough to miss you." She knew he was smiling though she couldn't see his face.

She lifted herself higher on her knees and moved her body closer to his. Her hands caressed his chest and pulled at the coarse hair that she found there. She pulled playfully as her tongue circled his ear. "Mmm . . . That's too bad. I had something really special planned for you, but since you didn't miss me . . ." Her words trailed off as she found the knot in his towel and loosened it.

"What did you have planned for me?"

Hope rested her hands on his thighs, refusing to touch the flesh that she *knew* he wanted her to touch.

"Okay, I'll give you another chance. I missed you, Ray, even though you were only gone a few days. Did you miss me?"

"Of course I missed you, baby. I thought about *it*—I mean *you* every mile from Atlanta to Dallas. I got three speeding tickets trying to get here. I wet my pants because I didn't want to take the time out to stop for a piss . . ."

Before he could tell another lie, Hope fell back on the bed laughing. He was being too ridiculous.

Ray turned around and his towel stayed on the bed. He stretched his body out over hers. "Why is that funny? You don't believe I pissed on myself? Why do you think I was in such a hurry to take a shower?" Hope continued to laugh as Ray nuzzled the side of her neck. *This is so much fun. I wish it could be like this every night. Don't be greedy, Hope*, she chided herself, *four nights a week is plenty.* She struggled to get up when Ray started to part her legs and assume the position.

"Wait a minute." She pushed at his shoulders but he wouldn't move.

"What for? I know you're ready." He touched the soft material of her panties to prove his point.

She knew he was ready too, but she pushed a little harder and got off the bed and stood in front of him. She moved her shoulders and the robe fell to the floor. Ray was on his back. She wanted him sitting up.

Hope pulled him up by the arms and straddled him, then proceeded to roll and rock on his lap until he was as hard as she was wet. She kissed him as deeply as she could, and she was rewarded when he tangled his tongue with hers before breaking away.

Ray unfastened the front clasp of her bra and moved his mouth from one breast to the other. He reached down to feel the softest part of her body and slid his fingers back and forth. Hope moaned, totally into the sensations they were creating in each other. He grabbed himself and pushed his hard flesh forward. "Sit on it, baby. Show me how hard you can ride."

She started to do just that, but instead she moved her body until she was kneeling before him. *This* time they didn't laugh when she licked her lips. "What should I do now?" Hope took slow, deep breaths as she waited for his answer.

He guided himself toward her waiting mouth. She pretended that she didn't want it, and closed her wet lips, refusing access.

He played along gladly, rubbing it back and forth across her mouth as she turned her head from side to side. In a short time she allowed him to force it past her lips, past her teeth, and deep into her mouth. Ray murmured words of encouragement as she closed her mouth firmly over him.

"Oh, baby." Ray stroked her short hair as she moved her tongue, lips, and hands in the way that maximized his pleasure. "I love it when you suck my dick," he whispered.

No shit. She almost giggled. Almost, but she didn't. Ray would be really offended if she laughed while she had his dick in her mouth. *Dick* was a very serious matter as far as Ray was concerned.

"Play with my nuts," he instructed her roughly. If her hair had been longer she knew his hands would be tangled in it, but since she had cut it he started to squeeze her shoulders during their most intimate times. She caressed him lightly with her tongue, occasionally raking her teeth over him . . . just to scare him a little bit. Then she got down to business.

She pulled him into her mouth over and over again until she felt he was at the brink . . . and then she stopped. Through trial and error, she had discovered that if she delayed his orgasm he came harder in the end. Hope ran her tongue and fingers lightly over his most sensitive parts until his breathing was under control, and then she took him into her mouth again and sucked harder and deeper than she had before.

She was in a subservient position. On her knees in front of her husband, servicing him. But she was in

control. She could tease him, make him beg if she
wanted to. And she did.

"Come on, Hope," he said when she let him slip out
of her mouth to kiss and massage his sensitive inner
thighs.

"Come on what?"

"You know. Don't stop, baby. I was just about to
come." She knew the few seconds that she paused
seemed like hours to him. But still she played with
him, moving the beads that formed at the head of his
dick back and forth with her tongue. Blowing and
sucking, caressing and licking. And when his moans
got louder and his requests became demands, she knew
he was at the breaking point.

He stood up and she leaned her head back as far as
she could and accepted him into the back of her throat.
Ray thrust his hips forward and she grabbed his ass as
she continued to move her mouth over him expertly.
He grabbed her head and pushed forward one final
time, and Hope held on as she felt the shudder move
through him and his body go limp.

He laughed slightly and moved slowly back onto the
bed. She climbed into the bed to lie close to where he
had positioned himself. "It's been a *long* time since
you sucked my dick like that." He sounded pleased.
She shook her head mentally as she tried not to take
exception to his statement. *Ray is just spoiled. It's not
enough that I suck his dick on a regular basis . . . he's
concerned about the quality of the sucking.* She knew
more than one woman whose husband would be grateful to get it as often as Ray did. Some of her friends
were squeamish or uptight about the whole oral sex
thing; some sucked only on birthdays and one or two
major holidays.

"Don't I always make you feel good?" She pouted and hooked her naked leg over his.

"Yeah, but sometimes it's just *incredible*."

Hope's smile was self-satisfied. *Now how can I be mad at the man for recognizing quality work?* As she slid her legs back and forth across his, she remembered that only half of them was satisfied.

"I *love* to suck your dick. I love to hear you moan. I love it when you come. It makes me *so* wet." Her voice was warm and sweet in his ear. Ray took one of her hands and moved it until it was between his legs. She was not surprised to find that he was hard again. He never left her hanging.

After she had stroked him for a few seconds he pulled her on top of him and lifted her slightly so that he could remove her panties. "Are you ready for your ride, baby?" He pulled her face close to his for a kiss.

"I've *been* ready," she whispered against his lips. He placed his large hands on her hips and positioned her. She slid down onto her husband and inhaled sharply as he filled her and pleasure immediately coursed through her body.

Chapter Twelve

Hope got up early enough to fix breakfast for Ray. She knew she was laying it on a bit thick, but after the night they had, she *felt* like it. Ray walked into the kitchen, and when he saw her standing in front of the stove, frying *his* eggs, in high heels, an apron protecting her suit, a smile spread across his face.

He walked behind her and kissed her on the neck. "You're making *breakfast* for me? Do you know how long it's been since you've made breakfast for me?"

The hairs on the back of Hope's neck started to rise, and not from the kiss. *That's the second time he's started that "it's been a long time" song,* she thought as she slid his eggs onto a warm plate.

"Ray, I make breakfast *every* weekend. And *every* weekend you or someone who looks exactly like you sits right in that chair and eats whatever I place on the table." She was unaware that her head moved back and forth as she spoke.

"I know you do, baby, and I appreciate it. But that's

more for the boys. It's nice when you do something just for me." Hope *could* have pointed out that the boys were perfectly content when she served them Pop-Tarts and that it was *Ray* who had suggested years ago that it would be nice if she made a big breakfast at least one day of the weekend. So in reality the breakfast she prepared on the weekend was really more for *him*. She could have pointed this out, but she didn't.

Hope rolled her eyes toward the ceiling and shook her head in a "what am I going to do with you" manner. *Men are such babies,* she thought, smiling. She added bacon and toast to the plate and put it on the table.

"*Boy*, just be quiet and eat." She pretended to be exasperated, but she hoped she understood what he was saying. "You want tomato or grapefruit juice?"

"Tomato," he answered between bites. She poured his juice and joined him at the table with coffee and toast.

They shared their breakfast and pleasant conversation for the next twenty minutes. The time went so well that when Hope got to work she had a big smile on her face.

That evening they watched a movie and Ray rubbed her feet. Neither brought up the fact that they were getting along better than they had in a long time. In fact, Hope realized, they had never addressed the fact that they *weren't* getting along.

She jokingly told him that they should leave the kids in Atlanta for the entire summer . . . or at least she thought she was joking. He seriously told her that he loved her. And then they made love on the couch. And just as she was about to come, she told him there was nothing that she wouldn't do for him. And she meant it . . . or at least she thought she did.

* * *

After two days of wedded bliss, Hope felt confident enough to broach the career thing with Ray. She brought home Chinese takeout, rubbed his back, and they made love, this time with her leaning over the bathroom sink. And when he was about to come the thought occurred to her that if things continued as they were, she could leave well enough alone and not mention going back to school, feeling unfilled at home, but how could she?

Even though they had been flowing the last couple of days, Hope was inexplicably nervous. There were knots in her stomach and she didn't like the weakness she heard in her voice when she started to talk. So much was riding on his reaction.

They were sitting up together in bed. Ray was watching a sports channel and Hope was pretending to read a book. She put the book on the nightstand and turned toward him. "I had the strangest dream the other night, and I've been thinking about it ever since." He made some unintelligible sound and continued to watch recaps of the day's sporting events. "Ray!" Hope prodded him with her elbow to get his full attention.

"I'm sorry, baby. What did you say?" *He hasn't called me "baby" this much since he was trying to get with me for the first time*.

"I wanted to tell you about my dream." Hope could see that he was torn between the television screen and pacifying her. She felt a surge of confidence when he shut off the television.

"Well," she started, "I was living in a house with a few people who weren't related to me. Sorta like a dorm or college living arrangements. Anyway, I had the *weirdest* feeling that they didn't want me living there with them. I had this heavy feeling because I thought they were plotting against me, but I wouldn't say anything to them about it. But one day I got up enough nerve to ask them about it. I said, *do y'all want me here or what?*" Hope moved her hands and her head as she pictured herself doing in the dream. Ray was looking confused.

"They said, *no, we don't want you here, we want you out of here*. And then I didn't know what to do." Hope's voice held all the mixed emotions she had felt in the dream. "I went into the bathroom and my nose started to bleed profusely.

"I mean, my clothes were *soaked*. The blood was making puddles on the floor." Hope's voice slowed and her eyes watered slightly as she replayed the dream that had been so disturbing to her. "Standing in that bathroom, I *knew* . . . I was going to die. I opened the door and shouted out for someone to call 911. Then everybody rushed to the door to help me, but I noticed that two of the people who told me they wanted me out just stood in the background.

"I needed help, but I wouldn't let anyone come into the bathroom. I waved them away and asked them to just call 911. They all turned away to go, and I was standing in the bathroom with my life's blood pouring out of my nose. And then this lady stepped in and she said to me so calmly, *you know, if you pinch the bridge of your nose the bleeding will stop*. And when I did it, the bleeding stopped immediately. Before she left the bathroom, she looked at me, smiled, and said, *find somewhere else to live*."

When she finished recounting her dream Ray stared at her blankly for a minute. "That *was* a weird dream." She wasn't sure, but she thought she saw amusement lurking somewhere in the back of his brown eyes. He flipped the TV back on.

Hope grabbed the remote and flipped it off again. "I'm not finished."

Ray held up his hands in defeat. "Go ahead, Hope."

Yep, she thought, *he's definitely patronizing me.*

"Like I said, I've been thinking about the dream, trying to figure out what it means."

"And what *does* it mean, Hope?" His face was screwed up, and she was sure he was regretting turning off the television in the first place.

"I'm not sure," she chose her words carefully, "but I think it means that I'm not doing what I need to do to help myself." She looked at him closely to see if she was making any sense to him. She wasn't. "In the dream I didn't speak up about how I was feeling and then when I did, I discovered that the answer to my problems was right under my nose."

The amusement was no longer lurking. "Okay, Hope, first of all, what *is* your problem, and second, what's the answer that's right under your nose?" Ray sighed and looked at her in a way that she felt was condescending.

"I don't know, Ray. These last few weeks we've been walking around this house like we don't even know each other. We do what we have to do for the kids, we get together at night . . . and the rest of the time it's like we go our own way. I don't know what you're feeling and when I try to talk to you about how I feel, you're not interested." Hope remembered one of the rules of effective communication—only use "feeling" statements. "Well, I *feel* like you're not interested."

"When have you tried to talk to me about how you feel?" His tone was slightly elevated. *Now he's defen-*

sive. I should probably just smile and drop this. But she couldn't.

"Like work, for instance. When I try to tell you about how I feel about advancing my career, you get pissed. I tell you about needing more from you emotionally and you think I'm trying to irritate you. *You* decide when we make love, *you* decide what our roles are in this marriage . . ." *Whoa, Hope,* she cautioned herself, *you are bringing up the wrong things at the wrong time. Just tell him you want to go to graduate school and you would like his support.* But she couldn't.

"I feel like all I do is serve this family. I don't expect the boys to appreciate it, but it would be nice if you would say, once in a while, 'good job, Hope,' or 'I'm glad you're my wife.'" Hope put her face in her hands momentarily; she was surprised that tears had formed in the corners of her eyes. *This is some bitter fucking honey.*

"So basically what you're saying is that your problem is me?"

"No, Ray, I'm saying that *we* have a problem, and that we have to stop ignoring it and do something about it."

"I'm not ignoring *shit,* Hope. You create problems where there are none. I come home hoping we could spend some time together, like you're always on my ass to do, and you bring up this bullshit!"

"It's not bullshit, Ray." Her voice was low, defeated. "I can't believe that you're not even *trying* to understand what I'm talking about." She resisted the urge to cover her face again. Ray stood up.

"Well, let me say this, Hope." He made no effort to keep it casual. "I understand that every few months you come to me with this same bullshit. Do I love you?

Do you make me happy? Do I think you look good? And every time I tell you the same thing . . . Yes! Yes! Yes! Well, yes, yes, yes, and yes again!

"You can try and disguise it by talking about a dream, but I know you're asking the *same* questions. Now ask me this: Do I work my fucking ass off to provide for this family? Yes. Do I want to be left alone when I ask to be left alone? Yes. Do I think your main priority should be caring for your family? Yes. Since you're so fucking *curious*, ask some questions about what *I* want sometime." And with that he left.

Hope sat on the bed for a minute. She could not believe their nice quiet evening had changed so quickly. The venom with which Ray said the words frightened her. The last few days she had allowed herself to be lulled into a false security . . . she had forgotten that there were eggshells littering every floor in their home.

She walked into the bathroom and turned on the water to let it heat up for a minute before she stepped in. She was going to take a shower, and it didn't matter that she had taken a shower less than an hour ago. After standing under the sharp, hot spray for a few minutes, Hope slid onto the marble floor of the shower. Her mind was blank. She was so numb that she couldn't begin to consider what Ray had said. She couldn't even remember if he had said it before.

She plugged the drain with her towel and thought that if she didn't have to work the next day, she would let the water run until it reached the top of the shower. When she dismissed the idea, all she could think of was that she needed a change, that she was going to *make* a change and it didn't matter . . . it didn't matter.

Chapter Thirteen

"I can't think of anything else to do." Hope examined the pattern on her office ceiling as she listened to Stephanie's voice on the other end of the phone.

"Why did you bring it up like that? You know men don't like to talk about anything when they're trying to relax."

"Well, the thing is, Stephanie, anytime Ray is at home he wants to relax. So there is *never* a good time to bring up *anything*. And I'm just tired." The empty feeling had remained with Hope throughout the night and had followed her to work.

"Well, try bringing it up again tonight, but this time don't criticize him. Relate what you want to do to him and the kids."

"Did you hear me, Stephanie? I'm tired. Shit! I have to always figure out how to approach him. Do you think he's sitting in his office right now trying to figure out how he could have handled our conversation differently?" And since it was a rhetorical question, Hope answered before Stephanie could. "No, he's not!"

"I think it's quite possible that he is. Call him and ask him."

"I'm not calling him. I have been so nice to him these last few days, and it didn't make a bit of difference."

"Wasn't he nice to you too? From what you said this past weekend, you had made up your mind to take a whole new approach to the situation. From what you told me, it sounds like you did the same thing that you always do."

Hope took a deep breath. "And what do I *always* do, Stephanie?"

"You get mad if Ray doesn't react exactly how you want him to react."

"What? You know what, Stephanie—" Hope cut off her angry words when she remembered that her friend was at home with a new baby and shouldn't be upset. She sighed. *Nobody understands me.* "Let's just forget it. I'll figure something out."

She made her voice deliberately cheerful. "How is our baby girl?"

"Why are you changing the subject?"

"Because, Stephanie," Hope shook her head in frustration, "I didn't call you for a lecture. And I'm not in the mood for another argument. I don't have the energy." Stephanie was quiet for a moment and Hope knew she was considering whether to press the issue. Thankfully, she did not.

They spent the next ten minutes talking about the new addition. Hope put her hands over her eyes after they ended the conversation.

She had a headache, and she was beginning to wonder if Ray had not chosen the wrong woman that first day on campus. When she took a minute to think about it, she realized that her best friend and her husband were very similar in terms of their values and personalities. Stephanie had decided that it was best for her family if she stayed at home—Ray wanted a stay-at-home wife. They both wanted large families, they had the same dry sense of humor, and they both spent a lot of time telling her what she was doing wrong.

She realized that last statement was not fair to Stephanie. Her friend had been very supportive, but she could never just *listen* . . . she always had an opinion. And Hope didn't want to hear any more opinions about how she should handle her business.

The clock on her desk told her it was almost time for the meeting she had scheduled with her staff. She was not in the right state of mind to hold a productive meeting. She couldn't recall a time when she had felt so much apathy. Just when she was about to call Helen and have her cancel the meeting, her phone rang.

"Hope Williams," she answered.

"Hey, Hope." Her body tensed when she recognized Ray's voice at the other end of the line. She took note of the slight cheerfulness in his tone. *Obviously he doesn't know that we're not speaking to each other.*

"Yes, Ray?" She kept her voice cool and dry.

"Are you going straight home after work?" Her body relaxed somewhat. *Maybe he's ready to talk.* She mentally crossed her fingers.

"I think so. Why?"

"Because I have to work late and I need you to pick up my gray suit from the cleaners."

This mother . . . Hope took a deep breath before she spoke to her husband. *I refuse to let him fuck with me.*

"Yeah, Ray, I'll go to the cleaners. Is it just the suit?"

"Yeah, thanks, babe."

She hated it when he called her *babe. Well, since you're in such a good mood . . .*

"Oh, Ray, before you hang up . . . I forgot to tell you that I'll be at a seminar in Houston tomorrow."

"For work?"

"Well, actually, it's something that I'm doing on my own. I plan on networking and finding out what I should be looking into when I sign up for some classes this fall."

"Sign up for classes? When did you decide this?"

She was pleased that his voice had lost its cheeriness. "I tried to tell you about it last night, Ray, but apparently you weren't interested."

"Hope . . . whatever." She could almost see the expression on his face. She could almost see him throwing his hand up. "Yeah, Hope, just do whatever the hell you want."

"I know, Ray, just as long as I pick up your suit. *Right?*" She hung up the phone and did not say goodbye.

Chapter Fourteen

Hope helped herself to the coffee that was laid out and found a seat toward the front of the hotel conference room. After all her big talk to Ray, she was not in the mood to network; in fact, she had almost decided not to come. Forcing herself to sit up straight, Hope fixed her face into what she hoped was an interested expression.

Around the room, others appeared to be doing the networking Hope had planned to do. People were standing in groups or pairs talking excitedly, sipping coffee, and passing out business cards.

I didn't even think to bring a business card. She shrugged and smiled politely at the woman taking the seat next to her and then turned her attention back to the people who were quickly filling the room. The people were mostly well dressed, but Hope spotted at least one brother with a royal purple suit on. That was enough to make her lips turn up into a slight smile.

"Excuse me. Excuse me." The woman sitting to the

left of her was trying to get her attention. Hope considered ignoring her, but she wasn't trying to be a bitch that morning.

When she had gotten home with Ray's suit, she had turned up her bitch factor full throttle. If she was like a bitch in training before, then last night she had been like a bitch on the fast track to management.

Hard stares, cold shoulder, rolled eyes, sarcastic comments . . . she swore Ray had muttered *Thank God* under his breath when she had announced that she was going to bed. She had been surprised—disappointed, actually—at how quickly she had tossed aside her resolve to put some sweetness back into her marriage.

"Excuse me," the woman said again.

Before Hope turned around she fixed a polite smile on her face. "Oh, I'm sorry . . . are you talking to me?"

"Yes, I am." The woman sounded impatient. "Are you here by yourself?"

Oh Lord, I hope she doesn't want us to buddy up. "Yes, I am," Hope admitted reluctantly.

"Well, I hate to ask, but . . . the room is almost full, and my friend and I would like to sit together. Do you mind moving to one of the other empty seats?" In what Hope presumed was an attempt to be helpful, the woman pointed out a more *suitable* seat for her. *Talk about a bitch.* Hope answered the woman with a *look* and turned around without saying a word.

Now that was ugly, she told herself.

So? She told herself right back.

Go ahead and be a bitch, then.

Thank you, I will.

"Excuse me." This time the voice was to her right and it was male. Hope looked up and recognized him immediately. The smile on her face was . . . strange.

"Hello." She stood up too quickly and some of her coffee sloshed out of the cup and onto his square-toed shoe—brown leather. The small purse that had been resting in her lap fell to the floor. They bumped heads when they both reached down to pick it up, and the bitc—*woman* sitting next to her laughed under her breath.

"Hey, what did I do to deserve this?" He smiled teasingly at her just as he had done at Ralph and Lisa's party. He rubbed the spot on his head that had made contact with hers. "Ouch!"

"I'm sorry." There was laughter in Hope's voice, as she stooped, alone this time, to pick up her purse. She stood up and shook his outstretched hand.

"Remember me? Anthony Bolden. I met you at Ralph and Lisa's anniversary party a couple of months ago."

"Yes, I do." Her smile was bright. *Let the networking commence.* "Hope Williams," she offered, sure he had forgotten her name. "It's good to see a familiar face."

"Let's go and get you another cup of coffee." Hope looked back at the sitting woman and smiled at her as though they had been having a friendly conversation.

"I guess your friend can go ahead and take my seat." She pretended that she didn't see the woman's sarcastic smirk before she turned around.

"So, did you come to Houston just for the conference or are you here on other business?" He made small talk as they walked toward the table that held refreshments.

"Just for the conference. I took a flight out of Dallas this morning." His suit was a summer wool, and Hope thought that he had done a great job coordinating the chocolate in the suit with the rust in his shirt and tie.

"What about you?"

"I live here. Not too far from the hotel, in fact. Sugar? Cream?" He was actually making her a fresh cup of coffee. She took her coffee black with artificial sweetener.

"Yes, thank you." After he added just the right amount of sugar and just the right amount of cream, he looked at her with a friendly glint in his eye.

"If I give you this coffee, do you promise not to burn me again?"

Hope took the cup, laughing. "I guess you'll just have to chance it." She caught her bottom lip with her teeth and released it before sipping from the cup. He glanced at his watch, and Hope couldn't help but notice that he wore the same expensive brand as Ray.

"Listen, if you haven't made any plans for lunch, I'd like to take you to this place I know of around the corner. Then we can talk."

About what? she wondered, but didn't ask. "Sure."

"We're about to get started, so I need to take my seat."

"Is there a seat near you?"

"Well, there is a seat next to mine, but it's occupied." He pointed to the makeshift stage set up in the front of the conference room. "I'm speaking today."

"Oh, I didn't realize." She smiled, a little embarrassed.

He smiled back at her, not embarrassed at all. "As vice president of the Houston chapter of African Americans in Banking, it would be my pleasure to help you find another seat." He placed his hand lightly on her back and urged her forward. "Come on." Anthony found her another seat close to the front with very little effort. "I'm going to keep my eye on you. Don't make me have to look for you during the break," he warned.

Hope smiled. *Is he flirting with me?* "Thank you. Is everyone involved with the Houston AAIB so solicitous?" She drew her teeth across her bottom lip as she waited for his answer. *Am I flirting with him?*

"Solicitous?" He raised his eyebrow. His smile was warm. Too warm. "I like a woman with a vocabulary." He nodded his head approvingly and walked away without answering her question.

He is flirting with me.

Hope paid close attention as Anthony Bolden again took center stage. He was serving as a sort of facilitator for the conference. He had made the welcoming remarks and so far had introduced each of the speakers. She couldn't help but be impressed with his easy style and apparent comfort in front of an audience. *And his good looks and his commanding voice and his humor and his . . . Okay, okay . . .* Hope tried to hush the voice in her head and concentrate on what Anthony was saying. *He's attractive and well spoken, let's leave it at that.*

No. The brother is as fine as hell and you know it.

Whatever. Hope dismissed the thought with a mental click of her tongue.

Anthony spoke at length about his work as an investment banker; he also talked about his background and what kind of credentials were needed to hold his position. The more he spoke, the more fascinated Hope became. He made the work sound exciting and important. *Just what I want . . . what I need.*

* * *

A couple of hours later, Hope sat across from Anthony—*Tony,* as he had insisted that she call him—at a Mexican restaurant. It was close to the hotel, as he had promised, and Hope noticed that some of the other conference-goers had decided to eat there also. The restaurant was festively decorated and the waiters and waitresses wore traditional Mexican garb. Hope thought the jalapeño lamps were a bit much. Her survey of the restaurant was cut short by the sound of masculine laughter coming from the opposite side of the table.

"What?" Hope was eager to be in on the joke.

"You should see the look on your face." His laughter was pleasing. "I know this place is kinda cheesy, but *I swear* I've never had a better enchilada in my life. You like enchiladas don't you?"

"I *love* enchiladas and I think the place is . . . charming." His look told her that he didn't believe her. "Okay," Hope admitted, "the food had better be good, because this place is pretty damn cheesy." They laughed again, and Hope realized she had never been so comfortable with . . . the only word that she could think of was *stranger*.

Tony ordered beef for himself and the cheese that she had requested. He looked to her for approval and got it before ordering margaritas on the rocks for both of them. "What do you think of the seminar so far?"

"I've really enjoyed it. I'm almost ashamed of how little I know about the opportunities that are out there. I've become so complacent at work." Hope shook her head. "I know I need a change."

"Did anything in particular pique your interest?"

Hope was nodding before he finished asking his

question. "Well, actually, I'm really interested in learning some more about mortgage lending, getting the word out to people who don't think they would be able to qualify for, much less afford their own home. Before I leave today, I'm going to get the number of the last woman who spoke this morning. Find out some more about what I need to do to get started. I mean . . ." Hope thought about how displeased Ray had been at the thought of her investing more time in her career. "If that's the course I decide to take." The waiter placed their drinks in front of them and Hope's eyes lit up in approval at her first sip. "This is *good*."

"Did I neglect to mention that they also have the best margaritas this side of Cancun?" He took a drink from his glass and Hope's eyes were drawn to his lips. They were full and very smooth looking. She liked the fact that they always appeared to be ready to smile. *Ray's lips are nice too, but most of the time he's looking so serious that . . .*

"What makes you think that you'd want to do that?"

It's nice to talk to a man who's interested in what I have to say. Hope took another drink from her glass, glad that he couldn't read her thoughts.

"Well, a few weeks ago a woman came into my office to complain because she had been turned down for a home loan." Hope started to get into the specifics, but decided against it. "Well . . ." She lifted her hands briefly to let him know she was telling only the most relevant parts of the story. "To make a long story short, she didn't qualify." Hope paused for a second and pretended to look at him suspiciously. "Wait a minute, before I go on, are you some sort of agent planted here by the banking industry to bust me?"

"Well." He shrugged and their eyes met directly.

Hope took note that there was no smile lingering in his. "You'll just have to trust me." He said it as though it were a challenge. He held her gaze for a long second, until she looked away toward the waiter bringing their food. She felt uncomfortable and comforted at once. They were quiet until the waiter arranged their food and left the table.

"You were saying?" he prompted.

What was I saying? "Oh . . . um . . ."

Come on, Hope!

"Oh yes!" Hope laughed at her short attention span. "She didn't qualify, but I gave her the loan anyway." She tried to gauge his reaction but realized she didn't know him well enough to do so.

"What made you decide to do that?" His voice held only interest, no judgment. Hope struggled to find the words to explain her actions.

"I just felt like . . . she needed a break. That she was caught between a rock and a hard place. That sometimes, you know, we all need . . ." Hope took a deep breath in order to better organize her thoughts and was surprised—and embarrassed—when tears welled up in her eyes. Anthony reached across the table and placed his hand lightly on hers.

"Then you did the right thing."

She hadn't known that a man's smile could be soothing, but his was. Her smile was brilliant. She was no longer embarrassed about displaying emotion before a virtual stranger.

"I think I did too." They agreed without words that they should start their lunch.

Chapter Fifteen

They made it back to the hotel before the seminar re-sumed, so Hope made contact with the woman who spoke about mortgage lending. The woman was warm and very knowledgeable and promised to give Hope a call once she made it back to Dallas.

In Hope's opinion the second half of the conference was a waste of time. At least for her. She couldn't con-centrate on what was being said. She was distracted by both the sudden raging thunderstorm going on right outside the hotel doors and thoughts of her new friend.

She and Tony had shared their enchiladas—literally *shared* their enchiladas. He had asked permission be-fore transferring some of her food to his plate and she had demanded one of his beef enchiladas in return. Ray *hated* to share his food. He would rather pay for another entrée than give up one bite of whatever he was eating. Hope shook her head mentally, as she had done for the last two days whenever thoughts of Ray popped into her head.

And the conversation they shared during lunch had been nice. She had learned that Tony had been divorced for four years, and that his ex-wife and nine-year-old daughter had relocated to Chicago the year before. He had tried to sound very casual when he imparted that bit of information, but Hope thought she detected some bitterness. Apparently he felt his ex-wife had made the wrong decision when she decided to follow her new husband to another city. Hope had decided not to pursue that touchy subject and had started talking about her boys.

A light rain had started just as they were leaving the restaurant, and when Tony had offered her his jacket as protection she had accepted it without hesitation. As they walked hurriedly to his silver Mercedes, Hope had breathed deeply, enjoying the feel of fine wool and the smell of his spicy cologne. *And he's driving me to the airport after the conference.* Hope stopped replaying the events of the afternoon long enough to consider and dismiss any concerns that she had about allowing her thoughts to linger so much on a man who was not her husband.

By the end of the afternoon she had convinced herself that it was normal to occasionally be attracted to another man. *Not that I'm attracted to him. He's just a nice man who happens to be physically attractive. I would be blind if I didn't notice. It would be crazy for me to pretend not to notice.* Hope's lips took on a cynical curve as she searched for further justification. *And I'm sure Ray has had an occasional conversation— probably a few lunches—with an attractive woman in the last ten years. And what does it mean? Nothing,* she decided. *Nothing.*

* * *

Hope sat back further in the plush leather seats and turned her head toward the driver's seat.

"What?" He looked toward her and smiled slightly.

"What do you mean, what?"

"I felt you staring at me. Do I have something in my nose?"

Hope giggled like a schoolgirl. "I wasn't staring at you. I was actually thinking about this rain. It's coming down pretty hard." And it was; sheets of rain were beating against the car. They were almost at a standstill in the rush-hour traffic. "I hope my flight hasn't been delayed."

"In a hurry to get home, are you?" He smiled at her like he knew she wasn't.

"Kinda," she lied. In a sudden move, or what seemed like a sudden move to Hope—that's why she jumped slightly—he reached over and pressed a button and then started pushing the numbers on his console.

"You said you were flying Continental, right?" She nodded slightly. "I'm calling the airport for you. Did I scare you?" His smile was almost wicked.

He's fucking with me.

"No, you didn't scare me. I jumped because that last bolt of lightning looked like it was pretty close." Her voice was cool, and she had her best "whatever" expression on her face, but she couldn't quite keep the smile from her eyes.

"Oh really?" he challenged.

"Really," she countered.

"Continental Airlines, how may I help you?"

"What's your flight number?"

"616."

"I'm calling to check the status of flight 616 from Houston Intercontinental to Dallas." They waited a few seconds for the voice to come through the speaker on the hands-free phone system.

"That flight has been delayed, sir, due to inclement weather. Departure time is tentatively set for 8:25 this evening."

"Thanks." Tony ended the call and gave Hope a "what now?" look. "That's more than three hours from now."

"That flight was originally scheduled to leave at six o'clock. How can a fifty-minute flight be delayed for over two hours?" Hope could not disguise the irritation that she felt.

"I don't know. Do you want me to call back and ask to speak to the person responsible for the weather?" She cut her eyes slightly at him. She was not amused. She had told Ray she would be home by eight o'clock, and even though they weren't really speaking to one another, she didn't want to give him another thing to fault her for.

"Damn." She shook her head and muttered under her breath as she thought of the tense weekend facing her.

"You really are in a hurry to get home, aren't you? I thought you said your kids were visiting their grand-mother."

"*They* are, but my husband is not too pleased that I made this trip." *Now why did I tell him that? That's not his business.*

"Do you want to call him and explain the situation to him?" He seemed concerned.

Yeah, Hope. Call him and tell him how you are on your way to the airport with a man you don't even know, but now there's a storm so you don't know when you'll be home from a city that he didn't want you to come to in the first place. Call him. You may as well ask him to have a bath waiting for you when you do eventually get home.

"Shut up." The words slipped out and Tony's look was confused and a little amused.

"It was just a suggestion." He shrugged his shoulders. Hope laughed apologetically.

"I wasn't talking to you. I was talking to myself. I'll call Ray from the airport." *What's done is done,* Hope told herself.

"Well, I was thinking," he lifted his right hand from the steering wheel, "since your plane won't be leaving for a while, we could grab a bite to eat. That way you won't have to just sit at the airport."

Now why does that sound so appealing?

You know why. The little voice that had been working overtime all day refused to be silent. And it was starting to get an attitude. *Because the only other thing you have to look forward to is going home and pretending not to notice that Ray is pretending to watch TV so he doesn't have to speak to you when you get in.*

When did my life get so pathetic? she questioned herself before responding to Tony.

"I can't hold you up *that* long. It's nice enough that you volunteered to drive me. I'm sure you have plans this evening." *There's probably some sister at the mall right now buying up everything in Victoria's Secret.*

"No, I don't, but if I did I would change them." And when she still didn't accept, he tried another tactic.

"Look, I protected you from the rain, I found you a good seat at the conference, and"—he held up his index finger to emphasize his point—"I saved you at *least* forty dollars on cab fare. And you won't buy a brother a hamburger? Hope," he chided her playfully, "I thought we were friends."

"So you want *me* to buy *you* dinner?" She was amused, and a short, pleased laugh escaped her.

His eyes swept her from the soft silk of her blouse to the fine hosiery covering her toned legs. "You look like you can afford it."

She laughed again. *I'm already going to be late, Ray is already going to be pissed—what would I be proving if I sat at the airport alone for most of the evening? Nothing!*

"The leather in this Mercedes smells pretty new. I suspect that you can buy your own hamburger."

He smiled at her. *And his teeth are so white!*

"But I think"—she pretended to consider his proposal for a moment longer—"for your time and effort you deserve something a little more substantial than a hamburger." He looked at her for a long second before turning his full attention back to the rain-slick freeway.

"Don't think I won't remind you that you said that."

Hope decided that it was best not to ask for clarification.

Chapter Sixteen

Hope felt like a teenager coming home three hours late from a first date. She heard the television going in the family room, so she knew Ray was up pretending not to wait for her. She put her briefcase down near the island in the center of the kitchen and continued to consider her options for greeting her husband.

I can go in and give him a big kiss and pretend I don't know what's wrong when he pushes me aside. I can call hello from here and pretend I don't notice when he doesn't respond. I can pretend I don't care, say fuck it, and go to bed without saying anything to him . . . or I—

Ray solved her dilemma when he walked quietly into the kitchen. "Why didn't you let me know you were home?"

Hope was immediately on the defensive. "I *just* walked in, Ray." She let irritation creep into her voice to mask her defensiveness. "I was about to come in and say hello. Hello." Her voice tone and her body language said *bring it on*.

Ray let his eyes narrow slightly and got straight to the point. "So this thing you went to in Houston must have been riveting. I have to assume that, since it's ten and you're just getting home." He leaned against the kitchen counter and Hope knew he was asking for an explanation without asking for one.

"As a matter of fact, Ray, the *thing* that I went to *was* very interesting. But I'm here at ten because my flight was delayed. I'm sorry I didn't call." She had never gotten around to it and she wasn't sorry. "And I'm sorry you can't see how important this is to me, but I'm tired and I don't want to fight."

"I don't want to fight either, Hope." At some point during their dinner, Tony had started to call her Hope, and she had started to call him Anthony. "And if you are going to be traipsing all over the state . . ." And he had told the funniest off-color jokes, not dirty, just a little off-color. "All I'm saying, Hope . . ." And of course he had paid for dinner. "I'm glad you find this situation so amusing."

Hope forced her thoughts back to the present. "Hmm?"

"You're not even listening to me." Ray sounded disgusted.

"I *am* listening. I don't think it's amusing." She had heard him say something about her being amused.

"Then why are you smiling?"

"I'm smiling, Ray," she walked over to him and placed her hands on his shoulders, "because I said *I* don't want to argue, and you said that *you* don't want to argue, and here we are about to argue. Baby, I *really* don't want to argue." She massaged his shoulders firmly as she continued to speak. "I had a long day, but it was a good day. I'm sure you probably had a long day too." She had always loved his broad shoulders. "But I'm glad to be home, and I'm glad we're here together." *Now that's the total truth.* Hope was almost positive that it was. "Let's not be mad tonight." She widened her eyes pleadingly.

Ray shook his head and let out a sort of sigh/laugh, but she could tell that he was responding. He shook his head some more. "You're a trip."

She knew when he said that he was going to drop whatever it was that he had been talking about. "You're a trip" meant "what's the use?" in "Ray-ese."

"No, *you're* a trip." She smiled at him to let him know that she didn't mean it, although she *did* mean it. "You want to make us some margaritas while I take a shower?" She let her hands drop from his shoulders.

"And if I do, what are you going to do for me?" He looked up and down her body suggestively.

Not a damn thing.

"What?"

Oops! She had inadvertently spoken aloud.

"I was just kidding, Ray." When he looked as though he didn't believe her she put her hands back on his shoulders and slid them lazily across the thin cotton material covering his chest.

"I'm so thirsty," she said in her best imitation of an out-of-breath, helpless Southern prostitute. "I would just do anything for a tequila-flavored beverage." She turned away with an exaggerated swing of her ass. He slapped it playfully.

"I'll see what I can do, ma'am. I'll see what I can do." It had been years since they played cowboy and saloon girl, but she was willing. Anything to keep from arguing. As Hope rounded the corner to their bed-room, a picture of Tony in boots and a cowboy hat flashed briefly across her mind.

"How long is it going to take before you're ready for your new career?" Sunday evening found Hope duti-fully visiting her goddaughter. Ray and Lamar were in the driveway playing one-on-one.

"I don't know. Tony is going to send me some more information tomorrow . . ."

"Wait a minute." Stephanie switched her hungry in-fant to her right breast, then looked at her friend closely to gauge her reaction. "Do you know that this is about the fifteenth time that you've mentioned this Tony?"

"What do you mean?" Hope knew what she meant and was slightly irritated that she would go there.

"You *know* what I mean. You've said this man's name twenty-nine times. Do you realize I didn't know your secretary's name until last year?"

"Make up your mind, Stephanie, a second ago I had said his name fifteen times."

Stephanie would not be distracted. "What does he look like?"

"I don't know, Stephanie." Hope was irritated now and did not attempt to hide it. "What does it matter what he looks like? I told you he is going to help me out. Quite naturally I would mention his name if I'm talking about the conference and my future career plans."

"What does he look like?" Stephanie continued to press the issue.

"He's tall, dark, and handsome." Hope said the words sarcastically, but they were true.

"Just like your husband." Stephanie raised her eyebrow knowingly. "I thought so." She removed the now sleeping baby from her breast and eased her gently onto her shoulder to burp her. "Be careful, Hope," she warned.

"Be careful of what?" Hope narrowed her eyes, daring her to say what was on her mind; and of course she did.

"You *know* what I'm talking about. This is not the best time to be starting a new friendship with a man."

"And why is that, Stephanie?"

"Why are you playing dumb, Hope?" She waited a second for Hope to respond to the question. Hope folded her arms across her breasts and refused to say a word. "For weeks, months, really, all you've been talking about is how things aren't going how you would like between you and Ray. When you're going through a period of *real* tension in your marriage you don't bring another man into the picture."

"Well, since you know *everything*, Stephanie, and since you're obviously the self-appointed queen of marriage, you should already know that my building a business, *a business* relationship with anyone—male or female, cover model or bone ugly—has *nothing* to do with my relationship with my husband."

"Then why are you raising your voice, Hope?" Stephanie lowered her voice to illustrate her point.

"Because . . ." Hope took a second to lower her voice. "Because I can't believe this. I come over here to visit my goddaughter and to let you know I'm excited for the first time in a long time about something that could possibly happen in my life, and you jump down my throat."

"I'm not jumping down your throat." Her voice was gentle. "I just don't want you to lose sight of the fact that you love your husband and end up doing something stupid. I wish I could have put a mirror in front of you when you mentioned Tony's name. I don't know if you're excited about this mortgage thing or if you're excited because you're going to be in contact with this man."

"I've worked with men before. I work with men now, and I'm not going to . . ." Hope stopped mid-sentence and raised her hands in defeat. "You know, I don't even want to talk about this anymore. This conversation is just too ridiculous."

"Well, answer this question." Stephanie would not let it drop. "Have you told Ray that you basically spent your entire day with this man?"

"I haven't told Ray anything about yesterday because he's not interested."

"You see what I mean, Hope? There you go making snide comments about Ray again."

"Stephanie, that's not a snide comment; it's the truth. How many times have I told you that Ray—" Hope abruptly ended the conversation when Ray and Lamar walked into the kitchen. Stephanie gave Hope a *we'll finish this conversation later* look, and Hope's expression clearly said, *I don't think so*.

"Is that baby girl the only one who can get a decent snack around here?" Lamar playfully questioned his wife.

"No, but she is the only one here who can't get a snack on her own." Stephanie looked over her shoulder and smiled at her husband.

They make me sick.

"Hope, you about ready to go? Now that I kicked his ass again, Lamar wants to kick us out."

"Yeah, baby, I'm ready." Both Ray and Stephanie looked a little surprised. *I can smile at my husband too.* Hope stood and kissed the baby on the top of her feathery soft hair. She refused to make eye contact with Stephanie.

"I'll call you later, girl," Hope called out as they made their way toward the door.

"Call me tonight or tomorrow from work. I need to talk to you about something."

On the ride home, Hope thought about Stephanie's question, whether she had told Ray about running into Tony. She really didn't think she had some hidden reason for not telling him, she honestly felt that he would not be interested.

Stephanie had a particular way of planting seeds of doubt in her mind. Hope remembered having similar experiences with her mother before she died. After a conversation with her mother, she could have doubts about her most well-thought-out decisions. *Okay, so I'll just tell him.*

"I was just thinking about how much I enjoyed that conference. I met quite a few people there." Ray's sigh was barely audible, but Hope heard it.

"Hope, we've had a nice day so far; let's not talk about that."

"How can me talking about something that I'm interested in interfere with the nice day that we're having?"

"Hope . . ." This time his sigh was louder.

"Well, fine then, Ray, I won't say another word about it." *Don't I know my husband or what*? Hope posed the rhetorical question to herself. Whether Ray knew it or not, they were no longer having a nice time. As far as Hope was concerned, their nice time had ended with Ray's first sigh.

Chapter Seventeen

Subj: *Just checking your e-mail*
Date: *Mon. June 10*
From: *ABOLD@quickflash.net*
To: *Lwilliams@SnbankDallas.com*

Hope, just thought I'd hit you to let you know that I enjoyed meeting with you on Friday. I think that you are definitely on the right path. It seems as if you have a real desire to help people. If you get a mortgage business started, you will be able to do just that. I meant it when I said I am willing to help. I look forward to hearing from you. By the way, don't think I didn't notice that you weaseled out of paying for dinner. You owe me.

Anthony

Subj: Me too
Date: Mon. June 10
From: Lwilliams@SnbankDallas.com
To: ABOLD@quickflash.net

   Thanks for the e-mail. I enjoyed talking and breaking bread with you too. I'm anxious to find out anything and everything I can about this mortgage-lending thing. I have to be careful and pace myself. This weekend I was thinking about names for my company once I get it started. Do you think that's a little premature? And by the way (back) . . . if you recall, I offered to pay for dinner and you said no. And anyway you know what they say . . . as long as I owe you, you'll never be broke.

Hope

Subj: Some info for you
Date: Tue. June 11
From: ABOLD@quickflash.net
To: Lwilliams@SnbankDallas.com

   Hope, I have a contact in Dallas who is interested in the same thing that you're interested in. I'm sending you her e-mail address and her home phone number. In case you were wondering, my home phone is (713) 555-8814. My business phone is on my card. If you ever want to communicate the old-fashioned way, call me. I want to know what names you came up with for your company. I would agree that it's a little premature . . . you should start working on your license first. But I remember the look in your eye while we were talking, and I believe that you will hang your shingle on a door someday soon. How are your boys? Are you still enjoying your time away from them? I'm trying to make arrangements for my daughter to come down to see me. It's hard having her in a different city. I don't think it's fair to either of us, but that's a whole other subject. When I come to Dallas you're going to buy me lunch or dinner or something. Hit me back.

Anthony

Subj: Read it
Date: Thurs. June 13
From: Lwilliams@SnbankDallas.com
To: ABOLD@quickflash.net

Anthony, I'm sorry I didn't write you back right away. I've been busy at work. Life is so funny; just when I'm having a break from my kids, things shift into high gear at work. I can honestly say that I don't miss my boys yet. Usually, just when I'm starting to miss them, it's time for them to come back home. And then after about five minutes of hugging and kissing we're back to our same old routine. They're fighting and I'm fussing, but I love being able to care for them. I always worry about them when we are not sleeping under the same roof. Thanks for asking. I can't imagine how it would be to be away from them for long periods of time. I hope it works out and your daughter is able to visit with you. Kids need both of their parents close to them as much as possible. As busy as Ray is most of the time, my boys still want to reach out and touch him on a regular basis. I really really hope it works out for you.

Oh! I did have a chance to call your girlfriend. She seems really nice and of course she was very knowledgeable. We're going to meet sometime next week for lunch. If I haven't said it already, I really appreciate you taking an interest. You can call me at the bank anytime. My home phone number is (216) 555-2002, but I'm usually pretty busy in the evening . . . what with slaving over a hot stove and wrestling with three little and one not so little boys . . . I barely have time to watch the soaps that I've recorded. (That's a sad joke by the way. I gave up my beloved soap operas after the twins were born.) This is the longest e-mail I've ever written, and would you believe that I could go on, but I won't. Until next time.

Hope

"Hope Williams."

"Hey, Hope, this is Anthony."

"I'm so glad to hear your voice. Did you get my *long* e-mail?" She sounded surprised . . . pleased.

"Yeah, I did. I didn't think it was long *enough*. I look forward to checking my e-mail and having a message from you. I have started to think of you as my pen pal."

She laughed. "Oh, you're so sweet."

"You're not the first woman who has said that to me."

"I'm sure I'm not." Her smile was big. She crossed her legs under her desk.

"By the way, Jessie Latin is *not* my girlfriend. We used to work together years ago when I lived in Chicago. She was fifteen years older than me then, and last time I checked she and her husband were expecting their first grandchild."

"Oh."

"Oh what?"

"Oh, I didn't know that you had lived in Chicago."

"Yes I did, for a little while, straight out of undergrad. There are a lot of things you don't know about me. But we'll fix that. Look, I know you're busy, but I just wanted to say hi the old-fashioned way. It's good to hear your voice."

She felt special. "It's good to hear yours too. Thanks for calling."

"I'll talk to you later. Bye."

"Bye." She took a deep breath.

Subj: It's the weekend
Date: Fri. June 14
From: Lwilliams@SnbankDallas.com
To: ABOLD@quickflash.net

   Anthony, my friend Tabitha sent this e-mail to me. I thought you would enjoy it so I am forwarding it to you. Have a great weekend.

Your pen pal,
Hope

Subj: Some info for you
Date: Fri. June 14
From: ABOLD@quickflash.net
To: Lwilliams@SnbankDallas.com

   I couldn't let that e-mail go unanswered. Your friend Tabitha is sick . . . can I meet her? Ha ha. I have friends who send funny things like that to me. I'll send a few to you over the weekend. You have a good weekend, and get some rest. You sounded tired yesterday.

Anthony

Four weeks . . . Four weeks, a dozen phone calls, and about thirty e-mails later, Hope was ready to say that she had a real friend in Anthony. She had come to look forward to their almost daily contact. As promised, he had been supplying her with information about mortgage brokering and had even connected her to some people already working in the industry in Dallas. He was also genuinely interested in her personal life; he always made a point to ask her about the boys, and he listened without judgment on the few occasions when she had spoken to him about some of the issues that she and Ray were dealing with. And when she complained that she was tired, he suggested that she take time for herself.

He was a surprisingly sensitive man. She wouldn't have thought it to look at him, but he was. In a short time it appeared that he was more in tune with her mood than her husband. Hope knew that he wasn't, really, it just seemed that way.

And he cared so much for his daughter. He *had* been able to get his daughter to Houston for a week. He had taken her to his office one afternoon and Hope had had the opportunity to speak with her briefly on the phone. Her name was Tamika and she was a very articulate little girl, friendly and obviously proud of her father. During her visit, there had been a quiet satisfaction in his voice whenever they spoke.

When Tamika went back to her mother, Tony told Hope he felt cheated that he wasn't a part of her everyday life. Hope didn't have too much experience with men raising children alone, but she was in silent agreement whenever he mentioned anything about seeking joint custody of Tamika.

Stephanie had been wrong. It was the perfect time to start a new friendship with a man. The kids were having a great summer, she was refining her career goals, she felt stronger, more energetic, and less tense than she had in a long time. There hadn't been as many waves between her and Ray; Hope knew that somehow her friendship with Tony had something to do with those changes.

It was nice to have someone—a man—to talk to about some things. Nice to have a man find her conversation scintillating (he had actually used that word), nice to have someone validate her feelings. Nice.

Subj: The weekend
Date: Fri. July 19
From: Lwilliams@SnbankDallas.com
To: ABOLD@quickflash.net

Tony, this is the best potato salad recipe in Texas, if not the world. My mother used to make this on special occasions when I was growing up. You know I like you, because the only other person I've given this recipe to is Stephanie. Use fresh dill if you can find it. Do not, I repeat, do not let this recipe get away from you! If you do and I find out, I will have to think of an appropriate punishment.

I hope your barbeque turns out okay. I'm sorry I can't be there to sample your famous ribs. If you were a real friend you would fly to Dallas on Monday and bring me the leftovers. I hope your mom is feeling better.

Take care,
Hope

Subj: The weekend
Date: Fri. July 19
From: ABOLD@quickflash.net
To: Lwilliams@SnbankDallas.com

I don't know about this recipe, but I'll try it. Can I substitute pickle juice for fresh dill? (Just kidding.) I will not reveal your secret recipe to anyone. You can trust me with anything, not just this recipe. I wish you could come, but I know you can't. I'll tell you what . . . to let you know what a real friend I am, I will bring you some leftovers on Monday. I have some people that I need to meet with in Dallas, and Monday is as good a day as any.

I've been wanting to see you. Let me know if you can clear your schedule for a couple of hours around lunchtime. If you can take the afternoon off I'll treat you to a movie.

Tony

Subj: Okay
Date: Fri. July 19
From: Lwilliams@SnbankDallas.com
To: ABOLD@quickflash.net

I will take the afternoon off. I have worked my ass off this summer and I deserve a break. I have really been wanting to see you too. I'll buy you lunch, and I get to choose the movie. You don't have to bring the barbeque, but it would be nice.

   Call me this weekend if you change your mind. Otherwise call me in my office when you get here and we can decide where to meet. And on second thought, just go ahead and bring the ribs.

Can't wait to see you,
Hope

   Hope twirled around in her chair after she sent the e-mail to Tony. She sure hoped that he could make it on Monday. He had only been to Dallas once since she had taken that trip to Houston. She hadn't been able to see him because Karl had come down with a stomach virus and she stayed home from work. She glanced at the clock on her computer. She had made arrangements to meet Stephanie and Tabitha for lunch and she had to hurry if she wanted to be on time.

Chapter Eighteen

Tabitha and Stephanie were waiting for her when she walked into the small Cajun restaurant. Stephanie had Tamara under her shirt nursing and Tabitha was looking as if she would rather be anywhere but where she was. "Hey, girls," Hope said in their general direction. Both women looked relieved to see her. They were not friends; the only things they had in common were their mutual disrespect for each other's lifestyle, and Hope.

"We ordered seafood gumbo for you. I can't stay long; I have to get back to the store." Tabitha looked great, as usual. She had straightened her hair, and the style accentuated her almond-shaped eyes beautifully.

"You look good. When you're through with that dress, pass it on to me."

"Honey, this dress is a classic. I'll never be finished with it."

Hope stuck out her tongue. She hadn't bought one item of clothing since she had made the decision to go back to school.

"Stephanie, you look pretty too. You must be trying to get another baby." And she did. Her hair was pulled back and her silver earrings looked good against her skin. She was back to her between-baby weight.

"Thank you. This shirt is a classic too; I bought it two babies ago." Tabitha couldn't help but laugh at that one.

"Bring my goddaughter out so that I can see her pretty face."

"She's feeding her pretty face; she's almost finished." Stephanie smiled up at her. Tabitha did not miss the opening.

"You know they have pumps for that. You can pump when you're in the privacy of your own home and then when you're out in public, you can feed the baby from a bottle."

"Well, she likes her milk straight from the source. And if you ever have a baby of your own, Hope will have to remember to get you one of those pumps as a shower gift."

Hope rolled her eyes and sighed. No matter how much she wanted it, the two women would never be friends.

"If you two promise to play nice, I'll buy lunch."

"Then I'm taking dinner home for the kids." Stephanie slipped the baby from underneath her nursing shirt and placed her on her shoulder to be burped.

"Speaking of the kids, bring them over tomorrow to swim. I'll see if Ray will grill some hamburgers."

"What should I bring?" Tabitha chimed in.

Hope didn't miss the sarcasm in her voice. "Now, Tabitha, you know you couldn't stand thirty minutes in a house full of kids, but you're welcome to come. Bring a dessert . . . enough for twelve."

"I'll pass this time."

"I thought so." Hope smiled at both of her friends, glad that she had successfully changed the subject. She held out her arms for the baby once she heard her burp loudly.

"So have you heard from Tony lately, Hope?"

Hope tried to look nonchalant even though she was not pleased that Tabitha had brought him up. She was sure she had mentioned to her that Stephanie did not approve of their friendship. She saw Stephanie's eyes narrow at the mention of his name.

"I heard from him today." The waiter brought their food and took her drink order. She motioned for Stephanie to eat as she continued to hold the baby.

"How exciting. How is he?"

"He's fine, Tabitha." The disapproval in Stephanie's eyes pissed her off, so she decided to elaborate. Who was she to judge her? The last time Hope had checked, her mother was still dead. "He'll be in town Monday and we'll probably meet for lunch."

"Do you think that's smart, Hope?" Stephanie couldn't hold back any longer.

"Why wouldn't it be smart, Stephanie? We both have to eat lunch."

"You know what I mean. What do you think this man wants from you?"

"Stephanie," Hope asked with exaggerated patience, "don't you think that if he was after something other than friendship, I would know by now?"

Stephanie looked as if she was going to say something but remembered that Tabitha was at the table and decided against it. She started gathering her things.

"I'm not hungry anymore. I won't say anything else

about your *boyfriend*." She walked over to Hope and gathered the baby. "I'll let you know about tomorrow."

"Stephanie, sit down." Hope didn't understand why Stephanie was so upset, but she certainly didn't want her to leave in such a rush.

"I really have to go, Hope. I'll talk to you later." She got her baby and left her steaming catfish platter on the table untouched.

The next day Hope was making coleslaw when Stephanie and her family drove up. The boys went into the playroom immediately, and Lamar joined Ray on the patio where he was firing up the grill. Stephanie made a pallet for her sleeping baby on the family room floor before joining Hope in the kitchen.

"You need some help?"

"No, I don't, but you can give me the twelve dollars I had to pay for the lunch that you didn't eat yesterday."

"Fine. I'll get you your money before we leave today." She still sounded angry.

Hope quit cutting up the cabbage to give her friend her full attention. "Girl, you know I don't care about that money. But I do want to know what was wrong with you yesterday. I couldn't even enjoy my gumbo, I was so busy worrying about you. You jumped up and ran out of the restaurant like it was on fire."

"I don't want to talk about it, Hope."

They had been friends too long for Hope to let her get away with that. She and Ray had similar traits, but enough was enough.

"Well, if you didn't want to talk about it, why did you walk in here with an attitude?"

"We've already talked about it, Hope, and obviously

you're not going to listen to me. I wasn't going to sit there and listen to you and Tabitha make light of the situation."

Hope sighed and looked around to make sure they were still alone before speaking. "I've told you Tony and I are friends. If it sounded like I was making light of the situation it's because I was. The situation *is light*."

Stephanie stared at her for what seemed like a long time before speaking.

"Don't fool yourself, Hope. You are always complaining about how much you have to do, but all of a sudden you have enough time in your schedule to start a new friendship." Stephanie shook her head. "Girl, please."

"Tony doesn't take a lot of my time." *Here I am on the defensive again.*

"If he takes thirty minutes of your time, it's time you should be working on your problems with Ray."

"I've also told you, in case you don't recall, that things are better between Ray and me."

"Hope, things are not better between you and Ray. You just don't care. All you're focused on is getting to work so you can get an e-mail or a phone call from your boyfriend."

"That's a lie, Stephanie, and that's enough. Do me a favor and keep your damn opinions to yourself." Hope turned back to her coleslaw. She wished that there was a way she could tell her to go home without having to explain to Ray and the kids.

"Yeah, I know, the truth hurts. After I say this I'm not going to say anything else about it, because you've been grown for a long time and it's obvious that you're going to do what you want to do. Lamar pulled the same shit that you're pulling now. He started a so-called friendship with another dentist that he met at some training. To make a long story short, he ended up fucking her."

Hope put the knife down and looked at her friend with her mouth open. "Oh my God, Stephanie! I didn't know. Why didn't you tell me?"

"Because I found out around the same time that your mother died, plus Lamar begged me not to say anything, and I didn't feel like talking about it. I *still* don't want to talk about it. So please don't ask me anything about it. I'm just telling you because I know you love Ray and he loves you too, Hope. Marriage is just *hard* sometimes, and when you allow someone from the outside in, it may seem like it gets easier, but in the end it only gets harder. I still want to kick Lamar's ass sometimes for what he did, but I decided that I wanted my family intact. But Ray is a *man,* and men are not as forgiving as we are." When she finished speaking there were tears in her eyes and Hope's. Hope took Stephanie into her arms for a quick hug.

"Honey, I'm sorry. I wish that you had let me be there for you."

"Let me be here for you, Hope."

"Stephanie, I'm not Lamar," Hope told her gently. "I appreciate you being concerned about me, but I'm not going to start anything illicit with Tony."

Stephanie held up her hands. "You're a grown woman. I won't say anything else about it." She smiled sadly at Hope before going to check on the boys.

Late that night when all the paper plates had been thrown away and the boys were asleep, Hope thought about what Stephanie had said to her. She would have never taken Lamar for the type of man to cheat on his wife. She decided that you never knew what went on behind closed doors in a marriage.

She turned on her side to look at Ray on his side of the bed. "Stephanie told me today that Lamar had an affair." She looked at him to gauge his reaction. He looked up from the book that he was reading.

"Is she going to leave him?"

"No. It was a while ago. And she forgave him."

"Then why did she bring it up today?"

"I don't know," she lied easily. "I guess it was just on her mind. Would you cheat on me?"

"For what?"

"What do you mean, for what? That's a yes or no question."

"I mean what reason would I have to cheat on you?"

"You know we've been having some problems . . ."

"What problems?" He seemed genuinely confused.

"Well . . ." Hope searched her mind and came up blank.

Ray looked at her indulgently. "We don't have any more problems than any other married people."

Hope sat up straighter in bed. "*Exactly*, and a lot of other married people cheat."

"I have never cheated on you, Hope, and I *won't*. Just because Lamar got a little on the side doesn't mean that we all do." He chuckled and turned out his bedside lamp. Hope knew he was ready to make love. She waited for him to ask if she would ever cheat; when he didn't, she realized that the thought would never occur to him.

As he pulled her into his arms she remembered some of the problems they had been having. He didn't help her out enough with the kids, he never seemed to be interested in what was going on with her, he rarely told her what was going on with him, he saved his "I love you's" for Mother's Day and Christmas; he hadn't even bought her a gift for the Mother's Day that had just passed. He didn't respect her opinions or her work. The longer Hope thought about it, the clearer the situation became. *They* didn't have problems; *she* was the one with the problems.

On Sunday night she was standing in her closet trying to decide what to wear to work the next day. Tony had not called over the weekend, so she assumed he would be in town the next day as planned. She smiled and pulled out a cream-colored pantsuit. It was one of her favorites; the pants were very slim and the three-button jacket hit her mid–thigh.

She took out and then put back a canary yellow shirt. The sandals she normally wore with the shirt wouldn't do for the office. Calvin Klein cranberry silk, V-neck, cuff sleeves . . . perfect. She had some pumps that were almost the exact color of the shirt.

Ray walked into the room as she was rummaging through her jewelry drawer looking for the small platinum hoop earrings that he had given her on some Valentine's Day past. He looked at the clothes that she had laid across the bed. "You wearing that to work?" Before she could respond, he continued. "I've never seen you wear that to work. Aren't those pants too tight?" She looked at him, a little surprised; she never knew that he noticed what she wore to work.

"They're not tight, they're just slim fitting."

"Oh, is that what they're calling them now?"

Hope couldn't help but laugh. *Why is he teasing me? He hasn't done that for a while.*

"Whatever, Ray, just leave my wardrobe to me."

"Do you have a meeting tomorrow or something?"

She closed the drawer and looked at him. "Since when are you interested in what I do at work?"

"I'm just trying to help you out. If you have a meeting and you want people to take you seriously, you shouldn't wear that."

"Everyone who works with me takes me seriously. I think I've been there long enough to have proven myself." *He should just take his ass to bed.* He opened his mouth to say something else, but she cut him off. "Ray, I know you don't mean to be insulting . . . or at least I hope you don't. So let's just drop the subject. I have enough sense to know what *is* and what is *not* appropriate to wear to work."

'I'm just messing with you, baby. You always look good when you go to work."

She looked at him suspiciously. "Thank you."

He walked behind her and started to nibble the side of her neck. "You fell asleep before I finished with you last night. You have to make up for it tonight."

"I'm tired, Ray, and I have to get up early tomorrow."

"It won't take long." He continued to kiss and bite her neck. He slipped his hands down her side and into the boxer shorts that she was wearing.

"Stop it, Ray!" Hope moved his hands away. She hadn't meant to sound so rough, but damn . . . he never wanted to take no for an answer. *And that's another problem, he thinks I'm his damn sex machine.*

"What's wrong with you?" The irritation in his voice further irritated her.

"I've been on my feet for most of the day. I'm *tired* and I don't feel like making love." *Shit!* she added silently for her own benefit.

"Fine, Hope, go ahead and get your rest." He walked out of the room and she picked up her clothes from the bed and hung them on the back of the closet door.

Chapter Nineteen

She checked her lipstick before she got out of the truck. Earlier that morning Tony had called and suggested that they have sushi for lunch. She wasn't crazy about sushi, but she did like Japanese food. The restaurant had an Asian motif and waterfalls bubbled in the background. The soft smell of exotic flowers scented the air.

Hope scanned the tables nearest the entrance searching for Tony before walking quietly to the hostess stand. "I'm meeting Anthony Bolden here for lunch," she told the Asian-looking woman who stood there. The hostess looked down at a seating chart and nodded for Hope to follow her.

Tony's eyes lit up as she approached the table. He stood up to greet her as the hostess placed another menu on the table and turned away. He took her into his arms to hug her like they were old friends. *We are old friends.* He released her and then looked her over from the top of her shiny hair to the tips of her shiny patent leather pumps.

"Wow!" He squinted his eyes and smiled. "You look great." Hope was glad she had chosen the outfit. She smiled so big that she thought her face would crack.

"Thank you. The boys don't call me eye candy for nothing." They laughed at her joke as they took their seats.

"Eye candy you certainly are. Eartha Kitt you're not."

"For your information, that was my Mae West impression."

He shook his head. "Mae West had more shoulder action going on. Look and learn." He moved his shoulder up and down and around, presumably like Mae West.

"Stop it, stop it. You look absolutely ridiculous." They were silent for a few seconds after their laughter had quieted. He was the first to speak.

"It's good to see you."

"It's good to see you too." The waitress came to take their order, interrupting their quiet talk. Tony ordered his sushi, and though she protested, he ordered the eel and a California roll for her. She ordered teriyaki chicken; they both ordered sake.

"Did you have any trouble getting off today?" he asked. Hope shook her head in response.

"No, I didn't. What about you? Did your meeting go well?"

"Well, actually, I have a confession to make. After I spoke with you on Friday, I had a conference call with the people I was planning to meet with."

"So you didn't have a meeting here today?"

"No, but I really wanted you to sample my ribs." She was flattered that he would make the plane trip just to see her.

"I thought that you were dressed sort of casually for a business meeting." He was wearing khaki pants and a short-sleeved polo shirt. "Thanks for coming." Hope thought for a moment that the gesture had some special significance, but she pushed the thought out of her mind. She was not going to let Stephanie's words or her paranoia taint an innocent friendship.

"No problem. Oh, by the way," he started and paused as the waitress placed the sake before them, "that was *the* most awful potato salad that I have ever made." Hope held up her hands, delighted that he was teasing her.

"Oh no! That is the best potato salad recipe in the world! I've never met anyone who didn't like it. You must have done something wrong."

"No, I didn't. I followed the recipe to a T. I even found the fresh dill that was *so* important."

"Well, how long did you boil the eggs?"

"What?"

"If you boil the eggs too long, it can ruin the potato salad."

He looked at her doubtfully before responding. "Yeah, right, Hope. No disrespect to your mother, but it's just a bad recipe."

For the next hour and a half they enjoyed a leisurely lunch, laughing and teasing and relating in a much more personal way than was possible over the phone or through a computer. He spoke in detail for the first time about his concern over his mother's health. His family had recently discovered that his mother had heart problems that began when he was in his late twenties, and after years of treatment her condition was getting worse.

"She's just seventy, and she's so weak that she's practically bedridden. I know that seventy seems old to some people, but when I see or hear about people who are active and healthy way into their eighties, I just want that for my mother."

"I understand. When my mother got sick, I was so angry. Just when she was starting to *live* her life, it was over. Ever since then, I've been thinking about how much of our lives we waste. Don't misunderstand me, I don't feel like my mother wasted her life, I just know that she would have made some different choices if she had known what was down the road for her. "We talked about it before she died. And I was sad for her."

Tony reached across the table and took her hand in his, and she was comforted. "Why were you sad for her?"

"Because she wanted things that I never knew about. She wanted more children, but after my father, she was never able to have enough faith in a man to take that step . . . and when she did, of course it was too late. She wanted to go to college; she wanted to have a convertible Mustang. I guess I was so sad because she didn't want anything that was unattainable. These last two years I have been really thinking about the things that I want from life, and I think that I have finally made the decision to just go for it.

"She didn't have enough confidence in herself, and there was nobody in her life to tell her she could do whatever she put her mind to. Including me. I was there and never told her . . . never encouraged her . . . never even asked her about her life or her dreams until it was too late." Hope took a deep breath to try to hold back the tears that were stinging her eyes. Tony squeezed her hand to let her know it was all right.

"Yes, you *were* there, and knowing what I know about you, I'm sure you let her know that you loved her. Sometimes, Hope, that's more important than all the encouragement in the world. Just having someone in your life . . . a child, a parent, a husband, or a wife who you know with certainty loves you no matter what."

Hope shook her head sadly. "I guess that's true, but I think it's easier to get that kind of unconditional love between a parent and a child. Love between a man and a woman *is* conditional. Like Ray, for instance . . ." She had shared with him at some point that Ray was not thrilled about her career plans. "I feel like he would love me more if I would just do what he wants. If I stayed at home, took care of him and the boys, cooked every day, and was ready for sex anytime he wanted, I think he would love me more."

Tony shrugged as if to say maybe so. "What about you? Would you love him more if he just did what you wanted? If he were supportive of your plans, took care of you and the boys, and was available for sex whenever you wanted?"

Hope laughed. "Yes," she almost shouted. "That would make my life easier and it would be easier to concentrate on the love."

"I feel you. Marriage is hard. Anytime you have two people with two different sets of wants and needs, two different personalities trying to make a life together, there are going to be problems."

She was intrigued by his intensity. "What about your marriage, Tony? What happened?"

He shrugged. "We should have never gotten mar-

ried. I knew that we wanted different things in the beginning. It takes two people to make a marriage work,
and I know that it takes two people to fuck it up. So I'm
not saying that Naomi was the only one at fault, but it
was hard being married to her. *Shit,* it was hard dating
her."

"What do you mean?"

"I mean *everything* had to be her way. We had to live
where she wanted to live; we had to eat what she
wanted to eat. We only had one child because she only
wanted one child. If things didn't go her way, it was
hell at home. When I finally said that some things were
going to have to go my way in order for us to make it,
she filed for divorce. We had other problems, but this
thing with her taking our daughter to another state
against my wishes is classic Naomi."

"How long were you married?"

"Eight long years."

"Well, excuse me for being nosy, but if you knew
what she was like before you got married, why did you
get married and why did you stay married for eight
years?"

Tony smiled at her and drank the last bit of his sake.
"Because you're a friend, and because I've had three of
these"—he lifted up his empty cup before placing it
back on the table—"I'm going to be real with you. It
was the pussy!" Hope sat stunned for a minute, and
then fell back in her seat laughing. He started to laugh
with her, glad that she wasn't offended. "A man will
put up with a lot of shit for some good pussy."

Hope laughed so hard that tears rolled down her
cheeks. "So in other words, you were pussy whipped."

"Some would call it that. My friends did."

"How did you . . . what made you . . ." She searched for polite words. "What changed that situation?"

"I had to work too damn hard for it. She put me on rations, like we were in a depression and she had to save it for harder times." He shook his head. "She started doing that when I stopped giving in to everything she wanted, and when *that* didn't work, like I said, we were in divorce court."

"Do you miss it?"

"What, her pussy?" He pretended to be confused.

"No, crazy boy! I mean being *married*."

He smiled at her as he shook his head. "No, I don't miss being married to Naomi, because we weren't a good match. I would like to be married again, though, now that I know what type of woman I need."

Hope found something to look at on the floor; she couldn't hold his gaze.

They were the last of the lunch crowd to leave the restaurant. They shared another sake before walking to the movie theater around the corner from the restaurant. The movie that she had chosen had subtitles, and she was pleased when Tony didn't complain.

In the middle of the movie and three quarters of the way through a huge tub of popcorn, Hope discovered that there was something practically sinful about leaving work in the middle of the day to see a movie with a friend. She loved it.

They got back to the restaurant parking lot at around five fifteen and Tony walked her to her truck. "Next time *I* get to choose the movie."

"You didn't like it?" She was disappointed.

"It was great. I still haven't figured out the significance of the ending, but it was a good movie. I'm glad we saw it."

She smiled at him, pleased that he was a good sport. "If you haven't figured it out by tomorrow, let me know and I'll tell you."

He stood directly in front of her and took one of her hands in each of his. She couldn't account for her sudden nervousness.

"I had a good time." He leaned in, and she offered her cheek for his kiss. His warm lips lingered against her soft skin. "I have to say, Hope, this is the best afternoon I've had in a long time. It's a good thing you live in Dallas, or I would be calling you all the time asking you to play hooky from work."

"I had a great time too. It *is* a good thing we live in different cities." She didn't say why, though, and he didn't release her hands.

"Maybe I should come again in a couple of weeks?"

"No. I know it's a short flight, but even short flights are expensive. Don't come unless you have a meeting or something."

"Don't worry about the expense. I have a little extra spending money since I gave up smoking crack."

Hope laughed like she was supposed to. "I like you, Tony. Well, come if you want," was all she could think of to say. He kissed her cheek again before letting go of her hands.

"I'll talk to you tomorrow," he said softly.

"Okay." Hope got into her truck as Tony walked toward his rental car. As she was leaving the parking lot of the restaurant, Tony pulled behind her and started blowing his horn. She stopped her truck and he got out of his car carrying a blue cooler in one hand.

"I almost forgot about the ribs. I have them on dry ice. Let me know what you think."

"Thanks." Hope took the cooler in through the window. "I'll give you my *honest* opinion," she threatened. She left him standing in the parking lot looking after her.

She served the ribs to her family for dinner. They were excellent—so excellent in fact, Ray asked her where she bought them. And because she didn't want to explain where she spent her afternoon, she told him a half-truth.

"Oh," she said casually as she passed the beans that she had made to go along with the ribs to Jordan, "one of my coworkers had a barbecue this weekend and brought ribs for me."

That's not a total lie. Tony and I are in the same line of work, so we could be considered coworkers. And anyway, since when has Ray been concerned about where dinner comes from . . . just so long as it comes.

Chapter Twenty

The rest of the summer seemed to go by without Hope noticing it. The twins went to camp for a week and Hope found a special summer program for David to attend. They swam every night, and a couple of times Ray took them camping in the backyard. She made sandwiches practically every night for dinner; on the nights that she didn't make sandwiches, she bought hamburgers.

For David's fourth birthday they had a party for his summer class at the Y, and the entire family went to Six Flags Over Texas. She worked harder and more efficiently at her office so that she wouldn't get behind, and she registered to take two classes during the fall semester, both on Monday night so she wouldn't be away from her family too often. When she told Ray about her classes, he nodded, but didn't make any comment.

Of course, he did comment on her no-fuss approach to cooking. One evening after she had placed a platter

of tuna sandwiches and chips on the table—good alba-
core tuna—Ray looked at her with an expression of
what could only be described as disgust and said, "So,
I guess you're never going to cook again?"

"I did cook, Ray." She looked pointedly at the sandwiches on the table. *Boiling eggs is considered cooking
in some countries.*

"I mean *real* food, Hope. These boys are growing
up." He looked pointedly at the three boys staring at
them with great interest. "They need real food."

"What do you mean by *real* food, Ray? I think most
people would consider this *real* food."

"I mean chicken, fish, potatoes, green beans, pork
chops—"

"Pork chops?" Hope couldn't help but interrupt
him. "I thought you said you were trying to stop eating
pork?"

"No, I didn't say that, Hope. What I said was, I am
trying to stop eating *beef.*"

She looked at him for a long second, wondering if
he was kidding or if he had actually turned into an idiot
behind her back. She walked to the refrigerator for the
milk, and when she placed it on the table she saw that
Ray had placed two of the sandwiches on his plate.

"Tuna is an excellent source of protein, by the way."
She smiled at the boys before taking her place at the
table. The next night she served tuna sandwiches again.

Her marriage was changing. She and Ray had put
their arguing aside, but they hadn't replaced it with
anything. They ate together, they made love, but she
felt disconnected, like—like a foreign-exchange wife

trying to get along with her host husband. She wondered often if Ray felt what she was feeling . . . or not
feeling. They never talked about it, they didn't talk
about anything but the kids and their schedules and
whether or not they should plant something other than
Mexican heather on the side of the house.

She was grateful she had Tony to talk to. Their
friendship had blossomed that summer, in great part
because he traveled to Dallas practically every week.
She didn't tell anyone about his visits, not Ray, certainly not Stephanie. She didn't want them to get the
wrong idea. Plus it was exciting having a secret friendship. When he came to town, they did things she did
not normally do.

One afternoon they went to the planetarium and
shared a bag of candy as a voice in the background
pointed out all the interesting constellations that she
hadn't taken the time to appreciate since she was a girl.
When she got home that night, she took her boys into
the backyard and pointed out the same stars to them.

They went bowling, and roller-skating, and to the
movies. Mostly they met in the middle of the afternoon, sometimes they met for the entire day, a couple
of times they shared a very early dinner. She started
taking lunch at her desk so she didn't feel guilty about
the time she spent away from her office.

They flirted with each other, but it was the kind of
lighthearted flirting that didn't mean anything, Hope
rationalized. They had only had one conversation that
Hope felt they shouldn't have had, and she had started
it. They were talking about sex, specifically about a
woman he had recently gone out with, and somehow
the subject turned to *her* sex life. She said something

that she should not have, and he volunteered to help out if Ray couldn't "get the job done." She asked how he would help, and he told her she didn't want to go there; she agreed that she didn't. It was their most provocative conversation.

Tony never asked to be introduced to her friends and family, and she never offered. She wasn't a stupid woman; she had admitted to herself after his first visit that there was some tension between them. She just chose not to define the tension; she chose not to examine it. And she chose unconsciously not to wonder why the more she looked forward to hearing from her new friend, the less she wanted to hear from her old husband.

Her friend told her that Ray was lucky to have a wife like her, that the kids were lucky to have her for a mother, that the people that she supervised were lucky to have her for a boss. That he was lucky to have her for a friend . . .

"I have a dinner meeting this evening, Hope. I won't be home until after eight," Ray said one morning toward the very end of summer. Hope was busy getting the boys ready to leave the house.

"Why do you wait until the last minute to tell me these things? Didn't you know you had a meeting yesterday? What if I had plans this evening?" she complained.

"Which one of those questions do you want me to answer first?"

"Forget it, Ray." Hope felt tears forming in the corners of her eyes and turned away from him.

"What's wrong with you, Hope?" He was concerned, but she was too irritated to hear it in his voice.

"Nothing Ray. Just do what you have to do."

"If you have plans, Hope, I'll call Stephanie and see if I can drop the boys off before my meeting. You didn't say anything about doing something tonight."

"Don't worry about the boys. I guess what I planned to do is not really important.*" I thought you'd know,* Hope thought sadly. He didn't protest or ask her anything specific before leaving the house. Her movements were slow as she finished her morning routine.

Almost as soon as she sat at her desk the phone rang. "Hope Williams."

"Hey you."

She relaxed a little when she heard his voice. "Hey back at you."

"What's wrong? You don't sound like yourself."

She heard the concern in his voice and it was genuine. She told him what Ray should have known. She wanted to talk. "Today is my mother's birthday, and I guess I'm feeling it."

"Oh man." She sat back in her chair and listened while he continued talking. "I'm sorry that she's not there with you. I lost my father a few years back so I know how it is to lose a parent. You never really get over it." They were silent for a minute. "What was she like?" She had spoken to him about her mother only in reference to herself.

"My mother?" It had been so long since anyone asked her about her mother that she was surprised. Up until this point, everyone who was significant in her life had known her mother.

"Yes, your mother." He laughed a little at the tone of her voice.

"Well, she loved tulips. I remember she would have tulips every spring when I was growing up. She would sacrifice to buy those flowers, I know, because I also remember the peanut butter sandwiches we had for dinner. Imagine having fresh tulips in a government apartment." Hope laughed as she considered the ridiculousness of it. "She was a hard worker, proud, alone most of her life." Tears Hope had been holding at bay for days worked their way onto her cheeks. "She spent the majority of her life just . . . surviving, and just when things had started coming together for her, she got sick."

"You told me before that she had not been married too long. Do you still keep up with your stepfather?"

"Yeah, Arthur, I talk to him occasionally. He's a really nice man, but my mother didn't marry him until I was long grown, so we don't share a lot of memories. But I know he was the type of man that my mother thought she'd never find. That was a big thing with her—men. She was always telling me how lucky I was to have found Ray."

"They got along well?"

"Yeah, they did . . . they really did." Ray had always been extra respectful toward her mother. He never forgot her birthday. *Which is why it is so ironic that he forgot this morning. I have visited my mother's grave on her birthday since she died.* "He would send her flowers for Valentine's Day even after she met Arthur."

"Well, from what you've told me about her, she sounds a lot like you."

"We were alike in a lot of ways."

"I hate to hear you sound so down. If there's anything I can do, just let me know."

"Just talking about it has helped. I appreciate that, Anthony. I really do."

"Call me later if you feel like talking. I'll be in my office for most of the day."

"Okay, bye."

"Hey!" He almost shouted into the phone.

"Yes?"

"Did you ever ask your mother why she loved tulips?"

All of a sudden Hope felt sad again. "I never did. My mother and I didn't have the type of relationship where we confided in each other or asked each other a lot of personal questions. I think I regret that more than anything."

Right before lunch Helen knocked softly on her door. When Hope called for her to come in she walked in with a beautiful bouquet of tulips in a tall crystal vase. Hope knew immediately that they were from Anthony. She didn't reach for the card until the door closed behind her secretary.

> *Hope, keep your head and your spirits up.*
> *These are for your mom.*
> *Love, Tony*

If she felt disconnected to Ray before, it was nothing compared to how she felt once she received the flowers from Tony. *How is it,* she wondered more than once, *that a man who has known me only a few months knows more about, and is more sensitive to my needs than my husband, who has known me forever?* She wondered—again, more than once—what it would be like if Ray were more like Tony: friendly, nice, respectful . . . At some point Ray had to have been like that, or else she wouldn't have married him.

He had gone to his meeting that night and Hope had picked up the boys and taken them to McDonald's. She half thought that he would come home and take her in his arms and tell her that he forgot about her mother's birthday, and that he was sorry; that they would both take off work the next day and go to the cemetery. He didn't, and she waited the entire week for something to jog his memory, because she certainly wasn't going to.

On Friday that week when Tony came to town she met him at the airport . . . outside the security gate. When she saw him, she started to cry immediately, quiet tears, and asked him to drive her to the cemetery. He hugged her close to him as they made their way to her truck. Once she gave him directions, she closed her eyes, tears still seeping from the corners down her cheeks.

At her mother's gravesite, Tony stood silently behind her, supportive but not intrusive. That day she did not go to work and she didn't call to say that she wouldn't be going in. The plan had been for them to have breakfast and for her to take him to his ten A.M. meeting. They spent the day at the zoo. She didn't remember his meeting until she was in bed that night. She thought back and couldn't remember him making a call, and she knew that he had not mentioned the meeting at any time that day. She appreciated him putting her needs before his business.

That day their relationship changed; at least it did for Hope. But she did not acknowledge it consciously. *It's normal,* she told herself, *as you get to know someone to rely on them and to look forward to seeing them.*

Chapter Twenty-one

Several days before school was to resume for the boys, Ray approached her about taking them camping. "I thought you said Lisa was having a birthday party for Ralph this Saturday?" She hadn't seen the couple in several months, she didn't particularly *want* to see them, but it seemed to her that the only time she and Ray went out together in the evenings was to attend one of their parties.

"Please, Hope, I know you don't want to go to that party."

"Maybe not, Ray, but it would be nice to do something other than sit around here all weekend."

"I agree, that's why I want to go camping."

"You know I can't stand camping, Ray. Let's go to New Braunfels, you know the boys love that water park."

Ray sighed and closed his eyes to let her know that she was trying his patience. "It's the last weekend before school. Everybody is going to be in New Braunfels. I don't feel like dealing with that crowd."

"And I don't feel like dealing with mosquitoes, and fleas, and snakes."

"I'm not surprised that you don't want to go camping—"

She cut him off before he could finish his remark. "You *shouldn't* be surprised, Ray. I've told you over and over again that I don't like to camp."

"As I was saying, Hope," he stared at her coldly, "I'm not surprised, because lately if I say *blue* you say *green,* if I say *stop* you say *go.* Everything has to be an argument with you."

So you have noticed. Hope put one hand on her hip.

"Well, I know that you like things to be different. I know if you say *blue*, you think I should say *true.* I hate to camp! The times you have dragged me out to the Piney Woods of East Texas, I have had a miserable time."

He ignored her sarcasm and shrugged his shoulders casually. "You don't have to go; I'll just take the boys." His attitude made her furious.

"I've been asking you all summer to go somewhere. You wait until summer is over and then you get an attitude with me because I have the nerve to voice my opinion and say that I don't want to go camping. All I'm suggesting, Ray, is that we do something that we can all enjoy."

His voice remained level. "I don't have an attitude, but you know what, Hope, nothing is ever good enough for you lately. You say things deliberately to piss me off, you act like here is the last place you want to be, you don't even give the boys any real attention . . ."

Oh, wait just a fucking minute, he just went too far.

"So now I'm not a good mother. Is that what you're saying?" He was looking at her as if she had shit on her head and she thought it was a hat. He continued to speak in the same level tone. Hope was sure he was doing it only to irritate her.

"Listen to you. I ask you to go camping and you go off. I don't know what's wrong with you, Hope, maybe you're going through a crisis or something, maybe this mortgage loan thing is not going like you wanted . . . I don't know, but I do know that you need to do whatever you have to do to get your shit together."

Her mouth fell open. "I need to get *my* shit together? Oh my God, Ray, oh my God." She shook her head, almost speechless, as he walked away.

Friday morning Ray loaded up her truck with camping supplies. The boys were excited about the trip and pleaded with Hope to go, but she continued to refuse. She kissed them good-bye and waved at Ray; he didn't return her wave or look in her direction as he drove off.

Chapter Twenty-two

Hope called in sick. She *was* sick. She climbed back into bed and pulled the covers over her head, grateful her family was gone and sad at the extent of her gratitude. Ray was right, about the boys at least. She *hadn't* been giving them her full attention. She couldn't remember one funny thing that the twins had done or said the entire summer.

She hadn't taken the time to spank David, and Lord knew the boy was getting out of hand. And when she took them to see a movie on the weekend or to some other activity designed to appeal to children, she spent most of the time praying that it would be over soon.

Her eyes started stinging, and Hope knew that she was about to start crying. She had been crying a lot lately, almost every day. A sad song on the radio would bring tears to her eyes. Once she had started to cry from frustration because the deli added mustard to her chicken salad sandwich. She had been so upset over the incident that she refused to eat the replacement sandwich that they sent over.

Her shit *wasn't* together, and she didn't know why and she didn't know what to do about it. She closed her eyes tight and waited for her mind to go blank. Hope wanted to go back to sleep. Tiredness weighed her entire body even though she had just gotten out of bed.

Hope sat up in bed, startled by the telephone. She wondered where and who she was for a minute. She still hadn't figured it out when she picked up the phone. "Hello." She didn't recognize her voice—it was hoarse and her mouth felt like someone had wiped it with cotton while she slept—but she recognized the voice on the other end of the phone.

"Hope?"

"Tony?"

"Yeah, it's me. Are you okay?"

"Yeah, I'm fine."

"I was worried about you. I called your office and your secretary told me that you were out sick."

"No, I'm not really sick. Just a little tired. God, what time is it?"

"Almost one o'clock."

"No wonder my head is killing me, I've been asleep for more than five hours."

"Well, something must be wrong with you."

She was touched by the concern in his voice. "Not really, just the same old thing." She wondered if Ray had left her a message at work to let her know that they arrived at the campsite. *Probably not.*

"Did Ray and the boys get off all right?" By now he

knew what the "same old thing" was. She appreciated that he listened to her periodic complaints but did not offer advice.

"Yeah, they left really early this morning." She sat up on the bed and twisted her body from side to side. Her muscles were aching also. If she didn't know better, she would think she had a hangover.

"So do you have any plans this weekend? Or will you be sleeping?"

"I think I've had enough sleep to last the entire weekend." She took the cordless phone with her and walked into the bathroom. "I don't know. I need to clean up around here." She looked at the mess covering the bathroom sink and made a mental note to call a cleaning service. "Are you going to that party tomorrow?"

"Ralph's birthday party?"

"Are you going?" She stood up a little straighter, and some of the pounding in her head stopped.

"I was thinking about it. I think it would be good for you to get out."

"And why is that?" She looked at herself in the mirror and smoothed her hair down.

"Because you've been so down lately. I'm worried about you."

"Well, if you say I need to get out, I guess I do." They arranged to meet at the party and spent a few more minutes talking about things that friends talk about. When she got off the phone her headache was completely gone and she had a smile on her face.

Hope adjusted the rearview mirror so she could take another look at herself. Her hair was freshly trimmed and she had had her make-up expertly applied at the Bobbi Brown counter. Daryl, the make-up artist, had said that she needed an edgy, modern look to complement her hairstyle. He had applied "gloss" everywhere. Eye gloss to her lids, neutral pencil and lip gloss to her soft lips, and a foundation that made her skin look so dewy and fresh that she didn't blink twice when he told her how much it cost. She wore a beaded T-shirt, form-fitting indigo jeans, and three-inch open-toed sandals. She thought she looked sort of like a rock star.

She took a deep breath, grabbed the bottle of scotch that she had picked up for Ralph, and opened the car door. She had never visited Ralph and Lisa without Ray. She didn't know if Lisa would want any unescorted ladies hanging around. *Hopefully Tony is already here,* she thought just before she rang the doorbell.

Lisa opened the door after only a few seconds. She smiled politely at her guest before looking over her shoulder. The disapproval in her voice was almost imperceptible. "Hope, I'm glad y'all could make it. When I didn't hear back from you, I thought you and Ray weren't coming."

Hope returned her polite smile with one of her own. She just wanted to get inside and look for her friend, but Lisa did not stand aside. "I'm sorry I didn't call to RSVP, I've just been so busy."

Lisa looked past her shoulders again. *Is she going to let me pass through the fucking door or what?*

"Is Ray still in the car?"

"No, he took the boys camping. I hope it's okay that I came alone." The expression on Lisa's face let her know that it was not, and Hope thought for a minute that she was going to close the door in her face, but Ralph walked up behind her.

"Hope, come on in. I thought y'all were going camping?"

Hope smiled at him as she stepped inside. "No . . . not all of us. Ray took the boys, so I decided to come alone." She held up the bottle for him to see. "Happy birthday." Ralph took the bottle and checked the label.

"This is the good stuff! We won't be serving this tonight. Thanks." Their conversation faded when the doorbell rang again. Hope allowed them to continue to play host/hostess and went to find a drink. She was pouring herself a glass of wine when Tony found her.

"Hey, beautiful." She put the glass down and gave him a hug. She saw that Lisa was watching her and wished that the woman would get some business of her own.

"Hello, handsome."

"I'm glad you made it." He stood back from her and looked her up and down appreciatively. "Wow! You look great." He laughed a little and shook his head and repeated his words. "You look great." Hope was a little embarrassed, but mostly she was pleased at his reaction. He stood beside her and poured two glasses of wine and handed one to her. He pointed to an empty love seat in the corner of the room and guided her toward it.

"I didn't talk to you today, so I didn't know if you were still planning on coming." Hope took a deep drink from the glass and sat back into the sofa. Tony sat close to her. So *close* that if another person wanted to sit with them there wouldn't be enough room between them. She didn't feel uncomfortable. She enjoyed the smell of his cologne and the look of admiration in his eyes.

"I've been traveling to Dallas to get my Hope fix all summer. Did you really think I would pass up an opportunity to spend an evening with you?" He *sounded* serious, but there was a big smile on his face.

"Is that what you've been doing?"

"Mmm-hmm. Finish that wine so we can dance."

She took the last swallow and placed the glass on the floor. Tony stood up and pulled her by the hand and continued to hold it as they walked to the space that served as the dance floor. Hope felt as if all eyes were on them as they moved to the fast-paced music. She was only concerned about one pair of eyes—Lisa's. She didn't see the other woman, but she felt sure that she was somewhere in the room watching her.

"What's wrong?" Tony leaned in closer to ask.

"I don't know. I guess I'm not as comfortable as I thought I would be, being here without Ray. I don't think Lisa is too happy about me coming here alone. Everyone here is in pairs."

"I know what you mean. I think that when she invited me she assumed I would bring a woman. If you hadn't come, I would have been standing on the wall all night. This is definitely a couples party, but I don't care. Do you?"

"I do feel a little uncomfortable."

"Do you want to leave? We could go to a dance club that I know of. It's not too far from here."

"I just got here. If we leave it'll look like we just came to meet each other."

"That *is* why we came, isn't it?"

She made a face at him. "You *know* what I mean."

She couldn't help but smile back at him. "I'm married, and these are my *husband's* friends. Even though we wouldn't be doing anything wrong, I still have to be concerned about appearances."

"Listen, I'll sneak around back and find the main breaker. When I turn off the lights, you feel your way to the front door. I'll meet you at the corner. I'll be the man with *this* shirt on with no car."

Hope laughed out loud at the silly suggestion. "You didn't drive?"

"No, I took a cab here. My hotel is close to the airport; I didn't see the need to rent a car. I'm depending on you to give me a ride back."

"No problem. I'll pick you up on the corner. I'll be the woman in *these* jeans. I'm driving a vintage Porsche."

"You're going to be wearing *those* jeans?" he said in his best Mac Daddy voice . . . which wasn't too bad. "I *could* start a fire to cause a diversion. When the smoke alarm goes off, run outside and I'll be waiting. Of course, the fire would cause severe property damage, and some people could die, but we'd be out of here."

Hope laughed until tears came to her eyes. "You are *so* ridiculous. Why don't we just stay for an hour and then leave? Are you sure you don't mind leaving the party? I know Ralph is an old friend."

"I didn't come here to see Ralph, I came to see you."

The mirth left her eyes. "Are you flirting with me?"

"You could call it that."

Chapter Twenty-three

Hope took the attendant's hand and stepped out of the car. Tony waited for her on the passenger side and they walked up the short flight of stairs into the club. She was pleased with what she saw when she looked around the room. Small tables were positioned strategically against the walls; the dance floor was small, but large enough to accommodate quite a few couples. The waitresses were sexy, but not over the top. She smiled her approval as they made their way to the only available table in the place.

A waitress came to the table immediately to take their drink orders. Hope ordered an Amaretto sour and Tony ordered a vodka on the rocks. They talked and laughed quietly about nothing while they waited for their drinks. Hope thought about the conversation they had with Lisa before leaving the party. Lisa had walked up to them sitting on the love seat talking quietly. She said that she didn't know that they were friends, and stood there as if they owed her an explanation.

Hope told her that they were business acquaintances
and left it at that. She was sure that she would hear
about it from Ray sometime next week. *But so what,
I'm allowed to have friends.*

They listened to the music for a while and enjoyed
their drinks. She wasn't listening closely to what he said;
she was trying to remember the last time she and Ray
had gone out dancing. "Hope . . . Hope." Hope jumped
a little when she realized Tony had asked her a question.

"I'm sorry. What did you say?"

"Nothing important. I can tell that you don't really
feel like talking. Why don't we dance?" Tony pushed
his chair back and helped her out of her seat. He was
right, she didn't feel like talking. She was better able to
focus on dancing than she had been at the party. A gig-
gle escaped her when she realized that Tony was rhyth-
mically challenged.

"What are you laughing at?" he asked over the music.

He asked, so she couldn't resist teasing him. "Where
did you learn to dance?"

He laughed back at her. One of the things she liked
about him was that he didn't take himself too seriously.

"I know . . . I know. I do the best I can with what
I've got." He narrowed the distance between them
when the D.J. played a popular love song. "I appear to
be a better dancer close up." He took her into his arms,
but left a respectable distance between them. He was
right; he was an excellent slow dancer.

They were dancing too close and she knew it. The
music was medium tempo and they were the only couple on the floor dancing so closely. She liked dancing
with him like this, her arms wrapped around his neck
and his hands resting on her hips. They moved well to-

gether and were keeping perfect time with the music. "I knew you had it in you. Now, aren't you glad we left the party to come here?" She was almost surprised to hear his voice; they hadn't talked much on the dance floor. She nodded slowly.

His breath was too close to her ear. Their bodies were too warm and it was too much of an effort to continue to hold her neck straight, so she let her cheek rest on his shoulder. They had been at the club for almost two hours and she told herself that she was getting tired.

They kept their silence. And as one song blended into the next, Hope had to ask herself was it right for them to be dancing like they were. Did friends dance so close? Did they make each other feel so warm? She couldn't stay focused long enough to answer the questions, so once again she gave herself up to the music.

Anthony pulled her even closer and moved one of his large hands to stroke the short hair at the nape of her neck. Something was happening, and because she was a married woman with three children, she couldn't afford to pretend she didn't know what it was. She tried to put some distance between them, but he wouldn't let her. "A little longer. Please, Hope . . . don't you want to dance with me?"

"Anthony . . ." She moved her head so that he could see her face. "We shouldn't be dancing like this. Look what's happening."

He didn't avoid her gaze. "I know. I'm not designed to hide what you do to me. I'm not ashamed of it." He waited for a second while she absorbed his words. "Are you hiding something, Hope?" He moved his hands between their bodies and ran them over the thin material covering her breasts. They responded instantly. Then she was mad and embarrassed. She pushed his hands away and almost stomped her way back to their table. When she got there she had to breathe hard and count to calm herself.

"Hope, I'm sorry. I shouldn't have done that. If you're not ready, you're not ready." His words angered her more.

"Ready for *what*?" Her hands were in the air to stop him before he could say anything. "You know what— don't even answer that." She closed her eyes to continue her counting and when she opened them and saw him staring at her from across the table her anger left her as quickly as it had come.

They looked at each other, and then with all the sincerity that she could muster, she said, "Anthony, I am married, and you're my friend. I'm not going to say we're *just* friends because . . . I mean . . . you mean a lot to me. But my family means a lot to me also. I'm glad I met you, but I'm not looking for anything other than friendship."

Tony had the same casual expression on his face when he responded. "Are you telling me, Hope, that I'm alone in this? You left your house to be with me tonight. I've arranged my entire schedule so that I'm able to see you every week. Don't tell me that you don't feel that we've *already* made a connection that's deeper than simple friendship." He waited for her to answer and when she couldn't, he continued. "The first time I saw you, I walked over to talk to you because I thought you were fine as hell. And when we started talking, I was thinking, *Damn, I want to get to know her,* and now that I have . . ." He shook his head slowly, all the while looking into her eyes. His expression was no longer casual.

"I have women friends, but I don't think about them like I think about you. I know what I'm feeling, and when we were dancing I felt the same thing coming from you."

"We shouldn't have been dancing like that," was all she would say.

"I'm not talking about the dancing. I'm asking you to be honest with me . . . be honest with yourself. Talk to me. *Please, Hope.*"

"Anthony, I think you're very attractive. I'll even go a step further and say that I'm attracted to you. I like a lot of things about you. I like talking to you and I like spending time with you." Hope blinked quickly to hold back tears. "But I have a family, and I'm committed to them." She took a deep breath and released it slowly before she continued. "I feel like . . . if we would just continue to focus on friendship and friendship *only,* the other thing will eventually fade away."

"I don't want the *other thing* to fade away." He reached across the table and took her hands in his. "I know you're married, Hope. I think about that all the time. And I know that if I were still married, I wouldn't want another man talking to my wife like I'm talking to you. I wouldn't want another man to feel for my wife what I feel for you." He shook his head. His earnestness was seductive. "I'm not trying to interfere with what you have going on at home. I just want us to take something for ourselves."

She didn't take her hands back, because the touch felt warm . . . innocent. "We can't have anything else. We're lucky that we've been able to have this friendship."

He started to caress the back of her hands; she left them where they were. "We could have a lot more. I don't want to play this game anymore. I want to be with you and I believe that you want to be with me. I want you to be my lover. You can say when, where, how much . . . how often." When he said the words, Hope knew she was in trouble. The words sent a jolt through her body, like when she was fifteen and Henry who was in her algebra class snuck up behind her and whispered on the side of her neck that he wanted her to go to the football game with him.

How had she gotten here, she wondered. Sitting across the table from a man she hadn't known for very long, away from her children, away from her husband, holding hands, being intimate . . .

She pulled her hands away roughly. "Stop it, Anthony! Don't do this. I already have a lover—*my husband.*" She lowered her voice to a harsh whisper when she saw that two women at the table nearest them were very interested in their conversation. "We can't be lovers, and if you keep talking about this we can't even be friends." She hoped that he didn't notice that her words sounded a little hollow.

He held up his hands, defeated. "Okay, okay. I won't mention it again. Your friendship is important to me. And I'll just, like you say, redirect my feelings and focus on that." He looked as if he was going to say something else but changed his mind. "But right now I need to get out of here, before I put my foot deeper in my mouth." He stood up and took his wallet out. "I'm going to get you in your car and call a cab to take me back to my hotel."

Hope stood up, protesting. She didn't want their evening to end with so much negativity between them. "I can drive you to your hotel, Anthony; you don't have to call a cab."

He stopped counting his money and looked up at her. Hope held his gaze for a second before looking away to find her purse.

Anthony tossed some money on the table and asked quietly, "Are you ready?"

"Yeah." They walked out of the club, careful not to touch.

No polite conversation, no singing softly along with the music playing on the radio, no friendly laughter. The twenty-minute ride back to the hotel was completely silent. And all Hope could do was think. She thought about how Ray had refused to do something they could all enjoy. She thought about the way he had driven off without looking back. And how she had been so lonely, and how Tony had relieved so much of her loneliness. She thought about how Tony's body had responded to hers and she thought about how Ray hadn't touched her in three weeks. Maybe he didn't want her anymore. And here she was sitting with a man who had practically begged to be with her.

Maybe Ray is having an affair. Maybe that's why he's making everything so difficult. Hope put a stop to her line of thinking. She knew that she was looking for an excuse. That Stephanie had been right and that she had known almost from the start the direction that her relationship with Tony would take. Why make excuses for the inexcusable? If she wanted to be with Tony . . . why couldn't she just be with Tony? And she did want to be with him. She had been a good daughter, a good mother, and a good wife. And if she decided to be with him and it turned out to be a mistake, wasn't everyone allowed to make a mistake? And who would know?

Her stomach was tied in knots by the time she pulled up to the valet station in front of the hotel. She prayed that Tony would say something and she prayed that he wouldn't. He didn't get out of the car immediately; instead he leaned back until his head was resting against the soft leather on the bucket seat. He kept his eyes open and looked straight ahead. She barely heard him ask, "Are you coming up?" She paused for the longest, most important second of her life and then she turned the key in the ignition to shut off the engine.

She didn't have one last chance to change her mind once they got into the hotel room; Tony took her into his arms immediately and kissed her like they were starting something real. He held her waist lightly as if he knew she wouldn't try to get away. Her tongue moved easily with his. It had been more than thirteen years since she had kissed a man other than Ray. *It's like riding a bike, no matter how long it's been since your last ride, get on and it all comes back to you.* Tony bit her lip playfully before he ended the kiss.

"I want to make you feel good tonight. I want to make your toes curl. I don't want you to hold anything back."

"Tony, I don't know . . ." She was scared of what she saw in his eyes. Scared to let him know that he had been making her feel good since their first conversation.

"You *do* know. If you really don't know you shouldn't be here." He dropped his hands from her waist and stepped back to look at her. "It's on you, Hope."

"I don't want to go, Tony. I know we shouldn't be here like this, but we are. Maybe . . ." She looked up at him for agreement. "Maybe if we did it once and relieved some of this tension that's been building be-

tween us we could go back to being friends. And nobody has to know."

His expression hardened for a second. He was not
about to let her off so easily.

"Nobody has to know, Hope, but I'm not willing to
put a limit on this."

"Damn." Hope almost laughed. "Can you give me
something? Make me some false promises, get me
drunk—something—so I don't have to go into this
with my eyes wide open."

He moved close to her once again and took her in
his arms. "Don't worry, baby. It'll be all right." And
when he kissed her the second time it was.

And he kissed her again, and she kissed him. And
they moved to the bed and they moved their clothes
away from their bodies. He kissed the right side of her
and she kissed the left side of him. And when they
made love to each other he kissed the tears that rolled
down her cheeks.

By the time it was morning he had made her toes
curl two or three times and she felt perfectly comfortable lying naked in his arms.

Chapter Twenty-four

"Where are you going?" Tony pulled her back just as she was about to stand up. She looked back at him lying on the bed. The sheets were tangled around the lower half of his dark body, and Hope couldn't help but notice that he had an early morning erection. She turned away from him but didn't try to get up.

"I thought you were sleeping."

"I *was* sleeping, and then I was watching you get dressed. By the way, you put your panties on backward," he teased. His good mood irritated her. Hope heard the sheets rustle as he turned on his side. He rubbed her back through her shirt. "Were you going to leave without waking me up?" He tried to pull her back down, but she resisted. "Now, you know that if I had tried to do that, you'd think I was a dog."

"No, I wouldn't, Tony." She turned to look at him again. "If I were a man and I woke up to find the married woman that I had been with the night before not in bed with me, I would assume that she had either gone

home to her family or gone to church to pray for forgiveness."

He sat up straight in the bed. His voice was low.
"Don't do it, Hope."

"Don't do what?"

"Don't be one of those women who do exactly what
they want and then pretend that they're embarrassed or
sorry about it. Or worse, pretend that it never happened. You made a decision last night . . . we made a
decision together. You being pissed at me is not going
to change it."

There was evidence of their lovemaking strewn
around the room: gold condom wrappers, his pants, her
sandals—one near the front door and one under the
table—there was no way she could pretend that it didn't
happen.

"I'm not pretending, but I am embarrassed. Now I
have to do my walk of shame through the hotel lobby.
Everyone will be staring at me because I'm wearing
the same clothes that I wore last night."

"If they stare at you, Hope, it's because you're beautiful." He shoved the sheet from his body and got out of
bed. He stood in front of her for a second before
pulling her up and against him.

"*Don't* be embarrassed. We're not in high school.
This is between the two of us." He rubbed his hands up
and down her back and kissed her softly on the mouth.
She started to push him away, but allowed her hands to
rest on his naked shoulders. He kissed her mouth again
and then moved his lips, sweet and moist, along the
side of her neck. Tony unsnapped her jeans and started
moving her back toward the bed.

"Tony . . . no!" She moved away from him. "I have

to get home . . . I can't." She snapped her jeans again and moved quickly to put on her shoes.

He continued standing near the bed. "You gonna leave me like this?"

She looked at him standing naked, making no attempt to hide his erection. If she hadn't been so ashamed of herself she would have been tempted. She shook her head before lifting her purse from the back of a chair. She walked to the door and in a barely audible voice said, "I guess I'll talk to you later."

Hope did not allow herself to think on the way home. She turned the music up loud and thought only about the words of the songs. When she turned on her street, she was happy to see that none of her neighbors were out. She opened the garage door and set the car's emergency brake. She did not turn off the engine until she heard the final strains of a song that she particularly liked.

The first thing she did after dropping her keys and purse on the floor was head straight to the shower. She turned the water on before taking a disposable douche from underneath the sink. It seemed to her that the smell of condoms and Tony's Dolce and Gabbana cologne was everywhere. Ray did not wear Dolce and Gabbana. She made a note to herself to have his car cleaned later that day.

She took off her clothes and stepped under the running water. She washed every part of her body that Tony had touched, from her hair to her toes . . . at one point during the night her toes had ended up in his mouth. He had been an excellent and considerate lover.

He hadn't taken anything for granted. Hope felt guilty remembering the pleasure they found together.

When she got out of the shower she inspected every inch of her body for scratches, hickeys—any mark that was sexual in nature. When she found none, she brushed her teeth. She turned away from the mirror on the way out of the bathroom.

As if on cue, the telephone started ringing. Hope looked down at herself and saw that she had forgotten to put clothes on. She sat down on the side of the bed naked and reexamined her thighs as she picked up the telephone. "Hello."

"Hey, this is Tony. Do you have a few minutes?"

"Yes, what is it?" It was the second time he had called her at home in all the weeks that they had been friends.

"Are your boys back home?" Hope knew that translated into "is your husband home—is it safe to talk?"

"Ray won't be back with the boys until after five this evening." Her voice held no expression.

"In that case, can we meet somewhere? I need to talk to you."

"No, I'm not leaving the house today. What is it, Tony?" Now her voice was impatient. He paused a minute before speaking. Hope thought that he had hung up.

"Listen, Hope, I'm sorry about how I handled things this morning. If it seemed to you that I was making light of the situation, I want you to know that was not my intention. Waking up with a married woman is not something that I do—in fact, the only married woman that I've ever been with *before* last night was my ex-wife. I'm sorry, I should have been more sensitive." Hope got under the covers and listened without interrupting as Tony finished speaking.

"I'm not going to lie and say that I regret what happened—I don't." He sighed before continuing. "But I won't get into that. I just wanted to let you know that if I had to do it over again, I would have held you, and talked to you . . . I wouldn't have let you leave the room until we were okay with each other."

His sweet words didn't make her feel any better. Her head was pounding like it had been on Friday. She felt sick to her stomach and could hardly open her mouth to speak.

"I'm not upset with you, Tony. I don't think you could have done anything to make me feel okay this morning." *God, my head is killing me.* "I don't mean to sound rude, but I really can't talk about this right now."

"Can I call you later?"

"No!" She tossed the sheets back and sat on the side of the bed. "I'll call you in a few days."

"Hope—"

She hung up the phone before he could finish the sentence. Hope stumbled into the bathroom and fell on her knees in front of the toilet. After a few minutes of dry heaving she realized that she was not going to throw up. The rumbling in her stomach was guilt . . . and fear.

She paced for most of the morning. She was tired but couldn't sleep. A swim didn't help; another shower didn't help either. Hope dressed and left the house to have Ray's car cleaned and stopped by the grocery store to get some things she needed to make a welcome-home dinner for her family. When she heard the truck pulling into the garage she was taking a sweet potato pie out of the oven.

The boys ran into the kitchen to greet her, hugging her and talking all at once. Ray stood back from the group and she knew that he was waiting to see what kind of reception he was in for. She smiled gently at him over the boys' heads, and she saw surprise light his eyes. "Hey, how was the trip?"

"Crazy, hot . . . we missed you."

She was touched and moved the boys aside so that she could kiss her husband. She pressed her lips firmly against his. When she tried to end the kiss he put his arms around her and kissed her deeply. The twins were happily disgusted with the display of affection between them, but David tried to pull them apart so that he could once again be the center of attention.

Ray ended the kiss, but kept his lips close to hers as he spoke. "You were right. Next time we'll do something that we can all enjoy."

"We're hungry, Mom. Can we have a snack?" Karl and Jordan were vying for space in front of the refrigerator.

"No! Dinner is almost ready. I made a very *nutritious* meal for you guys." She looked up at her husband teasingly, and he smacked her on her bottom.

"I hope you have something special for Daddy to eat."

"Cute, cute, I'm sure I can find something." Guilt caused her to hold fast to her smile, like guilt would put smothered pork chops, okra gumbo, garlic mashed potatoes, homemade biscuits, and sweet potato pie on the table. She turned back to the boys when she felt her façade slipping. "You guys go and take a shower, and when you finish dinner will be on the table." The boys left the kitchen immediately, grumbling but not wanting to do anything to delay their dinner.

Ray went to the stove to check the pots. "This looks good, baby. Do I have to take a shower before I eat too?"

"No, you don't." She wondered if he sensed how uncomfortable she felt. He took a plate and started to help himself. "You *could* wash your hands, though." He put the plate down and went to the sink to wash his hands. She sat at the table with him, a silly smile still pasted on her face.

"What did you do while we were gone?"

Does he know something? Her heart was pounding so hard and fast that she looked down at her chest to see if it was moving. It wasn't. *Easy, Hope, easy*, she cautioned herself. To lie or not to lie was not the question—the question was how big of a lie it was safe to tell. *I have to tell him that I went to the party . . . should I tell him I ran into Tony? What if that bitch Lisa tells Ray that we were talking at the party? Yeah, right, Hope, she's the bitch, but I bet she wasn't out last night fucking a man who was not her husband. True . . . True.*

"I went to Ralph's birthday party for a little while. I didn't stay very long."

"How was it?" Ray was eating like it had been ages since he had had a decent meal. *The truth is, it has been,* Hope admitted to herself.

"It was all right." Hope sighed and shrugged. "I took Ralph some scotch." She watched her husband as he continued to enjoy his food. "Since school is about to start I guess I need to start cooking more often."

Ray looked up from his plate with his eyebrows

raised. "Aren't you about to start school too? I would think that you would be cooking even less often."

"No . . . actually, I've been thinking that instead of taking two classes, I'll just take one. I'm gonna try and see if they have something that's a different night of the week. The time away from home won't be as inconvenient."

His eyebrows went up another half inch, and there was a smile on his face. "What brought this on?"

Guilt.

"I've just been thinking about what you said."

Yeah, right.

"And you're right. The boys need me right now, and I don't have to be in such a hurry to get my MBA."

Ray smiled at her like he hadn't in a long time. "You know what I said earlier about next time going somewhere we can all enjoy? Forget that. I'm taking the boys camping every other month."

"The boys asleep?" Ray put down the book he was reading.

"Yes, they are. The boys are asleep, the dishes are washed, and Hope is tired!" She yawned and started walking toward the bathroom.

"Where are you going?"

"I'm going to take a shower." *Another shower.*

"Uh-uh." He patted the sheet next to him. "I want you right here."

"Ray, I'm tired," Hope whined. *That happens when you're up all night screwing.*

"I have an energy pill for you."

Hope smiled tightly and walked over to the bed. She

really, *really* did not want to make love. But it was the least she could do.

When he took her in his arms she was stiff. He nuzzled her neck, she was stiff. "What's wrong?"

First of all, I just told you I was tired. Second, I think that we should wait a while before we make love, because I think I can still smell Tony on me . . . even though I know that's impossible.

"I'm fine." She took his face in her hands and kissed him deeply, and then she kissed him again. She could feel his body responding under the sheets.

Hope stood up and shimmied out of her shorts and T-shirt. She left her bra and panties on and joined him under the sheets. *Here goes nothing.* She wanted to ask God to make sure that everything was the same or better when they made love, but she refused to bring Him into her mess. She did, however, decide to put her heart—and everything else she had—into it. She reached down and stroked him firmly; she licked her lips seductively when she felt him harden in her hands.

"Mmm, I love you, baby." She put her lips against his again, but this time she bit him firmly. He tried to catch her tongue, but she moved away before he could.

"I love you too." Ray stretched out in the bed, more than willing to let her take the lead. She kissed his stomach and nibbled on his pelvic bone before taking him into her mouth.

"Oh baby, that feels so good." Ray sat up a little so that he could watch her; he placed his hands on either side of her head, and she allowed him to move it up and down. She was excited by his moans of pleasure, and some of her fear subsided. After a few minutes she moved his hand away and kissed him again. Then she pulled her panties aside and eased herself down on him.

She waited a minute . . . she waited for him to push her aside and ask, "What the fuck is going on? Who have you been screwing?"

When he didn't, Hope realized that she was the same to him. Tony hadn't knocked any new groove in it, it didn't fit around Ray any differently, it was the same to him as it had been the last time he used it three weeks ago. She had halfbelieved him when he said a man would know if his wife had been with another man . . . but until yesterday she never thought that she would ever put his theory to the test.

Hope moved her hips with more confidence and reached behind to caress him. Her deliberately slow movements were driving him crazy, so he placed his hands on her hips and forced her to ride faster and harder. When she felt that he was about to come, Hope shook her head mentally in wonder. *He really doesn't suspect a thing.*

"That was great, baby," Ray said to her as soon as he regained his breath. "Did you come?"

"No. I guess I'm too tired." She yawned to prove it.

"Give me a few minutes and we'll go again."

"No, babe, you go on to sleep. I know you're tired too." In a few minutes, after he drifted off to sleep, Hope got up to take a shower. In the bathroom, she couldn't bear the thought of yet another shower that day. She wet a towel and wiped the stickiness from her thighs and went back to bed.

I fucked my husband and another man in less than twenty-four hours. I wonder, does that make me a whore? It was the last thought on her mind as she fell asleep.

Chapter Twenty-five

For two weeks she played the perfect wife and mother
. . . for two weeks. Then she told Ray she had not been
able to get a class that met on a suitable day of the
week, and his response brought to the surface the resentment she had been suppressing as part of a self-in-
flicted penance.

"I *know* what I said, Ray!"

"Why can't you wait until next semester? I told you
about always waiting until the last minute to do something." In the last e-mail that she had gotten from Tony,
he had asked about her classes. Though she hadn't answered it, the note had been very encouraging.

For two weeks, Hope avoided Tony's phone calls
and did not respond to his e-mails . . . for two weeks.
She didn't know what to say, plus she was not the type
of café woman that her mother always talked about
when she was growing up, a woman who would screw
her husband—when she had one—and anybody else's,
always with a smirk on her face. A selfish woman with

no morals who left her children unattended so that she was free to go "cattin' around."

But Ray didn't make it easy. Apparently he was oblivious to the effort . . . to the *sacrifice* she was making for him. Apparently he didn't see how depressed she was. Just as long as she cooked something he liked for dinner and sucked his dick on demand, he was happy.

When Ray accused her of being irresponsible *again*, she looked at him for a long time; she couldn't decide whether it was disappointment or disgust on his face. In the end it didn't matter. What was the point, she wondered, in giving up something that brought her so much pleasure for someone who acted as if he had no interest in pleasing her?

Hope sighed and stood up from the table. "I'm so tired of this, Ray. I can't take it anymore."

"What does that mean?" Ray looked surprised.

"It means we have to figure out a way to stop arguing about everything."

"*We* don't argue about everything, *you* argue about everything. All I said was that I don't like the fact that you are going to be away from the house more often than you said a few days ago. I *am* still allowed to express my feeling in my own home . . . or is that a problem for you?"

"No, Ray, it's not a problem."

The next day she called her friend.

"Anthony Bolden." His voice was professional and crisp. She had been very hesitant about making the call, but as soon as she heard his voice she relaxed.

"Hey you." She was smiling.

"Hey back at you. How are you?" No recriminations, just a man who was glad to hear from her.

"Working. I got your e-mails. My class meets on Monday, and the boys are doing fine. Thanks for asking."

"And how is Ray doing?"

"Ray is Ray."

He laughed when she said that. "What does that mean?"

"It means that he is the same as he was . . . the same as he has always been."

"And are you the same as you have always been?"

She knew he was talking about what happened between them. "I'm not the same." Her voice was quiet. "I'm glad to be talking to you. I've been thinking about you every day." She had decided that if she called, she had to be honest.

"I guess I don't have to tell you that I've been thinking about you *all* day. Do you have some time this week? We need to talk."

"I know. I was thinking maybe I could come to Houston this weekend." She hadn't thought about going to Houston until just that second, but as soon as she said the words, she knew it was the right thing to do—well, at least it was what she wanted to do.

"I would love that, baby. Do you want me to send you a ticket?" He had called her baby over and over again the night they had made love, but it sent a jolt through her to hear it in the light of day.

"No, thanks. I think I need to drive. It'll give me some time to think."

"Are you sure you can get away for the entire weekend?"

She knew he was asking what she would tell her husband. "At this point, Tony, it doesn't even matter. It's what I need."

* * *

Ray *didn't* understand why she wanted to get away for the weekend. She made up a story about a woman's conference in Houston that she had been thinking about attending. He didn't argue with her; instead, he let his displeasure be known in a thousand different silent ways.

She took a page from his book and remained silent as she made arrangements for the boys to spend the weekend with various friends. Ray would be alone for the weekend, free to do anything he pleased.

When they got up Friday morning he didn't say anything as she told him he would have to drop the boys off because she wanted to drive his two-seater. He also didn't say anything when she put her overnight bag in the trunk of his car, or when she handed him the slip of paper telling him where and what time he should drop off the kids.

A good-bye kiss was out of the question. She told him he could reach her by cell phone if he needed anything, but she knew he wouldn't be calling. And by Friday afternoon she was on Highway 45 traveling eighty miles an hour to Houston.

She called Tony when she was about thirty minutes from his house according to the directions he had given her earlier that day. Pleasure was clearly evident in his voice when they spoke.

"Do you want me to meet you halfway? I don't want you to get lost."

"I won't get lost, I am very good at finding my way around."

"Well, I'm waiting for you. Get here soon."

She released the breath it seemed she had been holding since she started the trip. Hearing his voice had reassured her . . . they would have a good weekend. She stopped just short of telling herself she had made the right decision.

Tony was waiting outside when she pulled into the driveway of his Memorial town home. A grin spread across her face that rivaled his. He waved for her to stop and got into the car on the passenger side. "What are you doing?" she asked laughingly as he reached over the seat and grabbed her face. He kissed her loudly along her face and neck, leaving her giggling. "Stop it! Stop it!" Hope closed her eyes and opened them again, trying to control the pleasure she was feeling.

"Pull into the garage," he instructed, still smiling. She pulled the car in next to his Mercedes. She gave him the key so he could get her bag out of the trunk before getting out. She stretched and yawned, a little tired from the long ride.

"Damn, girl!" Tony walked behind her and put his hands around her waist. "I didn't know you had legs like that." She was wearing shorts . . . hot pants. After making an appearance at work for a couple of hours that morning, she had stopped at a department store to buy something to sleep in. The boxer shorts and T-shirts in her bag had been thrown in for Ray's benefit. She didn't know *too* much about having an affair, but she felt it was safe to assume that sexy lingerie was a plus.

The hot pants and halter top she was wearing had been an afterthought. She had loved them so much that she had left them on and gone to the shoe department and found a pair of sandals that matched the red outfit.

Hope held one of her legs out like a dancer and twisted it from one side to the other so that he could fully appreciate them. She leaned back into his bear hug, enjoying the closeness.

"That's right, you've never seen my legs."

He kissed the side of her neck. "No, I haven't, not in the light. I do, however, remember how exquisite they felt wrapped around my back. I should have known they were perfect."

"Are you flirting with me?"

"Nope, just stating the facts, madam." He released her and she followed him inside. Hope was immediately impressed with his home. The garage led to a rather large family room. It had oversized, plush-looking leather furniture and what looked to Hope like a very expensive home theater system. There was a gourmet kitchen downstairs and a very elegant eating area.

"Wow, this place is great, Tony. Did you go out and get it just to impress me?"

"No. I have something else that I hope to impress you with." His wink was wicked. "Actually, I bought this place after my divorce. My ex-wife got the house, which she has since sold. I didn't want to be bothered with a big lawn and neighbors; this place is pretty low maintenance."

"This place is low maintenance?" Hope looked around and up and down doubtfully. "How many floors is it?"

"Three. Come on, I'll show you where you'll be living for the next two days." There were two bedrooms, two bathrooms, and a small wet bar/refrigerator area on the second floor. One of the bedrooms was his and one was obviously for his daughter. Hope was impressed by the rich color scheme and the immaculateness. He told her that he had a decorator and that his housekeeper came once a week. The third floor had another bedroom and bath and an open space that Tony used as a combination workout area and home office. She loved his home and felt completely comfortable as they retraced their steps to his bedroom.

"Do you want to unpack?" He dropped her bag on the floor and flopped down on his king-sized bed. He looked up at her with his hands folded behind his head. He hadn't stopped grinning since he had met her outside. Neither had she. She half screamed, half laughed, flung her hands above her head at the sudden surge of freedom that she felt, and ran toward the bed, flopping down beside him.

She covered her face with her hands, trying to control her urge to scream again. "I can't believe I'm here." She turned on her side to look at him, wanting to touch him but needing some reassurance. "Do you think I'm crazy for coming here?" She didn't allow him to answer the question; instead she vocalized some of the feelings she had been experiencing for the past two weeks.

"We haven't talked about what happened between us." He met her eyes but remained silent. "You must think I'm the most fickle woman in the world. After all I said about being devoted to my marriage and my family, I sleep with you at the drop of the hat and then I call you up and . . ." She took a deep breath and turned so she was resting on her back. She examined the texture on the ceiling as she tried to gather her thoughts. Her mood had gone from exuberant to almost despondent in sixty seconds. "I don't know what I'm doing."

"I don't know what you're doing either, Hope, but

I'm glad to be doing it with you." He put his hands across her stomach and pulled her back onto her side so she faced him. "I don't think you're crazy, and I know this is hard for you. I don't know what *I'm* doing. I know what kind of woman you are, and I believe that you are committed to your family.

"I may have been wrong to open this thing up between us, but I don't regret it. I've been beating myself up these last few weeks thinking that I had ruined our friendship, but when I think about making love to you that night, and when I think about having the chance to be with you again . . ." They were looking directly at each other, and Hope was warmed by the intensity that she felt coming from him. "It's like I have to have you. I'm willing to risk anything." He ran his fingers across the bare flesh on her arms and she shivered.

"What are *you* risking Tony?" Another mood change. "I'm the one with the husband and the three boys who need their daddy."

Tony didn't let her go, and he didn't turn away from her sudden anger. "You're right, Hope. You're risking a lot." That's all he said.

Hope let her body relax. What was the point in driving hundreds of miles to argue? "I can't promise you anything. I can't even promise you that I'll see you again when I get back home."

He smiled softly and kissed her on the cheek. "I'm not asking you to promise me anything. I'm just glad you're here *now*." He moved her face and kissed her with very little pressure on the mouth. Hope opened her lips against his and he swept his tongue around the inside of her cheeks and the roof of her mouth. He flipped on his back again and pulled her on top of him.

As their kiss deepened, his hands warmed the bare skin on her back that the halter top left exposed.

The lower part of her body started moving against his and she was very aware of his response, as she was very aware of her own. Tony moved his hands down and slipped them under her shorts. "I want to make love to you," he groaned against her mouth. He moved his long fingers up and she jumped slightly when he found what he was looking for. "I think you're ready for me." She was ready physically . . . but not mentally. She reached behind her and grabbed his hands to keep them still.

"I want you too," she told him honestly. "But give me a little time."

He slipped his hands out of her shorts as easily as he had slipped them in. "Whatever you say. I can wait." He started to smooth her back in a less sexual way. "If you don't want to make love this weekend, we don't have to." She laughed at that. "I'm serious. I *want* to make love to you, and I'll be disappointed if we don't, but I know how hard this is for you. There's no pressure, baby."

And she felt like he was being truthful. It had been like that with him since they had started talking. It seemed as if her needs were always first with him. She had discovered that being put first made her feel . . . safe.

She kissed him once more in a way that was very sexual before rolling off him and standing up to straighten herself. He looked her up and down as she did so. "You're a beautiful woman, Hope." The look on his face made her blush. "I know I've told you already, but I'm glad you're here."

"I'm glad I'm here too, Tony." She decided then to put her guilt and misgivings aside and to fully enjoy their time alone together. She pulled him up from the bed. "I hope you have something great planned for the weekend." He kept his hands in hers as they walked out of the bedroom.

Chapter Twenty-six

After they showered and changed clothes, Tony took her to a steakhouse very near his home. He ordered a bottle of delicious soft red wine for the two of them to share and a porterhouse steak for himself. She changed her order to filet mignon after he teased her about ordering chicken at a steakhouse. "I was trying to save you some money," she teased after their waiter left.

"*You're* paying for this dinner," he teased right back. "The last time you were here, you skipped out on the check." His words sobered her momentarily. It seemed like such a long time since that first lunch, and that first dinner, but in reality it had only been a few months. She wondered again how was it possible for a life to change so quickly.

The restaurant was very romantic. Dim lighting and a single candle flickering in the center of the table made everyone look wonderful. Couples laughed and sipped wine or cocktails over low conversation. Hope wondered how many of the other couples sitting at the tables around the room had no right to be there with each other . . . how many others were having an affair. She visibly stiffened when the word "affair" flashed across her mind.

That's what you're doing, girl, having an affair.

"Are you okay?" Tony asked. Hope started to say yes, but then she wondered what the point was of not being honest with Tony.

"I was just wondering how many people here are in the same situation we're in. Look at them." Hope nodded slightly toward the couple sitting to the right of them. They were holding hands across the table and appeared to be having an intense conversation. If it weren't for the hand holding, Hope would have thought they were having an argument.

"You know, I was wondering the same thing. I'd bet one hundred dollars that they're not married." He laughed a little. "When I was married we didn't come out to hold hands or argue over a nice dinner. We had a lot of rooms at home to argue in."

"What did you go out for, then?"

"To *eat*. And then we started going out because my daughter liked to go out . . . and then we stopped going out altogether." He shrugged as if he thought that was the natural progression of a marriage. *Maybe it is.*

"Did you argue a lot before you divorced?"

"No, we didn't. We didn't argue, we didn't talk . . . and in the end we rarely made love." He smiled to change what was quickly becoming a serious conversation. "Remember I told you that the sex was a major part of our marriage. And when that was gone . . ." His words trailed off, signaling that was all there was to tell about his marriage, but Hope wasn't willing to drop the subject.

"Do you miss her?"

He didn't miss a beat before answering her question. "I can't honestly say that I miss Naomi, what I *miss* is having my daughter in the house with me, being able to see her every day. I don't think that Naomi was ready for marriage; maybe I wasn't either. I was so into what I thought marriage could be, given time, that I waited too long to express what was important to me." He took a sip of wine and looked at her. "What about you, Hope? How often do you and Ray argue? How often do you go out? How often do you make love?"

She looked at the flame on the candle as she thought about his question.

"At some point I remember us arguing about almost everything. Now it seems as if we have been agreeing to disagree. Our house is so quiet after the kids go to sleep—I know at some point that we couldn't wait for the kids to get to sleep—we would talk or watch the news together." She shrugged. "We don't go out unless it's something to do with the kids or something to do with his job. We still make love, but not as often as we used to." She looked up to see how he reacted to her last statement. He read her mind.

"Don't worry about me, I wouldn't have asked the question if I couldn't handle the answer." He took her hand so they looked like the couple that had sparked their last ten minutes of conversation. "You know that I love you, don't you, Hope?"

She couldn't hold his gaze. *Now what am I supposed to say to that?* she wondered. *I can't declare love for another man as long as I'm still married. As long as I'm still married . . . as long as I'm still married. Where did that come from?* She didn't know if she loved him;

she didn't know how she felt about anything or anyone anymore.

"I don't want to talk about love, Tony, and I don't want to talk anymore about marriage—yours or mine. I just want to eat and finish this bottle of wine." She placed her napkin in her lap as their waiter approached with their food. Suddenly she was famished. As she cut into her steak, she remembered her resolve just to enjoy the weekend.

Chapter Twenty-seven

The first thing that Hope saw when she stepped out of the shower was a huge gift basket on the double sink. She walked toward it like an excited child, forgetting momentarily that she was dripping wet. The card lying next to the basket said.

*Hope, I want you to have everything
you need while you're here.*

A smile spread across her face as she ripped through the silver cellophane. Obviously Tony had brought a variety of different products and had someone assemble them beautifully. Luxurious body lotions and bath oils, skin care products, French soaps, body sprays . . . He had even selected two lipsticks from her favorite cosmetics line, and in the center of the basket was a huge bottle of Coco by Chanel—her favorite. She never remembered a man taking time out to do something so special and personal for her.

Hope selected one of the body oils and tucked a towel around herself before leaving the bathroom. Tony was lying on the bed when she walked into the room. He looked and smiled at her. "You're all wet."

"I know." She held up the body oil for him to see. "This stuff says that it works well when applied to slightly damp skin. Thank you for the basket. I won't need to buy any more lotions for a year."

"You're welcome."

She sat on the edge of the bed and tossed the body oil back at him.

"I bet this stuff works best when it's applied by someone else." She tried to sound casual, but he could probably tell by her breathing how anxious she was to have him touch her. She didn't look, but she felt Tony moving toward her. He kissed the back of her neck softly before applying the first drop of the fragrant oil. His large hands massaged the oil into the skin that was exposed by the towel, and once he had her shoulders feeling like jelly, he reached around her and loosened the knot on her towel so it fell around her hips.

He rubbed oil on her back and stomach before he found her breasts. He had positioned his body so she was sitting between his legs, and she felt his heart beat against her back. Hope leaned back into his caress and he moved his lips, tongue, and teeth along the side of her neck as he continued to massage her breasts and then her thighs.

He murmured things like "you're beautiful" and "I need to make love to you" against her ear. She didn't respond with words, but she was sure he could feel the heat from her body. Tony moved smoothly across the side of the bed to stand in front of her.

The first time they had been together she hadn't allowed herself to look at him. Now she looked from head to toe, and the view made her weak. He wore drawstring pajama bottoms. The silk clung to the muscles in his thighs. Hope lifted her arms until they reached his shoulders, then she ran her hands down his arms and back up again. She put her face to his stomach and kissed the hard muscles that she found there.

"You're beautiful," she muttered into his stomach. "I love the way you feel." Tony stepped back and poured more of the body oil into his hand. As he warmed the oil, he looked at her. Her face, her stomach, her breasts were all exposed. The white towel covered her from the bottom of her waist to the very top of her thighs.

Tony knelt in front of her and slid his oil-slick hands across her stomach and through the towel's loose knot. Now she was fully exposed. She hadn't allowed him to look too long at her body before either, and he didn't look now—instead he looked into her eyes as he continued to massage the oil into her thighs and along her side.

"You're making me weak, Tony."

"You make me weak every time I look at you." He oiled his hands again, and this time slid them down her legs and across the top of her feet several times. She squirmed and giggled when he picked up her feet and rubbed oil on her heels and between her toes. The giggling stopped when he sucked gently on one toe and then another until all ten received adequate attention.

When he finished he rested her feet on his chest, and she curled her still-tingling toes so she captured some of the hair and skin that she found there. She pushed him back so she could extend her legs. The movement of her feet down his chest and to his crotch area was awkward, but he didn't seem to mind, especially when she slipped her soft feet into his pajamas and moved them against his sensitive skin.

"I see you're ready for me."

He reached down and held her feet still. "I'm almost *too* ready."

Tony pulled her feet out of his pajamas and stood up. He pulled her up after him, and the towel remained on the bed. He kissed all of her face and then her mouth. Hope reveled in the gentle pulling and prodding of their tongues. He massaged her buttocks and she put her hands around his neck, pulling him closer.

Tony put one of his hands between them and pulled the string on his pajamas. They fell to the floor and he moved her back so he could step out of them. The feel of his completely naked body against hers was beyond erotic, as was the sound of his heavy breathing and her own moans.

"Are *you* ready?" he asked before checking for himself. "Yeah, you're ready." Tony backed her up along the side of the bed, all the while kissing her deeply. When they got to his nightstand he changed their positions. He held on to her with one hand as he looked behind him and opened the drawer to remove a condom. He tore the small package with his teeth and released her for the two seconds it took him to slide it into place.

He backed her against the nearest wall and lifted one of her legs up the side of his hip. They both groaned when he slid into her. He moved furiously and with delicious force, pulling her away from the wall and lifting her other leg off the floor. Hope latched her legs together behind his back and he grabbed hold of her buttocks, supporting her and pushing her closer.

She kissed and licked away the sweat that formed on

his forehead. "Come on, baby," he encouraged her. Hope concentrated fully on the tension that was building somewhere in the center of her body, savoring the feeling and wanting it to last forever—or at least for a few more minutes. But when Tony said, "Come on, baby," with real urgency, she knew that it was her cue to release the tension and allow sweetness to flood her body.

"Oooh, Tony! Oh God, Tony!"

Tony bit into the side of her neck to muffle the sounds he made as he let go of the tension that had been building in his body. And when it was over, he kissed the smile he had put on her face and she moved her legs slowly down his sweat-slicked thighs. He kissed her mouth again before pulling out of her. "I'll be right back."

Hope let her body rest against the cool wall for a moment, but the lingering weakness in her legs caused her to sit on the edge of the bed. Tony walked back toward the bed in less than a minute. He pulled her up so he could turn back the covers on the king-sized bed. Then he picked her up and tossed her into the center and jumped in after her.

"Watch it, boy!" She covered her head with her hands and giggled when he landed near, but not on her. He pulled her close to him and they settled into a spoon position.

"Are you okay?" He kissed her affectionately on the side of her neck, and she giggled some more.

"I'm fine." She stretched luxuriously while he held tight to her waist. She loved the way his hairy legs felt against her smooth ones. "I don't remember you making love to me like that the last time."

"I didn't want to scare you." Hope felt a little uncomfortable at his words—he sounded to her a little bit like Ray. And then he laughed into the back of her neck and she felt his tongue moving against her skin, and all thoughts of Ray left her mind.

The next morning he made her breakfast . . . and brought it to her in bed. When she revealed her secret love of Saturday morning cartoons and music videos, he got back into bed and watched with her—the perfect host.

Before she got dressed for the day, she went into the bathroom and called her boys from her cell phone. She was pleased that each of them was in a hurry to get off the phone—that meant they were having a good time. She assured them that she would see them on Sunday night and that she would have a surprise for each of them. Ray did not get a call.

Tony knocked on the bathroom door just as she was about to put on her lipstick.

"You can come in."

His smile told her he approved of her outfit. Her cream cotton sundress was sheer—very sheer, something she would not dare wear out with Ray. Her legs and thighs were visible through the bottom panel of the dress; two broad bands of opaque material covered her breasts and were tied together behind her neck.

"Wow!" She twirled around in her chocolate sandals, delighted at his approval. "I was going to take you to shoot some craps, but I guess that I have to think of something a little bit more sophisticated."

"Yes, I guess you will." She looked into her make-up bag and took out another lipstick. She held them up for him to see. "Which one do you like best?"

"I like the red."

"I like the red too, but don't you think that brown is a little more appropriate for the afternoon, I mean, especially with this dress."

"What do you mean?"

"I mean the dress is kinda bold, maybe it's best to offset it with a muted lipstick."

Tony took the lipsticks from her and took her face into his hand. The brown lipstick he placed on the counter, and he shaded her lips with the bold red color. He turned her back toward the mirror so that she could see herself.

"You look beautiful in red . . . and if you like it, then it's appropriate."

She did love the red; she noticed also that he had applied it with less than an expert hand. "You're right . . . thank you."

"Are you ready?"

"I just need a few more seconds and I'll be down." She kissed him softly on his lips. The more she kissed him the easier it became. When he left the bathroom, Hope wiped off the lipstick and lined her lips carefully with a slightly darker lip liner before reapplying it.

He took her to the Fine Arts Museum and treated her to a light lunch at the café on the ground floor. From the gift shop he bought her a pair of earrings made by a local artist. They held hands throughout the afternoon, and on several occasions he lifted her hand to his mouth to kiss it.

That night before dinner they were running late, so to save time they showered together. They stayed in the shower until the water ran cold, and in the end they lost their dinner reservation. He took her to dinner at the movies instead of dinner and a movie, and they had a movie-food feast—nachos, dill pickles, Milk Duds, chicken strips, pizza . . .

They made out like teenagers, sweet kisses and surreptitious touches. They were like honeymooners; she couldn't get enough of him and he couldn't get enough of her.

After the movie Tony looked at her, smiling. "I'm glad you came. I know I keep telling you that, but every time we kiss, it's truer."

"Every time we kiss it's truer?" Hope's head went back with her laugh. "Even though that *has* to be the corniest thing you've ever said to me—no, wait." She stopped in the middle of the parking lot as she pretended to consider. "No, the corniest thing you've ever said to me was that knock-knock joke about the horse." She laughed again as she remembered the silly joke he told during their first lunch at the Mexican restaurant. "But I have to agree with you. I am thoroughly enjoying myself."

He squeezed the hand that he had been holding since they left the theater. "Well, if you think that was corny, listen to this. When I first saw you at that party, I felt like we would be good together. You were standing near the wall trying hard not to look like a wallflower, and I saw that you were missing something. I just felt like I could give you what you were missing."

"Wait a minute . . ." She took her hand from his and stopped again in the middle of the parking lot, placing one hand on her hip and leaving one free so she could point at him. She didn't know whether to be flattered or insulted.

"*First* of all, I was *not* trying not to look like a wallflower, I was *not* a wallflower. I *was* having a good time. And you don't sound corny, you sound like an old-school playa." She lowered her voice in a deliberately horrible imitation of him. "I felt like I could give you what you were missing." Arguing that she had not been "missing something" would be ridiculous, considering that at that very moment she was about to go home with her lover. "And you told me that when you first saw me you thought—I *believe* your exact words were, 'Damn, I want to get to know her.'"

He laughed and grabbed her hand again, and then she decided that she was amused and not insulted. *Ray never holds my hand.* "I love a sister with an attitude, and baby, when you move your neck like that—mm-mm-mm." They laughed together and he pulled her close and they walked slowly to his car. "I thought that too, that I wanted to get to know you. I thought some other things that I haven't gotten around to telling you yet."

He pushed her against his Mercedes when they made it to the car and kissed her along the side of her neck. She closed her eyes and tilted her neck, actually savoring the sensations he was creating. *Ray has never kissed me like this in public, not even when we were in school. And making out at the movies . . .*

Hope broke away from his kiss and took his face in her hands so she could kiss *him*. Their kisses were firm and tender. She didn't know how long they stood there in the parking lot kissing, or how many people saw them going at it, but she knew when they came up for air that she was happy. At that moment standing in the parking lot with her lover . . . *her love,* she was happy.

* * *

Later that evening, just after they had made love, Tony took her hand in his and held it up to the stream of light that filtered in through the open curtain. "You know I love you, don't you, Hope?" he asked casually, and turned her hand over so they could both see her sparkling wedding ring. "That I'm in love with you?"

She didn't know what to say. She didn't want to explore the feelings she had for him any more than she already had. The thought of hurting his feelings was unpleasant, but she already had one man in her life that she had to tread as if she were on eggshells whenever she said something to him—she was not about to have two.

"I thought we said we wouldn't talk about love. I don't want to talk about love, Tony, I don't want to talk about my marriage. I don't even want to talk about what it is that we're doing. I just want to lie here and be quiet." Saying exactly what she wanted to say made her feel powerful.

He brought the back of her hand to his mouth and kissed it. "We didn't agree not to talk about love . . . you said that you didn't want to talk about it. I don't expect you to say anything about love, I just had to be sure that you know how I feel . . . that this is real for me."

His feelings were not hurt. Hope closed her eyes and took a deep breath, savoring the moment as she had savored others during the last two days. How long had it been since she had been able to say what she wanted and get it without arguing or feeling guilty? *Too long*. He wasn't asking her for anything, he was just expressing himself.

He took the hand he had been holding and slid it

under the sheet, down his stomach, and rested it between his thighs. "I want to make love to you again."

She squeezed the skin under her hand before she responded. "I guess that's okay. But I'm on top this time."

"You make the rules . . . we'll do whatever you say."

I could get used to this, Hope thought as she rolled on top of him. *I could really get used to this.*

Chapter Twenty-eight

Hope left Houston early Sunday afternoon. Her intention was to get back to Dallas in enough time to spend a couple of hours with her boys before their bedtime. The memory of Tony's good-bye kisses kept her warm for two hundred miles, but during the last one hundred miles of the trip she evaluated the hours that she had spent with him.

She considered in depth for the first time why she had allowed herself to become involved with Tony. In the past, men had made advances toward her and she had been totally unaffected. Tony was good looking, financially secure, funny, sexy . . . but then so was her husband. What made the difference, Hope concluded, was her state of mind. Since Tony had stepped into her life, everything that she had been missing for so long had been magnified.

The male attention and conversation . . . *the approval*, Hope admitted reluctantly to herself, that she craved had been suddenly put within reach. And she had reached out and grabbed it. There had never been a time in her life when she had been so completely selfish. Over the last day and a half, she had thought mostly about satisfying her own needs, although Tony had looked completely satisfied when she had left him. *She* had decided where they would eat, what movie they went to see, when, how, and where they made love. She had removed the word "compromise" from her vocabulary, at least for the last thirty-six hours, and she was basking in the aftermath.

As far as she and Ray were concerned, she vacillated between anger and numbness. She thought about how she felt several weeks ago after her first encounter with Tony—how afraid she had been, how determined she had been that it would never happen again—and her smile was ironic. Driving home she felt none of those negative emotions, no apprehension, no fear, no second thoughts about the wonderful, passionate weekend she had just experienced.

She did not know what would happen with her marriage or how the situation would play itself out with Tony, but she did know that every smile she shared with Tony brought them closer together, and that every night she spent with her husband—lying on her side, sometimes with tears sliding down her cheeks—drove them further apart.

The house was unusually quiet when she walked in. "Mommy's home!" She put down her bag and prepared herself for the onslaught of her boys. No one came running. "Ray," she shouted and went to look for him in the living room. The truck was in the garage; unless he had gone somewhere with one of his friends, he had to be somewhere in the house. She looked into the backyard before heading toward the bedroom. "Ray!" she called again. He was sitting in the chair his mother had sent to them two Christmases ago, reading the paper. He didn't look up when she walked into the room.

"Did you hear me calling you?" In the house for four minutes, and already her good mood was fading. Irritation was heavy in her voice.

"If you mean did I hear you bellowing like you are in a county field, yeah, I did." He looked up from his paper and looked her up and down.

Hope started to feel slightly uneasy. "Where are the boys? I thought you would have picked them up by now." It was a little after five o'clock. "You know they have school tomorrow."

"I *did* pick them up, and then I called Stephanie and asked if she could baby-sit. I dropped them off an hour ago."

"Why would you do that?" Hope kicked off her shoes and left them on the floor. "You know Stephanie is busy with the baby." Hope was trying hard to ignore the sinking feeling in the pit of her stomach. She tried to focus on bitching, but it wasn't working. Ray had something on his mind and would not be distracted.

"I told her we needed to talk." He had the *strangest* look on his face. Hope wiped her hand across her forehead nervously. The bitching was *really* not working. She tried to look cool and disinterested. Then she switched to calm and concerned before she spoke.

"What is it?"

He watched her closely as she talked. "I went to the movies yesterday . . ." He paused and looked at her even closer.

"And?" She almost shouted. She couldn't pretend to

be calm when all she wanted to do was wipe her now-sweaty palms on the comforter.

"I went to the movies *and* I ran into Ralph and Lisa. Lisa asked about you. When I told her that you were in Houston for . . . What was it again?" He waited for her to answer before going on. The little voice that said "a retreat" could not have been hers. As soon as he said "Ralph and Lisa" she knew what they needed to talk about. She had suspected when she saw his face. *I can't do shit and get away with it.*

"A *retreat*? I thought it was a woman's conference." Ray laughed sardonically before going on. "But anyway, Lisa wondered if you'd get a chance to see *our* friend Anthony while you were there."

If I ever see that bitch again . . . Hope sat on the bed to keep herself from falling.

"I told her that I don't have a friend named Anthony. Then she said something about the two of you at their last party. Ralph dragged her away before she could finish. I started to call him and ask him about it, but I thought it best that I give my *wife* the benefit of the doubt and ask her directly." He moved to stand directly in front of where she sat on the bed. "Who is Anthony, and what was Lisa talking about?" His words were tame, but Hope saw that Ray was making a great effort to control his breathing.

Calm down, Hope, he doesn't know anything.

But he will if you just sit here looking like a deer caught in headlights.

"You've met Anthony before—remember, I was talking to him at Ralph and Lisa's that time, and you came up. I think you asked me to dance and then he left. He's Ralph's friend, but he's in baking . . . I mean *banking.* He's been giving me some advice about this thing that I'm interested in. I tried to tell you, remember, but you said you didn't want to hear anything about it."

Way to stay fucking cool, Hope. Shit!

"Did you see him this weekend?" Ray was cool.

She opened her mouth to lie but couldn't. Her lies so far had been mostly by omission. *I should have known that Lisa's nosy ass would find a way to say something to Ray. I did know.* She had been lulled into a false sense of security because a couple of weeks had passed since the first incident with Tony, and for some reason she thought that if Ray was going to find out, he would find out immediately.

"I did see him." Tears stung the back of her eyes. She had never been so frightened. She was trying to think of a plausible reason, but his next question took her by surprise.

"Did you fuck him too?" Ray was no longer cool. She looked up at her husband and tears fell on her cheeks. She couldn't speak, but she didn't need to.

"Oh my God, Hope!" A vein she had not noticed in all the time she had known him started pulsing in his forehead. His fists were balled and it seemed as if his entire body was trembling . . . or maybe it was hers. "I've been racking my brain trying to figure out what the fuck is wrong with you. You've been walking around here bitching for months. And you walk in here *still* bitching even after you've been on a weekend fuckfest. I oughta kick your trifling ass." She looked at his fists that he was clenching and unclenching and she backed up on the bed. She was frightened, but she had to defend herself. The best defense was a good offense. She started to speak and was glad that she sounded strong, almost righteous.

"And I've been racking my brain trying to figure out a way to tell you that something is wrong with me . . . with us, and have you take it seriously. All you do is cut me off, shut me off, tell me off." Her voice grew louder as the words started falling unchecked out of her mouth. "Do you realize that I have three damn jobs, Ray? I work at the bank, I take care of the kids, and I take care of your unappreciative ass. I work to keep this family together. I work to keep the kids happy. I suck your dick every time you crook your fucking finger. And you don't have enough respect for me to ask me how I feel on my dead mother's birthday."

Ray looked at her as if she had two heads, stunned at the bitter words that were directed at him. Hope got up from the bed and stood up in front of him. She felt a surge of power when he took a step back.

"And *I'm* always the bitch. Yeah, I've been walking around here bitching. Why shouldn't I? That's all *you* ever do. Tell me what I do wrong, tell me to fix it, and then go about your damn business. You stopped giving to me a long time ago. And just like you're a man and you need certain things"—she curled her lips as she spit out part of the speech that he had given her more times than she could count—"'Hope, I pay the bills around here, don't you think I deserve some respect, some understanding, some space?'

"Well, I'm a *woman,* Ray, and I need things too—loving, understanding, appreciation, soft words, compliments, support, help with your damn kids—none of which I get from you!"

Ray shook his head, disgusted, but Hope didn't care. She had never expressed herself to him as she had just done, and she felt almost cleansed.

Somewhere in the back of her mind she recognized

that a part of her hated Ray. She didn't know when or how it had happened, and standing in front of him with adrenaline and venom flowing through her veins, she didn't care.

"I can't believe you. You stand in a house that I bust my ass to pay for and tell me it's my fault that you're fucking some other man. I guess next you're gonna tell me that I put his dick in your mouth?"

And before she could stop herself the words had left her mouth. "No, Ray, *I* put his dick in my mouth." She almost didn't feel his open palm on her cheek, but she knew it hurt because the force of it knocked her back on the bed. The tears that had been streaming down her face dried up instantly. She looked up at her husband. Hope waited to see what he would do next without really caring.

His eyes were filled with hatred and something else . . . tears. Hope hadn't noticed them when she was talking. His voice was tired and sad when he spoke. "I believe that you have lost your mind." He walked quietly out of the room.

Hope put her hand to her cheek and rubbed it. The last time she had been slapped she had been fourteen years old. Her mother had been ranting and raving at her about her closet being dirty and how she need to do more to help around their small apartment. When she had had enough of her mother's ranting and raving, Hope had turned to her mother and had asked sarcastically, "When are you going to clean out your closet, Ma?" Her mother had responded to her impertinence by slapping her hard across the face, just as Ray had. Hope remembered her walking away without a word, just as Ray had. She hadn't cried then because of the slap, and she wouldn't cry now.

* * *

Hope pulled into Stephanie's driveway and sat in her truck for a moment to collect herself before going in to pick up her boys. She wondered how much Ray had told her . . . what kind of reception was waiting for her. Ray had left the house without saying another word to her. She had sat on the bed for what seemed like an eternity before deciding that she needed to pick up her kids—after all, they still had school the next day.

Hope looked up and saw Stephanie walking out of her front door. She got out of the truck and walked toward her friend. "Hey, girl." She put as much cheer as she could into her voice, which was to say not very much. "Thanks for watching the kids. Are they ready to go?"

"They're in the back playing." Stephanie looked at Hope and shook her head accusingly. Apparently Ray had told her more than a little. "Ray called and asked me did I know anything about you going to some retreat in Houston. Then he asked me if I knew anything about you having a . . . I believe he said 'male friend' in Houston. I don't know what's going on with you, because for the last several months you've been so secretive, but I'm telling you now—don't make me a part of your lies."

"I didn't make you a part of my lies. I haven't involved you in any way. And I don't appreciate you looking at me and talking to me like you're my mama."

"I don't appreciate being put on the spot like that." Stephanie raised her voice some. When she placed one hand on her hip, Hope knew she was in for an argument that she was in no mood for.

"You're right, Stephanie," Hope said with exaggerated patience, "I'm sorry that you were put on the spot."

"So why did you go to Houston?"

Hope looked past Stephanie's shoulder as though something caught her eye.

"Oh my God! You *did* go to see that man, didn't you? You're sleeping with him, aren't you?" Stephanie had a look of horror and disgust on her face. When Hope still didn't say anything she continued, "You know, I can't believe you." She shook her head in slow judgment. "I suspected that something was going on, but in my heart I never would have believed that you would do something like this. I told you to leave that man alone. You're gonna jeopardize your family and your marriage for some dick?"

It hurt Hope to her core to have her friend judge her so harshly. The tears that had dried up earlier started again.

"You don't know, Stephanie, what I've been go-ing through. *I* don't know what I've been going through."

"So I'm not a woman, Hope? I don't go through the same shit? You think that I don't know how hard it is to be a mother and a wife?"

Sarcasm came to her defense again. "Well, maybe you're just a better woman than I am, Stephanie. A better mother . . . a better wife . . . you have all the answers."

"No, I don't have all the answers, Hope, but I do know that whatever is wrong with a marriage, screwing around is not going to fix it."

Hope held up her hands and shook her head. "I don't want to talk about this anymore. I'm tired."

"You don't want to talk about it anymore because you know you're wrong. No matter what problems you have, no matter how you slice it, you're wrong." The two women stared at each other for a minute, Stephanie waiting for Hope to admit she was wrong and Hope waiting for some kind of sympathy and support from her best friend. Both women were disappointed. Stephanie was the first to speak.

"I assume by looking at your swollen face that Ray knows exactly why you went to Houston."

Hope put her hand on her cheek. It had started to tingle, but it hadn't occurred to Hope that it would swell. "Ray does know."

"What did he say?"

"Nothing." Tears streamed down her face as she spoke. "He didn't say 'I'm sorry that we've come to this,' he didn't say 'I love you and we can fix this.' He didn't ask me to stay and he didn't ask me to go. I think he said something about paying the mortgage . . . or maybe that was me." Hope felt bitterness rising as she thought about the encounter with her husband. "I don't even know if he cares."

"He cares, Hope. Believe me, I know. He cares." Just then Lamar walked out of the house. He stood behind Stephanie and placed his arm around her waist.

"Hope." He barely opened his mouth to speak to her. *Now if that's not the pot silently calling the kettle black.* "The boys are getting tired. They can spend the night if they want and Ray can get them in the morning." He spoke to his wife, as if she was responsible for them, and not their mother, who was standing in front of him.

"I think that's a good idea," Stephanie said just before she leaned back into Lamar's hug as if they were the all-American couple. Hope turned around and got back into her truck without saying good-bye.

Chapter Twenty-nine

Hope wasn't ready to go back home after she left Stephanie's, so she called Tabitha and asked if she could stop by and talk to her. There was concern in Tabitha's voice as she invited her to "come on over." Hope wouldn't have guessed in a hundred years Tabitha's response to her situation.

"You didn't get involved with him because I told you to go for it, did you?" Tabitha had a "I hope you're not blaming me for this shit" expression on her face.

"Of course not! I'm a grown woman. I make my own decisions."

"Good . . . because I never expected that you would get involved with somebody else. I mean, Hope, flirting is one thing—screwing another man while you're married is some serious shit." Tabitha was looking at her like she had never seen her before. "Is there something wrong with Ray?" Tabitha squinted her eyes as if it would give her better insight into the situation. "Is he on drugs? Does he beat you?" She looked pointedly at Hope's steadily swelling cheek.

Hope placed her hand on the swollen area. "No."

"Well . . . is he impotent?"

"No! Why would you ask something like that?"

"I'm sorry, Hope, I'm just trying to figure out what's going on." Tabitha sat back in her leather sofa. "I thought you loved Ray, and women don't normally step out on a man unless he's doing something drastic at home."

"Maybe that's it, Tabitha. Maybe this situation with Tony happened because there's *nothing* drastic going on between Ray and me. I get so little at home . . . and Tony offers me so much." Hope closed her eyes and thought about how happy she had felt during the last two days. When she opened them again, Tabitha was seated on the edge of the seat leaning toward her. Why did I come here anyway? she questioned herself.

"You know, Hope, I try not to get real deep into people's personal lives because I don't want anybody getting too deep into mine, but I've been out here a long time and I've dated a lot of people They *always* offer you more in the beginning. Everything *new* is exciting, but familiarity breeds contempt." Tabitha took one of Hope's hands in hers.

"You're sitting here, tears streaming down your face, a swollen jaw, and what it sounds like you're telling me is that you don't know what you're doing. You haven't said you don't love Ray or that you can't live without this other man. If I were you, Hope, I would sit down and think about what you're doing."

Hope took her hand back and wiped the tears from her face. She hadn't asked her for advice. All she had wanted to do was to sit down in a cool place and have a friend support her, not judge her. And that's what Tabitha was doing. It may be judgment "lite," but she was being judged nonetheless. Hope looked at her friend, disappointed and hurt. "Well, thanks for letting me come over . . . thanks for listening." Hope looked around for her purse, but realized that she had left it in the car.

"Are you sure it's okay for you to go home? You're more than welcome to spend the night here."

"Don't worry about it, Tabitha. I'll be fine."

Hope drove to a gas station around the corner from Tabitha's and turned off the engine. She sat unmoving for several minutes before picking up her cell phone. Who else was she going to turn to? Who else would understand her feelings? Who else could she count on for support?

"Tony?" Hope's voice was barely a whisper.

"Hey, baby, I was hoping you'd find the time to call me tonight." And at the sound of his voice she burst into tears. She cried for a long time, cried so hard that she couldn't respond to his urgent demands.

"Tell me what's wrong! Are you all right? Are your kids all right? Talk to me, Hope!"

When she finally caught her breath after several minutes she whispered brokenly into the phone, "Ray knows about us."

"What?"

"I said, Ray knows about us! Lisa told . . . asked him something about me going to Houston to see you. He asked me about it when I got home, and I just couldn't lie. I couldn't lie." Her words ran together and the tears started again.

"Are you all right? Damn! Of course you're not all right. Where are you?"

Hope took a deep breath as she struggled to compose herself. "I'm at a gas station. I don't know what to do, Tony. I'm scared to go back home. I don't know what to do."

"Did he threaten you? Did he hurt you?" His tone was urgent. She decided not to tell him about her cheek.

"No, he didn't . . . I just—"

"Listen, baby." He cut her off before she could finish. "Don't go back home. Check into a hotel and I'll be there as soon as I can. If I can't get a flight out tonight I'll drive. Either way, I'll be there." The love and concern in his voice caused her tears to start again. She had been nervous about calling him . . . scared of his reaction. Relief flooded through her. At least she still had one friend.

"Hope! Hope!"

"Yes?" she responded through her tears.

"Did you hear what I just said?"

"About the hotel?"

"No. I said leave your cell phone on, and I'll call you when I think you've had enough time to get a room. Okay?"

"Okay." She wiped the tears from her cheeks with one hand.

"I know it's useless to tell you not to worry, but I love you, baby, and we'll get through this."

Hope ended the call without responding, but she felt better . . . much better.

Several hours later, Hope was startled awake by a terrible noise. She sat up in bed and looked around the dark room. It took her a minute to realize she was in a motel. "Who is it?"

"It's Tony."

Hope got up and opened the door without looking through the peephole. He took her into his arms immediately and held her tight and long in the dark room while she sobbed brokenly against his chest. "It's all right, baby . . . it's all right," he assured her over and over again. He walked her to the bed and they sat down. After what seemed like forever the tears stopped and they started talking in the still-dark room. "Tell me what happened," he requested gently.

"I told you. Ray ran into Lisa and Ralph and she mentioned something about us being at the party together . . . and how we were such good friends . . . and was I going to visit you in Houston. She knew *exactly* what she was doing," Hope added bitterly.

"So Ray put two and two together and came up with four?"

She moved her head affirmatively against his chest. "When I was standing in front of him . . . I couldn't think of anything to say at first, and then all of a sudden this meanness just . . . spewed out of me. I swear it was like I *hated* him. Like he was the one who . . . who . . ."

"Who had been with someone else?" He finished her sentence for her.

"Yeah. Yeah."

"What did he say when you left?"

"He left the house. I haven't heard from him. He hasn't tried to call me."

"Where are your kids?"

"They're with Stephanie."

Tony stroked her hair as they continued talking. "Did you tell her what happened?"

"Some of it." Hope laughed sadly as she recalled Stephanie's reaction. "Needless to say, she does *not* approve." Hope had told him previously about Stephanie's feelings about their friendship.

"You don't need to worry about her right now. What we need to do is get a plan together."

"You mean plan on begging and groveling and praying for forgiveness?"

"No." Tony got up and searched in the dark until he found the lamp. She closed her eyes briefly against the bright light. Tony looked around the room, at the worn carpet and yellow peeling paint and at the faded threadbare comforter, but he didn't say anything.

Hope had turned into the first motel that she had found—and it wasn't the Ritz.

"You don't have to beg and grovel. I'm here for you. If you need anything, and I mean *anything,* Hope, you can come to me. It rips me up to see you like this, but it's been ripping me up for months. Knowing that you're with a man who doesn't want to make you happy. You didn't cause this situation all by yourself. Do you really think you should go to him and beg him . . . for what, baby? To continue to treat you like he's *been* treating you?"

He looked at her with a sincere expression. "You may think that I'm not the best person to take advice from, but I'm a man, and I know how men think. If you go back to Ray groveling—trust me, you'll be groveling for the rest of your life." He lifted her face so she couldn't avoid his eyes.

"He should be the one apologizing to you. At the very *least,* the two of you should apologize to each other. If he wants you, Hope, he should ask you what went wrong . . . what *he* can do to make it right. Women have been buying into the hype about there not being many good men around, but what you don't *know* is that a good woman is equally hard to find. You're a wonderful woman—I knew that from the very beginning—and unless he's crazy, Ray knows that too."

As he spoke Hope could feel some of the tension leaving her body.

"This may sound selfish to you—hell, it *is* selfish, but I'm not sorry Ray knows."

She waited, wondering what he would say next.

"I'm sorry that you had to face him alone, and I'm sorry that I didn't have a little more time to show you how I feel about you, but I've been looking for you all my life." Hope couldn't help but smile at the much-used expression. He smiled back at her, sensing that her mood had changed.

"I mean it! Since I was in the second grade, I've been looking for a woman with beautiful brown skin and shiny hair." He turned her face to one side and kissed her cheek—the sore one. "Just your height, funny, smart, cool, sexy . . ." He blew in her ear, and she laughed for the first time since she had left him on his curbside in Houston.

"Wait a minute." He kissed her along the side of her neck and she giggled some more, almost forgetting about her troubles. "You mean to tell me that you were looking for a sexy woman in the *second* grade?" Her tone was incredulous. He stopped playing with her and looked in her eyes again.

"I've been looking for *you*. I love you, Hope." She stopped giggling, and this time she kissed him to let him know she accepted his love. She needed the love that he was offering—had been offering since the beginning—more than anything at that moment.

What he had said sounded like the truth to her. It was what she had tried to express to Stephanie, what she had been trying to express to Ray for months—even years. Her mother's favorite topic of conversation since her only daughter's wedding day until the time of her death had been how lucky Hope was to have found a good man like Ray. Not *once* had she told her that Ray was lucky to have found her.

She hadn't gotten any recognition for working . . . giving birth to and raising three children . . . keeping a clean house . . . being a loving and faithful wife . . . and here was another *good* man giving her all the props she had silently longed for.

"You don't have to stay with Ray, Hope; you have options, and you should think about them very carefully before you make any decisions."

Isn't that what Tabitha told me, to take some time to think about what I'm doing? His kiss left no doubt in her mind about what one of her options was. Being in the motel room with him seemed to be her best option at that moment.

"I want you to make love to me." Hope couldn't believe the words had come out of her mouth, couldn't believe that she would be thinking about sex at a time like this, but it wasn't the sex she was after. She needed to be skin to skin with him, to know for certain if what he was offering her was real.

"I'm not trying to make love to you right now. You have too much going on." He kissed her gently on her forehead. His lips tickled her skin. She had not known her forehead was an erogenous zone. Maybe it *was* the sex that she needed. Her behavior and her thoughts were totally outrageous, but she didn't care anymore.

"You don't understand. I *need* you to make love to

me. I don't want to think anymore about what's going on . . . at least not now."

Tony was still reluctant.

"I don't have any condoms with me."

Hope laughed. "Look around you, Tony." She waved her arms around the room casually. "You can pay by the half hour here. I'm sure that if you ask, the attendant will have condoms to sell."

"Are you sure?"

She appreciated his concern, but it occurred to her that he hadn't been so concerned about her state of mind the first night they had been together. He had been determined that they would be lovers and now that they were . . .

"I'm sure."

Tony left the room and came back in less than five minutes with condoms. He made love to her slowly and reverently . . . he told her he loved her so many times that she couldn't help but believe him. She didn't do anything but lie back and accept the pleasure that he offered so expertly.

And before it was over, she had decided that it would be better if she did not go back to Ray groveling; he had slapped her face and blamed her for everything. *Everything* was not her fault . . . he had never told her he was glad that she was his wife. Never asked as she had so many times what had gone wrong with them. It was better for her, she decided, if she did leave her options open.

Chapter Thirty

Hope was relieved that Ray was not home when she got there midmorning. She needed some time to compose herself. She had called in sick to work, something she had been doing a lot more than she realized. Tony had left his car parked at the airport and would fly back the following day to check on her and to drive it back home. He had an afternoon appointment he couldn't miss.

Hope looked around her home and thought about the love she had put into it, and snorted ironically. *What's love got to do with it?* She took a shower and had a long nap. Ray came home just as she was dressing to pick up the kids. He had on jeans and a T-shirt; obviously he hadn't been to work either.

"Where are you going?" There was hostility and something else in his voice.

"I'm going to pick up the kids." She answered his question without looking at him and continued to search for the slippers that she always left under the foot of the bed.

Are you really going to act like nothing has happened? she questioned herself.

Why not? was her response.

"Don't you think we need to talk?"

"About what, Ray?" She looked at him as if she were confused. He looked at her as if he would like to slap her again.

If he asks me to sit down and tells me that we can get through this, then I'll tell him I'm sorry and I will ask him to forgive me. If he says anything other than that . . .

"About this man you've been fucking . . . about how long you've been fucking him." Derision made his lips curl.

Tony was right. He doesn't want to fix our relationship, he wants me to grovel and explain. Well, I won't. If he can't talk to me respectfully, fuck him.

"I know you're upset right now, Ray, so maybe now is not the best time for us to talk." She kept her tone polite.

"You don't think I should be upset? I find out my wife is fucking around, making a *fool* out of me, and you don't think I should be upset!" It wasn't a question. He screamed the words at her and Hope cringed inside, but she kept her resolve.

"I have not been trying to make a fool out of you, Ray, and I'm sorry if you think that." She could give him that. "You know things haven't been right between us for a long time."

"So when things don't go like *you* think they should, that gives you carte blanche to start fucking around?"

"No, Ray, I'm not saying that. I'm saying that we both need to calm down before we discuss this."

"What the *fuck* do you have to calm down about?"

She ignored his question and looked at her watch. "I'm going to be late picking up the kids." *If he wants to leave, he should leave. If he wants me to leave, he should say so. It's not like I don't have options.*

"What are you planning on doing about this situation?" She could see that he was making an effort to try and calm himself.

"I don't know." She looked him straight in the eye and shook her head. It was the truth. Some—*most*—of the fire went out of him at that moment. It had not been the response he had expected. She could tell that he wanted to say something else, but he didn't know how. It was because she had always been the one to start the conversations, express her emotions in regard to their relationship, thinking that by doing so she could get him to do the same. And now she wasn't saying anything.

"I don't know what to say to you, Hope." He shook his head sadly.

"You never have, Ray," she said, equally sad, before walking out of the bedroom.

That night she fixed dinner for the kids and they talked to her excitedly about how they had spent the last several days. She managed to smile and pretend she was listening to them. David was the only one who asked about her face, which was still slightly swollen. She told him that she had had an allergic reaction to a new lotion.

He asked her what allergic meant and Jordan stepped in to explain, happy that they were having fish sticks and macaroni and grabbing the opportunity to play the smart older brother. They accepted her explanation without question. It would never occur to them that their dad would hit their mom . . . it was not in their realm of experience.

After she checked on the boys one final time to make sure they were fast asleep, she grabbed her purse and told Ray she needed to pick up something from the drug store. He didn't look up from his paper. She hadn't expected him to; they hadn't said a word to each other all evening.

She drove around the corner and parked at a corner store. She dialed Tony's number but hung up before she was connected. She made a collect call on the pay phone instead; she didn't want Ray to get Tony's number from the cellular phone bill. Then she remembered that she had already called him from the phone. *I'll just open the bill this month.*

After Tony agreed to pay for the call, the operator connected them. "Hope?"

"Yeah, it's me."

"Is everything all right?"

"Yeah, I called collect because I don't want Ray to get your number and start calling you."

"I don't care if he has my number."

"Well, I care." She had promised when she left him that morning that she would call and let him know that she was okay.

"I'll get you a calling card."

"You don't have to do that," she protested. "I'll get one for myself."

He moved on to what was really on their minds. "Did Ray come back home?"

"Yeah, he did."

"Sooo . . ." he prompted.

"It was nothing, Tony. He asked me what I was going to do, I said, 'I don't know,' and went to pick up my kids. It was nothing," she repeated.

Tony was silent for several seconds. "Do you think he's going to move? Do you need to move?"

"I don't know, Tony." Hope sighed, weariness catching up with her. "I'm just going to see what happens."

"Did you tell him that we were going to stop seeing each other?"

"No, I didn't, Tony." She heard relief mingled with hope in his voice when he spoke.

"I know this is hard for you, Hope, but I promise things won't stay like this forever."

"I hope not."

"Listen, I'm not going to be able to get my car tomorrow, I really need to get some work done, but I'll be there Wednesday and I want you to meet me for dinner."

"I can't meet you for dinner"—she felt like she needed to be home in the evenings right now—"but I will meet you for lunch."

"Just as long as I get to see you. I hate that I'm not there with you right now." Hope couldn't help but be glad that she had someone in her life who . . . who wanted her. "I love you, baby." The words sounded so sweet to her that she almost said them back, but who knew how she felt anymore? She certainly didn't.

"Call me at work tomorrow," was the best she could do.

Hope walked back into the house without the "thing" that she had gone to get from the drug store. Ray was in the kitchen when she walked in and looked at her empty hands pointedly. *Message to self . . . plan your lies more carefully.*

When she got out of the shower, she heard the water running in the kids' bathroom. She walked down the hall to the guest bedroom and saw that Ray had taken clothes from his closet and laid them across the bed. It was a relief to her that he would be sleeping in another bedroom.

She walked back down the hall and got into bed. She replayed the events of the last several days in her mind over and over, until numbness washed over her and she fell into a dreamless sleep.

She woke up the next morning, still numb. Jordan asked why his daddy slept in the other room when she was taking them to school. She said she didn't know. After she dropped them all off she drove back toward home. *I'll call in sick again today*, she decided. Besides, she had left her shoes at home.

She called Ray midafternoon and left a message that he needed to pick the kids up, and fell back into the pillows. *I hope he gets the message.*

When the kids got home she was still asleep. Jordan and Karl came into the bedroom to ask what they could have for a snack. "Anything you want. I'll be in there in a minute."

"Are you all right, Mommy?" Jordan asked from the doorway.

"Yeah, baby, Mommy's fine. I think I must have a cold or something." *Or something.* She had fallen into bed with her clothes on; her silk blouse was wrinkled and her pantyhose were ruined. She wanted to fall back into bed, but it wouldn't be fair to the boys.

Freshly showered and flossed, she walked into the kitchen twenty minutes later. All three boys were sitting at the table. Chips and cookies were on the counter and on the floor, and a half gallon of ice cream sat melting in the center of the table.

"Who took all of this food out?" She looked at all three boys accusingly. Jordan looked up at her with wide, frightened eyes.

"Everybody wanted something different. You said we could have whatever," he whined.

"You should have put this up after you got what you wanted. You guys are old enough to know better. Where is your father?" Hope snatched the ice cream from the table and tossed it in the trash.

"Mommy!" All three boys protested; it was their favorite flavor.

"Don't 'Mommy' me. If you wanted it, you should have put it back in the freezer before it melted. Where is your father?" she asked again.

"I'm right here." Ray's tone was almost expressionless. He looked her up and down and shook his head; obviously he had heard her fussing at the boys. "Why don't you go back to whatever it was that kept you so occupied that you couldn't pick up your children? I'm taking the boys out for dinner."

"Why don't you go back to whatever keeps you so occupied that you can *never* pick up your children?" She didn't wait for his response. She looked around the kitchen and back at him. "Are you going to clean up this mess too, Super Dad?" She wanted to fight with him, she didn't care that the kids were in the room.

"You need to get out of my face, Hope."

She looked toward the table. The boys were looking at them, waiting to see what was going to happen next. Something was wrong . . . they could feel it. Hope couldn't help but laugh at the expression on their faces. She put one of her hands across her face and laughed until tears streamed down her cheeks. Their eyes looked like they were about to pop out of the sockets, like Buckwheat in *The Little Rascals.*

"Fine, Ray." She wiped the tears from her eyes, but the smile remained. Ray was looking at her, disgusted. "Put them to bed while you're at it." She kissed each of her sons, apologized for "fussing" and for being "soo tired." And as crazy and as incomprehensible as it was, she blew him a "fuck you" kiss before she went on back to bed.

Chapter Thirty-one

The next several weeks were uneventful, normal almost. Except Hope and her husband no longer spoke to one another. Every day she was further amazed that you could live in a house with a person, care for children, but not speak. And except she missed so many of the classes that had been important enough for her to fight over that she had to drop them or face certain failure.

And except she did not talk to her best friend. And except she was making so many mistakes at work that she had been called on the carpet. And except she hadn't taken a good look at her children since the end of their last school year. And except she continued to speak to her lover every day, and he traveled to Dallas every week to see her and to make love to her. And except sometimes she found herself crying for no reason that she could examine without having her knees buckle.

Tony wanted to spend more time with her, but she insisted that the time they spent together be during work hours. She was there to pick the boys up, and she

spent her evenings at home with them and with her
silent husband. Tony didn't understand why they continued to stay in the house together. It would be much
better for both of them, he insisted, if either she or Ray
left the home. He offered to get a real-estate agent to
find a rental, either near her work or near the kids'
school. She respectfully declined.

"Does Ray know we're still seeing each other?" He
had asked her the question more than once.

"I don't know."

"How can you not know?" He was irritated.

"Damn it, Tony, I told you—we don't speak to each
other. I have enough going on right now without you
asking me the same question over and over again." She
was irritated also. She pushed the sheets back and
walked toward the bathroom. They were at "their"
hotel very close to downtown Dallas, and they had
made love. "I have to go. I'm going to be late getting
back from lunch . . . *again*." She looked back at him
accusingly.

During the last several weeks, Hope had mastered
the art of the "ho bath." She took a washcloth from the
towel rack and soaped it very well with the soap that
the hotel provided. She scrubbed the inside of her
thighs, her buttocks, and her vagina. She rinsed the
soap out of the washcloth and washed herself again
with water. She dried herself and then applied hotel lotion liberally to the area.

Tony walked into the bathroom just as she was fas-
tening her bra. "I'm sorry, baby." He stood in front of
her and ran his hands up and down her arms. "I know
this entire situation is hard on you, and I know sometimes I don't make it any better."

She loved it when he touched her. He was the only

person she could talk to about her feelings, and she didn't like to be upset with him. She smiled at him to let him know she was glad he understood and continued dressing, thinking about how their relationship had evolved over the last several weeks. They were more familiar with each other . . . more comfortable.

Ray's silence and what Hope had convinced herself was his refusal to deal with their problems had actually driven her closer to Tony. Sometimes at night after Ray and the kids had gone to sleep, she called him from home, just so she could hear a friendly voice before going to bed.

She depended on him and resented him, wondering where her life would be right now if he had never invited her out to lunch and if she had never accepted.

"Talk to you later, baby." She had started to call him "baby" sometimes. He kissed her full on the lips and smudged her lipstick, but she didn't mind . . . much.

"Next weekend I've been invited to a party in town and I want you to go with me." He wiped some of the smudge away with his thumb.

"You know I can't." She sighed and gave him a "please don't start" look.

"Why not?"

"Because . . . you know I like to be at home on the weekends."

Tony let out a frustrated sigh. "Yeah, and I know that you like to be at home in the *evenings*, and I know that you can't come back to Houston anytime soon, and I also know that you're not being fair to me."

Hope tried to put some distance between them. "You're doing it again, Tony!"

"What, Hope? Being honest with you? I thought we had agreed that we would be honest with each other?

It's what you wanted, remember? Time is passing, Hope, and I want to spend as much time as I can with you. The little time that you dish out for me is not enough anymore.

"You want to keep our relationship confined to afternoon lovemaking and telephone calls. I guess that way you can convince yourself that you're still being respectful to Ray in some way, but the truth is you're *my* woman. I've kissed and touched every part of your body; we've laughed together, had more than a few arguments. Right now you're more married to me than you are to Ray, and you know it." She didn't agree or disagree. He shook his head when he got no response from her.

"What we're doing is not respectful. I don't like it, and I know that you don't like it either, but if it's the only way I can be with you I'll deal with it . . . for now."

It sounded like a warning to her. "Don't you think I know that?" *Damn, I'm going to be late!*

"I understand that you're afraid, but take a chance on us. Go out with me . . . meet some of my friends. You're too beautiful for me to keep you naked in hotel rooms, as much as I love for you to be naked with me."

She laughed and blushed. He always made sure that they were on good terms before she left him. He could always make her smile.

"I'll think about going to the party, but I'm not *promising* anything."

Tony smiled real big and kissed her again. This time she didn't mind at all about her lipstick.

"That's all I'm asking, baby."

* * *

When she finally made it back to work there was a message from Stephanie on her voice mail. She didn't identify herself or ask how Hope was; she just started talking, her tone as dry and disapproving as it was the last time they had talked.

"I don't know if you remembered, but Samson's birthday was *yesterday*. Saturday we're having a little party for him at the house, and he wanted the twins to come especially. It's at four. If you're *busy*, maybe you can have Ray bring them."

Hope erased the message, immediately put her face in her hands, and cried. It hurt her not to talk to her best friend. It hurt her to be reminded that she had turned into a selfish fuck-up, as Stephanie had implied, who was so caught up in the drama she had created in her own life that she couldn't be bothered to call a boy she had known before he was born and wish him a happy birthday.

She was too ashamed to call her back. What if she asked her about Tony? What if she asked her why she had shown no interest in her goddaughter? What if . . .

Her secretary knocked once on the door and peeped her head in the door without waiting for a response.

"Hope . . ." Her words dropped off when she saw that her boss was crying. "Oh . . ." It was obvious that she was at a loss for words. "Um . . . I'm sorry . . . are you all right?" she asked timidly.

Hope wiped her tears and tried to·compose herself.

"I'm all right." She took a deep breath before continuing. "What is it?" When your personal life was like a soap opera it was hard for some of the drama not to spill over at work.

"Everyone's waiting in the conference room."

"For what?" Hope was genuinely confused.

"For your staff meeting."

"Oh damn!" Hope put her face back in her hands and fought back the tears. There was no way she could conduct a staff meeting. She was just . . . not interested.

"Tell everyone that the meeting is canceled." The secretary looked as though she disapproved; she opened her mouth, Hope thought, to remind her that she had canceled the last meeting also. "I'm sick!" Hope snapped, not giving the woman a chance to speak.

"Okay, I'll let everyone know." She closed the door hastily.

Hope remembered the conversation she had had with her superiors at the bank not long ago. They had encouraged her to take a more hands-on approach with the men and women she supervised—translation, *get your shit together*. They would not appreciate the fact that she was no longer holding regular meetings with her staff. *But what can I do about that?*

Even though Hope had only been back from lunch fifteen minutes she started gathering her things. She was going home. She was sick. "Sick," as her mother used to say, "in the head."

When Hope pulled into the garage and saw Ray's car there, she started to turn around. She didn't because she knew she had to rest before she went to pick up the boys. He looked surprised and angry when she walked into the house. He was warming up some of the chicken casserole she had made for dinner the night before . . . he hadn't eaten it the night before. She almost laughed, but she had forgotten how to laugh when Ray was in the room.

"What are you doing home?" He stared at her hard for a minute before not speaking. He took the plate out of the microwave and dumped the food in the trash. Apparently her presence ruined his appetite.

"I live here." Her stomach was in knots. She didn't know how much longer she could keep it up, this not speaking, this open contempt from the man she had spent almost half of her life trying to love. She took a deep breath and tried again.

"Stephanie and Lamar are having a party for Samson on Saturday and they want the boys to be there. Can you go?"

"Are you going?" he asked coldly.

"No, I'm not."

"As long as you're not going I'll be happy to take my sons." When he walked out of the room Hope leaned on the counter nearest her. The knot in her stomach seemed as if it would consume her. Ray hadn't asked why she was home early. He had not asked how she felt in the last several weeks. It seemed to her that he had turned off all of his emotions . . . that he no longer loved her. The fact that he could turn off his love so quickly and so completely made her wonder if he had loved her at all.

Wouldn't a man fight for his wife if he really wanted her? Wouldn't he say something . . . reach out to her in some way? Hope felt tears forming in her eyes again, and she willed them not to fall. She was not going to let Ray see her crying again. If he could be stoic and uncaring, then so could she.

She picked up the cordless phone. That knot that had been in her stomach had taken over her entire body. She looked over her shoulder before dialing Tony's home number. The answering machine picked up, as she knew it would. "Tony, I thought about it, and I *would* like to go to the party with you. Call me tomorrow with the details." After she hung up she stood in the same spot for a long time, listening to Ray moving around the house they had made together. Wanting desperately at that moment to be somebody other than who she was.

As soon as Ray left to take the kids to the birthday party on Saturday, Hope went into her closet and grabbed the first dress she felt was suitable for a small house party. It was a lavender silk wraparound; she also took out the silver strappy sandals that she usually wore with the dress. She put everything else she needed for the evening into a knapsack. She wrote out a note and left it where someone would be sure to find it.

> *Hope everything went well at the party. I decided to go out. Will be back later.*

Hope backed Ray's car out of the driveway and steered it toward Tony's hotel. For a minute she felt bad that she was using her husband's car to get to her lover, but then she remembered that she had done it before.

Tony hugged her and took her bag from her at the same time. "I'm glad you decided to come with me." He was smiling like a little boy who had asked for a second ice-cream cone and gotten it. She returned his smile as best she could. She was not really in the mood for a party, but once she told him she would go, she felt that she couldn't back out. She couldn't have her only real friend mad at her.

He kissed her full on the mouth and she pushed him gently away. "What's wrong?" He was still very responsive to her mood.

"My stomach is a little upset." She tried to massage some of the knots out of her stomach.

"I'll get you a Sprite."

"Thanks." Her stomach was upset, but the real truth was she didn't want him kissing and rubbing on her, because then he would want to screw. And her desire for sex was nonexistent. Sex was a major part of having an affair, and though it was good with Tony—excellent when she was able to shut her mind down and concentrate solely on the feelings that they created inside each other—she didn't like how she felt afterward.

He handed her a Sprite from the minibar and she thanked him again.

"We have a couple of hours before the party, baby, what do you want to do?" It was obvious what *he* wanted to do. He was massaging her shoulders from behind, and she could feel the heat coming from his body. *In some ways men are all the same,* she decided. She reached behind her to still his hands.

"Could you go down to the little store and get me some Pepto-Bismol?"

"Sure. If you don't feel up to it, we don't have to go to the party. We can stay here. I'll order room service for us—"

"No . . . just get me the Pepto-Bismol and I'm sure I'll be fine." When he left the room Hope leaned back into the chair and closed her eyes. She hadn't been sleeping well, she hadn't been eating well—really, she hadn't been doing anything well lately. She smiled to herself right before she drifted off to sleep. *And what kind of an adulteress finds excuses not to make love with her lover? I'm not doing this well either.*

Hope sat straight up and for a minute couldn't remember where she was. Then she looked over at the king-sized bed and saw Tony lounging casually on the pillows. "Hey!" she called out to get his attention. He smiled at her immediately.

"Hey back at you." He got up from the bed and walked toward her. "Are you feeling better, or do you still need the Pepto?"

"I'm okay. Maybe I was just tired. How long was I asleep?"

"About an hour."

"I better hurry and get dressed."

"You don't have to hurry. It won't matter if we're a few minutes late."

"Well, still . . ." She let the sentence trail off, grabbed her bag, and practically ran into the bathroom. She leaned against the bathroom door for a minute. Ray and the kids were probably on their way back home from the party. If things were right between her and Stephanie, she would have been at the party—in fact, she would have gone early to help her get everything ready—and then the kids would have probably stayed the night and she and Ray would have gone to a movie or somethingafterward. And she would have been happy to be sitting in a cool dark theater alone with him, even if he did always have to pick the movie. *But things aren't right, Hope,* she reminded herself. *You know that because you're practically hiding in a hotel bathroom.*

* * *

Before they left for the party, Tony told her to hold her arm out and close her eyes. When she opened them she saw that Tony had clasped a beautiful platinum and diamond line bracelet around her wrist. She noticed that it went well with her wedding ring and wondered absurdly for a moment if he had chosen it with her ring in mind.

"Thank you Tony, it's beautiful," was all she said.

"I wanted you to have it. I appreciate you being here with me. I know going to this party tonight is a big step. I promise you won't regret it."

On the drive to the party, Tony dispelled Hope's theory about him choosing the bracelet to match her wedding ring. He looked down at her ring and spoke as though he knew he was broaching a delicate subject. "I told Mike and Ellen that you were divorced. Could you possibly not wear your ring for the next few hours?"

Hope only took off her ring to have it cleaned. She had cried when Ray had surprised her with it. That he would think her worthy of such a ring . . . Hope looked down at her beautiful ring and slipped it off and into her small evening bag without a word. Tears stung the back of her eyes. *What am I doing?* she questioned herself. She felt Tony smiling in the seat next to her, pleased that she would do as he requested without argument, and she didn't like it.

Chapter Thirty-two

The house that the party was being held in was lovely. It was a dinner party, so there were not very many guests. Three other couples and the host and hostess were there when Tony and Hope arrived. Ellen was a tall, very slim woman. She had a beautiful smile and her nose and cheeks were sprinkled with freckles. Hope liked her immediately. She and her husband Mike looked so much alike that Hope mistook him for her brother.

Soft music filtered through the comfortable living room as appetizers were being served. After a minute Hope realized that the music had a Christian theme . . . Christian love songs that had become so popular. Tony left Hope sitting on the couch enjoying crab puffs while he went to the bar to pour her a glass of wine. She was surprised when her hostess sat down next to her.

"So how are the crab puffs?"

Hope finished her last bite before speaking. "Delicious. Maybe I'll get the recipe from you later."

"I can give it to you now." Ellen laughed. "Call Jade's Lighthouse . . . they're in the phone book. And if you want the recipe for the pork and vegetables or the rolls that we're having for dinner, call them too."

Hope laughed. "You didn't make dinner."

Ellen leaned in and whispered to Hope, "I'll tell you this because I have a feeling that we're going to be friends, but I never cook for dinner parties. Mike loves to have parties, but he's so busy at the church that he doesn't have time to help out with anything, so about three years ago I started ordering take-out."

"At the church?" Hope hoped that she sounded casual.

"Yes, he's associate pastor at New View Christian. Tony didn't tell you?"

"No, he didn't." *He knew I wouldn't bring my adulterous ass into a preacher's house.* Hope was glad she had chosen a modest red silk slip dress . . . then she thought about the way the silk clung to her thighs and her behind. *Well, semimodest*, she amended.

"I'm surprised, he told us a lot about you. Let me see . . . you met at a seminar, you're divorced, you're a bank supervisor—"

Hope interrupted her. "Did he tell you my shoe size?"

Ellen smiled softly at her. "Tony is a very good friend of ours. We lived in Houston until my husband accepted the associate pastorship. We knew his ex-wife too, and we've been very concerned about him since the divorce. So when he said he would be here *and* he was bringing a date, I'm not ashamed to say that I drilled him." Ellen's smile was approving. "How long have you been divorced?"

Where is Tony with that damn drink? Hope looked

around but Tony was nowhere in sight, so she was forced to add to the lie that he had started.

"About . . ." What was an appropriate length of time to be divorced before dating? Hope decided to play it safe. "Five years."

Ellen looked confused. "Tony mentioned that you had three boys and that one of them was not really school aged."

Oh shit!

"Well, that's true. My ex and I tried to reconcile after the divorce and I ended up pregnant. You know how that goes," Hope ended lamely.

The expression on Ellen's face left no doubt that she did not.

"I have to finish taking the food from the cartons. I'm glad that Tony found you." She seemed very sincere as she patted Hope's knee before getting up. Hope looked after her . . . and shook her head mentally at her own stupidity.

She saw Tony walking up with her glass of wine out of the corner of her eye. He handed her the glass and sat down next to her.

"What took you so long?" She was very irritated, and embarrassed. Her tone caused him to frown.

"I was getting your wine. Are you okay?"

"No, I'm *not* okay." Hope took a sip of the rose-colored wine, but did not taste it. "Why did you leave me all alone with her?"

"You're a big girl, Hope, I figured you'd be okay." Tony laughed, but Hope was very serious.

"I made a fool of myself. If you were going to leave me alone with her, you should have told me what lies you made up about me."

"The only thing I told her that wasn't true was that

you were divorced. Everything else I told her was the truth." He leaned over to kiss her, calming her nerves. "I told her that you were beautiful, intelligent, a great mother, and a wonderful lover."

Hope looked at him, horrified.

"You told her *what*?"

"I told her that you were a wonderful lover and that our bodies fit together perfectly, and that your tongue is like raw silk—"

Her laughter interrupted him. "You're insane." She accepted another kiss on the cheek from him and decided to relax and enjoy herself. She held out her hand and examined the sparkling bracelet on her wrist. "Did I thank you for the bracelet?" She wondered where she would hide it. Maybe Ray would think it was cubic zirconia . . . maybe he wouldn't notice.

"No, you didn't, not properly, but I promise to give you the opportunity later."

During the forty-five minutes before dinner was served, Hope met the other guests, had another glass of wine and had another . . . smoother conversation with their hostess. She liked her and she liked the reverend. She had never met a minister who was so down to earth.

Tony didn't leave her again. He stayed close to her side, laughing softly if she made a funny comment, caressing the back of the hand he was holding, periodically kissing her on her forehead, her cheeks, once lightly on her lips. She was almost totally at ease when the doorbell rang.

Ellen broke through the swinging doors that led to the kitchen with a smile on her face. "You guys can go on into the dining room, and grab a seat. Dinner is ready. I'll be there as soon as I see who this is at the door." Her comment was directed at the people positioned in various spots throughout the room.

Hope and Tony did not move immediately to follow the other couples. He continued to sit on the arm of Hope's chair, holding her hand. She was in no hurry to eat; she was enjoying Tony's loving glances and the relaxed atmosphere.

Her soft smile froze in place when she heard a familiar voice in the hallway. She snatched her hand from Tony and stood up quickly, so quickly that she almost fell back into the sofa.

"What's wrong?" Tony was confused, but Hope couldn't answer his question—she was too busy praying that for just one minute God would grant her the power to make herself invisible.

By the time Ellen rounded the corner with her last guests, Hope was trembling inside. *It is them*! When Ralph and Lisa walked into the room, Hope's heart fell out of her mouth and landed somewhere near her knees. She guessed it was her heart that caused her knees to buckle. She tried to sit back down casually, but she knew her movements were awkward.

"Hope." Lisa's eyes moved from Tony to Hope. When her assessment was complete she gave her husband an "I told you so" look. She didn't miss a beat as she continued speaking. "I didn't expect to see you here. Is Ray in the other room?"

Hope stood up and tried to pretend that she was happy to see the couple, but she couldn't pretend. She wanted to run out of the room like Cinderella at midnight, but the satisfaction that was lurking in the back of Lisa's eyes was enough to keep her feet firmly planted in one spot.

"Hi Ralph, how are you?"

Ralph, who had been so friendly toward her despite his wife, looked at her and Tony with sad disapproval. "I'm fine, Hope. What's up, man?" The nod that he directed toward Tony was almost imperceptible.

They stood around looking at one another, Ellen looking confused—the tension in the room could not be mistaken. At that moment Mike walked into the room.

"Everybody's waiting to eat, baby." He smiled at Ralph and Lisa. "I thought y'all weren't going to make it. Come on, let's eat—"

"Just a minute honey." Ellen's look stopped her husband midsentence. "Do you know each other?" She spoke quietly, waiting for someone to explain . . . something.

"Of course!" Lisa responded too cheerfully. "Ralph works with Ray, Hope's husband, and he went to grad school with Tony." Lisa continued as if she didn't know exactly what was going on. "Ray *is* here, isn't he, Hope?" Her wide-eyed expression didn't fool Hope.

"No, he's at a birthday party with the boys." Hope wanted to scratch the smirk off the other woman's face, but she was too humiliated. And Tony didn't say a word. He just stood behind her looking at everyone in the room with a blank expression on his face.

Lisa looked pointedly at the small-faced watch that she wore. "Is it a slumber party?"

"You bitch," Hope muttered under her breath.

"Excuse me?" Lisa put her hands on her hips and looked at Hope with open challenge.

"I said, *you bitch*." Hope was not one to back down from a challenge.

"Oh! I'm a bitch. Well, Hope, at least I'm not the kind of bitch who walks around thinking that she's *all that*," she looked pointedly at Hope's clingy dress, "and screws over her husband without a second thought." She paused for a second as she pretended to consider. "You know, where I come from, we have another word for *females* like you. And my mother always said it's better to be a bitch than a whore."

Tony continued to stand silently. Ellen must have known that Hope was about to kick her ass because she put her hands up to stop the two women.

"That's enough! Ralph, why don't you take Lisa in and tell everyone that it's okay to start dinner. We'll be there in a minute." Ralph did as she requested and led Lisa by the elbow into the dining room. Hope and a still-silent Tony remained to speak with the reverend and his wife privately.

"Is that true, Tony? Is Hope married?" Mike looked at Tony, waiting for an explanation. Tony nodded slowly.

"Yes, she is, but they're basically separated." He moved closer to Hope and put his arms around her shoulders. Mike and Ellen looked at each other doubtfully. Hope wished that Tony would move his arm. She knew he was trying to be supportive, but it made her feel worse, more ashamed.

"Does your husband know you're here with Tony tonight, Hope?" Ellen asked the question quietly and with little judgment.

Hope felt her body shrink underneath Tony's arm. "No, he doesn't."

Ellen looked at her husband again . . . it was his cue to finish the conversation.

"Look, Tony, we're not exactly sure what's going on here, but you know we can't allow you to bring a married woman into our house." Tony stood before them unapologetic, his arm burning a hole in her bare flesh. Ellen looked at Hope, who tried to avoid her eyes.

"Hope, can I speak to you privately for a minute?"

How could she say no? She smiled stiffly, almost grateful for a reason to move away from Tony. She followed Ellen to a corner on the far side of the room; she looked back briefly and saw that Mike continued to speak to Tony quietly. He looked more repentant that he had seconds earlier. Hope looked back at Ellen, who was looking at her with a soft expression on her face.

"Hope, like my husband said, we don't know what's going on here. Well . . ." She paused to amend her statement. "We don't know *all* of the circumstances, but no matter what, we hold certain things sacred. Marriage is one of them. If we allow you to stay here with this new knowledge, it would be as if we approved." Ellen placed a soft hand on Hope's shoulder. "Not that it's our place to judge, but it is our home, and we *certainly* don't approve." Hope could barely meet her eyes.

"We have a very exciting couples ministry at our church. I'd like to invite you and your husband. We meet every Thursday at seven P.M., and bring your children." Hope finally met her eyes, and she was surprised to find no judgment there. Just understanding. "Marriage is hard, Hope, it's hard for all of us."

Hope appreciated the woman's kindness, even though she was being kicked out of her house. All she could think of to do was to try to alleviate any ill feelings that the woman might have toward Tony.

"You've been friends with Tony for a while . . . I don't want you to think any less of him. He has been a friend to me."

Ellen looked doubtful. Hope's appreciation vanished and she felt a surge of resentment. Why was she trying to offer explanations for Tony's and her behavior to this . . . stranger?

"This is not about Tony. I'm speaking to you not as someone who has known and been friends with Tony for years, but as one married woman to another. It's always a mistake to let someone of the opposite sex become privy to the intimate details of your marriage, but it's never to late to do the right thing. I don't know you, so I couldn't hazard a guess as to what the right thing would be for you, but I know it couldn't be this." Ellen patted her once again on her shoulder, and Hope turned around and walked toward Tony.

Hope didn't know what the reverend had said to Tony, but whatever it was, it was enough to keep his hand off her shoulder and firmly at his side as they walked though the front door.

They rode in silence for several minutes before Tony spoke. "Well . . . that was an adventure. Do you want to stop at a restaurant and get something to eat or do you want to order room service back at the hotel?"

"Is that all you're going to say?"

He cast her a sideways glance. "What do you want me to say?"

"How about, 'I'm sorry, Hope, I shouldn't have put you in that position' . . . or how about, 'are you okay.' I know you're not okay, and I am sorry, but—"

She couldn't let him finish his sentence. "Did you know that when you say 'but' it negates anything that you said before?"

"What?" Tony was trying to concentrate on his driving, and his face was scrunched up as if he had a headache.

"If you say 'I'm sorry, *but,*' it means that you're not really sorry."

He let out a long breath. "Hope, I *am* sorry. How was I supposed to know how the evening was going to turn out? I had no idea that Lisa and Ralph would be there. I didn't even know they knew Mike and Ellen."

"Well, answer this. Did you know that Mike was a minister?"

"Yes, I did. I get your point, Hope. I probably shouldn't have invited you to the party, but I want to be with you. I want you to meet my friends."

She leaned back in the seat and covered her face with her hand. She was too tired to argue.

"Do you realize what just happened, Tony?" She removed her hands and looked over at him. "I just pray that Ray doesn't find out about this."

Tony didn't respond for long seconds. "Why not?" His lack of concern irritated Hope.

"What?"

"I asked why you don't want Ray to find out. He already knows we're seeing each other. What difference does it make?"

Now she was furious. She raised her voice like she had never raised her voice to him. "I can't believe you can ask something like that. He's my *husband* . . . do you think I want to hurt him?"

"And what am I, Hope, a convenience . . . a diversion?" He raised his voice to match hers. "How long do you think you can straddle the fence?"

"*What? What? What?*" It wasn't a question, it was a statement of disbelief. She could think of no other way to respond to what she considered his outrageous question.

"You heard me. You've been playing both sides

against the middle for months. It's time for you to make some decisions . . . some choices. You can't have your cake and eat it too."

She was silent and tears of anger and hurt formed in the corners of her eyes. "I can't believe you. Aren't you the man who said to me. 'I don't want to interfere with what you have going on at home, I just want to spend some time with you'?" She did a poor imitation of him through her tears. "And now you sit here and tell me I'm trying to have my cake and eat it too. Well, tell me *this:* where is the fucking cake, Tony?"

"Calm down, Hope. I didn't mean to upset you. You misunderstood me. We can talk about this later."

"No, Tony, let's talk about it *now.*"

Tony sighed and tightened his hands on the steering wheel. "We're *almost* at the hotel, Hope. Let's talk about it once we get to the room."

She didn't like the way he said her name; he used the same patronizing tone she sometimes used with her children. She took several deep breaths and wiped the tears from her cheeks. She had learned from years of experience that a woman could not make a man talk when he did not want to, and, Hope realized suddenly, Tony was just a man after all. So she waited and did not say another word as they walked through the hotel lobby, rode up to the eighth floor, and stepped into the room.

Chapter Thirty-three

"I'm going to make myself a drink." He looked back at her as he was walking toward the minibar mounted on the wall. "Do you want something?"

"No." Hope shook her head and sat down on the bed. She needed to change back into her casual clothes, but she didn't have the energy. Tony took out a miniature bottle of vodka. He busied himself making his drink . . . a screwdriver.

She watched him for a minute through partially closed lids. He was an attractive man, strong, confident, but no more so than the man she had at home. He took his time making the drink. Hope felt like he was moving in slow motion on purpose; trying to avoid the conversation that she was determined to have for as long as possible. She held her tongue for as long as she could, about seventy-two seconds, before speaking.

"Tony, you said we would talk once we were back in the room. I don't have all night. I need to be home at a decent hour."

He drank from the glass before speaking. "That's just it, Hope. You say that you need to be home at a decent hour, but there is nothing decent about this entire situation." He looked angrily at her from across the room.

Hold up! Sirens were going off in her head. Hope stood up from the bed. Her look was equally angry.

"Are you preaching to *me* about decency? Tony, *you* were the one who pursued *me*! You're the one who's been making all the promises, not me. You knew I was married! That wasn't even a bump in the road for you."

"*You* knew you were married too, Hope." His words were quiet, but for her they were deadly.

She stood stock-still in the middle of the hotel room, filled with anxiety, shame, and anger. The truth hurt. It hurt a lot.

"What does that mean, Tony?"

He put the drink on a side table and walked toward her and put his hands on her shoulders.

"Hope, I love you. I want you with me all the time. Every time I see . . . every time I talk to you I love you more." He moved his hands up and down her shoulders. "I thought I could control my feelings, but I can't. And I have to be honest with you and tell you that I don't think you're being fair to anyone in this situation. Not me, not Ray . . . not even to yourself. I've seen how stressed you've been these last several weeks. You don't like being in this situation any more than I do."

"What do you suggest I do, Tony?" She knew before he spoke what his answer would be, and he didn't hesitate to speak.

"I think you should leave him. You've already left him *emotionally*. I want you to pack your things and leave. I want you to give *us* a *real* chance." She looked at him strangely. She had never considered leaving Ray. It had occurred to her that he might leave *her* on several occasions, but she had never considered leaving. She looked at Tony with a half-smile on her face, lost in her own thoughts.

And anyway, what reason would she give for leaving him? He hadn't abused her in any way that a court would recognize—he provided for his children, the sex was good . . . or at least it had been when they were having sex. What reason could she give for leaving her house, for causing God knows what problems for her children—for hurting Ray more than she already had?

She could say that they didn't understand one another; she could say that he tried to control her, or that he never told her how pretty she was, that he never let her choose the movie, that he didn't like the way she made macaroni and cheese . . .

It didn't seem like enough to her.

"Are you ignoring me?" The roughness in his voice brought her back to the moment.

"I'm not ignoring you."

"Well, do you agree that you can't continue to be selfish like this?"

"I never knew you thought of me as selfish."

"If you allow this situation to continue as it has been, that's selfish." He looked her in the eye and spoke slowly. "You need to be a woman and make a choice."

"What do you know about being a woman, Tony? Better yet, what do you know about me?" As she waited for his response the answer came to her—*not much*. She held up her hands, no longer interested in the conversation. She moved from the bed and went to pick up her bag.

"I can't do this anymore. You're right. I have been

selfish." She looked at the handsome man standing in the middle of the room. Her face was sad and drawn.

"When you say 'this,' what are you referring to?"

She knew he was struggling to control his emotions, just as she was. "I mean I'm not going to see you any-more."

"So you think you can just go home and forget about these last several months? Do you think that Ray is going to let you forget? I don't know Ray, Hope, but if he's anything like most men, it would be hard for him to let things remain status quo when his friends know that his woman—his wife—is seeing another man."

Something in his tone made Hope look at him really hard.

"Did you know that Ralph and Lisa would be at that party?" The thought was almost incomprehensible to her.

The look on his face changed and he moved closer to her and placed his hands on her shoulders. "Hope, look . . ."

She shook his hands off roughly. "Answer me, Tony!"

"Mike and Ellen didn't submit their final guest list for my approval." His sarcasm made her more suspi-cious.

"Did you know there was a *possibility* they would be there?" The guilty expression on his face gave her the answer she needed. She was horrified.

"Oh my God, Tony! Why would you put me in that position? Do you know how humiliated I was?"

"Hope, I don't like what we're doing. Believe it or not, it's eating me up. I didn't know for sure that Ralph and Lisa would be at the party, but I knew it was a pos-sibility. I'm tired of sneaking around, of wondering what you do at night when we're not together. I wasn't trying to humiliate you. Maybe in a way I was trying to force your hand. I knew as soon as they walked through the door and I saw the expression on your face that it was a mistake to take you to the party.

"I'm sorry, Hope. I love you and I would never do anything to deliberately hurt you."

The enormity of what she had done fell over her and she stumbled back toward the bed. She sobbed sad, angry tears. She was mad at herself . . . mad at this man that she had taken as her lover.

"How can you say that you love me?" She looked up at him angrily, not attempting to wipe her tears away. "You don't know me. You don't know anything about me, and I don't know you either."

"We do know each other, Hope."

"No, we don't!" she screamed at him. "You don't know a fucking thing about me! Do you know that I almost died giving birth to the twins? Do you know that I'm allergic to almonds? Do you know why I've had to be responsible since I was a fucking girl? No, you don't, do you? Because if you knew anything about me, you would know that trying to force my hand by humiliating me would never work." At that moment she blamed him for all the bad decisions that she had made over the last several months, and at that moment, she hated him for it. "All you know about me is that I'm a woman who will betray her husband and her family for the first interesting invitation." The bitter words left her mouth and she stood up and gathered her bags once more. He didn't try to stop her as she walked toward the door.

"I've never seen you like this," he called to her back.

Her hand was on the doorknob, but she turned around to face him.

"That's just the thing, Tony . . . you've never seen me in a lot of ways."

His eyes squinted at her sarcastic tone, and he responded through clenched teeth.

"I know what this is really about and I'm not going to let you do this, Hope." He shook his head angrily. "You're upset—and rightly so; but you walked into this with your eyes wide open. I didn't force you; I didn't hypnotize you; I *invited* you, just like you said, but I won't let you pretend, in the middle of the party, that you didn't check the mail every day for the invitation."

How could she argue with the truth?

"True . . . true." Her smile was still bitter as she turned the knob and walked out the door.

Chapter Thirty-four

Hope didn't hear her children the next afternoon as they told her about the birthday party. "Aunt Stephanie baked two cakes, and I got to have a piece of each one. I wanted to bring you a piece of the chocolate, but Daddy said that he was sure you were having your own party. Did you have a party, Mom?" Karl asked innocently. She tightened the belt on her gray cotton robe. It was after two o'clock and she had not gotten dressed.

Ray had taken the boys to church while she was still pretending to be asleep. He dropped them off after the service, and according to the boys had gone to play basketball. "You had a party, Mommy?" Jordan asked. His tone was accusatory. Hope wished she had gone ahead and put vodka in her orange juice. She looked down at the three pairs of eyes looking up at her and wished also that Ray had kept them out all day. Then she would be free to drink vodka straight from the bottle, and climb back into bed.

"I *didn't* have a party." All three children looked as

if they didn't believe her. Maybe it was because she looked hungover. "I didn't have a party," she repeated. "I had errands to run yesterday."

She spent twenty minutes of not-so-quality time in the family room with the boys before she gave up. She stood up from the sofa and picked up the empty juice glass. She didn't have enough energy to be a mommy right then.

"Jordan, Karl, watch your brother. I'm going to lie down for a while. I don't feel very well," she called out to the two boys playing video games. "If you get hungry, make some Pop-Tarts or something. Use the toaster, but don't turn on the stove or anything, and don't go outside."

She took her glass to the bar and poured a little vodka in it . . . then she poured a little more. When she got into *her* bedroom, she drank it all before getting back into bed where she belonged.

She stayed in bed for the rest of the afternoon and into the evening. She heard Ray come into the house and ask, "Where is your mother?" Someone opened the door to the bedroom, but she didn't turn over to see who it was.

Later when she heard four car doors slam, she knew she was alone in the house. She went into the kitchen because she was hungry, but lost her appetite when she saw the mess the boys had made. She took another glass from the cabinet and went back to the bar. This time she poured tequila and took it back into the bedroom. When the boys came in to say good night, she waved them out of the room.

She was a little late for work the next morning. She had forgotten it was Monday, and Ray and the boys left the house without checking on her. When she walked into her office, Helen almost didn't look up at her when she said hello, and when she did the look on her face was almost embarrassed. Hope attributed the look to her appearance; she wasn't wearing make-up, not even lipstick, and the suit that she had pulled out of the closet was one that Ray's mother had given her two or three Christmases ago . . . one that she had always intended to give to the Salvation Army.

"Hope, Mr. Demarco has called twice this morning. He would like for you to call him as soon as you get in." Helen still couldn't quite meet her eyes. Hope's heart started to beat a little faster, but she didn't let on to Helen.

"Thank you," she responded politely before walking into her office. She leaned against the door and wondered what her supervisor could want with her so early in the day. And of course he would call on a morning that she was running late. She put her purse and her briefcase on the chair in front of her desk and took a deep breath before she picked up the telephone and dialed her boss's extension.

"Tom Demarco."

Hope swallowed and tried to make her voice sound as normal as possible before she identified herself.

"Hi, Tom, this is Hope, you wanted to speak with me?"

He paused for a second and Hope imagined that he was looking at his watch.

"Yes, I did. Could you come to my office . . . say in about ten minutes. There are some things that I need to speak with you about."

"Sure. I'll be there." Hope forced herself to smile into the telephone. The last thing she needed was a meeting. She sat behind her desk and decided that she would check her e-mail and then put on some make-up before meeting with her boss. There were three messages from Tony. The first one was so personal and so inappropriate for the workplace that she deleted the other two without opening them.

She didn't care about his promises to give her more time, to ease up some. She didn't care if he loved her or if he didn't love her . . . she didn't care if she loved him or didn't love him. She knew she was through. She was tired of the life she had been living for the last several months . . . just as tired as she had been of the life she had been living before she met Tony.

Hope forgot her plan to put on some make-up before meeting with her boss and walked into his office looking worn out, and disinterested. She read the look on his face when he saw her—surprised. In all the years she had worked at the bank, she had always arrived looking fresh and put together, even during the last months of her pregnancy with the twins. Everyone was allowed one bad day per decade, Hope thought.

She ignored the look on his face and refused to make any excuses for her appearance. Her body was clean and she *had* brushed her teeth. She smiled brightly and sat in one of the two empty chairs in front of his desk without being invited. "Good morning, Tom."

"Good morning, Hope," he returned. He sat up in his seat and cleared his throat. "Let me get straight to the point, Hope." Straight to the point was not a good way to start a conversation, in Hope's opinion. "We've been very concerned about you recently, Hope. You have been missing work, not showing up for meetings, coming in late . . . Your position as a supervisor de-

mands that you set a positive example for those that
you supervise, and quite frankly, Hope, you haven't
been doing that."

Hope sat across from him and did not say a word.
She felt so removed from the moment it was as if he
were speaking to someone else.

"That's *one* problem that we're facing, Hope. A
greater problem is that one of the people you supervise
has been stealing from the bank." He paused to gauge
her reaction to the news. Although the statement did
catch her attention, and she sat up a little straighter in
her seat, the first thought to cross her mind was "so?"

"Who?" It took all that she had to sound interested.

"I'm not at liberty to share that information with
you, Hope. We are still conducting an audit, and when
it's done we will decide how to proceed with this matter. From all indications, Hope, this has been going on
for months. Quite frankly, it's something that *you*
should have brought to *my* attention."

So?

"Well . . . what happened?" If she had stayed home
in bed where she belonged, she was sure none of this
would be happening.

"The employee in question made a series of loans,
and after one or two payments they were defaulted on.
We suspect that either the loans were bogus or that they
were relatives or friends of his."

*Well, the "his" narrows the list of suspects down to
two.*

"Well, what does that have to do with me?" As soon
as she asked the question Hope knew she should have
phrased it better. "I mean, why do you think that I
should have been aware of the situation?"

He looked at her in amazement. "*Because,* Hope, he

is under your *direct* supervision. You have a responsibility to review transactions and to investigate any suspicious patterns."

"Oh." No other response came to mind.

"I must say that I'm disappointed, Hope. Your attitude about your work and the bank has concerned me for some time." When she offered no excuse or explanation, he continued. "I wouldn't normally ask this, Hope, but you've been with us for a long time. Is there anything going on with you that would explain your apparent lack of interest in your work?"

Hope looked at her boss and considered what she should say. She could tell him that she was sorry and that she had spent the last several months focused on things that had absolutely nothing to do with anything. She could tell him that she had a serious medical condition, maybe a yeast infection that was threatening to turn into cancer—it was her experience that men generally stopped talking when the conversation veered to anything exclusively female. Or she could tell him that if he had just noticed her lack of interest in her job, his powers of observation were worse than hers. She had not been interested in her job for years.

"No, Tom. I don't know what to tell you." She sat back in her chair and almost smiled at his obvious discomfort.

"Well, Hope, I feel that there must be something wrong. Maybe you've become unhappy with us." He lifted his hands up in defeat. "I don't know, but we have a very efficient system of checks and balances here, and if one of the individuals who is responsible for checking is not doing the job properly, then the entire system is thrown off. Do you understand what I'm saying?"

"No, Tom, I don't." She wasn't about to let him off the hook. He sighed and shook his head slightly.

"I don't want you to think of this as something negative, Hope. It doesn't have to be. But we feel that it would be best if you took a leave of absence at this time. It's apparent that you are not committed to your work here at the bank."

Hope took a deep breath. His words reminded her that at this point in her life she wasn't committed to much of anything.

"Are you firing me, Tom?" Her words were dispassionate.

"No, Hope, you are not being fired. I am suggesting that you take a leave of absence. In a few months you can contact us for a meeting and we can talk about your future here at the bank."

"In these *few months,* will I continue to receive a paycheck?"

"No, Hope, we would have to pay someone to replace you while you're out." He was very uncomfortable now. She knew all about the personnel procedures at the bank; how it was unusual for someone to be terminated without a trail of documents leading up to the event. She knew that she could argue her side—Why hadn't she received written communication if he was unhappy with her work? Wasn't it customary for a long-term employee to be placed on probation before termination? She *could* pose those questions and she *would* . . . if she wanted her job. But she didn't—and in all areas of her life she never liked to be where she was not wanted.

"You know what, Tom? You can cut the bullshit. I *know* when I've been *fired.* I'll be out of here in less than an hour. I trust you've already found my replacement?" She sounded as if she was angry with him, but she wasn't. A more lengthy discussion would have only kept her away from her bed that much longer. "It's been nice. Sorry things had to end like this." The words were similar to the ones that she had said to Tony. She stood up, waved casually at him, and left the office.

She was on her way to the parking garage when she realized she had left her purse in her office. She also needed to clean out her office because she knew once she left she would not be back. Hope walked with determination back to her office. She walked past Helen without saying a word, sure the other woman had been spying and reporting to the higher-ups.

When she walked into her office she closed the door and leaned against it. Tears came from nowhere and streamed down her cheeks. It was one thing to be dissatisfied with a job . . . it was another thing entirely to be dismissed. She looked around the room where she had spent so many hours of her life, and a sob escaped her. Everything in her life was changing, and she was afraid.

She thought of all the arguments that she and Ray had about her working, how she had defended her work as *so* very important to her—when in reality it had not been. As she gathered her things, she thought about how Ray would react to her being fired. If she had been fired months ago—which she never would have been— he would have been elated. He would have shown as much pretend sympathy as he could muster, and then would have said something like, "well, now you can . . ." and he would have finished the sentence with something that he wanted her to do.

She went to her computer and sent Tony an e-mail, telling him she had been fired and he was not to send her any more messages at work. Then she trashed the messages they had sent each other over the last several months. She put the family pictures that had rested on top of the credenza inside an old file box. She considered taking some of the plaques that she had been presented with over the years, *but for what?* she asked herself.

It took her less than six minutes to clear an office she had been in for several years. It would have taken longer if she had been leaving under different circumstances. There would have been a party and she would have probably received another plaque and there wouldn't be a huge ball of anxiety, shame, and anger settling in the pit of her stomach. Her phone rang and she answered it one last time. It was Helen calling from the other side of the door.

"Yes." Hope's tone was hostile.

"There is a Ms. Rendale here to see you."

"I don't know a Ms. Rendale, Helen. If it's a bank matter, refer her to Rob." She hung up before Helen could respond. Less than a minute later the phone rang again.

"She would really like to speak to you, and she says it's a personal matter."

"Fine, Helen, send her in." Hope stood behind her desk in a position that made it clear she was on her way out. Her purse was on her shoulder and one hand rested lightly on the box containing her personal items. She called out "come in" to the soft knock on the door. She recognized the woman instantly as she walked through the door. It was the woman who had come into her office months ago questioning why she had been turned down for a home loan. It was the woman who had been the center of her first real conversation with Tony.

"Ms. Rendale." Hope couldn't muster a smile. "I

was just on my way out. Is there something that I can help you with?"

"I won't be a minute." The woman smiled hesitantly at Hope, who didn't return the smile. "I just had to stop by and tell you how much I appreciate what you did for me . . . the home loan, I mean."

Hope did try to smile then, but she couldn't make it reach her eyes.

"Things are going well for me and my kids. We *love* our house!" Hope looked closely at the woman and noticed that there were tears forming in her eyes. "You've been on my mind a lot lately, and I had to come by and tell you that I know I acted a fool that day in your office . . . crying and going on . . . like I am now." She wiped the tears from her cheeks. "I don't think you can imagine how scared I was at that time in my life." She shook her head, remembering. "And if you knew how unlike me it was to be so demanding . . . to even *ask* again after I've been told no . . ." She let the sentence fall off. "I wasn't going to go home that day."

Tears ran freely down her cheeks as she spoke. "I just couldn't face my children having failed again. *I wasn't going home that day.*" She looked at Hope intently to be sure she understood the full meaning of her words. "Do you ever wonder why you did that?"

Hope nodded, and said quietly to the crying woman, "I did wonder, and you've crossed my mind on several occasions. I'm glad you're all right."

"I just came here to say thank you, and to let you know that I've made *all* of my mortgage payments and in fact I'm trying to pay the loan off early." She laughed a little through her tears, obviously proud of herself. "That's all I came here to say." She took a deep breath before going on. "But now I have to tell you that

I believe God sends people to us at just the right time . . . to give us just what we need." She walked over to where Hope was standing behind her desk, and without asking, hugged her tight and long. Before she released her she said softly in her ear, "You were a godsend for me."

Hope knew the emotion that had settled in the pit of her stomach was struggling to reach the surface, but she refused to let it. She didn't know this woman, and she had never been one to open up to strangers—well, she hadn't been before she met Tony, and look what happened with that. She held herself as stiffly as possible throughout the embrace. After a while the woman stood back, smiling sincerely into her eyes.

"Thank you," she said again and walked out of the office.

Hope stood behind her desk, still and silent, for a minute longer before something white flashed in the corner of her eye. She looked down at her desk and picked up the small card that had been placed there.

Guest Card
New View Christian Church
"What a friend you have in Jesus"

10092 Freemont
Sunday worship
10:00 A.M.
&
1 P.M.

Chapter Thirty-five

Hope awoke from her nap and bolted upright in the bed. She looked around frantically for the clock on the nightstand; she relaxed when she saw that it was about one-thirty. She had several hours before she was due to pick up the kids from the Y. She lay back again, naked, in the sheets. Her eyes roamed the room as she tried to remember why she was at home in bed in the middle of the afternoon. She saw the clothes she had worn to work in a heap beside the bed and then she remembered. She had been fired. The box of personal belongings that she had removed from her office was still sitting in the front passenger seat of her truck.

There were other things that she needed to do at the bank, personal and financial matters that she needed to clear up, but it would have to be done over the phone or through the mail. She was never going back there again. She wondered, if under the circumstances, she would qualify for unemployment. If she did, she decided she would use the money to hire a mother for her children and take a trip somewhere, maybe to Georgia, or London, or Abilene—anywhere, just so long as it was away from all the mistakes she had made.

She sat up in the bed again when she heard the kitchen door slam. "Ray?" she called out hesitantly. No answer. She threw the covers back and went to the closet for her robe and put it on as she made her way down the hall to the room where Ray slept. Ray was standing in the closet, moving hangers around. "Ray," she said again, "why didn't you say something when I called earlier? I was scared."

The expression on his face when he turned around was enough to make Hope take a step back. His eyes were wet with hatred. He turned back to the closet without saying a word and started putting the clothes on the bed. It was obvious to Hope what he was doing, but she pulled the knot in her robe a little tighter and asked anyway.

"What are you doing?"

"What the hell does it look like I'm doing?"

"Are you going on a business trip?" Her voice was weak and her legs would no longer support her, so she found herself sliding down the door frame onto the floor. He looked at her with open contempt before answering.

"No, I'm getting the hell out of your way. I had actually convinced myself that I could ride this out. I figured that our family was important and that I had made a commitment for better or worse. I just never imagined the worst would be you flaunting the motherfucker that you've been screwing in my *face* . . . socializing with him with my friends . . ."

Sitting on the floor, dazed, Hope tried to remember if

it had occurred to her that somehow it would get back to Ray that she had been at a party on Saturday with Tony. Obviously it had.

"Look at you. What's the matter, Hope, your man not treating you right?"

"Ray," she tried to explain from her position on the floor, "I'm sorry. I'm not going to see him anymore. He knows that. I made a mistake." She couldn't look at him, and closed her eyes and let the salty tears run down her face.

"You made a mistake? Is that all you have to say? What happened to all that bullshit you were talking weeks ago?" He pulled a large suitcase out of the closet and started filling it with clothes. "You know how hard it's been for me all these weeks? I've been waiting in this room every fucking night . . . waiting for you to come in here and tell me that you were ready to put our family back together." Hope had never heard her husband sob, but there he was, hating her, sobbing . . . and leaving. "I'm not perfect, but I didn't do anything to deserve this. I could have never predicted that you'd do this to *me*, but for you to do this to our children . . ."

She didn't hear all of what he said, but the words that she did hear were like kicks in her stomach. She held her position on the floor as she continued to sob silently.

"It would have been better if you left, but you didn't leave because I'm here paying your fucking bills, letting you do whatever the fuck you want. Why wouldn't you try to have your cake and eat it too?" He closed the suitcase and picked it up from the bed. "Well, no more, Hope."

Hope pulled herself up from the floor. "Ray, you

don't have to leave. We never talked about this." He pushed past her, and she followed him and his suitcase down the hall.

"Yes, I do, Hope. If I stay here, I'll kill you." He turned around to face her and she knew he meant what he said.

"What about the boys? What are we going to tell them?" One last appeal—for what, she didn't know.

"*Tonight* you can tell them that I had some work to do out of town. I'm looking for an apartment. I'll pick them up from school on Wednesday, and when I do I'll tell them the truth: their mother is a whore, and I can't live with it anymore." And then he left.

Hope stood in the hall until she heard the sound as he started his car and screeched out of the driveway. Her legs failed her and she found herself on the floor again, this time flat on her back looking up at the ceiling in the hallway.

Images of her life played itself out on the ceiling: her graduations . . . her wedding . . . her babies . . . her arguments . . . her lovemaking . . . her mother's funeral. She stayed on the floor watching the movies on the ceiling until the phone rang. She knew before she got up that it was the Y calling to tell her that she was late picking up her kids.

Chapter Thirty-six

Ray kept his word. The weekend after he announced to Hope that he would be leaving, he found an apartment and moved most of his things out of the house. Her children were confused, and Hope could offer them no explanation that they understood or would accept.

"Why did Daddy have to leave?" Karl asked her so often in the weeks following his father's departure that it started to make her angry.

"Because . . ." Her face was expressionless. "Sometimes mommies and daddies have problems and they need to be apart."

"What problems did you and Daddy have?" Jordan asked.

"*Adult* problems." She tried to be patient, and attempted a "Mommy understands that this is hard" smile.

"What are adult problems?" David whined. This time, she turned away without answering him and went into her bedroom. It was like they were all ganging up on her. Blaming her—their looks were accusatory, suspicious. They called after her and she called back for them to watch cartoons. It was Saturday morning, and she didn't have any more answers for them. When Saturday afternoon rolled around Jordan opened the door to her bedroom and whispered to her that they were hungry.

"Eat some cereal," she lifted her head from the pillow to tell him.

"There's no more milk."

"Well then, make a peanut butter sandwich."

"We don't have any bread, Mom." She sat up on the bed, and the expression on her face caused her son to flinch.

"Jordan, you're almost nine years old. Surely you can look in that kitchen and find you and your brothers something to eat!" Tears welled up in her son's eyes and Hope felt guilty. She wasn't angry with him, she was angry with herself.

"*Please,* Jordan, help me out here!" Hope was on the verge of tears herself. "I don't feel well. Have a Pop-Tart, and then Mommy will get up and order a pizza in a little while, okay?" She lowered her voice slightly. Jordan wiped his tears, nodded, and closed the door just as quietly as he had opened it.

The first few weeks after Ray left, Hope always checked the caller ID before answering the telephone. She only picked up the phone when she saw that it was Ray, and then she would take a deep breath and speak with false cheeriness in her voice. "Hello?"

"Let me talk to the boys."

"Hello, Ray, how are you doing?" Or sometimes she would ask, "What time are you coming to pick them up?" He would never respond to her questions, he would just hold the phone silently until she called out for the boys. One day she whispered into the phone, "I'm not seeing him anymore, Ray. Can't we talk about this?"

It was the only time he had responded to her question. He asked, "Are you going to call the boys or not?"

After that she stopped answering the phone. She put a phone in the boys' room where they spent most of their time when they were at home, and they answered the phone when their father called.

She assumed that Ray was taking care of the mortgage and the car notes as he always had. He never asked her anything about her job; she didn't really know if he knew she spent her days at home like he had always wanted. Every Tuesday she got money from the ATM and sent the boys into the store for food. They could get whatever they wanted as long as they bought milk and cereal, bread and cold cuts, and canned ravioli, all of which could be enjoyed cold. When they needed something hot she ordered pizza or hamburgers.

Sometimes when the boys were at school, she would get out of bed and stand in front of the mirror naked, considering herself. She had lost weight, her skin was parched and itchy—she no longer slathered it with expensive perfumed lotions. Her hair had grown out of the sophisticated style she had taken so much pleasure in. It looked shaggy and unkempt; it was growing long the way Ray had always preferred it.

Tony called her for weeks, but since she only answered the phone for Ray, when she *was* answering the phone, she never spoke to him. She thought it was very arrogant of him to call the home that she had shared with her husband. He had heard through the grapevine that she and Ray had split—the grapevine of course being Lisa or Ralph—but *still,* she didn't appreciate him calling her house.

One day a package was delivered to her doorstep. It was from Tony. He had packaged all the bottles of perfume and lotions that had been waiting for her when she had gone to visit him at his house and sent them to her. *These are yours, Hope,* the note read. *I won't try to contact you again. If you ever want to talk, call me.* He didn't sign his name to the note. Hope immediately threw the box in the trash and used the little energy she had to rip the small note card to pieces. She opened her hands to let the small pieces flutter to the floor.

The leader of her pack, Jordan, started to wet the bed. Hope knew this because he and his two brothers had also started crawling into the bed with her sometime in the middle of the night. She never made them go back into their rooms; the only other time she spent with them was in the car, taking them to or picking them up from school or the Y, or their weekly trips to the grocery store. They didn't speak while they were riding in the car. In fact, Hope rarely opened her mouth.

She knew on some level that she was sick, but she didn't know what to do about it. She was sinking deeper into the hole that she dug for herself, and she didn't have the strength to even begin to pull herself out. And there was no one offering her a lifeline, a rope. Hope couldn't remember the last time Ray had stepped foot inside the house. When he came for the boys on the weekend he blew his horn and they all ran out. He was driving a dark green SUV now. She wondered whether he still had his two-seater, but by the time the boys got home, usually late Sunday night, the question was gone from her mind. She had stopped asking the boys about Ray a while back and assumed that he never asked them about her.

Tabitha had gotten a job at a major department store in New York, and from all reports—short messages she left periodically on the answering machine—was very busy living the high life.

After so many years, Stephanie had just stopped being her friend . . . just stopped after their last argument about Tony. Hope had never had a father, and her mother was dead. Her children were *children*. There was nobody to offer her a lifeline . . . nobody. At one time she had thought her life was so full, not enough time in the day to accomplish all that she had to accomplish. The phone rang off the hook, and she was always rushing to get somewhere or to get back from somewhere.

Her life had been filled with her husband, her job, her children, her friends, her mother—when she was alive—and then Tony. It was amazing to her that in the middle of life, a person could just *stop*, and life would continue on around them.

It seemed to Hope that her life had started grinding to a halt when her mother left her, and that Ray walking out of the door was the final screech of the brakes.

Chapter Thirty-seven

Hope sat on the side of the bed one Friday morning looking at the robe that she had thrown in the corner sometime the night before. She knew she was supposed to put the robe on so she could drive the boys to school. They were already late. She had told them over twenty minutes ago that she would be out in five minutes. It had taken her *that* long to sit up, and Hope knew that it would take her at least that amount of time to put the robe on. And then she would have to cover her hair with something . . . *another ten minutes*. And then she would have to find her keys . . . walk to the garage . . . She shook her head mentally. It was too much. She decided that her children would not be going to school that day.

Her body was dead weight as she moved back into the bed and lifted the covers over her as if she were an arthritic old woman. She turned on her side and watched the minutes tick away on the bedside clock as she did most mornings.

"Mom." Karl stood just inside the door, his brothers behind him. "Are you coming?"

Hope shifted her eyes from the clock to her children. "No, baby. I don't feel good. You can stay home today."

"But, Mom, we have our spelling test on Friday, and you never feel good anymore."

"I'll write you a note Monday, and Ms. Lester will give you a make-up test." Hope wanted them to leave so she could get back to staring at her clock.

"Ms. Lester was my teacher last *year*! And I don't want to take a make-up test." Karl screamed at her from the door.

In the past Hope would have jumped from the bed and demanded to know who he thought he was talking to in that tone of voice . . . but in the past she would not have been in the bed. In the past the boys would already be sitting at their desks at school. In the present she ignored him.

"What's wrong with you?" He half screamed, half shouted. She heard David, her littlest one, start to cry. *Heard* because her eyes were focused on the ceiling. "Mom! Mom! Mom!" She counted Karl scream about three times. She had never known a child to go on about missing a damn spelling test. She was relieved when Jordan told him, "Come on, Karl," and led him sniffling from the room, closing the door quietly behind them. Hope turned back to the clock and watched time slip away.

She was still looking at the clock forty-six minutes and twenty-two seconds later when Ray opened the bedroom door.

"What's wrong with you, Hope?" She moved her eyes but not her body to look at him; she hadn't actually laid eyes on him for several weeks.

"What are you doing here?" Her voice was hoarse.

"Jordan called me. He said you weren't taking them to school today." He stood in the door staring at her accusingly, waiting for an explanation. She didn't need a mirror to know how she looked. She could see it in his eyes. She struggled to sit up in bed and tried to smooth her hair some.

"I think I may be coming down with the flu," she lied. He didn't even pretend to believe her.

"The boys say you don't do anything but lie in the bed all day. This house is dirty, there's no food in the refrigerator . . . and Jordan is ready to go to school smelling like piss."

"Jordan wet the bed. He was supposed to take a shower."

"When did Jordan start wetting the bed?" He sounded outraged.

"I don't know."

He walked into the room and closer to the bed. Hope knew he was angry.

"Well, do you *know* that if he wets the bed it's *your* responsibility to make *sure* that he takes a shower?"

Hope let herself collapse against the pillow and closed her eyes before speaking again. "I can't do everything, Ray."

"The problem is, Hope, you ain't doing *shit*. I'm getting my children out of here." She opened her eyes long enough to see the disgust in his. His lip was practically curled. "I never would have imagined that you'd let yourself get like this."

"Fuck you, Ray." She muttered the words. He ignored her and walked back to the door.

"You need to get yourself together." It was the only advice he ever gave her. Whenever something was wrong, he would tell her to "get yourself . . . your shit together." He never had any suggestions as to how she should do it, just that it needed to be done.

"Did you hear me, Ray?" she shouted after him. "I said *fuck you* . . . fuck you!" She didn't know why she was angry with him, but she was. She stared at her clock angrily until she heard three car doors slam, then she relaxed against her pillow and counted the pieces of texture on the ceiling, unaware that tears were sliding down her cheeks.

Hope woke to the soft cries of a baby and a finger poking her in the shoulder. "Hope. Hope." The poking became more urgent and Hope was forced to open her eyes.

"Stephanie?" She was confused as she looked up at her former friend. She thought for a minute that she was dreaming until she heard another baby cry. *It's*—Hope had to search for the name of her goddaughter, it had been so long since she had seen her or her mother—*it's Tamara, Stephanie is here with Tamara.* Hope sat up and wiped her hands across her face. "What are you doing here?"

"Ray called me yesterday. He said that he had to pick up the boys because you were sick." Hope could tell by Stephanie's tone and facial expression that that was not all Ray had said. Stephanie sat down on the edge of the bed and looked at Hope closely. Concern was written all over her face. She put a pacifier in Tamara's mouth and placed a gentle hand on Hope's leg through the covers. "What's wrong?"

"There's nothing wrong with me."

"Ray said you stay in bed all day and that he thinks you quit your job."

"Well, you can tell Ray that I didn't quit my job. I got fired the day he walked out on me."

"Do you really think Ray walked out on you? He didn't walk out on you, Hope, he had to leave. From what I understand, he didn't have a choice."

Hope looked at her former friend angrily. "Is that what you came here for, Stephanie? To tell me how wrong I was? To tell me that I deserved everything that I got or didn't get? Well, you can save your breath."

"No, Hope, I came here because you're my friend and I love you, and I'm concerned about you."

"Yeah, right, Stephanie. The kind of friend that judges and deserts you if you do anything that she doesn't approve of." Hope continued to stare at Stephanie accusingly. Stephanie laid the baby on top of the comforter and stroked her back, encouraging her to sleep before speaking again.

"I'm sorry, Hope. You're right, that's exactly what I did. I judged you and I deserted you." Stephanie had tears glistening in her eyes when she looked at Hope. "I thought I was so mad at you . . . I *was* mad at you, but I was really still mad at Lamar for screwing around on me. And I was mad at myself for not having the courage to tell him what I needed to tell him. Then it seemed like you were doing the same thing that he had done . . . I don't know, Hope, but I know I've been wrong these last months and that I want you to forgive me. I should have been there for you; it was not my place to judge."

Hope started crying herself when Stephanie finished apologizing. She had needed to talk to her friend so many times over the last several weeks, but anger, shame, and the fear of being judged again had kept her from doing so. The two women embraced for long minutes, both smiling through their tears, relieved to be talking again.

After a while, Stephanie pushed Hope away gently and looked at her again. "What's going on, Hope? Why are you like this?" By "this" Hope knew Stephanie meant unkempt, too thin, crumpled.

"I just don't have any energy. All I want to do is sleep."

"I think you're depressed."

Hope laughed a little at that. The first time she had laughed in weeks. "I believe that that is an understatement."

Stephanie laughed too, but quickly became serious again. "I *mean* . . . you have to get up. You have to get yourself together."

"Get up for *what*?" Tears started rolling silently down Hope's cheeks. "Do you know what I've done, Stephanie? I've *ruined* my life! I betrayed my husband, I lost my job, and I've changed the way my children were supposed to live their lives. I figure if I stay in this room long enough it'll all go away." That's what she had been doing for the last several weeks, praying that "it" would go away.

"Hope, you've made some mistakes, but your life is not *ruined*."

"Look what I did. I risked everything and lost. And the saddest thing is I don't know *why* I did it. I'm so ashamed, Stephanie, and I'm so afraid." The enormity of the changes she had brought about in her life overwhelmed Hope. Stephanie held her in her arms until her sobs subsided.

"Hope, you haven't lost everything. You have your children—"

Hope cut her off. "I can't even look them in the eye!"

"Hope!" Stephanie's voice was strong and loud in the room—so strong it startled Hope. "You need to get up! Sometimes things happen in our lives that make us want to lie down and never get up. I felt like that when I found out about Lamar, but I didn't have that luxury. I had children who needed me, and so do you. Your children are scared to death. They don't know what to think. If you need to cry, cry at night, like we all do. You have too much to do during the day. You fucked up, Hope, I can't argue with you about that, but your life is not over, not unless you want it to be."

Stephanie wiped the tears from Hope's face and from her own and then reached over to pick up her sleeping baby. "I'm going out to get some food. I'll be right back to help you clean up. *You* get up and pull these sheets off the bed. Then you need to take a shower." Hope nodded thankfully before Stephanie left the room.

Hope sat on the shower floor and let the warm water pelt her head and body for several minutes. When she felt her legs were strong enough, she stood up slowly and reached for the soap. As she soaped her body she tried to form a plan, but found it was too difficult. She washed her hair with the same soap she used on her body, rinsed, and sat on the bathroom floor to dry off.

By the time Hope made her way to the kitchen, Stephanie was back from the store. Stephanie looked up from the kitchen sink and frowned at Hope's choice of clothing. She wore a robe and house shoes. "Why don't you go back and put on some jeans, Hope?"

Hope saw the baby carrier sitting on the bar and sat on one of the stools in front of the baby, ignoring Stephanie's question.

"I can't believe she's so big." She pulled off the sock

and stroked the soft skin on Tamara's foot and leg. The baby shifted in her sleep. Hope could hear the pride in Stephanie's voice when she spoke.

"She can stand up for a few seconds on her own. She may start walking any day now."

"They grow up so fast." It hurt Hope that she had missed so much of her goddaughter's first year, but it was her own fault. "What are the boys up to?"

"Nothing, driving me crazy as usual."

"And how is Lamar?" Hope thought about how he had looked at her the last time she saw him.

"Driving me crazy too." Something in Stephanie's voice changed and Hope looked back at her.

"Is everything all right?"

Stephanie's smile was tight. "Here, drink this." She took the bar stool next to Hope and handed her a glass of orange juice.

"Is everything all right, Stephanie?" Hope asked again.

"I didn't come here to talk about *me*. How are your boys? Ray brought them by the house a couple of weeks ago for a barbecue."

"Oh really? They didn't mention it." Hope laughed at herself and drank some orange juice. "Or maybe they did and I just don't remember." Tears filled her eyes again. "To be honest with you, Stephanie, I don't know how the boys are. I . . . I haven't been able to focus on them in a long time."

The two sat at the counter for what seemed like a long time, both lost in their own thoughts, staring at the baby before them. Stephanie spoke first.

"What happened with that guy you were seeing . . . Tony?"

At the mention of his name, Hope fought the urge to

slink back to bed and pull the covers over her head.
"Nothing."

"Nothing?" Stephanie gave Hope a "come on, girl"
look.

Hope put her head on the counter. Her words were
muffled.

"Stephanie, I don't want to talk about that. I don't
even know *how* to talk about it. It's over with us . . . it
has been for a while." There was more silence after
that; it was awkward trying to restart a friendship.

"What are you and Ray going to do?"

"I don't know, Stephanie. I don't care anymore. He
left me . . . that's that." Hope lifted her head and looked
at her friend. The short conversation had exhausted her
and she was ready for Stephanie to leave so she could
get back in bed. "I'm really tired, Stephanie. Thanks
for coming—"

Stephanie cut her off in the middle of her sentence.
"Drink this juice and I'll make you a sandwich."

Hope took the glass and drank deeply. "Thanks, but
I'm not hungry. The juice was enough."

Stephanie ignored her and took cold cuts and bread
from a bag on the counter. In the middle of preparing
the sandwich she looked back at Hope.

"Hope, you need to eat, and you need to do whatever you need to do to . . . to . . . get yourself together."
Now where have I heard that before? Hope wondered.
"Ray is talking about taking the kids. He says he won't
bring them back until you're ready to take care of
them."

"How am I supposed to take care of them? I can
barely get up in the morning."

Stephanie looked at her with very little sympathy. "I
don't know, Hope, that's for you to figure out. Your kids

shouldn't have to worry about this. They shouldn't have to witness their mother fall apart because she can't live with the choices that she made." Stephanie continued to talk and Hope heard the same old anger and judgment in her voice. She got up from the bar stool and walked back into her bedroom, leaving her former friend in the kitchen alone.

In her bedroom she let her robe drop to the floor and stood naked, looking at her soiled sheets. She had been meaning to change them for . . . days. She pulled the sheets from the bed and lay on the bare mattress before dragging the comforter from the floor and wrapping it around her body.

When she woke the first time it was dark outside and her house was quiet. When she woke again it was a new day . . . six o'clock in the morning. For a minute she listened for the familiar sounds of her children moving around the house, and then she remembered they were gone. She hadn't heard from them since Ray had taken them away. And then she thought about what Stephanie had said . . . that he was threatening to keep them away. The sense of relief that flooded through her made her sit upright in the bed. Did she want her kids? The question frightened her; the fact that she was confused about the answer frightened her more.

It was Sunday morning, and she was all alone, no husband, no mother, no children, no friends. The last thing she remembered putting in her stomach was the orange juice Stephanie had poured for her, and she couldn't remember if that was yesterday or the day before, but she wasn't hungry. When she looked at her clock she was startled again to see that it was seven-thirty. She hadn't moved from the bed and she didn't know what she had thought about for the last hour and a half. And she knew then that if she didn't get up, she would spend the next hour and the next in bed. She thought about Stephanie's words and knew that she was right . . . it was not a luxury she could afford.

She knew she had to get out of the bed and out of the house. She moved faster than she had moved in weeks. She pulled sweatpants and a sweatshirt from her drawer and slipped on her sneakers. She ran as if someone was chasing her to the kitchen and got her keys and her purse. Hope got into her truck and left her home, forgetting to wash her face, brush her teeth, or let the garage door down.

She drove around her neighborhood and then the outskirts of her neighborhood trying to focus on something. *I don't have the number to Ray's apartment . . . or at least I don't think I do. Even if I did have it, it's too early to call. And what would I be calling for? What would I say?*

Hope focused her attention on the cardboard box that had been sitting in the passenger seat for weeks. She had left it there when she had left the bank . . . or the bank had insisted that she leave. White flashed in the corner of her eye and she leaned over and plucked the small card from the box.

Guest Card
New View Christian Church
"What a friend you have in Jesus"

10092 Freemont
Sunday worship
10:00 A.M.
&
1 P.M.

After reading the card several times, Hope made a U-turn in the middle of the empty road. She drove in the direction of the church almost desperately, the refrain "What a friend you have in Jesus" playing over and over again in her mind. Although she could count on her hands the number of times they had attended church when she was a little girl, her mother would half hum/half sing the song often.

The parking lot was almost empty when Hope arrived. The church was an impressive structure, expansive, with many annexes. The grounds leading up to the main entrance were beautifully landscaped. She turned off her engine and sat alone in the parking lot.

After a while cars started entering the lot. Her eyes followed the people as they moved toward the church. Well-dressed people. Couples, singles, couples and singles with children. One family in particular caught her eye. A single woman, smiling and talking to the occupants of the backseat of her gray Ford. She had on a blue dress and her hair was hanging straight on her shoulders. It was the woman from the bank.

Hope watched as two children climbed out of the backseat. The woman inspected both children, like Hope would do with her boys an eternity ago. The woman straightened the boy's collar and smiled approvingly at the girl. Hope watched her as she put her purse on her shoulder and hugged her children close. They walked into the church, a seemingly happy family. Hope thought of her own family, and tears from nowhere started coursing down her face.

Chapter Thirty-eight

Hope sat in the back of the church and listened to the choir sing as she waited for the minister to take his place behind the pulpit. She didn't sing along although she knew the words. Her hands were folded across her lap; she didn't want to move or speak. She didn't want to draw attention to herself.

Someone thanked the choir for their "inspiring performance" and asked that "God lead Pastor Mike during his sermon today." Then a casually dressed man stepped behind the pulpit and asked that everybody say amen. It was Tony's friend. She hadn't realized she was in his church. He led the church in a short prayer before telling them that the message today would be about harvest.

As he spoke, Hope continued to sit quietly in her seat, but she felt as if he was speaking directly to her. "My mother has been telling me since I was a little boy, 'what goes around comes around.' The Bible says, 'you reap what you sow.' Now, I'm sure that everyone in this room has heard that before, but periodically we have to be reminded of what it *means*. We like to use Mama's expression and we can quote the Bible book, chapter, *and* verse. 'She gon' get hers, Rodney has a brain tumor, they don't give him long to live . . . remember how he treated Debra? The Bible says you reap what you sow.'

" 'You reap what you sow' is a natural law, but we are so busy trying to see how it manifests itself in the lives of others that we don't pay attention to the seedlings we're throwing in the air. Our *actions* are the *seeds* that we plant. I want you to take a minute and think about what you've been planting lately."

And Hope did. She saw where she had planted seeds of judgment, and discontent, disloyalty, and unhappiness, and she had gotten it back twofold.

Before the sermon was over, Pastor Mike told them to think about what was missing in their lives and challenged them to start planting the seeds of whatever that was. If they needed love, he suggested that they be more loving. "If you wish for forgiveness . . . be more forgiving." He said other things that struck a chord in Hope's soul, and at the end of the service when he asked that anyone who needed to replant their garden and start again come to the altar for a special prayer, Hope stood up immediately and walked to the front of the church and fell to her knees.

"Dear Lord," Pastor Mike started, "we come humbly before you and ask you for the strength that we need to rebuild our gardens . . . our lives, Lord. We know, Lord, that we have sown seeds that are not to your liking, and we ask for your forgiveness, Lord, and forgiveness from those who our actions have affected."

Tears streamed down her face as she prayed sincerely with the minister. It was exactly what she needed in her life . . . forgiveness. She needed to forgive herself so she could make things right. She prayed for God to show her what was right; she asked for forgiveness many times over, and when the pastor was done, Hope stayed on her knees. When everyone else was back in their seats, Hope stayed on her knees. When the pastor left the pulpit to kneel beside her, she stayed on her knees.

"Please, God." Her lips moved silently as she made the simple request over and over again. When the pastor placed a hand on her back, she started sobbing. Sobs shook her body and she would have fallen on her back if the pastor had not been beside her offering his support. Hope was barely aware when someone else knelt beside her and helped her to her feet. She was led sobbing from the sanctuary. She had not done a very good job of not drawing attention to herself.

When Hope stopped crying enough to take the tissue that was being offered to her, she looked up and took note of her surroundings. Women stood on either side of her. The lady from the bank was there and so was Ellen, Pastor Mike's wife. They stood behind her, rubbing her shoulders, offering words of encouragement.

"Hope, right?" Ellen questioned softly from her left side.

"Yes." Hope's voice was quiet also. "You have a good memory."

"Not really. We just happened to have met under very memorable circumstances." Ellen laughed gently.

Hope was too exhausted to laugh and too exhausted

to be embarrassed. "Yes, it seems as if I can't stop making a fool of myself in your presence."

"You didn't make a fool of yourself. I'm glad you're here."

"I'm glad you're here also. Believe it or not, you've really been on my mind." It was the lady from the bank . . . Hope didn't know her name.

"I appreciate that." She tried to turn her lips up in semblance of a smile, but failed. "Well, I guess I'd better be going. Thanks again for your help." Hope rose from the chair and found that her legs wouldn't support her. She fell back into the chair awkwardly and covered her face with her hands.

"Clarise," Ellen whispered above her head. "Let me talk to her alone for a minute."

Hope heard the door close behind the woman from the bank . . . Clarise. She felt Ellen leave her side for a moment, and when she looked up, Ellen sat facing her.

"I take it that you don't think things are going too well for you right now. Do you want to talk about it?"

"There's nothing to talk about."

"If I remember correctly, you were having some marital problems. Has that been resolved?"

"Pretty much. My husband left me."

"And Tony? How are things going with Tony?"

"I don't know . . . I don't speak to Tony anymore. I haven't spoken to him since the night of your party." Hope's voice held no emotion. "I really need to get going."

Ellen held up her hand to stop Hope from moving. "Wait a minute, Hope. It seems to me that you need some help. Too often we try to manage things that are unmanageable or that we aren't able to manage on our own. I'm a therapist, Hope. A Christian counselor. I oversee a women's group here at the church, and I also have a private practice. I can look at you and tell that you've been crying for a long time."

"I have, and I'm so tired of crying." As she said the words, Hope felt more tears welling up inside.

"Then stop it." She said the words as if it were as simple as that. She leaned forward in her chair and took Hope's hands in hers. "I wouldn't normally offer this, because I know Tony and I have a feeling that he is some of what's bothering you, but I feel like you're here today for a reason. And I can't see you in such pain without offering my services. If you would like to come to my office next week and talk, I can make room for you on my calendar."

See a therapist? It was something Hope had never considered. "I don't know. I think I just need to go home."

"All right." Ellen patted her hand before releasing it. "But take my card and think about it." She handed her a simple white card. Hope folded it in the palm of her hand without looking at it, and waited with her head slightly bent while Ellen led her out the side door of the church.

Later that evening, Hope picked up the phone and called Ray. "Hello, Ray, I was calling to speak to the boys."

"Really, that surprises me."

Hope took the bait. "Why does that surprise you, Ray?"

He ignored her question and she heard him calling for the boys to come to the phone. She spoke to each of her sons in turn, from the youngest to the oldest. They asked how she was doing, but they didn't ask about coming home. Their conversations were strained, even with her youngest. It was as if she were trying to reestablish contact after being away from them for a long time. She realized that was exactly what she was trying to do. She said "I love you" to Karl before hanging up and he said, "I love you too, Mom." Her words and his response both sounded empty to her.

Twenty minutes later she called Ray again.

"Hello."

"Ray, it's Hope."

"What is it now?" He made no attempt to hide the irritation in his voice.

"I need to talk to you."

"So start talking."

"I was thinking that we could meet sometime tomorrow."

"There's nothing that we need to meet and talk about."

"Ray, *please*. I know how you feel, but we can't do this forever."

"You don't know a *damn* thing about how I feel. And I don't plan on doing this forever. I've hired a lawyer and I suggest you do the same." He hung up before she could say another word.

Hope sat in the middle of her bed and felt tears forming again. She remembered what Ellen had said earlier in the day and refused to let her tears fall. Stephanie had been right also, it was a luxury to wallow in self-pity and tears . . . a luxury she could no longer afford. She knew what she had to do. She was through crying.

*   *   *

The following morning Hope dressed as if she were going to work. She looked into the mirror before leaving her house and acknowledged that she looked better than she had in weeks; she also acknowledged that that wasn't saying very much. Her slacks hung loosely on her hips, and even though she had applied her make-up with a heavy hand she had not been able to do much to disguise the bags and circles under her eyes.

When she drove into the parking lot of Ray's office building, she sat in her truck for long minutes before turning off the engine. She had spent the previous night rehearsing what she was going to say to Ray. She had not told him she was coming to his office, but she was sure it was the only way she could get him to listen to her without causing too much of a scene.

When she reached his floor, a woman she didn't recognize sat at the receptionist's desk. It crossed her mind that when she and Ray were both working downtown they had very rarely had lunch together. "May I help you?" The polite smile on the woman's face didn't reach her eyes.

"Yes, I'm here to see Ray Williams."

"Do you have an appointment?"

"No, could you please just tell him that Hope is here." She couldn't fix her lips to tell the woman that she was his wife. The woman spoke quietly into the telephone before looking up and giving Hope permission to go in.

"What are you doing here?" Ray looked up from the paperwork strewn across his desk.

"I came to talk to you."

"I thought I told you last night that we didn't have anything to talk about."

"I know you did, Ray, but that's not true." Though he

didn't invite her to, Hope sat in one of the chairs in front of his desk. "I've been thinking about what you said a few months ago. Remember, you said that I needed to get my shit together." She laughed awkwardly as Ray continued to stare at her from across the desk. "Well, you were right in a lot of ways, but I wasn't listening. I want the opportunity to try and do that now. Last night you said that you were getting a lawyer. I know I don't have the right to ask, but I would like to put that off for a while."

"I agree. You *don't* have the right to ask. Now, if that's all you came to say, I have work to do."

"Ray, please!"

"Please what, Hope? Give you some more time so you can figure out some other ways to destroy my family?"

"No, Ray. Give me some time to figure out what went wrong. I talked to Tabitha last night. She still has her apartment here, and she said I could use it if I needed to. I was thinking that you could move back into the house with the boys and that I could use her place for a few weeks."

"Are you saying that you don't want your children now?"

"It's not that I don't want them, Ray. I can't really care for them right now. It hasn't been good for them seeing me like this. I can't take care of the house. It would really be best if they were with you right now."

"You know, Hope, the one thing that I could always count on is that you would do exactly what you wanted regardless of how it affected anyone else. So now, because it *suits* you, you want to shirk your responsibilities to your children."

"That's not fair, Ray . . . that's not what I'm trying to

do. I'm trying to do what's *right*, not just for me, but for you and the boys too."

Ray's laugh was full of contempt. "I don't give a fuck what you do. I'll bring the boys back to the house tomorrow. It would be great if you were already gone."

"Ray—"

He cut her off before she could finish her sentence. "I'm not trying to hear what you have to say. I'll hire somebody to look after the boys when I can't. Just please yourself like you always have. Now, like I said, I have work to do."

Hope stood up slowly from the chair. She could tell from Ray's expression that it would do no good for her to continue to try explaining to him. She walked toward the door, and just as she was about to turn the knob Ray called out from behind her.

"I must say, Hope, you look like shit. I guess that grass is not as green as you thought it would be." His laugh was full of bitterness and spite, and she was glad that she had not turned around to face him.

Chapter Thirty-nine

"So how did it go this weekend?" Ellen directed the question to where Hope was sitting on the couch in her office. Hope had started seeing her the day after she left Ray's office.

"It was fine. The kids were happy to see me, and I didn't realize I had missed them so much."

"How long had it been?"

"Three weeks. I hadn't seen them since Ray picked them up for school that day. That's the longest period of time I have gone without seeing them since they were born."

"How is Ray doing?"

"I don't know. The kids say a lady picks them up from school and makes dinner every night."

"How do you feel about that?"

"About what?"

"About someone else taking responsibility for your children?"

"I don't necessarily like it, but I know I need this

time, and this week I'm going to talk to Ray about keeping them with me one night and taking them to school the next morning."

"That's great." Ellen smiled at her encouragingly before looking down at a notepad that she held loosely in her hand. "Friday you were talking about your mother and her expectations of you."

"Yeah. I've been thinking about that too. My mother never really had any good experiences with men until she met her husband. So all my life she told me what I needed to do to be okay, and then when I met Ray, her entire conversation changed."

"What do you mean?"

"When I was growing up she would say things like, 'go to school,' 'keep your panties up and your dress down.' That was her *favorite*." Hope laughed as she remembered the conviction with which her mother would repeat the instructions; then she continued soberly. "She told me what I should give a man."

"And what was that?"

"Nothing. She would say, and I quote, 'don't ever give a man nothing.' She made herself a living example for me. Every time something would go wrong in her relationship she would say, 'see what I mean?'"

"Sometimes mothers tell their daughters things to try to protect them. Is that what you think your mother was doing?"

"I understand that. But she changed without any explanation. She *loved* Ray. When I told Ray I would marry him, I told him I wanted to wait until I finished grad school. He didn't want to wait, but my *mother* . . . I think she thought that if we waited, Ray would change his mind. She kept telling me how lucky I was to have a man who was willing to take care of me."

"Do you think maybe she was projecting some of her own desires and feelings onto you? From what you've told me so far, her life wasn't very easy."

"I don't know, but I do know it made me feel bad . . . unsure." Hope shifted gears suddenly and sat up straighter on the couch. "I don't want to talk about my mother anymore. She died long before I got myself into this mess."

"Why don't you want to talk about it?"

"Because I don't want to be one of those women who come to therapy to complain about my mother or cry about the fact that I never had a father."

"What's wrong with that?"

Hope opened her mouth and closed it several times before speaking again. "I don't know."

"If you have some negative feelings about your mother, it doesn't mean that you didn't love her or that you didn't appreciate the things that she did for you. I know from personal experience and from many of my clients that not having a father can have a profound impact on us."

Hope picked up her purse from the seat next to her and stood up. "I have to go."

Ellen stood up and smiled softly. "We have more time, but if you need to go, I'll see you on Wednesday?"

Hope knew it was a question, but she left the office without answering.

Hope sat in the living room of her friend's apartment flipping through the channels on the TV. It was seven o'clock and she hadn't eaten dinner. She was waiting for the clock to strike eight so she could call her children and ask about their day, and wish them sweet dreams. She could hardly remember the time when her daily routine had included working all day, picking the boys up from the Y, cooking dinner, getting the boys to bed at a reasonable time, and doing whatever she needed to do to entertain her husband. She never really had time to sit down and rest; now all she did was rest, but she was more tired than she had ever been. She wondered if it was possible to have some sort of happy medium.

She had been determined to put her life back together, but sometime during the last several weeks she had realized that it was almost impossible to do because her life was on the opposite side of town. Ray still refused to say more than two words to her. She had told Ellen that her weekend visit with the boys had gone well, and it had . . . as well as it could go with sullen, angry children.

She went to Lighthouse two times a week— Wednesday for Bible study, and Sunday for morning service. But every night when she got on her knees to pray, she became scared. Scared to ask God for what she really wanted, thinking that she didn't really deserve forgiveness, didn't deserve another chance with her family. And there was always that voice that came from nowhere telling her that she didn't really want a family, that she never had been committed to being a wife and a mother. That she should cut her losses and leave it alone. The voice frightened her more than anything, because sometimes it made the most sense.

"Are you ever gonna come home, Mommy?" Jordan whispered into the telephone so as not to be overheard.

"I told you, Jordan. I don't know what's going to happen. But I do know that I love you and your daddy loves you and you'll always be taken care of. I'm going to see you again tomorrow."

"I know you don't like Daddy anymore, but can't you come home anyway?"

"I never told you that I don't like your daddy. Who told you that?"

"Nobody, I just know. You're never coming home . . . why don't you just say it." His voice was no longer hushed, he was sobbing into the phone.

"Jordan! Jordan!" Then he was gone and Ray was on the line.

"I would appreciate it if you would not call here and upset the boys. They have enough to deal with, and you constantly add to it." He hung up without giving her a chance to respond.

"I've been thinking a lot about our last conversation about my mother. And I think you were right. I am mad at her. I tried to make my life everything that she wanted for me, and I never took the time to think about what I wanted for myself."

"I'm not sure I understand." Ellen smiled encouragingly at her.

"I mean she wanted me to have this *husband* and this *house* and this *job*, and if I ever hinted at wanting something different, she just shut me down. I don't think she really wanted those things *for* me, I think that she wanted them *through* me. And then she was dead and I had all of these *things* and I didn't even know if I wanted them . . . if I had *ever* wanted them. Now it just doesn't seem fair. Sometimes I think I should just forget about everything and start over."

Hope looked up, surprised, because Ellen was chuckling softly to herself.

"Is what I just said funny to you?"

Ellen sat up straighter in her chair and looked Hope directly in the eye. "I'm going to do you a favor. I could allow you to continue to come here for months and examine *every* aspect of your life, and then you could come here for several more months and examine every aspect of your mother's life, and then your *marriage* and so on and so forth, but you don't have that much time. I'm going to be totally honest with you. You came here to figure out what went wrong in your life. Let me tell you—you were greedy and spoiled.

"Many women come in here with your same problem. Their husbands don't give them the attention that they desire, they work hard, their children get on their last nerve . . . they become *discontent*. To deal with their discontentment, some women work obsessively, some women start to mistreat their children, some women tune out, and some women like you, Hope, have affairs. That's the easy way out, Hope.

"I've listened to you talk about your husband, and I can see that there were some problems in your marriage. I also know by listening to you that you *contributed* to the problems. Every marriage has problems. It's hard for people to live together. You met Tony and decided to step out and see if the grass was greener on the other side of the fence. Men and women do that every day.

"And when it turned out that the grass was not only *not* greener, but that it was the same *type* of grass, you became depressed. I could send you to a doctor who could prescribe a pill for your depression, but that's not going to fix the problem."

Hope was offended. "I didn't come here for you to

judge me. You invited *me* to *your* office . . . you said that you could help."

"Hope, I *can* help you; that's what I'm trying to do. I'm not judging you . . . it's not my place. I'm telling you what I've observed in the weeks that I've been seeing you. You haven't *said* it, but I know that you want what you gave up. Your home, responsibility for your children, your *husband*."

"Ray has made it clear that he doesn't want me anymore. He's not even civil toward me. I've told him that I'm sorry, I've told him that I don't see Tony anymore . . . I've told him that I'm trying to get my life back together. What am I supposed to do? Beg him?"

"Yes, that's exactly what you're supposed to do. You're supposed to tell him over and over again how sorry you are until he hears you. You're supposed to put your pride aside and listen to what he has to say to you without becoming defensive or angry. You are to *truly* humble yourself and wait for the true healing that can happen in your marriage. You are not supposed to come in here and examine everything but the actions that got you into your present situation so that you can shift the blame to your mother, or your husband, or anybody other than yourself. I can't let you take the easy way out again. That's how I can be of help to you."

Hope sat with her eyes closed as she absorbed what she had just been told. Ellen was right—she did want her family back, but she wanted things to be better if possible. The total truth was that if things could not be better than what they had been, she still wanted her family back . . . she wanted her husband back. "What do I need to do?"

"You need to get a job. You need to start being a mother to your children again . . . they really need you. You need to have some sort of closure with Tony—"

Hope cut her off. "Are you saying that I need to see him again?"

"No, I'm not. You don't have to meet with him to let him know that you're never going to see him again. Write him a letter, explain to him what happened. Explain to him what's really important in your life."

"Have you seen Tony?"

"We've seen Tony, and I think that he needs some closure also."

"How is he doing?"

"He's not doing well, but that's not your fault. He knew what he was getting involved in. As adults we reap the consequences of our actions."

"I don't miss Tony. That's so strange, because for months I thought he was my only friend. I believe at one point I may have thought I was in love with him."

"Sometimes the price you pay for a relationship ruins it."

"I guess so." Sitting on the sofa talking with Ellen, Hope felt more in control than she had in months; she felt in control enough to voice the question that had plagued her since Ray had left their home. "What if Ray doesn't want me back? What if it's really over?"

Ellen walked around her desk and sat with Hope on the sofa. She took her hands gently into her own and smiled softly at her.

"Then that's the consequence that *you* reap, and you learn to live with the choices that you made."

Hope thanked the therapist with her eyes for her honesty. "Should I come back next week?"

"No, the next time you come back I expect that you will have your husband with you. I'd like to see the two of you together."

Chapter Forty

Tony,

I'm sure you're surprised to get this letter from me. I'm surprised to be writing it myself. I hardly know what to say, so if I ramble on please forgive me. I hope that your business is doing well and that everything has worked out or *is* working out with your daughter.

I guess I'm writing to explain to you from my point of view what happened between us, and *why* it happened. I really felt a connection with you. I know we ended very abruptly and there are some things that I need to say to you.

You came along at a time when I was lonely and scared . . . I don't believe I knew how lonely and scared I was until I met you. I was confused about my marriage, and was unsure about what form I wanted my life to take during the next thirty to forty years.

I was lost and I didn't know why or what to do

about it. To be honest, I still haven't figured it out. I had three children and a husband who wanted me to depend on him and consult him about *everything*. I was so uncomfortable with that, with letting go and allowing myself to be a wife and a mother. For me that was hard . . . remember, I'm a woman who grew up with a mother who was living proof that a woman should not depend on a man. And it seemed as if Ray wanted me to give up my job and my dreams and depend on him for everything . . . he did want that. I know for some women that's a dream come true, but I wasn't one of them. The thought of him having so much control over my life scared the shit out of me. I couldn't say that to him, though, and I couldn't admit it to myself, so I fought against him, and he fought against me.

Now here you come, and suddenly there's a man in my life who thinks what I want makes sense. I had something separate and apart from Ray and the boys, something he couldn't control or criticize because he didn't know anything about it. And then when he did find out—I don't know why, but I felt like if I stopped seeing you at that point it would be him making the decision for me, that I would be giving up control to him. Does that sound crazy? It sounds crazy to me, because now I know that I should have stopped seeing you at that point—that I never should have started seeing you in the first place. I think I was trying to prove something to him. Your attention was nice, flattering, and so good mainly because I knew it was something that I shouldn't be entertaining.

Didn't I tell you that I would probably ramble on? What I guess I'm trying to say is that I'm sorry for allowing you to involve yourself so deeply in my life. I got caught up, Tony. We got caught up together. I was looking for an escape. You were something to look forward to.

When I would have an argument with Ray or he did something that I didn't like, I would think about you. Sometimes I think that I *stayed* mad at him deliberately so I would have an excuse to go on seeing you. Wait! That sounds like I was using you, doesn't it? I don't believe that I used you any more than I think you took advantage of me. We're both adults. Remember you told me that first night we were together that I needed to go into it with my eyes open? I thought I could, but now I realize that at that point in my life it was impossible for me to go into anything with my eyes open.

You asked me several times when we were seeing each other if I loved you. I never answered you because even in the thick of it I knew I didn't love you like family . . . not like I love my husband . . . not like I love my children. I knew that, but I pushed it to the back of my mind. I liked you, Tony, maybe I even loved you for a while, but that's not enough.

I'm trying to put my life back together. Ray and I are still living in separate places. I'm staying in a friend's place for now. Sometimes it takes getting what you *think* you want in order to know what you *really* want. I don't want to be apart from my husband and my children, and I'm committed to doing whatever I need to do to put my family back together. I guess that includes letting you know what my plans are and making sure you know that we made a mistake and that I'll never walk down that road again.

I made a commitment when I married Ray, I made a commitment when I had my children, and it was childish and selfish of me to allow myself to become involved with something that could prevent me from seeing it through.

Please don't write me back, Tony. I know that may seem unfair, but I can't be concerned about that right now.

I wish you everything good that life has to offer.

Hope

Chapter Forty-one

After she dropped the letter to Tony in the mail, it took Hope another month to figure out exactly what she wanted to say to Ray and then another week to build up enough nerve to broach the subject.

She had started spending more time with her boys and had been looking into getting her real-estate license. She decided she needed a job more flexible than any she could find in the banking industry, and she could fulfill her dream of helping people find afford-able housing, *and* she could work from a home office. Where exactly the home office would be depended en-tirely on Ray's reaction to her . . . *proposition?*

As she drove closer to the house, the tension in her stomach grew. She was taking the boys back to Ray after spending a three-day weekend with them. She was so busy practicing her speech in her head that she didn't realize she had passed the house until the boys started protesting loudly in the backseat.

"Okay, okay!" Hope's voice was equally loud. She pulled into a neighbor's drive and turned the truck around. Ray had to have been waiting at the door because as soon as she pulled into the drive, he walked out of the house and toward the truck. He motioned for her to open the back door but did not look at her. The boys climbed out of the car excitedly, ready to get back to their room and video games after being without for the weekend.

He didn't speak to Hope and waited on the side of the drive as the boys said their good-byes. He was following the boys back into the house when Hope called out to him. "Ray. Ray," she called a second time after he didn't respond.

He said something to the boys and they went into the house before he turned around to face her. "What is it?"

He won't even say my name. "Do you have a few minutes? I need to talk to you about something."

"What is it?" he repeated again with even less patience.

Hope opened the door and stepped out of the truck. She smoothed the fabric of her pants. She had taken special care with her make-up and her clothes that morning; she didn't want to give Ray the opportunity to say that she still looked terrible.

"Is it okay if we go inside?"

"I have a lot to do, Hope."

Her instinct was to get back into the truck and leave, but she remembered what Ellen had said about taking the easy way out. "Please, Ray. I promise that I won't take up too much of your time."

He walked away from her without answering, but he left the door open and Hope walked in after him. She

followed him to the den and he sat in one chair and she
sat in a chair opposite him.

"So how was your weekend?" She tried to sound
pleasant, but her voice broke.

"I don't have the time or the desire to make small
talk, Hope. What is it?"

Hope opened her mouth to speak, and the speech
that she had been practicing for days deserted her, so
she started speaking from her heart.

"I'm so sorry about the way things are between us. I
never thought in a million years that we'd ever be like
this."

"What did you think, Hope? That I'd sit back and let
you fuck other men to your heart's content without ever
saying a word?"

He is not going to make this easy for me. "Ray,
please, can you just hear me out? I know that you're
angry and that this is hard for you, but believe it or not
it's hard for me too." She paused for a minute, and was
encouraged when he didn't say anything negative. "I
haven't seen Tony since before you left the house that
time. That was the biggest mistake of my life."

"Not seeing your lover?" He was being sarcastic,
deliberately misunderstanding her. But she remembered what she had decided was important and kept her
tone humble.

"No, Ray, getting involved with him in the first
place. Betraying you . . . betraying myself. I wish that
there were some way for you to look into my soul and
see how sorry I am. I was confused and angry with you
for a lot of reasons that didn't make sense—"

He cut her off midsentence. "So you wanted to tell
me again that this shit is all my fault."

Hope closed her eyes briefly and tried to remember the important parts of her speech, but she couldn't.

"What I did was not your fault, Ray. I made my own choice. What I'm saying is that I've never regretted anything so much in my life. I know that you're a good man and a good father, and I was stupid because I didn't appreciate what I had. And at some point I would like for us to sit down and talk about what happened with our marriage. Whenever you feel ready."

You're supposed to be doing that now, she reminded herself. But she couldn't continue with Ray looking at her with such dislike. She decided to put off the conversation until another time. *Easy way out! Easy way out!* Hope shushed the voice in her head and smiled politely at Ray. He didn't return her smile.

"I don't have any questions about what went wrong in our marriage." He stared at her pointedly for a few seconds before standing up. "Like I said, I have things to do."

"I'm thinking about going to real-estate school. That way I can have a flexible schedule, possibly work from home." She spoke to his back as she followed him to the back door.

"Is that right?" His tone let her know that he couldn't care less. "I wondered how a woman so concerned with having a career could stand doing nothing all day."

She let his comment go by without one of her own. He opened the door and stood aside so that she could pass. She didn't want to leave.

"Well, I'll just say good-bye to the boys again before I leave."

"Boys!" he shouted toward their bedroom without

releasing the doorknob. "Your mother wants to say good-bye . . . *again*."

The boys came running out of the bedroom to kiss and hug their mother again. She still didn't want to leave. She stood in the doorway and realized that though it might not be the right time, she couldn't leave without saying what she really needed to say. She looked down at her three sons and back up at their father before speaking.

"I have something that I need to say to you." She took a deep breath and swallowed hard, stalling as she searched for the words that would make him understand how she felt.

Ray looked at his sons near her, almost surrounding her. "You boys go back to your room. Apparently your mother and I aren't quite finished talking."

She needed their support. When she looked down at her boys again she found the words that she needed. When she looked back up at Ray, her eyes were glassy with unexpressed emotions.

"I know we've been through a lot. I know that I've put you through a lot. I love you, Ray, with all my heart—I always have—even though I did what I did." She let go of her son's hand to wipe the tears that had fallen on her cheeks.

"I've never asked you to forgive me. I said I was sorry and I meant it, but I've been too arrogant to ask for forgiveness. I asked God every night, but now I'm asking you. *Please* forgive me."

She crossed her palms in front of her. The boys were perfectly still beside her. "And if you can forgive me, let me come home. The boys need me here. I need you." She wiped her nose with the back of her hand.

The boys moved closer to her as her tears started to fall more rapidly; they started to whimper at her side.

"I can't promise you that things will be perfect. I'm not perfect. But I promise that what happened before won't *ever* happen again, and if you let me, I'll spend the rest of my life making it up to you." What else could she say? What else could she do? If she knew how to be more humble, she would be.

"It's not that easy." He said the words quietly; it was obvious to her that he was struggling with his own emotions.

"Why not? Why can't it be that easy? We're a family."

"Boys, go to your room." They walked away reluctantly, but they knew from their father's tone that there was no room for argument. When he was sure the boys couldn't hear him, he started speaking.

"I can't believe you just did that. Obviously you have no idea of what we've been going through around here."

"I do, Ray," she protested.

"No, you don't!" he shouted back at her. "Because if you did, you wouldn't have pulled that bullshit stunt. I can't believe how selfish you are. To say what you just said in front of the boys? I guess you thought if you put me on the spot I would *have* to take you back. Say, 'Oh yes, Hope, I've been keeping your side of the bed warm.' Hell no!

"Now it's going to look to the boys like I'm the one who split this family up. It kills me that you think you can come back here, bat your eyes, drop a few tears on the floor, and all is forgiven. Well, I *don't* forgive you, Hope, maybe I never will."

His words dripped with anger and contempt, but she was startled by the fact that they didn't scare her. She had said what she needed to say. She *hadn't* taken the easy way out.

"I'm not going to press you about it. I'm just going to wait for your heart to open so that we can be the family that we're supposed to be." She smiled at him and let her hand fall back down to her side. "Have I told you how much I appreciate you for keeping things stable for the boys?" His eyes narrowed, and Hope knew he was trying to figure out if she was setting a trap for him.

"No, you haven't."

"Well, I *do.*" She didn't say anything, but stood looking at her husband for a minute longer. "Kiss the boys goodnight for me," she requested. "I'll call them tomorrow."

Ray nodded his head, and his expression told her that he wanted her to leave. She wanted to hug him, to smooth her hand over his head and tell him again that she loved him, but it wasn't the right time.

She walked through the door and heard him close it behind her. When she was well on her way back to her temporary residence, a smile lit her face. The trees seemed taller and the flowers were more vivid than they had been in months. It was time for her to enroll in that real-estate class. *As soon as possible,* she decided.

The short conversation that Hope had with her husband played over and over again in her head. Ray had said that he might never forgive her. The more she thought about it, the broader her smile became. For some women his words would have been disheartening. But Hope knew Ray; he had made no attempt to hide his anger, but she had looked beyond the anger and caught a glimpse of something else . . . the possibility of forgiveness. He hadn't laughed at her, he hadn't thrown her out of the house, and he hadn't told her to look for divorce papers. *Maybe, Ray said maybe.* For now that was enough.

Chapter Forty-two

There was no room in Hope's new life for unaddressed situations. She had given Ray an opening—whether he took it or not was solely up to him. Three days before, she had dropped by the bank to see her former boss. Not to plead for her old job; she didn't *want* the job. She wanted to let him know that she was grateful for the time that she had spent at the bank . . . that she had learned a lot, and to let him know that she could smile . . . that she was okay.

There was another unaddressed situation in her life. She had weighed the positives and negatives for leaving things as they were between her and Stephanie. They hadn't talked in months. Initially, Hope had been fine with that, but at the end of the day, she wanted her friend back.

She lifted the nickel plated knocker and rapped hard on the door four times. After thirty seconds, she did it again. When Stephanie opened the door, Hope could tell from the expression on her face that she had seen her through the peep hole. Stephanie stood with one hand on the door and one hand on her hip.

"Yes?" Stephanie challenged her.

"I'm mad at you," Hope told her quietly. A look of surprise and then anger crossed Stephanie's face. She took two steps out of the door and closed it behind her.

"You're mad at *me*? I haven't done anything but try to help you. You may not remember this, but I came to your house to help, and you left me standing in the middle of your kitchen. I took it that you didn't *want* my help."

"You came to my house to say, 'I told you so.' That was the *last* thing I needed to hear. You judged me and left no doubt that you found me lacking." Hope looked at her best friend and realized that she was not as mad as she was hurt. "I didn't think that was the kind of friendship we had."

Stephanie took a deep hard breath. "So I'm not supposed to express my feelings? I was supposed to pretend that I didn't know that you had screwed up your life?"

Hope sat down on where she was standing and leaned her head back against the warm brick. "No, you were supposed to say, but then you were supposed to be there for me. You weren't *there* for me, Stephanie."

Stephanie opened her mouth to protest, but instead she sat on the step next to Hope. "I was mad at you. That had to be the *stupidest* thing you've ever done."

Hope gave Stephanie a warning look from the corner of her eye. "I think you were mad at Lamar." Stephanie shrugged her shoulders. "You *had* to forgive him, so you transferred all your negative feelings about cheaters to me. I was your scapegoat."

Stephanie started laughing. "Please, Mrs. Freud, can

we do this without the amateur psychoanalysis? Looks like you think you've got *you* all figured out, but let *me* figure me out. Okay?" Hope laughed too.

"Fine with me, but I was just trying to save you some money." The women laughed together. Hope's expression sobered and she looked at Stephanie. "I just want my friend back. I want to move forward and let bygones be bygones. I want to see my goddaughter. You know when she gets older, she's gonna need me to sneak her out of the house to take her to get her hair relaxed when you refuse to," Hope teased.

"That'll happen over my dead body or yours." They sat in silence for a minute, and then Stephanie said, "I'm sorry, Hope. I want my friend back too." Hope grabbed Stephanie's hand and squeezed it. They would always be friends.

"What's happening between you and Ray?"

"You don't know?"

"Well, the last I heard, you told him you wanted to come home."

"I did, and I do." Stephanie looked doubtful.

"You think he'll go for that?"

"I think it's a *possibility. Your* marriage survived infidelity."

"Yeah, but the difference is, I'm a woman and Ray isn't. Men aren't as forgiving as we are, Hope."

Hope sighed and stood up. "I know that, but I also know that Ray loves me. You know what I've been discovering Stephanie?" She didn't wait for her response before continuing. "I've discovered that if we *let* them, one way or another, things always work out." She offered Stephanie a hand up. "Now can we go inside so I can see what you've been doing to my goddaughter?" Stephanie took her hand and Hope pulled her up.

"Yes, we can go inside. She probably won't recognize you with all that hair on your head. Are you going to go back to wearing it short?" Hope thought about the question for a second as she followed Stephanie into the house.

"I don't think so. Right now, I think it's fine just like it is."

Every woman's got a secret in Layla Jordan's
scandalous debut novel
The Liar's Club

Coming in December from Dafina Books

Turn the page for a preview of *The Liar's Club* . . .

Chapter One
Sinclair

Who ever said "money can't buy you love" has never so much as stepped a pinky-toe onto Rodeo Drive. Prada, Dolce & Gabbana, and Christian Dior—their mere existence is proof that there's heaven on earth. Every time I strut down the pristine three-block stretch of expensive boutiques I feel and look like a billion bucks. And why shouldn't I? I'm a dime diva. Long locks (weave), golden honey complexion (MAC), and coke bottle curves that make even the white boys' tongues in this Barbie doll infested town roll out of their heads. Hell. I don't mind. My big tits, small waist, and round ass are about the only real things my momma gave me. My street smarts and hustler mentality are courtesy from my father, God rest his soul. Add all those fabulous attributes together and you get a fierce bitch that has landed herself an insanely rich producer husband, Omar Fines.

Omar. The first thing that pops into my mind whenever I think of him is *'cha-ching'*. I mean mad loot.

None of the hood rich bullshit that's an epidemic in my hometown. I'm talking no limits. We have four homes in the states: Beverly Hills, Manhattan, the Hamptons, and Palm Springs. Two homes in Europe: Paris and Barcelona. Not to mention the yachts, Lear Jets, and Italian cars. I'd like to say this is the lifestyle that I've always dreamed of, but before I met Omar, I didn't know people lived like this—let alone black people. I mean, I've heard of rich people, but you really have no idea what money can buy unless you have it.

Money can't buy you love. Puh-lease. I *love* my homes, jets, boats, and cars. I love my apartment-sized walk-in closets that look like mini-boutique stores. I love my jewelry. I *love* this entire lifestyle. But if the question is do I *love* my husband, Omar? Well, that's a little more complicated. True, he looks a hell of a lot like that actor in the old Rocky movies, Carl Weathers. Tall, chocolate, and totally ripped from the hours he spends pumping iron in the gym—well, that and his extensive steroid use. The latter left his dick so small that the first time I saw it I thought about filing a missing person's report. Don't laugh. Marrying a small dick is a serious adjustment and it's not something that a woman should do all willy-nilly without weighing the pros and cons.

PROS: Money

CONS: Sexually fuckstrated

Okay. So there wasn't that much deliberation. I snatched that five carat, emerald-cut diamond ring before Omar's knees hit the floor. Hell, in that moment, I thought, *I can do this. I'll just buy tons of sex toys.* Sheeiit.

I totally underestimated how much I love a good dicking down. If you don't agree, then I hate to be the one to tell you that you just ain't had a brother that hit it right. I *love* sex—and not just the standard three positions: missionary, cowgirl, and doggie style. I'm a certified freak; an unrepentant dick addict that needs a helluva lot more than what my husband is working with. So . . . I creep.

Surprise, surprise, right?

And don't judge me. I hate that shit. All that finger-pointing and gossiping bullshit when you know damn well deep-down inside that if you were dealing with a grown man with a dick the same size as a toddler's you'd be doing the same thing. Hell, most of America creeps nowadays. The trick is not to get caught, which is difficult in the age of camera phones, YouTube, and saved text messages. Pulling off a successful creep is equivalent to obtaining a Ph.D. in neuroscience out here. So far, you can call me Dr. Sinclair Fines, and as long as Omar's money is raining, I'm not going anywhere. I'm going to keep it right and tight, and play my position as the perfect Hollywood trophy wife for as long as the position is available.

It's another sunny California day when I step out of my custom-made, Bentley Mulsanne dressed in a baby blue scoop-neck dress that hugs my hips and caresses my swaying black girl booty. My matching pumps add four inches on my five-foot nine frame while my wrists, neck and ears are blinged out by that patron holy saint Harry Winston.

To look at me, one would make the mistake that I was born into the lifestyles of the rich and famous instead of the hard streets in the South Side of Chicago, but what people don't know won't hurt them. All that matters now is that Beverly Hills is my new playground and I have no intention of jumping out of the sandbox.

"Sinclair!"

Who the hell is screeching my name out here? Turning, I remove my shades and flutter my mink lashes at Brijetta Hamilton's loud ass as she races down the sidewalk to ctach up with me. Now don't get it twisted. I love my girl. Ever since I first met her at a Vanity Fair Oscar party, I knew that she was, to coin the phrase, good people. Sure, it's easier to detect that things weren't exactly what they appeared to be between her and her action star, and recently ranked *People's Most Beautiful list*, hubby Trey Hamilton, but I let her go on with her pretense because I live in a glass house my damn self.

"Oh, hey, Brijetta. I didn't even see you." I lean in for a quick hug and air kiss. When I feel my girl's tits brush against me, I jerk back, stunned. "Damn, girl. When did you get those?" I reach out and give her new silicon babies a soft squeeze right there in the middle of the sidewalk. Trust me, that's a compliment in this town.

Brijetta strikes a pose that thrusts her new DDs up high in the air. "You like? Trey bought them for me for my thirtieth birthday."

I sweep a critical gaze over my girl, who looks like she went two sizes too big and is in danger of tipping over. I don't have it in me to tell her that she looks like a stick with tits, so I take a dive. "Girl, if you like it I love it."

"In that case, the jury is still out," she says. "I didn't know getting these babies would hurt so damn much. I'm popping percocets like candy. But, shit. Trey loves them. The bandages came off yesterday and last night he wore me and these babies out."

I fight like the devil not to roll my eyes. As far as I

can tell, her beloved Trey is never satisfied. He clearly views his wife as his blank canvas because every time I turn around he's trying to get Brijetta to do one crazy, drastic surgery after another. Case and point, when I first met Brijetta at that Oscar party two years ago, she was a three hundred pound, fashion-challenged, lonely virgin who was still working as a RN at Cedars-Sinai. Now, she weighs a hundred pounds, is a complete label whore, married, with her days of working a nine to five firmly in her rearview.

The tabloids had a field day with her and her steady transformation. Trey Hamilton had broken a lot of hearts when he upped and married Brijetta sixty days after meeting her. Most headlines labeled him a chubby-chaser and then speculated that Brijetta was just the rebound chick from his highly publicized and doomed relationship with supermodel Camilla. So every week the rags reported or made up stories about marital spats and a pending divorce.

It's no wonder Brijetta is always fighting to prove her marriage was on solid ground. Nobody is buying it—including me. But in Beverly Hills creating the perfect lie is important.

"You look like you were lost in your own world. Where are you headed?" Brijetta asks.

"Armani. I'm picking up a suit for Omar and then I have to head out to The Ivy to meet Jaleesa for lunch. You want to come?"

"I thought Jaleesa was still filming that Denzel thingy out in New York?" Brijetta starts walking with me. "She didn't get fired again, did she?"

"Don't know. She called me last night and said that she wanted to meet for lunch." Now in truth, I wouldn't be at all surprised if that heifer did get fired. That girl put the D in diva. Once upon a time she might have been considered a good actress; now all the tabloids talk about are her drunken antics in the clubs and on movie sets. That old adage: *'there's no such thing as bad press'* isn't true any more. Bad press has killed many careers out here in the city of bright lights and I'm afraid that my girl is next on the chopping block.

"Honestly, I don't know how she keeps landing acting gigs," I add.

"According to her it's because she has a mean head game on the casting couch." Brijetta snickers.

"Do you believe that shit?"

"What—that Jaleesa is a hoe? Girl, I know it. I've known Jaleesa since we were in junior high. The day she got breasts she was pushing them up on every guy that walked past her. And the night she realized the power she held in between her legs, forgetaboutit."

"Humph. Some women go a whole lifetime and never realize their power."

"Some misuse it," Brijetta volleys.

"And some try to conquer the world." I smile. "That would be me."

We crack up as we enter Giorgio Armani and of course buy more things than what we came in there for. Two hours later, Brijetta and I are escorted to our seats by The Ivy's white picket fence. Without a doubt the restaurant is a celebrity magnet, drawing a list of who's who of the Hollywood elite. A lot of people hail the place as the best restaurant in Los Angeles; for its food and for the paparazzi accessibility that tended to camp out across the street.

We already know that Jaleesa's ass is going to be late so we go ahead and order our usual Cajun shrimp salads and margaritas.

"So how are things with you and Omar?" Brijetta asks taking her glass before the waitress has a chance to set it down. "I read in the trades that he'll be producing the Hughes brothers' film."

I instantly perk up as my husband's latest achievements inflate my own ego. "Yes. Liongate greenlighted the deal. Filming starts next week. Omar is thrilled to have a strong contender for a summer blockbuster."

"Well, let's drink to that," she says cheerily holding up her glass.

"Damn straight." I tap my margarita glass against hers and then moan aloud when the chilled alcohol slides down my throat. The first sip of alcohol is an euphoria like none other. "Ahh. Now this is how to spend an afternoon."

"Afternoon, ladies!" Jaleesa sing-songs, strutting her stuff toward us. She's dressed in a strange combination of street casual and haute couture. Add in a gaudy Mardi-Gras looking beads and a pair of bumble-bee styled Chanel glasses and you have a hot mess that is Jaleesa. "I didn't know you were coming, Brijetta." She leans down and gives both of us air kisses while pressing our cheeks together. "How are . . . ahhh. What are these?" She gropes Brijetta's silicone twins. "Nice. Nice. Who did your work?"

"Dr. Oxford on Rodeo Drive. Brilliant surgeon," Brijetta gushes. "I'll definitely be using him again."

"Again?" I hike up a brow. "Don't tell me that Trey already has you signed up for something else."

Brijetta shrugged her thin shoulders. "Just a little nip and tuck. Nothing major."

Bullshit. I can tell just by the sudden way she's avoiding making eye contact. But I gotta hand it to

Trey, I'm curious to what his final masterpiece will look like when he's finally finished with her.

"I hope you don't mind me playing tag with Sinclair. My afternoon was free."

"Don't be silly." Jaleesa waved her off and finally sat down. "I haven't seen you in ages. Well, at least since . . . did you get a new nose, too?"

Brijetta gushed as she struck a couple of profile poses. "Well, you know I suffered from a deviated septum."

I had to speak up. "Child, please. That's what Jewish girls say for a nose job. Just admit you pulled a Li'l Kim and leave it at that."

Jaleesa laughs. "Ain't that the truth? No need to fake the funk with us. Keep it real and we'll keep with you."

More bullshit. The last thing any of us do is keep it real. These little get togethers only serve two purposes: to gossip and brag. Let's face it, I like these girls but I wouldn't call either one of these heifers if I was in a real jam. They aren't like the ride or die chicks I grew up with in Chicago. Telling either one of these chicks the real 4-1-1 meant that it will be all over Los Angeles before the eleven o'clock news came on. No, what we have here in this sunny paradise is The Liars Club. In this town, there is no lie too big to fail in order to survive. It's a prerequisite to be able to tell it with a straight face and a sincere voice. As for me, Sinclair Fines, I'm the biggest liar of them all.

Chapter Two
Jaleesa

I love having lunch at The Ivy. It's absolutely the best way to guarantee my name in the hot gossip rags and blogs—well, at least a casual mention. A lot of celebrities like to pretend there's some made up war between them and the paparazzi but let me tell you, it's all bullshit. We love the paparazzi, we adore them. We lay awake at night dreaming up all these fantastic ways to get their attention. They are the life blood that feeds our vampire thirst to be in the spotlight; which is why I'm sitting here wondering if this table is giving those snapping photographers my best angle.

"So what are you doing in town?" Brijetta asks, leaning back in her chair and sipping on a margarita.

I can't help but wonder how many drinks the secret alcoholic has already downed before I arrived. I've known this vapid heifer since her Nell Carter look-alike days and I think it's just some weird cosmic joke that she landed on the arm of Trey Hamilton instead of me. Really, what the hell does she know about the industry? How can she boost his image? I mean, really. Creating the perfect power couple is essential in any industry. Think: Will and Jada, Jay-Z and Beyonce or heck, Barack and Michelle. Trey Hamilton needs to upgrade to someone like me.

"Jaleesa?" Brijetta presses, snapping me out of my wild musings about her man.

"Girls, those assholes can kiss my ass. The script is bullshit and is getting stupider with each daily rewrite. How the hell do they expect me to memorize my lines if they're changing them all the damn time?"

Brijetta and Sinclair exchange looks.

"Well fuck both of you too then," I snap and then glance around. "Where the hell did our waitress go?"

"All right. Calm down," Sinclair says. "Why don't you just tell us what happened?"

"Puh-lease. The same bullshit that always happens. The lead actor and director on some dynamic duo bullshit trip that leaves the rest of the crew feeling like we're just squirrels in their world trying to get a nut." I finally see the waitress that led me to my table. "Hey, honey, I need an orgasm over here!"

Every head turns.

"What?" I ask, laughing.

Brijetta and Sinclair crack up behind me. I turn and wink at them. "I love ordering that drink in public," I admit and then laugh at myself.

"So what happened?" Sinclair asks. "Were you out partying every night again?"

"Ha. Ha. A bitch can walk and chew gum at the same time, you know."

"I'm going to take that as a *'yes'*."

"Believe what you want to believe." I reach for my purse and remove my lipstick and compact mirror. "I told those bastards what they could do with their stupid movie and I stormed off the set. The director is a major asshole anyway."

"You stormed off a Denzel Washington movie? Have you lost your mind?" Brijetta asks. "Do you know how many actresses would kill to be in a movie with Denzel?"

"Don't you start in on me. My agent has been blowing up my phone for the last twenty-four hours. Fuck them. I have principles you know. Those bastards snuck a nude scene in the script and that shit ain't in my contract."

"Since when have you objected to showing your tits to anybody who wants to see them?" Brijetta asks, smirking.

"It'll cost an extra cool million to put my shit on the big screen. Believe that."

"A million? Girl, you're smoking something fierce. They don't pay that kind of money to see black titties. Are you crazy?"

"They will if they want to see *these* titties. My shit is real. I'm not double bagging like you are, sweetheart." That shut the bitch up. She finally gets some titties and she's suddenly a fucking expert on shit? Give me a fucking break. "Anyway, the whole thing is bullshit anyway."

"Here's your drink, ma'am," my waitress says, smiling. It's a damn shame that you have to look like a model in this town just to get a waitressing job. "Would you like to place an order?"

"That won't be necessary. I'm on a liquid diet this week. Just keep the drinks flowing."

"I'll have another margarita," Brijetta says and then goes back to fluffing her lace front to make sure that her curls are holding steady. "So what are you going to do? You know that they're going to sue you for everything you got."

"Shit. Line up. Hell, if my own damn daddy is suing me I don't know why I should give two cents in hell why some studio with its head up its ass should faze me." I down my drink in one long gulp; savored the rich, creaming coffee flavor and then smile at my two girlfriends. "This is how a bitch starts an afternoon."

Sinclair shakes her head. "I don't get you. You begged for this job and now you're just blowing it off. Pretty soon the only work you're going to be able to get is on Celebrity Rehab or . . . porno."

"Well I'm sure as hell not going to any damn rehab. So you can forget that shit." I lay my best Hollywood smile on her. "But I did happen to thumb through the trades and read about Omar's latest project: *Defiance*. It's already generating quite a buzz around town about it being a posible summer blockbuster."

"Crossing our fingers and toes," Sinclair says.

"So . . . I was thinking that you have to know which dick I gotta suck to get my hands on a copy of that script. My agent Maury ain't worth shit." Sinclair gives Brijetta another one of her sneaky sideway looks before she busts out laughing in my face.

"Please say your flaky ass is joking."

My heart and hopes drop. "I'm not flaky—just a little misunderstood." I shrug. "C'mon. I'm your girl. Surely you can hook me up." Here I am giving my best sister-girl pitch and this heifer is looking at me like she doesn't know me from Adam. "Oh, you gonna play me to the left like that?"

Sinclair rolls her eyes. "I'm not trying to play you,

but I don't get involved with Omar's business. You know that."

"But you can put in a good word with Omar." I smile. "You know. A little pillow talk here and there?" I pull on all my acting skills to keep my desperation out of my voice. No way am I about to let these two bitches know my real situation. So what I didn't walk off my last movie, but was instead fired. The most important thing is to get ahead of the story and to lock down my next job before the studio's vow that I'll never work in this town again has a chance to take root. Damn it. I'm an actress—a damn good actress. I was nominated for a Screen Actors Guild Award for my first film: *Blue Skies* ten years ago. I was hot. The black *It* girl was going to be the next Halle Berry. All these director and producers gassed me up good with that shit. I have the looks and the talent. Every party I walked into, they were tripping over themselves trying to get at me. Now they play crazy and try to act like I have to audition or screen test for D-listed films. What the fuck?

Next thing I know I have to pull bullshit drunk stunts outside clubs and conveniently forget to wear panties in order to get any kind of love in the tabloids. But let's face it; the shit doesn't work as well as it does for blond, blue-eyed white girls. The truth, though this isn't the type of town that wants to talk about the truth, is that there's only a handful of African American women that even work steadily in this town. The other handful of black actresses packed up and moved to Atlanta so they can remain on heavy rotation with Tyler Perry.

Sinclair finally huffs, "I'm not going to make any promises, but I'll see what I can do."

I jump out of my seat and throw my arms around my new BFF. "Thank you, thank you, thank you."

"I *said* no promises."

"Understood." I *need* a part in *Defiance* like a crack-head needs a five dollar hit and I'm not afraid to do whatever it takes to get what I want. That includes me throwing myself on Omar's casting couch. Sinclair will just have to understand that the shit ain't personal. It's just business.

Chapter Three
Brijetta

Jaleesa knows her ass is trifling. She's thinks that she's pulling the wool over a muthafucka's eyes, but her game is whack as hell. Her ass up here trying to tell us that she just walked off a major movie set. C'mon now. Do we have Boo Boo the Fool stamped on our heads? Jaleesa's ass has always been foul. It's one bullshit scheme after another and she's not above using and abusing anyone to get what she wants. She thinks my ass is her friend, but nothing is further from the truth.

Yeah, we go back a ways; junior high, in fact. Trust. She was just as trifling then; a back-biting, boyfriend stealing, hoe is my middle name, daddy-tease bitch. Yes, I threw in daddy-tease because my mother claimed to have caught her more than once trotting her little ass in front of my dad in just panties and a bra when I'd foolishly invited her over for sleepovers. My monogamy-allergic dad was practically nipping at the bit to get at her young pussy—so much so that my mother eventually had to ban the trick from coming back over to the house.

Admittedly, at first I didn't want to believe the shit. Me and my mother battled all the time back in those days. Typical teenage shit. Then Jaleesa set her sights on the boy she *knew* I had the biggest crush on: Darrin Savoy. Sure I was a little chubby back then and Darrin didn't know I was alive, but Jaleesa got me to admit that shit on a truth or dare game and the very next day she was rubbing her stank-ass titties all over Darrin. She got that boy so pussy-whipped that when she moved on to one of her other BFF's boyfriends, Darrin was so heartbroken that he put a .38 to his temple and threatened that he'd kill himself if she didn't take him back.

She didn't

He blew his brains out.

That shit alone rocketed her to fame in Culver High. The girls wanted to know her secrets to get a boy to fall that deeply in love and the boys wanted to sample what hooked a brother so bad that he'd take his own life. Hell. It was a win-win situation for Jaleesa. She still used that whole tragic episode in her movie biography as some great triumph that she had to get over to become the great piece of shit actress she is today.

Foul.

And no. I'm not a hater. I'm watching from the sidelines waiting for this bitch to finally get what's coming to her. It's coming. Karma is a bitch. Believe that. Don't think that I don't know that it's fucking killing her that I married one of the hottest actors in the business. Shit. Jaleesa sat at my wedding with her nose damn near ready to twist off her face.

How did *fat* Brijetta hook someone like Trey Hamilton? Hell that's what the whole world wants to know. My answer? I put up with a lot of bullshit. Anyone that's been in this town more than two seconds should know that not everything that glitters is gold. Dating actors, let alone marrying them, is like having a lobotomy . . . daily. Their vanity, their God complexes and their constant need for love and attention is not for the faint at heart. But . . . I love my husband . . . just as I love the life being married to him has afforded me.

I grew up with nothing . . . less than nothing. A broken home with an alcoholic and constantly cheating father left me and my six siblings to deal with a deeply bitter mother. The kind of mother that never missed an opportunity to tell me how I was never going to amount to anything and don't bother with ever trusting a man. I get it. She was hurt, but her words battered my fragile self-confidence until I found myself repeating her hateful words to myself in the mirror.

It's no wonder I found comfort in food. A little pizza to smother the loneliness, a little ice cream to mute the pain of my dead-end career. Before I knew it, I was tipping the scales at three hundred and fifteen pounds and trying to convince myself that the pain in my back and legs were no big deal. Trey saved me and in return I try each and every day to save him right back.

And don't think I'm foolish enough to ever leave Jaleesa alone with my husband. Not going to happen. Hell, I don't even invite this trick over to my house and I certainly don't discuss what projects Trey is working on so she can beg me for a muthafucking job. This bitch could be on fire and I wouldn't bother to piss on her to put it out. Believe that shit.

I don't know Sinclair that well, but she's going to have to learn her own lessons when dealing with

Jaleesa. I threw out a couple of hints and I'm going to leave it at that because bitches in this town love nothing more than to shoot the messenger.

"Oh look at the time," I say, glancing at my watch. "I gotta head back. We're doing some renovations on the west wing of the house and I have a team of contractors coming."

Jaleesa frowns. "Aww. But I just got here."

"We'll just have to catch up next time." I stand and brush a brief kiss against her cheek and stretch my fake smile as wide as her own. "Take care and good luck with your audition."

"Oh, I'm not going to have to audition. My girl, Sinclair is going to hook me up. Ain't that right?"

Sinclair frowns. "I didn't say that. I said that I'd get you a copy of the script."

I shake my head, but then hug and kiss Sinclair goodbye. Like I said, she's gonna have to learn her lessons the hard way. "Check you later, girl."

A few minutes later, I'm in my blue Mercedes and flying up Santa Monica Boulevard, basking in the afternoon sun and replaying Jaleesa's desperation over and over in my head. Damn. I should have busted out my camera phone and taken a picture of her begging Sinclair for a script. It's not much, but I have the sneaking suspicion that it's just the tip of the iceberg.

I pull up to the gate of my estate and punch in the code. When the wrought iron bars swing open, I get hit with that same wondrous disbelief that this is my place. My home. It's gorgeous. Emerald green lawn neatly manicured and landscaped with blankets of flowers I don't even know the names of. Water fountains, Cupid statues, sculptured hedges were nothing compared to the French-Chateau styled mansion nestled on the three acre estate.

My house. How you like me now, momma?

Parking the car in one of the nine car ports, I rush into the house certain that I have about ten minutes before the first contractor gets here. Plenty of time for a quick wardrobe change.

"Ah, Mrs. Hamilton, thank God you're home."

I look up at the top of the winding staircase to see Amaya, our four foot, husky-build housekeeper, looking like she's in a near state of panic. "What's wrong?"

"It's Mr. Hamilton. He no come out the room. I think that something may be wrong."

I'm already running up the stairs before she even finishes talking. "Where is he?"

"In the bedroom. That man came by again this morning." Amaya struggles to keep up with me while I run to my bedroom. "I don't like that man. He scares me."

"Why didn't you call me?" I reach the door and sure enough the muthafucka is locked. "Trey?" I knock. "Baby, are you all right?"

KNOCK. KNOCK.

"Trey?" I turn to Amaya. "Find me a screwdriver."

"Yes, ma'am." She takes off.

KNOCK. KNOCK.

"Trey, baby. Open the door." I press my ear against the door and I think I can just barely make out Trey whispering my name. Fear seizes control of me as I rattle the knob and bang on the door harder. "What did you do, baby?" Tears splash down my face because I'm already imagining the worst. "HURRY UP, AMAYA!"

"I'M COMING!"

My knocking is now a raucous bang. It doesn't do any good since the door is solid oak. "TREY, CAN YOU HEAR ME, BABY?"

BANG! BANG!

Amaya races back to my side, red-faced and out of breath. "Here you go, Mrs. Hamilton."

Shakily, I snatch the screwdriver out of her hand and get busy dismantling the doorknob. "Hold on, baby. I'm coming." Shit. I'm so fucking nervous, I can barely get my hands to stop shaking.

"Do you think he's all right?" Amaya asks nervously over my shoulder.

I don't bother answering her because I really don't need my mind going there. I stab my fingers a couple of times, chip a nail but I finally get the doorknob off and rush inside. My gaze instantly flies to the large mahogany bed where Trey is face down with a needle still protruding out of his arm.

"Shit. Shit." Rushing over to him, I still try to push all negative thoughts to the back of my head. *He's okay. He's okay.* I desperately need to believe this. I snatch the needle out and, with Amaya's help, get Trey flipped over onto his back. I quickly try to find a pulse, but I'm having trouble and he's clearly turning a purplish color. "Help me get him into the bathroom."

Amaya starts to back away. "I dunno. Maybe we should—?"

"Don't argue. Grab his feet." I swear to God I'll beat the holy hell out of her if she bolts.

Amaya hesitates for just a second, but then hops to it. Together we manage to carry Trey off the bed. Getting to the bathroom is more of a challenge. I even break a heel off my shoes, trying to lug Trey's dead weight. Eventually we make it to the king-sized tub and Amaya turns the shower on while I'm still sitting in the tub behind Trey and trying to slap him awake. The minute the cold water hits us, Trey springs to life, sputtering and gasping.

"What the fuck?" He gasps and then sputters under the icy current. "Goddamn it. TURN THAT SHIT OFF!"

Startled, Amaya quickly shuts off the water and then looks me dead in my face and says, "I can't do this no more, Mrs. Hamilton. It's not right. I quit!" She turns and runs off.

"Amaya, please come back!"

"Let her ass go. Fuck." Trey huffs and then eases back against my heaving chest; like us hanging out in the tub with our clothes on is something we do everyday. My clothes are ruined, I broke my favorite pumps and chipped a nail, but Trey is all right. Thank God.

How did I snag a man like Trey Hamilton?

I put up with a lot of bullshit.